SKELETON HILL

This Large Print Book carries the
Seal of Approval of N.A.V.H.

SKELETON HILL

PETER LOVESEY

THORNDIKE PRESS
A part of Gale, Cengage Learning

GALE
CENGAGE Learning™

Detroit • New York • San Francisco • New Haven, Conn • Waterville, Maine • London

LIBRARY OF CONGRESS CATALOGING-IN-PUBLICATION DATA

Lovesey, Peter.
    Skeleton Hill / by Peter Lovesey.
        p. cm. — (Thorndike Press large print basic)
    ISBN-13: 978-1-4104-2231-6 (alk. paper)
    ISBN-10: 1-4104-2231-3 (alk. paper)
    1. Diamond, Peter (Fictitious character)—Fiction. 2. Police—
England—Bath—Fiction. 3. Bath (England)—Fiction. 4. Large
type books. I. Title.
PR6062.O86S554 2010
823'.914—dc22   2009037661

Published in 2010 by arrangement with Writer's House LLC.

Printed in the United States of America
1 2 3 4 5 6 7 14 13 12 11 10

SKELETON HILL

1

Two men lay dead on a battlefield and one said 'Hey!'

The other stayed silent.

'I'm talking to you.'

There was no response.

'You with the head wound.'

Now the other one stirred. 'I'm dead,' he said through his teeth like a ventriloquist.

'Me, too. So?'

'So we're not supposed to talk.'

'Get real. No one's looking at us. The action is all over there.'

Both were in the royalist army commanded by Lord Hopton. The re-enactment of the Civil War battle for Bath had moved closer to the spectators, some distance from where the pikemen had first clashed, leaving the so-called dead and dying as background decorations. The setting was spectacular, high on Lansdown, seven hundred feet above the city of Bath and with views across three counties. Unconstrained by even a breath of wind, the July sun belted down, catching the flash of pike, sword and armour but overheating everyone.

The one who had spoken first was on his back on the turf and the other was face down two yards away. The stage blood on his head wound was drying. 'Some of us had to fall, I was told.'

'You're new to this, aren't you?'

'My first time.'

'I thought I hadn't seen you before. You're a mess.'

'When I was given my uniform, the officer told me it's expected for a new recruit to get killed at least once, so I came prepared with a bag of blood. I'm trying to look as if I took a shot to the head.'

'I'll go for that.'

'You can have some if you like.'

'No thanks. I'll be up again soon. The reason I'm dead is that I want to cool off. I'm Dave, by the way.'

'Rupert.'

They didn't shake hands, seeing that they were supposed to be slain.

'*Rupert*. For real?'

'Of course.' Rupert hesitated, then gave a forced grin. 'Oh, I see. You thought the name was made up specially for this. Unfortunately, no. I'm stuck with it. Should we get up and join in again?'

'You can if you want,' Dave said. 'I'm thirsty.'

'It's the armour, isn't it? Makes one sweat.'

'Fancy a can of lager?'

He smiled. 'Don't I just? I'd die for one — all over again.'

'I got here early and put some by.'

'Really?' Rupert had raised his head off the ground.

'It's not far off.'

He didn't hesitate long. 'Which way?'

'Follow me and keep your head down. Leave your pike. You can pick that up later.' With that, Dave got up and with a stooping gait trotted further down the hill in the opposite direction from the fighting.

'We look like deserters,' Rupert called from close behind.

'So what? You bet they had some in those days.'

Their raised voices caught the attention of a couple of women kneeling beside the wounded, but they were supposed to be camp followers giving comfort to their own, the despised parliamentarians.

'See that fallen tree? That's where it is.'

There was no question that they were breaking the rules by quitting the battlefield.

Rupert had the sense not to mention any more of his anxieties to his new friend. With luck, no one had spotted them except the women. The spectators were massed behind ropes a few hundred yards away.

The fallen tree must have been blown down in one of the great storms of recent years. Its exposed root system, stark against the sky, formed a canopy ideal to hide under. They sank down in its shadow.

'Should still be reasonably cool,' Dave said. He burrowed in the earth and took out a can of Heineken and handed it to Rupert.

Rupert removed the ringpull and gulped some down. 'This is a lifesaver.'

'Brought you back to life for sure.'

Rupert laughed.

Dave raised his can. 'To good King Charles.'

Rupert did the same. 'The King, God bless him.'

Even though the lager wasn't chilled it was bliss to drink. Dave explained that on battle days he usually found a spot where he could stow some away before anyone got there. 'In weather like this you've got to look after yourself.'

'I can see I've got a lot to learn,' Rupert said.

'I'm in the cavalry normally and we smuggle the odd tinny into our saddle holsters, but you can't risk it as a pikeman. You wouldn't get past the inspection.'

'What are you doing on foot if you're in the cavalry?'

Dave laughed. 'Slumming. I'm a Captain of Horse.'

'Wow.'

'If you get a boil on your arse as I have, you don't want to think about mounting a horse. Today I'm infantry and grateful for it.'

'Some of the men have knapsacks, I noticed.'

'That's the first place an officer would look. If you were desperate you could stuff a tin down your breeches. I'd rather get here early and put down my own store.'

'And you're serious about joining in again?'

'That's why I'm in it, for the fighting. Aren't you?'

'Well, I'm a historian,' Rupert said. 'They had what they called a lecture day in October and I was invited to give a talk. I thought it would be interesting to come along and get a sense of what it's like to re-enact a battle.'

'And is it?'

'Is it what?'

'Anything like?'

Rupert the historian smiled. 'Not if I'm brutally honest. This is put on mainly for the spectacle, so the audience has to have a view. The real point of interest in 1643 was Sir William Waller's brilliant tactics.'

'Waller? He's the enemy.'

'Yes, and in the real battle we outnumbered him by a couple of thousand, yet he moved his army in the night and outflanked us. When our side woke up, the parliamentarians had the high position along the top of Lansdown. You saw the little copse behind the Grenvile Monument?'

'Yes.'

'It wasn't there in 1643. There were clumps of trees at either extreme, where some of Waller's musketeers were deployed, but the main route of attack was a bare hillside. Our royalist army was on Freezing Hill, that one to the north. When we attacked we had to come down from there and fight our way uphill. We took a lot of casualties.'

'But we saw them off.'

'Finally, and at great cost. Not much of that is being shown here. I suppose a battle on a steep hillside wouldn't work as a spectacle.'

'Flat ground is better,' Dave said, looking across the plateau of Lansdown to where the sound of the action continued. 'Safer for the horses, too.'

'And the scale is so different,' Rupert said, his focus much more on the past. 'We don't have anything approaching the numbers they did. The royalist army had come up from the West Country under Sir Ralph Hopton's command and they had upwards of six thousand men, against about four thousand defending Bath for the parliamentarians.'

'Is that so?' Dave said in a voice that was beginning to lose interest.

'Yes, today's turnout looks pathetic beside those figures. Hopton lost about three hundred in the real battle. I doubt if we started with that many this morning.'

'This is only a minor muster,' Dave said. 'We do have bigger turn-outs.'

'Each army had masses of artillery. According to the accounts, there was so much smoke from the cannon and muskets that they couldn't see more than a few yards ahead.'

'Hell on earth by the sound of it.'

'Most battles were. A far cry from this little show.'

'Stop knocking it. We go to a lot of trouble

13

to get the uniforms right. You should see my cavalry gear. Hand sewn.'

Rupert smiled. 'I was given mine on loan. I know the rules. If I carry on, I'm expected to supply my own.'

'Quite right, too. And make sure you get the proper fabric. You'll be inspected. Real leather belt and boots. All the weapons have to be accurate replicas.'

'Firing blanks and thunderflashes.'

'What do you expect?' Dave said, increasingly put out. 'I tell you, I wouldn't be here if there were cannonballs flying about.'

Rupert smiled. 'True.'

Dave said, 'We're putting on a show for the public, and we do the best we can with what we've got.'

'The real thing wasn't very satisfactory anyway. They fought to a standstill and nobody won on the day. You saw that drystone wall up to the left?'

'Yeah.'

'His musketeers used it as cover and held off the royalists until late in the evening. It's known as Waller's wall even to this day. If you look at it closely you can see where it's been repaired, to fill the holes they made. When it was dark they slipped back to the city, leaving some burning tinder along the top to give the impression they were still

14

camped there.'

'You couldn't re-enact that,' Dave said. 'Nobody would stay that long. Fancy another?' He dug his hand into the loose soil again.

A shake of the head from Rupert. 'One was good. That's my limit.'

Dave was groping up to his elbow among the earth and dead leaves for his second drink. The search was increasingly agitated. 'I can't find it. There were six here.' He used both hands, exploring every part of the hiding place. 'Some tosser must have nicked them.'

'One of the enemy?' Rupert said.

'You could be right. Bloody roundheads. None of our lot were about earlier, but I did see one of them.'

'At least he had the decency to leave the two cans we had.'

'You call that decent?' Dave was still scrabbling in the hole. 'There's something down here, but it isn't a can. It isn't a tree root either.' He lifted out an object over a foot in length, narrow and with bulbous ends. After picking off some caked earth, he said, 'Only an old bone.'

'Some animal must have buried it,' Rupert said. 'A fox, I expect.'

Dave held the bone in both hands. 'Well,

15

whatever this was, it was bigger than the fox when it was alive.'

Rupert said, 'It's a femur.' Not wanting to sound too much of an academic, he added, 'Thigh bone.'

'But of what?'

'Might be a deer.'

'You know what?' Dave said. 'I've just had a spooky thought. It could be human.'

'Up here on Lansdown? How would it get here?'

'This is the spooky part. What if it belonged to one of the soldiers who was killed in the battle?'

There was a moment when nothing was said. The sounds of the fighting were distant now, muffled by a sudden breeze.

It was Rupert who spoke next. 'Nasty.'

'But not impossible?'

'You could be right. There must have been corpses scattered all over the down. The army would have buried their dead up here before they moved on. They were in a campaign. They couldn't take them home for burial.'

Dave shook his head. 'Makes you think, doesn't it? Here we are, all dressed up and playing soldiers, and this was a guy who really bought it.'

'That does put a different perspective on

the day,' Rupert said. 'If it is human.'

'I've a gut feeling it is.' He placed the bone respectfully between them, as if he didn't wish to handle it any more. 'What shall we do with it?'

Secretly excited by the find, Rupert decided to appear indifferent. 'Put it back, I suggest.'

Dave was a bit of a mind reader. 'One of them archaeologists might be interested. There could be more stuff buried here.'

'I rather doubt it,' Rupert said. 'The tree was growing over it.'

'Three hundred years ago that tree wasn't here.'

'I don't know. How long does a tree live?'

'They could arrange a dig here and find more bones, even some of his armour.'

'Along with your missing beer. Should confuse them.'

Dave shook his head. 'Some bastard had the beer.'

'I wasn't serious.'

'You're right,' Dave said. 'I vote we leave it here. We can't join in the battle again with a thing like that in our hands.'

'You agree to bury it again?'

'Leave the poor guy in peace.'

'That's the decent thing,' Rupert said. 'I'm with you, Dave. He's rested here for over three hundred years. We don't have any right to disturb him.'

Dave dug out more of the leaf mould and they replaced the bone at about its original depth and covered it.

'RIP, whoever you are,' Dave said.

'Amen to that,' Rupert said.

They slung their empties a respectful distance from the internment and returned to the battle.

After the fighting was over, the King's Army picked up their casualties, assembled behind the standard and made a dignified withdrawal from the field, marching to the slow beat of a single drum. The cavalry went first, followed by the artillery hauling the guns and then the foot soldiers and finally the camp followers, mostly women. This wasn't true to history, but in contrast to the noise and confusion of the fighting it made an impressive spectacle for the crowd watching from higher up. There was spontaneous applause. The parliament army would make a similar exit later.

When they reached the road that runs along the top of Lansdown, the marchers broke step and headed back to the car park at the racecourse where they'd left their transport: rented buses as well as horse boxes, vans and flat-top lorries for the cannon. Many had come in their own cars. While some loaded up and stowed away the weaponry, others attended to the horses or prepared barbecues. At least a couple of hours would pass agreeably in banter and debate about the fighting.

Rupert, new to all this, took his cue from the regulars, assisting where he could before slipping away to his car and changing out of his sweaty battle costume into a cool shirt and shorts. He was still curious about the femur Dave had unearthed. If, as they had speculated, it was part of the remains of a Civil War soldier from the original battle, this was an exciting find. In all the years he'd spent as an academic he'd never felt the touch of the past in such a direct way.

There was a good chance of finding more bones — perhaps a complete skeleton — lower down. And, if so, surely there would be metal objects preserved, a breastplate, a helmet or a sword.

How pleasing it would be to bring a group of students to the site and supervise them in a dig. Good for them and good for his career. He could visualise himself writing a paper about the discovery, giving a slide lecture, doing an article for *History Today*.

First — not wishing to make a fool of himself — he would need to establish beyond doubt that the bone was human in origin. And then find out if it really was as old as he hoped. Carbon dating ought to establish its age. The university had the technology, so why not make use of it?

His conscience troubled him a little. He and Dave had talked about putting the dead soldier's femur to rest where they'd found it. He'd gone along with the suggestion. To return to the place and secretly retrieve the bone would be underhand. Dave wouldn't approve, but then who was Dave? Just a simple guy who liked playing soldiers. He wouldn't understand the pursuit of historical truth.

Rupert joined in the barbecue for a while, made himself a burger and chatted to the others, then slipped away as if for a call of nature. Using the parked buses to shield his movements, he crossed the car park and the golf course and made a detour so as to cross the road out of sight of everyone. The flat top of Lansdown Hill was all too open for his liking, so he moved in the direction that had the steepest descent until he could be certain he was no longer visible from the car park.

The light was softer now, fading slowly, a

glorious summer evening, cooler by some degrees and comfortable for walking. The birds were putting on a show of diving and soaring after the insects. Below was a valley through which one of the tributaries of the Avon flowed and beyond that a steep rise to the old RAF station at Charmy Down. Rupert had studied the map only the previous evening to get a full appreciation of the battleground and its all-important contours. Disappointingly, the re-enactment had not followed the original action with any precision. If he ever had any say in the planning, he'd insist on a more authentic approach, but he doubted if he'd want to play soldiers again.

He had entered a field, staying roughly parallel with the road, when there was a rich splash of red in the evening sun as a fox broke from its cover and dashed in front of him only a few yards ahead. The sight uplifted him. He didn't have the countryman's contempt for such animals. Anything that survived in the wild by its own efforts would get his support. This one seemed symbolic of the lone adventurer, encouraging him to complete the mission — or so he told himself, preferring not to think about the fox's reputation for slyness.

He crossed two stiles, still well short of

the true site of the infantry action, the valley between Lansdown and Freezing Hill where a counter attack by the royalists had forced Sir William Waller's army to retreat. The terrain had played a key role in the battle. Fighting up those steep slopes, with little more than drystone walls for cover, must have been hellish. At the end the royalists were in control of Lansdown, but at the cost of the most casualties. It was believed Waller had lost as few as twenty men, with about sixty injured.

The uprooted tree came into view and he quickened his step. Nobody was in sight and the light was fading fast. Higher up the slope, on Lansdown Road, the drivers were using their headlights as they travelled down into Bath for their Saturday night out.

The vast root system was silhouetted like some beached sea creature with tentacles, sinister and monstrous. In its shadow he had difficulty locating the precise place where the bone was buried. He knelt and poked his fingers in to find where the earth was loose. There was a place where both hands sank in easily.

Terrier-like, he scooped out a sizeable hole. This wouldn't take long.

His fingers touched something solid and bulbous. Definitely one end of the femur.

He got a grip and pulled the bone from the hole.

Job done.

He brushed off the dirt. Sorry to disturb you again, my friend, he addressed it in his thoughts. Just finding out if you're a victim of the real battle.

He stood up again — and froze.

A hand was on his shoulder.

2

'For a start, you're overweight,' the doctor said.

'I don't need you to tell me that.'

'Quite a bit over for a man your height. How do you exercise?'

'I lift the odd pint.'

'It's not funny, Mr Diamond. You could be killing yourself. Your blood pressure's too high. Are you regular?'

'What?'

'Motions.'

There was no answer.

'Big jobs,' the doctor explained.

Peter Diamond said after a crushing pause, 'Young man, how old are you?'

The doctor twitched. 'My age isn't under discussion.'

'Well, let's discuss big jobs, seeing that you mentioned them. Mine is a big job. I'm in charge of CID in the city of Bath.' He'd slipped his thumbs behind his braces —

ridiculous for a man without a shirt, so he removed them. 'My employers are the Police Authority and they insist on this annual medical. And your not-so-big job is to give me the once-over and declare me fit for work. Correct?'

'Not entirely.'

'Okay, the fitness is not guaranteed.'

'Agreed.'

'But let's get one thing clear. You're not my doctor. I haven't come to you for treatment or advice about my bowel movements or my blood pressure or my weight. I just need your signature on that form.'

'You may see it that way.'

'Believe me, I know about forms. I spend a large part of my time filling them in and most of them are pointless. I should be catching criminals and you should be looking after people who are sick.'

'You won't catch anyone if you're unfit.'

'I don't run after them. Younger men and women do that. Most of my work is done in my head, or on paper. Yes, I'm a few pounds overweight and have been for years. Some of us are built that way. It doesn't stop me doing my job. So why don't you sign me off and call in the next guy?'

'I can't do that.'

'Why not?'

This doctor wasn't completely cowed. 'Unless you take your state of health more seriously, it may not be just your job you lose.'

Diamond picked up his shirt. 'Are you telling me I'm ill?'

'Unfit is a more accurate term.'

'And we all know what happened to the man who wrote that famous book on jogging.'

'I wouldn't suggest you take up jogging, Mr Diamond, not in your present condition. Some sensible eating would be a start.'

'Don't go there,' Diamond warned him.

But the doctor was back on the attack. 'A brisk walk at least once a day. Do you drive to work?'

'I live in Weston, over a mile away.'

'Ideal.'

'I don't have the time to walk.'

'Get up earlier. Do you live alone?'

'These days, yes.'

'Then you won't disturb anyone by setting the alarm.'

'Didn't I make myself clear? I don't need you to tell me how to run my life.'

'You need somebody, Mr Diamond. That's *my* job.'

'Are you going to sign that certificate?'

'With misgivings.' The doctor picked up his pen.

Diamond should have left it there. Instead, he asked, 'Why didn't they send the regular man? Hold on, I don't mean regular in your understanding of the word. The doc we've seen for years, about my own age, who I sometimes meet in the Crown & Anchor?'

'He died.'

'Oh.'

'Heart. He didn't look after himself.'

Difficult to top that. 'Well, at least he had warm hands.'

The doctor looked over his half-glasses. 'Not any more.'

Back with his team, still buttoning his shirt, he said, 'Passed.'

'With flying colours?' Halliwell asked.

'With misgivings.'

'Miss who?'

'He's not the quack we usually get. Looks fifteen years old, just qualified, out to make an impression.'

'He didn't impress you?'

'That's putting it mildly. How about you? Have you been in yet?'

'Next but one.' An anxious look crossed Halliwell's features. 'It's just pulse and blood pressure, isn't it?'

'That's what I thought, until . . .'

Halliwell's eyes were like port-holes. 'Until what?'

'He put on the surgical glove.'

'He's kidding,' John Leaman said. 'Can't you see the grin?'

Diamond switched to Leaman. 'So when's yours?'

'I'm excused. They gave me a medical at Bramshill when I did the weapons training.'

Diamond rolled his eyes. Typical, somehow, that Leaman should escape. 'You can hold the fort, then. I need some lunch after what I've been through.'

Still nettled by the young doctor, he asked for extra chips with his burger. 'I just passed my medical,' he told Cressida in the canteen. 'While I'm at it, I'll have an extra spoonful of beans.'

'Building up your strength?' she said, smiling.

'It's a good principle. In my job, you never know what's round the next corner.'

'Could be a nice young lady, Mr D.'

'I'll need the strength, then.'

'If you like I'll spread the word among the girls that you passed your medical.'

His romantic prospects were fair game. The kitchen girls knew about his friendship with Paloma Kean. What they didn't know was how much he missed his murdered wife Steph.

He paid, picked up his cutlery and looked for a table, always a tricky decision. If he joined other people, they would be lower ranks and uncomfortable in the presence of a superintendent, but an empty table left him vulnerable to Georgina, the Assistant Chief Constable. Many a burger and chips had been ruined by Georgina arriving with her salad and some sharp questions about the way he was running his department.

A face from the past looked up from a newspaper, not a face to be recalled with much affection, yet not easy to ignore. A Lord Kitchener moustache flecked with silver. Brown, unforgiving eyes. The man had once been Head of CID Operations.

'John Wigfull, for all that's wonderful. I thought you'd long since left the madhouse and gone back to Sheffield, or wherever it is.' Diamond placed his tray on the table.

Chief Inspector Wigfull had been given extended sick leave three or four years ago after receiving a head injury and being left for dead in a cornfield near Stowford. He'd spent almost a week unconscious in Bath's Royal United Hospital.

Wigfull didn't move. There was no handshake, let alone a hug. They'd never been that friendly.

'They brought me back as a civilian,' he said.

'You were always good at paperwork,' Diamond said, and it wasn't meant as an insult. No one had ever come near to Wigfull in filing and form-filling. 'What will you be doing?'

'I'm the new media relations manager.'

'Are you, indeed? I should have realised when I saw you reading the *Sun.*' He popped a chip into his mouth. 'So I can look forward to you keeping the press boys off my back.'

'That's not the idea at all,' Wigfull said. 'In the modern police we encourage openness.' He'd always had this talent for making Diamond feel he was one of a dying breed.

'You feed them stories, do you? We've had some juicy ones since you were here.'

'Oh, yes?'

'Like the crossbow killer we called the Mariner. And the Secret Hangman. You could have made something of those.'

'I don't "make something", as you put it. I communicate facts.'

'Too right you do.'

'In the past we haven't maximised our use of the media,' Wigfull said, and the phrase

30

could have come straight from his job interview. 'It's a two-way process. There's potential for information-gathering from the public.'

'Like the old Wanted posters?'

Wigfull looked puzzled, then pained. 'We're more sophisticated.'

'*Crimewatch*?'

'We're in the twenty-first century. My brief is to make the police more approachable.'

'You wouldn't be thinking of giving out my phone number?'

'Not at all, but I may at some point arrange for you to be interviewed by a magazine or newspaper.'

'You're joking. What about?'

'About you — as a human being. They'll do a full page profile.'

Diamond frowned. 'You can stuff that.'

'You are a member of the human race.'

'Yes, and I value my privacy.'

'Don't look so worried, Peter. You're not top of my list. Not even halfway up, in fact.'

A putdown calculated to injure Diamond's pride, and it succeeded. 'What's the matter with me? Okay, you don't have to answer that question.'

'The interviews are only one of many innovations I'm making.'

31

Diamond lifted the top from the burger and and poured on some ketchup. He wished he'd sat with someone else.

'I'm feeding titbits to the media as well,' Wigfull added. 'Human interest stories like the missing cavalier.' He spoke the last two words in a throwaway tone, as if Diamond should have known all about it.

'What's that — an oil painting?'

'Please.'

'A dog, then?'

'Dog?'

'Cavalier King Charles spaniel.'

'It's what I said — a missing cavalier. You won't have heard of this because it hasn't come to CID. There's no crime that we know of . . . yet.'

'But it could come to pass?'

'When I release the facts to the press there's a chance they'll take up the case and someone will know something.'

'Go on, then.'

'Two weekends ago they re-enacted the Civil War Battle of Lansdown.'

'Missed it.'

'You would, when all you think about is rugby and old films. The real thing was in 1643 and they had a major muster three hundred and fifty years on, in 1993.'

'A what?'

'A muster. That's the term they use. It made a very colourful spectacle, I'm told. There are societies like the Sealed Knot who take it very seriously.'

'Pathetic,' Diamond said. 'Cut to the chase.'

'As I was trying to tell you, they had another muster this year. One of them fell in the battle and hasn't been heard of since.'

'Killed?'

'If he had been, you'd have heard about it. There would have been a real corpse when the fighting came to an end and they all got up and marched away. No, this man doesn't seem to have been injured.'

'You just said he fell in the battle.'

'It's all pretence. They lie down for a while and then get up and join in again. Somehow this one went missing. No one reported it at the time, but two days later his car was found in the race-course car park. His armour, the authentic costume, was in the boot.'

'Pity.'

'Why?'

'It spoils your story, doesn't it? You're not looking for a missing person in a big hat with a feather.'

'He was an infantryman. They wore helmets.'

'Doesn't matter, does it, if his stuff was in the car? You say his motor was found, so you must have checked with Swansea for his name.'

'Yes, we know who he is. Rupert Hope, a history lecturer at Bristol University. They have no idea where he is.'

'Family?'

'Parents living in Australia. They haven't heard from him since the incident. Neither have any of his university colleagues.'

'Another missing person. I expect he'll turn up.'

'But why would he abandon his car?'

'Any number of reasons,' Diamond said. 'Has anyone tried it, to see if it starts?'

'I wouldn't know.'

'If the car was giving trouble, he may have got a lift with someone else.'

'That doesn't explain why he disappeared.'

'You asked me why he left the car there.'

'He's been gone twelve days.'

'Try this for size, then. After the battle, they all get together for a few drinks. What's the pub up there? The Blathwayt. Your cavalier gets stonkered and in no state to drive. One of his mates offers to drive him home, but on the way back to Bristol they have an accident.'

'We'd have heard.'

34

'Hold on. His friend the driver is killed, but your man gets out and walks away. He's hit his head, lost his memory. Nobody knows there was a passenger.'

'So where is he now?' Wigfull said with scorn.

'In the funny farm. Check for the guy with delusions that he's a cavalier.'

Wigfull took him seriously, as usual. 'We don't have time for that. After all, he's only a missing person, not a suspect on the run. But if the press take up the story, they might make something of it.'

Diamond smiled. 'John, they'd make something of that little patch of shaving foam under your tash.'

The satisfaction of watching Wigfull check with a finger brightened Diamond's day.

3

The next morning a woman called Miss Hibbert walked into Manvers Street Police Station with three greyhounds and a large bone. 'I've always obeyed the law,' she told the desk sergeant, 'and I want to know if I can keep this.'

Sergeant Austin, with eighteen years' experience, had seen some shocking things across this desk. He eyed the bone without much interest. 'You want to keep it?'

'For these chaps. They're rescue dogs. Life hasn't given them much in the way of treats. Do you have any idea of the disgraceful way so-called sportsmen treat greyhounds when they can't race any more?'

Sergeant Austin sidestepped the question with one of his own. 'Where did you get the bone, ma'am?'

'Up on Lansdown. I give them a good run whenever I can. It's the ideal place to take them. I thought it was a piece of wood at first, and then I saw it had the shape of a bone and I thought I'd better check with you in case it's human.'

'Human? Let's hope not,' Sergeant Austin said, turning the thing over in his hands.

Catching sight of the bone again, one of the dogs reared up and tried to take it back.

'Get down, you brute!'

'Who are you calling a brute? There's no need for that,' Miss Hibbert said. 'He's muzzled. He can't bite you. Down, Hector.'

Sergeant Austin rubbed the back of his hand. 'He got me with his claw.'

'Your own fault. You shouldn't have shown him the bone. Has he drawn blood?'

'If you really want to know, he has.'

'Then I'm sorry, and I'm speaking for Hector as well. It wasn't intentional. We kept within the law by wearing the muzzle.'

'It's a claw mark, not a bite,' the sergeant said, rubbing at the spot. 'He needs restraining.'

'I hope you're not suggesting I tie up his paws as well as his jaw.'

'That's not the point.'

'Let me see, sergeant.' The speaker was the police doctor, who happened to be on his way into the police station to carry out more medicals. 'One of these dogs attacked you?'

Miss Hibbert, outraged, said, 'Absolutely not. Hector was being playful.'

To his credit Sergeant Austin said it wasn't a problem.

The doctor said, 'Let's see. Just a scratch, then. Are you up to date with your tetanus jabs?'

A silence.

'I'll see to that shortly. I have some anti-toxin on the premises.'

'It's nothing. I don't need a jab.'

'Sorry, sergeant, I must insist for your own safety.'

'Okay, thanks,' the sergeant said without any gratitude at all.

'And what are you doing with that femur?' the doctor said. 'It looks human to me.'

The bone was taken into the CID office and shown to Peter Diamond. He had no training in forensic anthropology, but if the doctor thought the thing looked human it had to be taken seriously. He went downstairs to speak to Miss Hibbert, who by this time had taken the dogs outside to the car park. Silver-haired and sturdy, with a pale full moon of a face, she was in a Bavarian hat, tweed suit and brogues.

'What I'd like to do,' Diamond said, when he'd heard her story, 'is go up to Lansdown with you and see exactly where you found the bone.'

'I just walked all the way into town,' she said. 'That was downhill. If you think I'm tramping all the way up again, you've got another think coming.'

He offered to drive.

'With the dogs? I'm not leaving them here.'

'Are they all right in a car?'

'They're angels . . . if you treat them right.'

With the angels on the back seat, he managed the drive without anything worse than a damp nose prodding the back of his neck. True, in the excitement when he stopped the car he felt a drumbeat on his shoulders, but no permanent damage was done.

Lansdown was at its most enchanting under a cloudless sky.

Miss Hibbert said, 'To hell with the law. I'm going to take off the muzzles.'

Diamond said, 'I didn't hear that.'

'The muzzles,' she said, as if to a deaf man. 'There's no one in sight except us, so I'm taking them off.' And while he was locking the car she released the dogs altogether. They raced away across the open down.

The cool air at this altitude was as good as champagne after the humidity of the city. 'I should come here more often,' he said, filling his lungs. 'Is this their regular walk?'

'Every day, rain or shine. Thanks to you, they're getting it twice over.'

He asked to be shown where the bone had been found. She led him across a field and down a steep incline towards a fallen oak tree much covered in lichen. It must have been down for some years. The fine parts of the root system had long since succumbed to the weather and children at play, leaving only the major roots exposed in a display reminding him of the Gorgon's head in the Roman Baths Museum.

'Here?'

'I didn't see precisely where they got it from,' Miss Hibbert said, 'but they were fighting over it when I caught up with them, so I think it was hidden here somewhere.'

On cue, Hector raced in and started burrowing in the soil below the roots. He was joined by the others. The ground looked soft.

'Stop them doing that, will you?' Diamond said. 'This could be a crime scene for all I know.'

Miss Hibbert produced a rubber ball from her handbag. 'Try throwing this down the hill.'

'Me?'

'They like you, I can tell. Besides, men

are better at throwing.'

'I'm supposed to be working,' he said, secretly pleased to win the dogs' approval. He flung the ball as far down the slope as he could and the dogs chased after it. Gratifying. He'd never thought keeping a dog was worth the trouble of exercising it. Now he wasn't so sure. His cat didn't chase anything except birds and mice. Try throwing a ball for Raffles and you'd end up fetching it yourself, watched with disdain by a superior being.

He paced the area, studying the ground, thinking back to his lunchtime conversation with Wigfull about the missing cavalier. The re-enactment of the battle must have happened here or hereabouts. But he couldn't imagine the femur having anything to do with the lost lecturer, Rupert Hope. The stained off-white appearance suggested it had been in the ground for years. Miss Hibbert's greyhounds hadn't had a meal from it.

His search produced nothing more suspicious than some cigarette-ends, a flattened beer can and an empty Smarties tube. 'Have you ever seen anyone acting suspiciously here?'

'Doing what?' Miss Hibbert asked.

'I don't know. I'm asking you.'

41

'I've seen children climbing on the trunk and running up and down, but I wouldn't call that suspicious.'

'How long has the tree been down?'

'Years and years. As long as I can remember.'

The dogs returned with the ball and dropped it at Diamond's feet and gazed up at him with confidence. 'You win,' he said, stooping. The ball was damp to the touch. He threw it downhill again. 'I can't keep doing this. Do you live nearby, Miss Hibbert?'

'Only a short way off, in Upper Langridge. I gave my address to that policeman I first spoke to, the one who went for a tetanus injection.'

'Anti-tetanus, I hope.'

'I'm not going to get that bone for my dogs to chew on, am I?'

He smiled, admiring her nerve. Staunch single women like this, used to standing up for their rights, had his respect. 'Not now we're treating it as human.'

'You don't know for certain.'

'That's true. A fair number of the bones brought in to the police turn out to be animal. If that's the case, you could get it back.'

'If I'd been less public-spirited, no one

would have known.'

'True, but if it was your leg bone, or mine, we wouldn't want it thrown to the dogs, even charming dogs like Hector, would we?'

She appeared to agree, but was looking thoughtful. 'Do you think there could be more bones under here?'

He put up both hands. 'Don't go there. Don't even think about letting the dogs do any more digging.'

By the end of the day the area around the tree was marked off with crime scene tape and a luckless constable was posted to guard the scene overnight.

In the morning, a forensic anthropologist confirmed the femur as human, probably from an adult of average height. Further tests would yield more information. In theory that single bone could reveal its owner's sex, age at death, body weight, ethnic origin and how long ago death had occurred. 'Bloody marvellous,' Diamond said, to encourage even more co-operation. 'I don't know how you people do it.'

He was told they'd do it even better if he provided more bones from the same individual.

He returned to Lansdown with two of his team, DC Ingeborg Smith and DI Keith

Halliwell, and watched the white-suited crime scene investigators slowly sift the earth below the upended root system.

Diamond told his colleagues about the mass of information an anthropologist could get from a single bone. 'As a first step we want an estimate of the length of time since death. Carbon dating should establish that much.'

'Do you think it's ancient?' Halliwell said.

'It didn't look fresh to me. There was a Civil War battle up here three or four hundred years ago. I expect some bodies were buried in haste.'

'There were Iron Age settlements long before that,' Ingeborg said in one of those demonstrations of learning that didn't always go down well. 'The bone could be two thousand years old.'

'How can they tell if it's male or female?' Halliwell asked, getting back to the wonders of anthropology.

Diamond shrugged.

'Not obvious from a femur,' Ingeborg said. 'Much easier with a skull or a pelvis.'

Halliwell rolled his eyes upwards.

'You did ask,' she said.

'I'm in awe,' he said.

'Liar.'

Diamond stepped in. 'Look, I didn't bring

you two up here to knock spots off each other. Just enjoy the scenery. It beats sitting in front of a computer.'

The excavation was slow. After another hour, all the searchers had found was a ring-pull and bits of broken root. The man in charge, a cantankerous character called Duckett, reported that they'd reached a level where the earth was more compacted.

'You mean it hasn't been disturbed?' Diamond said.

'Listen up, will you? I didn't say that. The section we've just cleared was extra loose, as if someone had dug here in the past few weeks.'

'Like Miss Hibbert's dogs?'

'More than that. It's too much for animal activity alone.'

'Why would anyone come digging here?'

'Maybe it was something to do with the re-enactment of the Battle of Lansdown, troops digging themselves in and using the tree as a shield.'

'Good thought. Did any of you watch this event?'

Nobody had.

The digging resumed.

Twenty minutes later, one of the team in the trench said, 'There's something here.' She had exposed a patch of off-white.

'Another bone?' Diamond said. 'Hook it out and we'll see.'

Duckett glared at him as if he was a vandal. 'If you don't mind, superintendent, we'll do this the approved way, leaving everything in situ.'

Soon enough, the outlines of the object were revealed.

'It *is* a bone,' Diamond said.

'A tibia,' Ingeborg said.

Soon some foot bones were unearthed at the lower end of the tibia.

'Can we get someone else clearing at the top end where the skull is?' Diamond asked. The painstaking progress frustrated him.

'We'll do this in our own good time,' Duckett said. 'In all probability it's been here for hundreds of years. An hour or two more isn't going to make much difference.'

Almost as if it was done to provoke the police, the excavation slowed. Brushes, rather than trowels, were being used. At regular intervals photos were taken.

'What time is it?' Duckett eventually asked.

'Three thirty, just gone,' Diamond said.

'Is it, by Jove? Take a break, people. We've been going two hours.'

'You're on a job,' Diamond said.

'Yes, and it's back-breaking work. You

should try it.'

'All right, then.'

'I didn't mean that literally.'

The police were forced to watch the CSI team sit down, open their flasks and look at newspapers. Suspicion hung in the air that the break was being prolonged just to spite Diamond. 'At this rate, we'll be here all night,' he said to Halliwell.

'I heard that,' Duckett said, looking up from his crossword. 'You don't have to worry. We stop at five.'

'Five?'

'Terms and conditions of employment. We're a private firm. Will you be guarding the site overnight?'

'He's winding you up, guv,' Halliwell said.

'I think he means it,' Ingeborg said.

Duckett hadn't finished. 'Now that we've located remains, we'll need to put up a tent to screen off the trench.'

'How long will that take?' Diamond asked.

'Half an hour, no more.'

'We can do that, me and my officers.'

'No, thanks. Not while we're at work in the trench.'

'But you're not in the trench now.'

'It's a specialised job.'

'What — putting up a bloody tent? Ridiculous.'

'This isn't one of your boy scout tents, officer. This is a metal-framed inflatable job, property of the firm. I can't allow any untrained person to handle it.'

Diamond was about to erupt, but Halliwell said, 'Leave it, guv. He's going to have the last word whatever you say.'

'How do they find these people?'

The break came to an end about four. Ingeborg phoned the station to get a man out to guard the site.

'I was expecting answers by now,' Diamond said, pacing the turf. 'All I'm getting is high blood pressure.'

After another twenty minutes there was a clicking sound from the trench. Duckett was snapping his fingers.

Ingeborg said, 'I think he's asking for you.'

'He's asking for something, that's for sure,' Diamond muttered.

He went over. More of the skeleton had been revealed, enough to see that the leg bones were at an angle, as if the body had lain on its side in a foetal position.

Work on the dig was about to stop for the day. More photographs were being taken and one of the CSI team was unloading the protective tent from the van.

Diamond stood over the trench with arms folded. 'You've got something to tell me?'

'Only if you're still interested,' Duckett said. 'You asked about the skull. There isn't one — not where it ought to be, anyway. This would appear to be a headless corpse.'

4

That evening Peter Diamond had a pub meal with Paloma Kean, the one woman he'd been out with since his wife Steph had died six years ago. Their friendship — still more of a friendship than a relationship, although they'd slept together — had got them both through a testing beginning and tough times since. They drew strength from each other. She understood his moods, his brash manner, even his conviction that no one would ever replace Steph as the ideal woman. And he treated Paloma with the warmth that sprang from a shared sense of humour and physical attraction.

They managed to get a candlelit table on the patio at the Hop Pole, in Albion Buildings, off the Upper Bristol Road. This warm summer evening had brought out drinkers and diners in large numbers. With a pint of Barnstormer real ale in front of him and steak pie on order, Diamond was more expansive than usual, telling Paloma about his frustrating day.

'You got out of the office, anyway,' she said when he'd finished. 'It wasn't a bad day to be getting some fresh air.'

'Agreed,' he said. 'A simple walk across the down would have been very agreeable. Instead, we were standing around like dummies all afternoon in the hope that the crime scene people would find something.'

'Well, they did.'

'In the end.'

'It could have been worse, then.'

He gave a grudging nod.

'Personally, I like Lansdown,' Paloma said, doing her best to lighten his mood. 'The history isn't as obvious as it is down here among all the old buildings, but you get a sense of it whichever way you look.'

'The Civil War, you mean?'

'Not just that.'

'Iron Age settlements?'

Her eyes widened. 'You have hidden depths.'

'I was briefed today by Ingeborg, our pet culture vulture.'

'Did she mention Beckford's Tower?'

He'd often driven past the folly towards the city end of the hill, two miles from the crime scene. On the hill today he'd noticed its octagonal gilt lantern on the skyline catching the sunlight. 'He was a weirdo, wasn't he, William Beckford?'

'An extremely rich weirdo,' Paloma said. 'I provided some costume drawings for a TV company doing a documentary on him, so I read the books.' She had amassed a huge collection of archive material on historical costume and built a successful company much used by the lucrative film and television markets. 'An amazing man. He had a much taller tower built at his family seat, at Fonthill Abbey, twice the height of Nelson's Column. Can you imagine that?'

'A Victorian skyscraper.'

'Pre-Victorian. Early nineteenth century. But it lasted only about thirty years. Soon after he sold up, it collapsed.'

'Why?'

'Poor building, bad foundations, something like that. He'd moved to Bath by then.'

'He wasn't so daft, then.'

'Weird, but not daft.'

'You're well up on all this.'

'Another culture vulture in your life — is that what you're thinking?'

'Not at all,' he said. 'Don't forget I took you to the theatre once.'

She smiled. 'On two complimentary tickets. And it was *An Inspector Calls.*'

'What's wrong with that?'

'Nothing. I enjoyed it.' Another smile. 'Next time let's see something unconnected with the police.'

She told him more about the eccentric Beckford, how he created a mile-long landscaped walk across country to his tower and would set off each day from his home in Lansdown Crescent accompanied by a dwarf servant and four dogs. 'I'll lend you a book. You'll enjoy him — witty, wilful and scandalous, too.'

'Thanks.' He doubted if he'd do more than dip into the book. His preference in reading was true crime of the trench coat and trilby days.

The food arrived. Paloma's was a crab and prawn salad. For a while eating had priority over conversation. Only when they'd each confirmed that the food was up to Hop Pole standards did Paloma ask, 'What have you got lined up for tomorrow? Another day watching the dig?'

He shook his head. 'Some chance.'

She raised her eyebrows. 'But it's a murder case, isn't it? You said you've got a headless body.'

'A skeleton without a skull.'

'That's murder, surely?'

'War injury. My best guess is that the head

was blown off by a cannonball in the Civil War. A case for *Time Team,* not me and my lads.'

'Don't you have to investigate, even if it's history?'

'The forensics lot are doing that. They may dig up some bits of armour when they go deeper. Fun for them, but no help to us. I'm outta there.'

'Doesn't the coroner get involved?'

'Too true, he does. And when they report to him they're stuck with all the paperwork. I'm not daft. Anyway, I've got other fish to fry.'

'Keeping the streets of Bath safe?'

'Exactly.'

On cue, a patrol car's siren sounded from somewhere in the city.

'Here's a thought, then,' Paloma said. 'All this talk of Lansdown reminds me that one of my well-heeled clients offered me a free day at the races any time I want. How would you like a flutter on the horses?'

'He was chatting you up.'

'She.'

'Oops.'

'A lady owner, in a long term relationship with a very rich rock star, who shall be nameless. She really means it. She has a double annual badge for the Premier

Enclosure.'

'You think you can pass me off as the rock star?'

She laughed. 'That *would* be a challenge. No, it's perfectly legit. We go as ourselves. Shall I check the date of the next meeting?'

'Why not?' he said, thinking this was a long term suggestion. 'Do you know, I've lived in Bath all this time and never gone racing.'

She took out her mobile and fingered the keys. 'We can remedy that.'

It turned out that there was an evening of racing at Lansdown the next day. Cynic that he was, he suspected she'd planned this all along.

Police work has a knack of springing surprises. In the morning Diamond took a call from Dr Peake, the forensic anthropologist who had been given the femur to examine.

'You said it was found up at Lansdown?' Peake said in that way academics have of double-checking everything before committing themselves.

Diamond had nothing to hide. 'Correct — and now we've found the rest of him, bar the skull. It's a good bet he was a Civil War victim who failed to duck when a cannonball came his way.'

'Have you any evidence for that?'

'Heads don't get parted from bodies that easily.'

'I meant the Civil War connection,' Peake said. 'Are there relics as well as bones?'

'Give us time. We're still digging.' He made it sound as if he wielded a spade himself.

'Now that you've found more bones, I'd better visit the site and see for myself.'

'Be my guest.'

'Mr Diamond, are you certain that the femur I was sent belonged to the skeleton you're talking about?'

'Put it this way, doc. It came from the same hole in the ground and the headless soldier is missing a thigh bone. Why?'

'Because the first indications are that this bone is comparatively modern.'

Diamond said nothing for several seconds. 'What exactly do you mean by that?'

'Not from the Civil War era. More recent. Say within the last twenty-five years.'

'Are you sure?'

' "Sure" isn't a word much favoured in my profession. We prefer "probably" or "maybe". There are too many variables. Going by the state of the bone I wouldn't say it's been buried more than a quarter of a century.'

'Did you carbon date it?'

'I hate to disillusion you, but radiocarbon dating isn't of the slightest use for the short periods in forensic medicine. There was no indication that this bone is ancient.'

'We're not talking *ancient,* doc. A few centuries.'

'Anything over fifty years is classed as ancient in my work.'

'Ouch. You don't have to get personal.'

Peake didn't get the joke. To be fair he hadn't met Diamond to know he was over fifty. 'These are the terms we use.'

'What are your reasons?'

'For saying the bone is modern? For one thing, the appearance. A modern bone has a smooth, soapy texture. And for another, the density. Bones a hundred years old or more are lighter in weight and tend to crumble.'

'That's observation. Have you done lab tests?'

'On the femur? Indeed we have. The nitrogen content is a good indicator. It reduces with time. Typically, a bone three hundred and fifty years old contains a percentage of 2.5. Your femur came in at 4.3.'

'Too much for a dead cavalier?'

'Way too much. We also ran a fluorescence

test. A modern bone will fluoresce under ultraviolet light, but an ancient one fades away to nothing. The femur gave a positive result, not the strongest, but fitting into the time frame I'm suggesting.'

'Twenty-five years or less?'

'Approximately.'

'I don't know whether to thank you or not. You've made me look a bloody fool, but on the other hand you've given me a mystery to work on. Shall we meet up at Lansdown this afternoon?'

Later the same morning he went looking for John Wigfull and found him in a small office studying a computer screen. 'Is this urgent?' Wigfull said, his face with the big moustache rising above the screen like a surfacing walrus. 'I'm at work on a press release.'

'I didn't think you were playing online poker,' Diamond said. 'Is it about the missing cavalier, by any chance.'

'No, that went out yesterday.'

'Any response?'

'It's early days. Peter, if you don't mind, I'm in the middle of something. My time is precious.'

'Mine is as precious as yours, old chum. I'm not here on a social call. How long is it since the re-enactment man disappeared?'

'Rupert Hope? Over two weeks now.' He frowned. 'Why — have you heard something?'

'It's just a coincidence. I'm dealing with a buried skeleton found up at Lansdown. I thought he was a Civil War soldier — a real one — but I'm told the bones are modern.'

'My man wouldn't be bones already,' Wigfull said. 'Not in our climate.'

'I worked that out for myself.'

'So I don't see why you're bothering me. It can't be Rupert Hope.'

'This one is without a head.'

'I wouldn't attach too much importance to that. Ploughing of the land does it.'

'Under a fallen oak tree? That ground hasn't been ploughed in a thousand years.'

'You think he was decapitated?'

'You're a mind-reader.'

'Why? To hinder identification?'

'Probably.'

'Was he murdered, then?'

Diamond rolled his eyes. 'I'm trying to keep the proverbial open mind.'

'A headless corpse,' Wigfull said, beginning at last to be interested. 'It might make an item for the press.'

'Not yet, old chum. We're still digging. We

may get more information. Meanwhile I'm interested in your missing cavalier. Be sure to let me know when he turns up.'

'I doubt if there's a connection.'

'Even so.'

He let Wigfull reconnect with his screen.

Back at the dig, the crime scene team were on another break, flasks and newspapers out, when Diamond turned up. An inflatable tent the size of a small barn had been erected over the area of excavation. He took a look inside. Nothing seemed to have changed since he'd last seen it. The bones were still partially embedded in soil.

'How did you spend the morning?' he asked after emerging from the tent.

Duckett, the head honcho, looked up from the *Daily Mail.* 'What?'

'I said how did you spend the morning? To me it looks the same as it did last night.'

'Skeletons do, on the whole,' Duckett said, and got some grins from his team.

Diamond contained his annoyance. 'I don't know if this makes any difference at all to your rate of work, but we could be dealing with a recent murder here. I've got an expert coming out. A forensic anthropologist.'

'We heard. That's why we downed tools.

He won't want it disturbed any more than it has been already.'

This was probably true. Not often did Peter Diamond come off the worst in an exchange of opinions. He turned his back on them and gazed across the vast landscape as if something of much more interest was happening two miles away.

Actually the action was much closer. Ingeborg's head and shoulders appeared over the brow of the hill. Beside her, at about the level of her bobbing breasts, was a man in a white zipper suit carrying a cardboard box almost as big as himself. 'This is Dr Peake,' Ingeborg told Diamond when she was close enough.

'Lofty,' the small man said in a tone suggesting he'd heard every conceivable play on his name and settled for this one. 'Ingeborg kindly gave me a lift here. Let's have a look at what I came for.' He dropped the box, put on surgical gloves, dipped under the crime scene tape and entered the tent, followed by Diamond and Ingeborg. 'Ah, beautifully presented. Full marks to the diggers. Give me a few minutes with the young lady.'

Diamond had got accustomed to men making a play for the attractive Ingeborg, and it didn't amuse him any more. 'You can have your few minutes with me. I'm the SIO here.'

Lofty Peake said, 'I think we're at cross purposes. I was speaking of the deceased.'

'You said "young lady".'

'Look at the pelvis. Obviously female.'

Time for a rapid rethink. Diamond had convinced himself the victim was male ever since he'd linked the death to the Battle of Lansdown.

He turned to Ingeborg. 'You'd think that dozy lot would have recognised a female skeleton.'

'Maybe they did,' she said.

'And said nothing to me? That would be so unprofessional.'

'I wouldn't take it up with them, guv.'

'I don't intend to. I'm not giving them the satisfaction.'

Lofty Peake was on his knees beside the skeleton, his face so close to the bones that he could have been sniffing them. 'Has she had her picture taken?'

'The victim? Yes, repeatedly.'

'Soil samples taken? A search made for trace evidence? I think we can lift her, then. I'll find out more in the lab. First impressions suggest she was a young adult, average in height. I don't suppose there's much chance of finding the skull, but you'll make the effort, won't you?'

'Do you think it's hereabouts?' Diamond asked.

'Don't ask me. Try a sniffer dog. They're more likely to know than I am.'

'It was a dog that found the femur in the first place.'

'I know that. Its teeth marks were all over the surface. The chances are that she was killed elsewhere and the head removed to hinder identification and if they go to that trouble they're not going to drop the head into the same grave as the body. But you have to search the area.' He asked for his cardboard box and started the task of collecting the bones, lowering them onto layers of tissue paper. 'It goes without saying that the forensic team will collect the soil samples,' he said as he worked. 'We might learn something.'

'Fibres?' Diamond said.

'Hopefully. Clothing deteriorates pretty rapidly in damp, acid soil like this. Cotton won't last longer than a year and a half. Silk and wool are gone in three years. Synthetic fibres such as acrylic may last longer. Leather is fairly durable. The micro-organisms win in the end.'

'If you can estimate how long she's been here, we'll run a check of missing persons for the years in question.'

'In the fullness of time, superintendent. A lot of factors come into it.' He prepared to raise one of the large pelvic bones. 'Do you see how we know she's female? This area below the pubis has to be wider in females to accommodate the birth canal. The baby's head must pass between these two bones.'

'I'll take your word for it,' Diamond said.

'It's very obvious.' Lofty transferred the bones to his box and then turned back to the soil and lifted something that had dropped with a chunk of earth as he raised the pelvis. 'Hey-ho.' He held the thing up. Not bone, for sure, it was about six inches long. He gave it a shake to show how flexible it was.

About the length of an earth worm.

'Proof positive that she isn't ancient,' Lofty said.

'What is it?'

'It could do with cleaning up and then you'll know for sure. I think it's a zip fastener.'

5

The two-year-olds cantered down to the start for the main race of the evening and Paloma was looking at the filly she'd backed at 17 to 2, called My Stylist. 'Mine's moving well,' she said, holding the binoculars to her eyes.

'You've done this before,' Diamond said.

'Mm?'

'I said you've done this before. Are you sure these badges belong to your rich client?'

'I don't know about yours. It's looking nervous.'

'You're not listening, are you?'

'Not now, Peter. This is the exciting part.'

He'd been under pressure from Paloma to put his ten pounds on a runner called Lady Policeman at 25 to 1. Instead he'd preferred Best Brew, the 11 to 8 favourite. As a rare visitor to racecourses, he knew enough about gambling not to fritter away his money on a name with a chance connection to his life. Sentimental betting wasn't clever. Best Brew had the form, a top jockey and was tipped in the papers. It wasn't a bad name either, but that was not a factor, he'd made very clear to Paloma.

The course looked velvet in the evening sun. On a clear, windless day, Lansdown is unequalled. All three enclosures were well filled and there was a buzz of expectation about the main race of the meeting.

Down at the start the handlers were having difficulty persuading some of the young fillies into the stalls. Bucking and whinnying, one pulled back for the second time.

'I think it's yours,' Paloma said.

'I'm not worried,' he said, determined to stay calm. 'The frisky ones start the best.'

'If they start at all,' she said. 'It *is* yours, I'm certain.'

'It's the favourite. It's got to start.'

'Tell that to the horse.'

His calm was beginning to evaporate. 'May I borrow the glasses?'

Now he had the magnified view of another attempt to steer Best Brew forward. All the others were in position and the starter was gesturing to the handlers to hurry. They tried covering the filly's eyes and it reared up, almost unseating the jockey.

'For God's sake!' he said.

One of the lads slipped and fell.

Under pressure himself, the starter spread his hand and gestured at the reluctant horse and appeared to say something. His hand went to the lever.

'I think he's ruled her out,' Diamond said in disbelief. 'That's my money gone before they start.'

The gates crashed open and the field — apart from Best Brew — hurtled from the stalls for the five-furlong dash.

Diamond handed back the binoculars. 'So much for my ten pounds. See if yours comes in.'

Eleven runners thundered away to the loop at the far side of the course, their spindly forelegs thrusting them forward, urged on by their jockeys and the crowd's roar. Over the public address came the measured commentary of the track announcer. 'The early leader is Bluestocking, followed by Lady Be Good and My Stylist.'

'Go, baby!' Paloma said.

'Bluestocking still leads. My Stylist is moving up. Lady Be Good now third. Extra Portion and Reefer showing . . . Coming to the two furlong marker, nothing to choose between Bluestocking and My Stylist. Going well in third is Extra Portion . . . One furlong out, it's still My Stylist and Bluestocking . . .'

'Go, go, go!' Paloma shouted, and Diamond joined in.

'In the last hundred yards, My Stylist leads. Bluestocking fading. Lady Policeman is finishing fast on the outside . . . My Stylist and Lady Policeman. Photograph.'

Paloma was making little jumps. 'I think she got it. What was the other horse?'

'Lady Policeman — the one you told me to back.'

'We could have had a winner for sure.'

'And I didn't listen.'

'But it could have started an argument. Let's see them being led in. I feel sure mine stayed in front.'

'Have you still got your betting slip?'

'In my bag.'

They threaded their way through to the winner's enclosure. Everyone seemed to have an opinion which horse had won until the announcement settled the matter.

'The result of the Tipping Group Fillies race . . .'

The talking everywhere stopped.

'. . . first, My Stylist.'

Shouts of joy.

Paloma grabbed Diamond and embraced him. 'She won! She did it!'

They both did some jumping. 'Nice one.'

Feeling a big debt of gratitude to the horse, they watched her led in by her lady owner in a peacock blue hat and pink suit.

'Isn't she gorgeous?' Paloma said in a carrying voice.

The owner took it as a personal compliment and beamed at them, unaware that the hat had been decorated with a ball of foam from My Stylist's mouth.

Over the public address it was announced that the presentation of the Tipping Group Trophy would be made by Sir Colin Tipping.

'Local sponsor,' Paloma told Diamond. 'Heads a firm of chartered surveyors. Once owned a horse called Hang-glider that won one of the classics.'

Well informed, as well as a winner, he thought, wondering where she'd learned so much racing lore.

'And by a happy coincidence,' the announcement continued, 'the winning owner is Sir Colin's daughter, Mrs Davina Temple-Smith.'

'Talk about keeping it in the family,' Paloma said.

The grey-haired and grey-suited Sir Colin duly handed over a sterling silver model of a galloping horse on a black marble plinth.

There were coos of delight from some of the women in the crowd as the winning owner also got a kiss that gave a tilt to the peacock hat.

'Let's collect your winnings,' Diamond said in Paloma's ear.

'You think I'm heading straight for the champagne bar after that,' she said. 'Well, you're a smart detective. I am.'

Two long rows of bookies were standing in the betting ring among discarded betting slips paying out to the successful punters. Paloma found the right man and collected. Before they moved off, someone shouted, 'Watch out.'

The shout had come from beside the course.

The bookie turned to look and said, 'Flaming hell, what a twat!'

A scruffy-looking man in jeans and a hooded jacket had climbed the rail and was ambling across the racecourse from the centre to the Paddock Enclosure oblivious of the horses being cantered past for the start of the next race. A jockey yelled at him. People in the crowd were getting angry, too.

'A few beers too many,' Diamond said.

'Or he's found a way to get in free,' Paloma said.

If that was the object, it worked — up to a

point. The man was grabbed by one of the police and dragged over the rail and into the exclusive section, so close to Diamond and Paloma that they heard him say in quite a refined drawl, 'Thank you, officer, I'll be on my way then.'

'What the hell were you up to?' the constable asked.

'Crossing over for a bite to eat. All the food seems to be this side.'

'You must be nuts. What's your name?'

'Noddy.'

'Definitely drunk,' Diamond said to Paloma. 'And a stupid drunk. He could have been killed.'

'Serve him bloody right if he had been,' the bookie said. 'More serious, he could have damaged a horse. He's trouble, that one. He's been here and acting daft since I set up two hours ago. I don't think he paid to get in.'

'Neither did we,' Paloma murmured to Diamond as they moved off.

'But we're not misbehaving.'

'Yet,' she said. 'What will happen to him?'

'He'll be shown the gate. It's too much hassle to charge him with anything unless he turns violent. He's at the silly stage now.'

They found the champagne lawn where the winning owner was treating her friends, and she seemed to have a lot of them. They heard someone say, 'I'm so delighted for Davina. She looks every bit the socialite, doesn't she, and she was probably in surgery as usual this morning. She deserves this.'

'Dr Davina, then?' Diamond said to Paloma.

A woman near them shook her head. 'She's a local vet.'

'Lucky animals. My cat goes to a bearded Australian with red socks and sandals.'

A waitress was moving among them with a tray loaded with filled glasses.

'Shall we join them?' Diamond said.

'It's a private party.'

'Anyone with a horse like that is a friend of ours.'

'I couldn't,' Paloma said. 'Let's buy our own.'

When they'd got their glasses, he raised his and said, 'To My Stylist.'

She seemed to enjoy some joke at his expense as they clinked glasses. Whatever it was, he didn't mind. Her eyes were still shining.

He remarked that she'd clearly been racing before.

'What makes you say that?'

'For a start, you picked the winner.'

'Luck,' she said.

'And some judgement, I suspect. When we saw them parading you seemed to know what to look for.'

'There are too many variables for anyone to get it wholly right,' she said in a more serious tone, confirming his impression that she knew more than she'd said up to now. She was such a different personality from Steph, who'd never concealed anything. In his mind he immediately rejected the notion of concealment. Paloma wasn't sneaky. Rather, she chose not to air her knowledge unless and until it was useful. Hidden depths was a better way of putting it.

'You mean the weights they carry?'

'The going, the form they've shown in previous outings, the jockey and whether they're blinkered or tongue-strapped for the first time.'

'Sounds like a medieval torture.'

'Funnily enough, it can give them confidence. Then there's another factor: the stable. On a course like this one, which isn't as highly rated as some, you get expensive and blue-blooded young horses from top stables at places like Lambourn being sent here to win. They start at odds-on and tend to win by small margins to nurse their handicaps.'

'Was mine trained at Lambourn?'

She smiled. 'Doesn't matter, does it? If they won't start, they can't win.'

'Did you know it was highly strung?'

And now she laughed. 'Of course not. I'd have told you to save your money.'

'You advised me to bet on Lady Policeman.'

'For fun.'

'I'm not sure what to believe now. You know your horses.'

She glanced down and thoughtfully traced her finger around the rim of the glass. 'There's a reason I haven't told you about. Gordon, my ex, was a compulsive gambler. He knew practically nothing about racing except that you sometimes get lucky.'

'Sometimes, but not enough times.'

'Exactly. I soon found out he wasn't going to come to his senses, so I thought if I took the trouble to learn the basics the bets might be better informed.'

'And were they?'

'Immeasurably.' Another laugh. 'And it didn't make a blind bit of difference. My system was no better than Gordon's. But that's how I can bluff with the best.'

'You're telling me this win was down to luck?'

'Nothing else.'

Later in the evening, back at Paloma's

house on Lyncombe Hill, Diamond got lucky, too.

6

Two days later the police were alerted to a man trying to break into cars in the small car park behind the stands at Bath racecourse. It wasn't a race day so there weren't many vehicles parked there — just a few belonging to staff.

'Deal with it, will you?' the sergeant on duty radioed to a patrol car in the city.

'You want us to bring him in?'

'You heard what I said.' The modern police are knee deep in paper. Bringing in a suspect would indicate an intention of charging him and about two hours of filling in forms. 'What we have is a call from a Major Swithin who noticed what was going on and reported it.'

PC Andy Sullivan, the driver, was thankful for the job. He'd been stuck all week with a new 'oppo' who thought silence was the eighth deadly sin. He already knew more than he needed about Denise Beal's admiration for David Beckham. Even when he had the two-tone siren going she didn't stop. She simply raised her voice.

The sight of Major Swithin did the trick. When they drove up the approach to the racecourse, Denise went silent in mid-sentence. The major was in the middle of the road waving a shotgun.

'Doesn't it fill you with confidence?' Andy Sullivan said. He lowered the window and said, 'I hope you have a certificate for that, sir.'

'What? This? Of course.' The major was probably closer to eighty than seventy, a short, stout, silver-haired man in a Barbour and flat cap. 'Good thing I had it in the car. If you need some support arresting this scum, you can count on me.'

'Right now, I'm counting on you to step off the road and put the gun on the path. Is it loaded?'

'You can bet your life it is. I was a regular officer for thirty years. Served in six different war zones. I know about firearms.'

'Then you know it's illegal to have a loaded shotgun in a public place. Do as I say. Now!'

'For the love of Mike!' The major obeyed the instruction. 'Anyone would think I was the criminal.'

'Thank you, sir. Stand back, please.' Sullivan stepped out of the car, retrieved the gun, opened the breech and removed two cartridges. 'You are Major Swithin, I take it?'

'Who else would I be, looking out for you? I wasn't proposing to shoot you — or the car thief, come to that.'

'What's the gun for, then?'

'In case I spot a fox. The Socialists stopped the hunt from destroying them, so it's down to public-spirited people like me.'

Sullivan returned the gun and cartridges. 'Keep the breech open and unloaded. This man you saw. Is he still in the car park?'

'I expect so.'

'What exactly was he doing?'

'Trying to steal a car.'

'How do you know that?'

'It was blatantly obvious. He was going from vehicle to vehicle trying the doors. A rough-looking herbert, unshaven, shabbily dressed.'

'How long ago was this?'

'Ten or fifteen minutes maximum. He won't get far. My wife has him in her sights.'

'Your *wife?* Is she armed as well?'

'With the field-glasses. I left her observing him. She may have more to report by now. Shall I meet you in the car park?'

'You'd better get in the car. How old is your wife?'

'Does that have any bearing? She's a senior citizen, and well capable of looking after herself.'

With the major in the back seat they drove off at speed while he continued to justify his actions. 'These days John Citizen has to pitch in and help with law and order.'

'Up to a point,' Andy Sullivan said as they approached the line-up of cars in front of the turnstiles.

'That's Agnes looking out of the sun roof of my Land Rover.'

Agnes must have been standing on the seat, for she was very obvious, an elderly woman in a deerstalker peering through binoculars.

The police car drew up beside the ancient Land Rover. Major Swithin was the first out. 'Any sign of the blighter, Agnes?'

The old lady lowered the glasses. 'He's gone in. I spotted him heading for the grandstand end. I think he knows we're onto him.'

'That *is* a possibility,' Sullivan said, exchanging a look with his Beckham-obsessed colleague. She was still tongue-tied. 'We'll take over, then.'

'You're not proposing to go it alone?' the

major said in a shocked tone. 'We'll come with you.'

'No, you won't. You'll stop here, the pair of you. I'll need a witness statement from you.'

'You're mad.'

'Not to say ungrateful,' Agnes added.

Regardless, Sullivan walked away, heading for the open gates to the left of the turnstiles. 'Wouldn't you rather be in a job where the clients give no trouble, like grave-digging?' he said to Denise Beal.

He should have known better than to ask Denise a rhetorical question.

'Personally,' she said, 'I wouldn't enjoy digging graves, but I once had a part-time job doing a survey in Milsom Street, asking people questions about their favourite footballers, and, do you know, four out of every five — girls mostly, I must admit — nominated David Beckham, which gave me my opportunity because really I was only there to suggest they tried his new perfume. Isn't it amazing how easily you can get people to talk? Have you noticed it yourself?'

'I don't have to try,' he said.

And she proved it by going on some more about Beckham.

They faced the two grandstands along the finishing straight, the Premier — for the super-rich and sponsors — and the G & P — the Grandstand and Paddock — for those who prefer paying less. The whole complex had plenty of places where a fugitive from justice might hide. Sullivan's gaze also took in some low buildings away to the right.

'We'll split up,' he said. 'You check the stands and I'll do the stabling area over there.' The stables were a good two hundred metres away.

'What if I find him?'

'Keep him talking till I arrive. That shouldn't be any problem for you.'

'Is he dangerous?'

'Compared to that idiot with the shotgun, no.'

Few places are so bleak as a racecourse enclosure on a day of no racing. Denise Beal felt uneasy, for all Andy Sullivan's confidence. Typical of him, the senior partner, to send her to the place where the suspect was last seen. She fingered the handle of her baton. This was only her second month in the police. Some of them at the station had said she was lucky getting picked for car patrol duty, hinting heavily that her good looks had worked the magic. Others had said Andy Sullivan was the lucky one. But he'd made very clear that he was indifferent to her. He seemed to resent being partnered by a woman. Up to now, though, he'd done everything by the book. The less experienced officer always gets the rough jobs.

She thought about her obligation to keep the suspect talking, and wondered if she could cope. What do you talk about when you have to do it? The weather? The cars he's broken into?

A pigeon flew from a ledge so close to her face that she felt the rush of air. She gave a squeak of fright. Good thing macho PC Sullivan wasn't there to hear it. Moving on, she came to an industrial-sized rubbish bin, easily large enough for a man to hide inside. She debated whether to lift the lid, and thought better of it and walked on. Andy Sullivan need never know. He'd sent her to the danger area so what did he expect? She took a wide berth rounding the corner of the Paddock Bar and was relieved to see no one crouching there.

From here she had a good view of the course.

Not a living soul.

Putting herself through an ordeal like this wasn't why she'd joined. She'd pictured herself doing crowd control at a Spice Girls' revival gig, escorting the stars and their spouses to the VIP seats.

All looked deserted in the stand area at the front, so she moved on and down some steps. To her left was a recessed area, probably one of the entrances to the Premier stand where the celebs went. She wondered if Becks had ever been here. Probably not. Bath wasn't one of the fashionable racecourses.

Then she noticed a movement in the shadows.

A man was there.

Her heart thumped against her ribcage, but not because he looked like Becks.

He fitted the major's description, rough-looking, unshaven, shabbily dressed. Probably in his mid-forties. Torn jacket with hood, mud-stained cord trousers and sandals. His feet hadn't seen soap for a long time. He was leaning against the wall with arms folded, showing no reaction to her.

Denise knew where her duty lay. She looked ahead to see if by some miracle Andy was in sight, but he wasn't. She could summon him by radio, but he'd have to run all the way back from the stables before he could come to her assistance.

She stepped up to the man and said, 'Do you mind telling me what you're doing here?'

He was silent for some time. Finally,

without making eye contact, he said, 'It's a free country.'

She said, 'You're on private property here.'

'If you say so.' The voice was educated.

'What's your name?'

'They call me Noddy.'

He's sending me up, she thought. How do I handle this? 'Noddy who?'

'Just that. Noddy.' His expression hadn't altered. He seemed to be serious.

'Are you local, Noddy?'

'I must be, mustn't I? I'll be on my way, then.'

'Hold on a second.' She stared into the far distance. Still no Andy. 'Were you in the car park just now?'

'Which car park is that?'

'Behind me. Not many cars there today, so it may not look like a car park, but someone like you was seen there.'

'If you say so.' That phrase again. It didn't come across as defiance or evasion. This guy was passive to the point of resignation.

'Have you been drinking, Noddy?'

He shook his head.

She said, 'I'm trying to work out what you're doing here.'

He spread his dirty hands. He didn't appear to have an answer. Denise wondered if he was just some simple-minded guy unable to cope with modern life. And now she was stumped for another question.

She had a strong sense that no one would rush to congratulate her if she handcuffed Noddy and pulled him in. Even if he *had* been trying car doors it was probably because he was looking for food or drink. So she did what they'd advised at training school: used her initiative. 'On your way, then. Sharpish. And stay away from cars.'

He nodded three times. Was that how he'd got his name? Then he shuffled off — towards the end Andy Sullivan would come from.

'Not there,' Denise said and pointed her thumb behind her, towards the golf course. 'That's your best your way out.' Remembering the major and his wife, she added, 'Don't go through the car park.'

She moved on herself and eventually linked up with Andy Sullivan in the Grandstand and Paddock enclosure. He asked if she'd seen anyone and she shook her head. For all her compulsion to make conversation, she respected the old adage that all truths are not to be told.

'No bad thing,' Andy said. 'Saves us some paperwork.'

'The major won't like it,' Denise said.

'I'm backing you to silence the major. Tell

him about Posh and Becks.'

Lofty Peake phoned Diamond later in the week with his findings.

'Your victim was about five six in height and probably under twenty, but not much under. Leaving some margin for error, I'd say she was seventeen to twenty-one. The epiphyses — those are the bony caps on the ends of the long bones — were not fully united, and that's a pretty reliable test of age. Pity we don't have the skull because you can tell a lot more from that.'

'I doubt if we'll find it now.'

'Incidentally, the head was hacked off with some force, going by the state of the vertebrae.'

Diamond had a brief, vivid image. It wasn't long since he'd eaten breakfast. 'After death?'

'Let's hope so. I've no way of telling. She appears to have been a healthy individual. The skeleton was normal in development, with no evidence of earlier fractures.'

'What about her build? Was she sturdy?'

'No more than average.'

'Now the critical question,' Diamond said. 'How long is it since she died? When we last spoke, you said up to twenty-five years.'

'You know the answer, then.'

'But you had only one bone to work from.'

'Correct. Good, wasn't I?'

'You're standing by the estimate?'

'When it comes to telling the age, more bones don't necessarily yield more information. As you know, I carried out extensive tests on the femur.'

'Twenty-five years is a lot to work with.'

'Now you're asking another question.'

'Am I?'

'You want a time frame. The answer is — and this can only be an estimate based on observation — that the bones have been in the ground for more than ten years. No soft tissue remains and there's some coarsening and discoloration that I would expect from the temperature changes of a series of summers and winters. Yet there are still traces of the candle-wax odour given out by the fat in the bone marrow, so these remains are not all that old.'

'Between ten and twenty-five?'

'Best I can do for you.'

'You found the zip under the pelvis. Presumably it was a zipfly from a pair of jeans. I'd expect someone of her age to be wearing jeans. All of the fabric had rotted away, I suppose?'

'Completely. Nothing remained in the soil samples.'

'The zip survived because it was metal. Wouldn't she also have been wearing a belt?'

'We didn't find one. Not everyone wears one. They wear their jeans so tight that there's really no need for a belt.'

'If she'd had coins in her pockets, they could help.'

'How? What could they tell you about her?'

It was Diamond's turn to air some knowledge. 'They show the year they were minted, don't they? We could narrow that time frame.'

'I'm with you now,' Lofty said. 'But no joy there. I checked with the crime scene people who were at the site and they found nothing else of interest. No coins, jewellery, belt buckle, shoes. Not even the hooks and eyes of a bra.'

Diamond could picture the look on Duckett's charmless face as he announced he'd found nothing more. He thanked Lofty, put down the phone and went to look for Ingeborg. She was at her computer.

He told her about the fifteen-year time frame. 'We're looking for a young woman aged seventeen to twenty-one who went missing between 1984 and 1999.'

She turned to look at him. '1987, guv.'

'That isn't what I said.'

'That was the year of the great storm. October, 1987.'

'Well?'

'When so many trees came down. She was buried in the hollow left by a tree's roots.'

She was bright. He wished he'd thought of that. 'But can we be sure that tree came down then?'

She nodded. 'I checked with the Lansdown Society.'

'The *what?*'

'There's a society dedicated to keeping Lansdown unspoilt. I believe they're a mix of landowners and wildlife enthusiasts. They monitor everything up there, all the activities.'

'And they knew about that tree?'

'As soon as I asked.'

He raised both thumbs. 'So the time frame comes down to twelve years. You're a star, Ingeborg. And now you can become a megastar by checking the missing persons register for those years.'

'I already have, guv.'

'You'll get a medal at this rate.'

'Not when you hear the result. I looked at all the local counties, made a list of missing girls under twenty-five, but I'm not confident she's on it.'

'Can you show me?'

She worked the keyboard and four names with brief details appeared on the screen.

'Why so few? Hundreds of people go missing.'

'We narrowed the criteria. These are all the search gave me.'

'So what's the problem with them?'

'Look at the descriptions. The first girl, Margaret Edgar, was five foot eleven and Hayley Walters was only half an inch less. Gaye Brewster had broken her left arm and had it pinned some weeks before she disappeared. That would surely have been noticed by Mr Peake. Olivia Begg was about the height of our victim, but she went in for body piercings and nothing like that was found at the site.'

'Those rings people wear in their . . . ?'

'Places I'd rather not mention.'

'The killer could have removed them. He removed the head.'

'True, but Olivia went missing only in 1999, at the margin of our time frame, and even that's in doubt. There was an unconfirmed sighting of her in Thailand two years later. I doubt if she's ours.'

Diamond exhaled, a long, resigned breath. 'I've got to agree with you, Inge. They're not serious candidates. When you think about it, plenty of young women of this age leave their families and friends and quite often it doesn't get reported because no one is alarmed. It's their choice. They hitch up with a pop star or go travelling or end up on the game. They don't make the list of missing persons.'

She raked her hand through her long blonde hair and clutched it to the nape of her neck. 'So what else can we do?'

'Ask ourselves questions about the killer. Why choose to bury the body at Lansdown?'

After a moment's reflection she said, 'It's remote. He wouldn't be noticed if he picked his time to dig the grave.'

'True.'

'Where the tree was uprooted the soil would be looser to work with. He'd have a ready-made hole in the ground and he could use the soft earth to cover the corpse.'

'You're right about that. It was buried quite deep, not the proverbial six feet under, but all of three.'

'Deep enough.'

He nodded. 'Most murderers don't appreciate the difficulty of digging a grave in unsuitable ground. The body found in a shallow grave is a cliché of the trade.'

'So he chose his spot wisely, but he'd still have to transport the body there.'

'Well, the ground slopes down a bit, but

you could drive across the field in, say, a four by four.'

'This is looking like someone who knows Lansdown well.'

'Either that, or he got lucky,' Diamond said. 'The body was undiscovered for at least ten years and probably several more. It was deep enough to avoid the interest of foxes and dogs for a long time.'

'It was a dog that found the bone in the end,' Ingeborg said.

'Yes, and I wonder why, after so long. Had something happened to disturb the grave?'

'Dogs do go digging.'

'Not that deep. Miss Hibbert didn't say anything about the dog burrowing. She seemed to suggest he found it near the surface.'

'What are we saying, guv? Some person was digging there? Why would they do that?'

Out of nowhere he became confessional. 'When I was about eleven we used to make camps in the woods and smoke our fathers' cigarettes and look at girlie magazines.'

Ingeborg didn't really want this insight into his misspent youth and couldn't see how it impacted on the investigation.

'The space under the root system would make a good camp if you dug into it,' he said.

'Not my scene,' she said, with a mental image of the adult Diamond sitting in the mud reading soft porn. 'But I see what you're getting at.'

'Do kids still do that — make camps?'

'I expect so — but I doubt if they'd choose Lansdown. It's a long way from habitation.'

'The crime scene people found some ringpulls.'

'Adults?'

'You might have a picnic there on a warm day.'

'But you wouldn't go digging for bones.'

His thoughts went back to something John Wigfull had told him. 'A few weeks ago they re-enacted a Civil War battle up there. Grown-ups playing soldiers. If you were defending a stretch of ground and needed to dig in you'd be glad of a position like that.'

'It wasn't the Western Front,' Ingeborg said. 'The Civil War was all about man to man fighting, not trenches.'

'You'd need to store your supplies somewhere. You'd look for an obvious place like that, partly sheltered. I reckon they're the people who disturbed the grave. If they unearthed a femur in the heat of battle they're not going to give it much attention. That could be how it came to the surface.'

'Does it matter?'

He didn't answer that. He was on a roll. Thanks to John Wigfull, he could air his second-hand knowledge with impunity. 'Most weekends in the summer there's a muster somewhere. That's what they call it, a muster. The Sealed Knot came to Lansdown this year and they've been before, but not every year. Obviously they had a major muster in 1993, the anniversary.'

'Of the Battle of Lansdown?'

'Three hundred and fifty years on.' He paused, as if to weigh the evidence. 'We're looking for a killer who buried his victim in the hole left by the tree. Depth, soft earth to cover her with. She's been buried at least ten years. I'm thinking about 1993, right in the middle of our time frame.'

7

Unfortunately there was no better way of progressing the case of the headless skeleton than to employ the services of the new media relations manager. John Wigfull was still positioned behind his computer when Diamond came in.

'How's business?' Diamond asked.

Wigfull didn't look up from the keyboard. 'Early days.'

'Any results?'

'I don't know about that.'

Diamond picked up a paper from the desk. The *Bath Chronicle.* He'd noticed a Post-it note marking an inside page. 'Oh, yes. A definite result.'

The page he'd opened had the headline CLOCK THE CAVALIER, over some photos. The picture editor had superimposed Rupert Hope's face on several well known images. In one he was the Laughing Cavalier of Franz Hals and in another a Van Dyck portrait of Charles I. In a third he was given the resplendent hair of Brian May, of Queen.

'It's not the press release I gave them,' Wigfull said with bitterness.

'They've been creative.'

'I called the editor to complain. He said the story will get more attention this way.'

'Probably true. The phone will start ringing soon.'

'It already has.'

'Well then.'

'A number of people claim to have seen him locally. They seem to expect a reward. It's not a game.'

'But it's not too serious. I expect your Rupert Hope will turn up wondering what all the fuss is about.'

'Are you saying I shouldn't have released the story?'

'No, it makes good copy. That's what your job is about, isn't it — feeding juicy stories to the media?'

Wigfull twitched in disapproval. 'It's a whole lot more than that. I'm not just here to get publicity. I'm after results.'

'Which is why I'm here,' Diamond said as if he were Wigfull's guardian angel. 'I told you about my headless skeleton. I know some more now and I'm ready to go public.'

'You want me to inform the press?'

'Don't sound so gloomy about it. This is the big one, John, your chance to make the nationals.' He pulled up a chair and sat beside Wigfull. 'A young girl, under twenty-one, buried on Lansdown minus her head. We need to know who she was. An appeal for information. Who remembers a girl going missing in the nineties?'

Together, they drafted the press release. When it was done, Diamond returned to the CID office and spoke to Ingeborg. 'Something you mentioned the other day has been on my mind. The Lansdown Society. You said you'd been in touch with them about the fallen tree.'

She blinked twice and gave a nervous cough. 'That wasn't strictly true, guv. A friend of mine did some work for them. That's how I heard of them.'

'Not a problem. I was thinking they could be useful to us. I tried looking them up. They don't seem to have a phone number or a website.'

'I don't think they're a public organisation.'

'How did your friend get to hear of them?'

'Perry's a cartographer. They commission him to make maps of the land use up there. He told me he did one showing features of botanical interest. I thought of him when we went to look at the site.'

'He's your inside man?'

'He doesn't go to the meetings. It's all rather secretive as far as I can make out. But he knew about the tree and it definitely came down in 1987. It would have been sawn up and removed, only it has some rare lichens on the trunk.'

'Come again.'

'Lichen. That bright green stuff, isn't it, like a fungus?'

'Nature study passed me by at school. Getting back to the Lansdown Society, what's it about?'

'According to Perry, they want to keep the down unspoilt. Like I said, they monitor everything that goes on.'

'Does much go on?'

'More than you'd think, particularly at weekends. Football, golf, hang-gliding, kites.'

'It all sounds harmless enough. What are they afraid of — the ground getting scuffed up?'

She smiled. 'I wouldn't know.'

'One thing is certain. They must know all about the Civil War events. I bet that tests their tolerance, muskets and cannon going off and cavalry charging across the sacred turf. I'd like to know their take on it. How do I get to meet them?'

'I could ask Perry.'

'Do that. Is he, er . . . ?'

'Just a friend.'

Lansdown is, indeed, a place where much goes on. Sundays and Bank Holiday Mondays through the summer see a large car boot sale in the racecourse car park. The traders set up from 7.30 a.m. and the buyers are supposed to arrive from 9 a.m. onwards, although dealers have their ways of getting an early look. There's always the hope that a Hepplewhite chair or the first Harry Potter will be put up for sale by some innocent. After the dealers have swept through, that hope has gone. There isn't much chance of one of the public finding a real bargain. But the sale is still somewhere to go on a Sunday, a free show and a social occasion. The setting, with those views into Somerset and Wiltshire, is unequalled. But the downside is that it's exposed to the elements.

On this breezy Sunday anything that wasn't weighted down was taking to the air. The various wood and fabric structures used as rain covers or sunshades or just extra shelving were under threat from gusts.

More than one table collapsed. Some traders spent most of the morning rearranging their displays. It wasn't surprising that a visitor in a hooded jacket was able to move through the sale helping himself to food items. He'd got some way before one of the traders asked him for payment for a meat pie he'd picked up from a stall that sold hot food.

He replaced it at once.

'You can't do that,' she told him. 'It's got a bite out of it. That'll be one pound fifty.'

The man shrugged and moved on.

'Hey!' the woman said. 'That's no good to me. I can't sell it. That's theft.'

He was already some way off.

She asked the trader nearest to her to take over. 'He's not getting away with it. I'm going after him.'

'Leave it, dear,' the neighbour said. She was a peace-loving woman with a long chiffon scarf. She sold copper bracelets and good luck charms. 'He won't have any money on him. I've seen him nick stuff before. He's simple.'

The pie woman wasn't to be dissuaded. Snatching up the pie, she set off through the crowd and caught up with the man near a display of model cars. 'This is your pie, mister. You owe me one pound fifty.'

He shook his head.

'Here, take it,' she said, thrusting it at him 'Enjoy it. I can say it myself, because I made it, it's a good pie. It's no use to me or anyone else now you've bitten a chunk out of it. Just pay for it and that's the end of the matter.'

'Madam, I can't,' he said in a refined tone. 'I have no money on me.'

'That's great. What are you doing here anyway, if you've got no money? This is a sale, not a fucking free-for-all.' Her shouting was starting to get attention from the crowd and she felt compelled to take action rather than lose face. 'All right,' she said. 'Citizen's arrest. I'm nicking you for theft. Anything you say will be used in evidence against you. Someone call the police. Who's got a phone?'

The man under arrest shook his head. 'Not me.'

'I wasn't asking you.'

'I beg your pardon.' He was co-operative, if nothing else. He looked bewildered.

Uncertain what to do next, the pie woman grasped the man's arm and led him back towards her van. He came like a lamb.

It was the copper bracelet seller who reluctantly called the police on her mobile. 'It's not my name you want,' she said into the phone. 'It's the lady who made the arrest. What's your name, love?'

Before the pie woman could answer, the arrested man said, 'Noddy.'

'God help us!' the copper bracelet seller said, and giggled. Somehow, she got control of herself and gave the essential facts and ended the call. 'They said to keep him here if possible and they'll send someone.'

The result of all this was self-defeating. No trade was done in the next half hour. The man calling himself Noddy had his own aroma competing with the appetising smell of the pies.

When two police officers eventually made their way through the crowd, the pie seller explained what had happened. As proof, she showed them the pie with the bite out of it.

'And you arrested him?' PC Andy Sullivan said.

'Citizen's arrest,' the woman said. 'It's common law.'

'I know that, ma'am. Do you want to press charges?'

'I want to be paid for my pie, that's all.'

It's the job of uniformed police to defuse a situation whenever possible. Andy Sullivan spoke to the prisoner. 'Why don't you give the lady the money and settle the matter?'

'Because I haven't got any money, officer.' Shabby and strong-smelling he may have been, but the man was polite, well-spoken and logical. Not the usual troublemaker.

'What's your name?'

'Noddy.'

Sullivan revised his opinion.

A stifled sound of mirth came from behind the copper bracelet table.

While this was going on, Sullivan's partner, PC Denise Beal, wished she was a million miles away. Her stomach was churning. She could see her short career in the police coming to a quick end if Noddy recognised her. She was trying to avoid eye contact.

Sullivan moved his face closer to the prisoner's. 'If you mess with me, my friend, you'll regret it. Now tell me your name.'

'I'd rather not, if you don't mind.'

'Why?'

'Because I'll regret it.'

'Don't get smart with me. Who are you?'

'That's what I'm called. Noddy.'

'He's not right in the head,' the copper bracelet woman said. 'I've been trying to tell her.'

'Hold on,' the pie woman said. 'I'm the victim in all this, not him. I've lost half a morning's trade through him. I'm taking him to court.'

'Where do you live?' Sullivan asked the man.

The copper bracelet woman said, getting another fit of the giggles, 'Toyland.'

Sullivan told her to shut up. Then he turned back to the man. 'I'm waiting for an answer.'

'I'm living up here for the present.'

'But where exactly?'

'Anywhere that's dry on a wet night.'

'So you're homeless?'

The man nodded.

This touched the heart of the copper bracelet woman. 'Did you hear that? He's homeless. You can't take a homeless man to court.'

'I can and I will,' the pie woman said. 'He may sound like a smoothie, but he's a thief. You can't argue with the evidence.' She held up the pie. But such was the force of her feelings that her thumb and finger met in the middle and the evidence collapsed and fell in bits on the ground. 'Oh, buggery!'

'I was going to say "crumbs",' the copper bracelet woman said, in giggles again. 'Case dismissed, I reckon.'

This was all too much for the pie woman. 'You bitch!' Angry and defeated, she made a grab, caught hold of the other woman's scarf and wrestled her to the ground. They rolled over and over, screaming, in a flurry of bare legs and black underwear, all dignity gone.

'Get them apart,' Andy Sullivan said to Denise.

It took half a minute and some grappling, but at least Denise was in trousers. She'd had recent training in detaining a suspect resisting arrest and she succeeded in getting the pie woman's arm behind her back and forcing it upwards so that the other woman could squirm free.

'Okay,' Sullivan said to the pie woman, still on the ground. 'Are you going to be sensible and calm down?'

She said, 'Let go of me.'

The copper bracelet woman had retreated to the other side of her table and was brushing down her clothes. She said, 'I could do her for assault. She almost strangled me.'

'I don't think that's a good idea,' Sullivan said. He nodded to Denise. 'You can let go of her now.'

The pie woman got up, mouthing obscenities, but not giving voice to them.

Andy Sullivan was in control. 'And now I think you ladies should go back to doing what you paid your fee for, selling your wares.'

'Where's he gone?' the pie woman said. 'What happened to the thief?'

In all the distraction, the man known as Noddy had gone.

Late the same Sunday evening, Diamond took a call at home. It was Ingeborg, apologising for troubling him, and saying she'd made contact with her friend Perry, the link to the Lansdown Society. Two of the committee, Perry had told her, had a regular Monday morning round of golf and it might be an opportunity to see them. They met at ten.

'Who are these two?' he asked.

'A Major Swithin and Sir Colin Tipping.'

Thinking his own thoughts about ranks and titles, he wrote down the names. 'Tipping? I've heard of him. He sponsored a horse race I watched the other evening.'

'I didn't know you followed the horses, guv.'

'I was being sociable. Horse racing or golf, I take it all in my stride. Is that the course up at Lansdown? I don't really need to ask, do I? Thanks for that, Inge. I'll make it a threesome and ruin their morning.'

8

Early on Monday, Diamond looked in at Manvers Street and told Keith Halliwell about the press conference fixed for the afternoon. 'Basically we're going public about the skeleton in the hope it will jog someone's memory. John Wigfull is setting it up, but you may get enquiries during the morning. I'll be at the golf course, so you're in charge.'

He was amused by Halliwell's wide-eyed look, a mixture of mystification and umbrage, but nothing was said.

'Ingeborg will fill you in,' he added, not wanting to cause real hurt.

On the drive out of town he saw the morning traffic inching down Lansdown Road and for a short while felt what it was like to be on a private income and able to indulge in golf while most of the world was forced to earn a living. In truth he knew he'd soon weary of the life of leisure. Golf wasn't his sport, anyway. The only white ball game worth playing was table tennis — his sort, in the old ping pong tradition, with sandpaper bats and no crafty spinning allowed.

Not many cars were parked outside the clubhouse. He checked the time. Five minutes to spare. Rather than go inside he made his way around the building to the first tee. The two members he needed to meet probably kept good time, one being a military man.

Even on an August morning, it was cool up here, over seven hundred feet above sea level, and he wished he'd dressed as golfers do, in some kind of sweater and perhaps a baseball cap. Nobody was waiting to play when he arrived. In the distance, the pair who had started earlier had already played the first hole and moved on.

Two minutes to ten. No sign of the Lansdown Society. His assumption about good timekeeping was looking faulty.

Then a whirring sound came from the side of the clubhouse and a golf cart glided into view and across the trimmed turf to arrive at the tee precisely on time. One of the two riders was definitely Sir Colin Tipping. The other, at the wheel, halted the cart. Major Swithin was short and elderly, but had more than a hint of military swagger as he stepped off and approached Diamond.

'Is there a problem?'

'Not to my knowledge,' Diamond said. 'Would you be Major Swithin?'

'I would. We have our round booked for now. It's a regular arrangement. Are you a member?'

'Visitor.'

'You know visitors have to produce a handicap certificate?'

Not the friendliest of welcomes, Diamond thought. 'I don't want to play.'

Sir Colin Tipping was slower getting off the cart, as if arthritis had set in. He looked just as distinguished as he had in the winner's enclosure. Today he was in a loose-fitting yellow sweatshirt and check trousers. 'What's this, Reggie?' he said to the major. 'Have you hired the professional to improve your game?' He chuckled at his own humour.

Diamond showed them his warrant card and gave them a moment to absorb the shock. 'I don't want to hold up your round, gentlemen. If you don't mind, we'll talk as you go along. All I want is the benefit of your expertise.' This was a phrase he'd fashioned while shaving, the right touch of flattery, he'd decided.

'Detective Superintendent, are you?' Tipping said. 'He's a senior man, Reggie. You must have done something pretty serious this time. Did you try it on once too often with the barmaid?'

'He says he wants expertise,' the major said. In this comedy act he was definitely the straight man.

'If that means tips on golf, he's picked the wrong fellows,' Tipping said. He grinned at Diamond. 'Our combined handicap is bigger than the national debt.'

'It's about Lansdown,' Diamond told them. 'I understand you both take a personal interest in this area.'

'Who told you that?' the major asked. He was not going to be sweet-talked into co-operating.

'The reputation of the Lansdown Society is well known.'

'What do you know about the Lansdown Society?'

'That's what this is about,' Tipping said. 'He wants to join. He wants to be a member, Reggie. Shall I tell him about the secret initiation ritual with the custard pies?'

Diamond wasn't sure which of these was the more tiresome: the churlish major or the laugh-a-minute Knight of the Realm.

'We came here to play golf,' the major said

to Diamond. 'Can't this wait until lunchtime?'

Tipping immediately said, 'Good thinking. See you at the nineteenth hole.'

'My time is short and so is yours, I gather,' Diamond said. 'We'll talk as you play your round. Who goes first?'

'Reggie's turn today.'

'I don't care for this at all,' the major said.

'Get on with it, for heaven's sake, Reggie,' Tipping said. 'You just told him you came here to play golf. Some might not describe it as that, but that's why we're here.'

'He's got a damned nerve.'

'The neck of a giraffe, old man, and so have we, calling ourselves golfers. Let's make a start, or we'll never get round.'

Muttering, the major placed a ball on the tee and selected a club. Before taking his stance he took some practice swings. Then he wetted a finger and held it up.

'Checking the wind,' Tipping said to Diamond. 'He does everything right. It's the damned ball that gets it wrong.'

The major's ball travelled not very far and still managed to miss the fairway. He turned angrily on his colleague. 'You ruined that by speaking as I made my backswing.'

'Take it again, dear boy,' Tipping said. 'It isn't far off.'

'I might as well give up now,' the major said. 'No one can play under these conditions.'

'Watch me,' Tipping said. He positioned his ball, swung and struck it — not far, but at least twice the distance the major had. 'That puts me in charge of the buggy, I think. Why don't you hop aboard, Superintendent? Reggie doesn't have far to walk.'

The golf cart was a two-seater, as most are, with space at the back for the bags. Diamond hadn't foreseen the pair arriving on one. He'd been wondering in the last few minutes if there was a way he could perch on the back, holding on to the metal strut supporting the canopy. But there was no need if the major was on foot.

Tipping started up and they whirred up the fairway. 'Don't get the wrong impression of Reggie,' he said to Diamond. 'He's a good man. Our society couldn't function without him.'

'What does it do, exactly?'

'What was that you said about our famous reputation? I thought you knew all about us.'

'Only loosely.'

'Loose is what we are.' Another guffaw. 'We try to make sure that this historic hill is respected. We don't have any official status like park keepers, but we keep an eye on the multifarious activities people engage in up here — and I know what you're thinking. Who was the lady who said she didn't mind where people made love as long as they didn't do it in the street and frighten the horses? We take much the same view. But if someone tries holding a barbecue, or a motorbike rally, or anything that damages the turf, we tell them politely to find another place. That's fair enough, isn't it?'

'So do you patrol the down looking for offenders?'

'Impossible. We're a small group. We act on tip-offs, just as you fellows do. We're in touch with pretty well all the legitimate organisations that use the place. They know we're interested and they keep us informed.' He stopped the cart. 'I'll take my second, if you don't mind. Keep a look out for the major's ball. He has been known to connect. He can be lethal from the rear.'

Diamond watched him take a huge swing and miss the ball completely.

'Only taking aim,' he said, and laughed.

His second attempt failed to lift the ball, but sent it some way along the well-mown surface.

As the cart moved on again, Diamond said above the hum of the motor, 'Did you hear about the skeleton we found?'

'What a charming line in conversation you have. I was beginning to think "dem dry bones" might be behind your interest in us,' Tipping said. 'Yes, we knew early on that you people were up to something. This may sound uncaring considering some poor soul died, but your digging could have been a concern. It wasn't, because it took place under the roots of that fallen oak tree. Do you know who the victim was?'

'A young girl, some years back.'

'Why would anyone bury her up here?'

'Possibly because she was killed up here.'

'On Lansdown?'

The cart stopped again.

Diamond glanced behind. The major was in sight, still a long way off. 'Should we wait for him?'

Tipping shook his head. 'We meet on the green. We'd never get round if we waited for each other at every shot. He'll take one or two more than he puts on the card, and so will I, so it's better if we aren't too close to each other.' He chose a club and shifted the ball another ten yards or so. 'You didn't see that.' He strode the short distance to the ball and struck it again, with more success. 'Par for this hole is four,' he said. 'I take about nine usually if my putting is tidy and Reggie is out of sight.'

When they moved off, Diamond asked, 'How long has your society been in existence?'

'We formed in the year they staged the mock battle, the three hundred and fiftieth anniversary.'

'1993.'

'Yes. Some of us of like minds were concerned that real damage might be done to the land, with all the paraphernalia of cannon and horses and so on. We formed this group to meet the re-enactment people and lay down certain procedures — which I have to say they observed to the letter. Afterwards we decided to formalise the society and monitor some of the other activities.'

'Like the horse racing?'

'Are you a racing man?'

'No, but I saw you present the prize to the winning owner last week.'

'My daughter Davina. Wasn't that charming? She has three horses in training and I'm proud to tell you it's not my money that pays for them. She's a lady of independent means, with her own business. Works damned hard.'

'And you're still involved in racing?'

'I sponsor a few flat races during the year. It's nice to meet old friends, but I haven't owned a horse for some time.'

'Hang-glider?'

'That was a great horse. You *are* a racing man.'

'No, I just heard someone mention it in connection with you.'

'Sad story. Do you know it? He ran his first races here and showed such promise that I sent him to be trained at Lambourn. Won a few more and then a big one in Ireland. Everyone was certain he was set for greater things and then he popped a tendon in his near foreleg. Devastating.'

The force of the last word led Diamond to only one conclusion. 'Was he put down?'

'Lord, no. Don't confuse injured tendons with broken legs. He was fit to put to stud. Poor old fellow, he'd earned some sport with the ladies and I would have been a very rich man as a result. I had a certain Arabian sheikh lined up as the next owner. Then the worst of all things happened. I was asked to parade my horse in front of the crowd one last time at an evening meeting. He was a great local favourite, you see. A lovely tribute. You should have seen his ears prick up when they cheered him all along the straight. Sadly, it was the last I saw of him. My trainer returned him to his box and some evil-minded bastard broke in and stole him.'

'What for — a ransom?'

'No. We never heard a word. My theory is that they put him to stud secretly and his progeny are winning races at long odds.'

'Your deal with the sheikh fell through?'

'All I got was some paltry insurance money.'

'You lost a lot?'

'Getting on for a million. That horse was a thoroughbred, an investment. He didn't come cheap. But in racing you have to treat those two impostors just the same.'

'Who are they?'

Tipping gave Diamond a disbelieving look and then laughed. 'Triumph and Disaster, of course. Don't you know your Kipling?'

'Poetry isn't my strong suit.'

'I thought it was compulsory in the modern police. All the television detectives know their poetry.'

'I'm in the real world, sir. Did the experience put you off owning horses, then?'

'I couldn't afford another thoroughbred. I'm content to sponsor a few races.'

'What do you get for being a sponsor — a box in the main stand?'

He shrugged. 'Unlike most of them, I don't want anything out of it. I'm a chartered surveyor. You don't get new clients by sponsoring horse racing. It's not as if I've got a product to peddle, like beer or cigarettes. I do it because I like the sport. Always fancy I can spot a winner.' He stopped the cart beside his ball. 'How far off is the green, would you say?'

'Seventy yards. Maybe seventy-five.'

'One good hit, then. Why don't you go ahead and remove the flag?'

'If you want.'

'Joke. What's that white object near the pin?'

Diamond stared. Was this more of the humour? 'I don't see anything.'

'We need Reggie's wife with her field glasses. She's marvellous. Look to the right of the flag.'

There was something. 'I see it now. A plastic bag?'

'Could be. Just my luck if the ball hits it.'

'Do you want me to go ahead and clear it off?' Diamond asked.

'Not yet awhile.' He took his shot and struck the ball about halfway to the green.

It would have been simpler to walk, but they couldn't leave the buggy on the fairway. Getting on and off took up a lot of time.

'How many members are there?' Diamond asked when they were in motion again.

'Of the golf club?'

'The Lansdown Society.'

'Five now.'

'As few as that?'

'We started with eight, but people moved to other parts of the country, or fell off the perch. In the original group there were seven men and one woman, the formidable Augusta White, magistrate. I dubbed her Snow White, naturally, and we were the seven you-know-whats. No prizes for guessing which of us was Grumpy. Is the major catching up?'

'A magistrate must be a useful member.'

'Goes without saying — particularly when we have to deal with gypsies, as we do from time to time. What do they call themselves now? Travellers. Not many of them are true Romanies any more. Let them set up camp as they did at the old RAF station at Charmy Down and you have a real problem on your hands. Scrap metal, vehicles they can't move, dogs, faeces.' He halted and hauled himself out of the buggy. 'They've always been trouble. Lansdown had a famous annual fair, you know, and they came from miles around for that, so they think they can set up camp whenever they want.'

'You mentioned Mrs White. Is she still in the society?'

'Oh, yes. Have you met her?'

'In court from time to time.'

'Splendid woman. And, as you say, useful to have the law on our side. What *is* that wretched object on the green?'

Diamond could see it better now. Not a plastic bag, he was sure. Chalky white and unmoving, it lay close to the pin. Was his mind predisposed to death, or did it have the rounded shape of a cranium?

'I'm going to take a look.'

He'd not expected ever to find the missing skull. The whole point of decapitating the victim was surely to prevent identification. The killer would have disposed of it miles from here.

What could it be doing in plain view on a golf course?

He quickened his pace.

And was disappointed.

The round, white object was a partially deflated balloon. He picked it up. A label was attached. The wording was *Number 297. Bath Rugby Club Balloon Race.* This balloon hadn't travelled far. He wouldn't be ringing the number on the reverse. Unlucky for number 297 and unlucky for him, too.

'What is it?' Tipping shouted.

'Only a balloon.'

'Keep hold of it. We don't want litter on the course. At one time, we made a collection of all the rubbish collected off the down in a single week. You wouldn't believe the disgusting things we recovered. Are you sure it's a balloon?'

'Positive.'

'Take out the pin, then. I'm going to try a long putt.'

Diamond did so. The ball rolled past and off the green again.

'You could have stuck your foot in the way,' Tipping said as he approached. 'Reggie isn't far behind now.'

'I'm a little disappointed in you and your Lansdown Society, Sir Colin,' Diamond said, trying a different approach. 'I thought you missed nothing of what goes on up here, yet someone is killed and buried and you don't seem to have any knowledge of it.'

'I'm concerned, naturally, but it's a mystery to me.'

'You were one of the original members?'

'I was, along with Reggie and Mrs White, who are still very much with us. Do you want to wait for Reggie?'

'Aren't you going to take another putt?'

He winked. 'I'm taking it as holed.' He picked up his ball and pocketed it. 'That goes down as a seven for the first hole.'

There was a shout of 'Fore!' from behind them.

'That's Reggie,' Tipping said. 'I can't see him, can you?'

Another shout from the major: 'Move the bloody buggy. It's blocking my line.'

'As if he ever hits straight,' Tipping said. He returned to the golf cart and moved it off the fairway.

Diamond could see the major hunched over his ball now, not all that far from the green. By luck or skill the shot came off and the ball stopped inches from the hole.

'Not bad. Was that your seventh?' Tipping asked his opponent.

'Fifth.' The major held up five fingers.

'He's lying,' Tipping muttered to Diamond. 'Tap it in, then. That hole is halved.'

'You took six?' the major said. 'You've never done that before. Is that true?' He strode up to the green and asked Diamond, 'Did he really take only six?'

'I lost count,' Diamond said, not wishing to get involved. 'I was distracting him, anyway. Questions about the buried skeleton. Do you remember anything suspicious going on around the fallen oak tree some years back?'

' "Some years back" is far too vague,' the major said. 'Can't you be more precise?'

'All right. After 1987, when the tree came down, and before 1997.'

'What do you mean by suspicious?'

Tipping was quick to say, 'Your score for the first hole, old boy.'

Diamond said, 'A car or van parked near the tree. People digging.'

'No,' the major said. 'I would have noticed. Can we get on with the golf?'

'I'll not delay you much longer,' Diamond told them. 'I must get back anyway. You said Mrs White is the other founder member of the society. There were eight originally. Who were the other five?'

'Two of them are dead,' Tipping said. 'Roger Rhodes was a gentleman farmer. Crashed his light plane, poor chap, and Willy Drake-Allen, the BBC man, caught one of those hospital bugs. The others moved away. Jamie Fleming went back to his beloved Edinburgh. He was our policeman — before your time, I expect. George Philpot bought a villa in Italy. Who was the other one?'

'Underhill,' the major said. 'The vicar of St Vincent's.'

'Of course. He served his time locally and was given a new parish in Norfolk.'

'So you had the Church and the police on side as well?' Diamond said, impressed by the power base of this small group.

'Still do. We recruited the next incumbent at St Vincent's, the Reverend Charlie Smart.'

'And who is your policeman?'

'Policewoman,' the major said, 'Assistant Chief Constable Georgina Dallymore.'

Diamond's boss. He had to bite back a strong word. He couldn't believe it.

9

John Wigfull's day started in a promising way. The desk sergeant said two people were waiting in connection with the missing cavalier and there were phone messages as well.

Strictly it wasn't his job to interview witnesses, but — he reasoned to himself — everyone knew he was more than just a PR man. He'd worked in CID for years. Besides, the cavalier was his pet project. He didn't want some rookie constable taking it on and missing the significance. He would meet these people himself.

The first was a woman who'd seen the piece in the *Bath Chronicle* and was certain she recognised the missing man as a down-and-out who was caught stealing food from tables at Saturday's car boot sale at Lansdown. Wigfull soon learned that she was a witness with attitude. 'I had you lot come out to him after he helped himself to one of me home-made meat pies, but the bobbies you sent were woodentops. They asked him his name and he told them it was Noddy and they didn't turn a hair. They let him walk away scot-free. There's no respect any more. And when I got home and opened the paper there the thieving bastard was, all dressed up in a fancy hat.'

Wigfull decided not to go into an explanation about the hat. The Civil War connection would be lost on this lady. 'Are you sure we're talking about the same man? He isn't a down-and-out, as you put it. He's a university lecturer.'

'It was him. No question.' Her eyes widened. 'Now you mention it, though, he didn't sound like a dosser. The voice was posh.'

'Did he say why he'd helped himself to the pie?'

'Stole it, you mean. Let's call a spade a spade. No, he had no conscience. I asked him to pay and he said he didn't have no money. That much I believe, but he shouldn't have picked up my pie, should he?'

'How was he dressed?'

'Dead scruffy, in muddy old jeans and one of them hoodie things, and he smelt.'

'Don't you think you might be mistaken?'

Her face reddened. 'Are you calling me a liar?'

He was tempted to answer 'yes — and a time-waster, too.' He'd met plenty like her and they'd go on for ever if you let them. 'Frankly, madam, we know who the missing man is and he isn't the sort to behave the way you describe.'

'Is that so? Well, that's me and the fucking police finished!' she said in an explosion of outrage. 'You're all the same, on the side of the villains, looking for excuses for them. I came here out of the goodness of my heart, giving you important information, and you treat me like I'm a bloody liar. If that's the way you want to run the city, you can stuff it where the monkey puts his nuts.' She marched out, leaving Wigfull untroubled by the tirade. He'd been told on a PR course he'd attended that the majority of so-called witnesses are attention-seekers. The woman was a prime example.

His spirits improved when Mrs Swithin came in: one of those well-bred old ladies you know will keep their emotions in check. Dressed in a tweed jacket and pleated tartan skirt, she radiated good sense. 'Is the photo in the paper reliable?' she asked first. 'I'm talking about the face, not the way they dressed him up. Is that really the missing man?'

'Rupert Hope, yes.'

'And he's an academic?'

'Bristol University.'

'I have to tell you, then, that he's been behaving out of character, trying to open people's car doors. This was up at the racecourse, in the car park. Reggie, my husband — the major — was convinced he was up to no good, so we phoned the police. I happen to possess a powerful pair of binoculars and I stayed on watch while Reggie went to meet the police car. I had the man in focus for quite ten minutes and saw his face clearly. He was definitely the gentleman in the paper.'

'What was he wearing?'

'A hooded garment and blue denim trousers.'

The same man, apparently. Wigfull's promising morning took a roller-coaster plunge. 'Did the police come?'

'Yes, but unfortunately the man had left by then, in the direction of the main enclosure.'

'Was this on a race day?'

'Not at all. I'm sorry if I gave that impression. It was Wednesday of last week and very quiet at the time. People use the car park every day of the week. We're often up there keeping an eye on things. That's how I noticed his suspicious behaviour.'

'Did he actually break into any of the cars?'

'No, I think they were all locked.'

'And did the police catch up with him?'

'As it turned out, no. They returned later and took statements. We had to wait almost an hour. Reggie's a responsible citizen, but he gets testy if he's kept waiting. Anyway, we saw the item in the *Chronicle* and both agreed it was our duty to get in touch with you. The man wasn't behaving as one expects a university lecturer to conduct himself, but these days one never knows. They employ some strange types in so-called higher education.'

'You did the right thing.' Wigfull was thinking as he spoke that he'd done the *wrong* thing in letting the pie woman go.

'What will happen now?'

'I'll find out which of our officers answered your call and speak to them. We heard of another sighting as well. It begins to look as if our man is behaving erratically.'

'Either that, or he's a Trot.'

'A what?'

'A Trotskyist. The universities are full of left-wing people trying to change the world.'

The world had moved on a bit, since

Trotsky, but Wigfull had a rough idea what was meant and shared the sentiment. He still thought Mrs Swithin a dependable witness.

Just to be certain, he returned a couple of the overnight phone calls about the cavalier. More sightings. Rupert Hope must have been wandering about Lansdown for days drawing attention to himself through minor misdemeanours. Probably not as a left wing protest, but drunk, drugged, or unwell.

Why, then, hadn't the officers on patrol picked him up?

Smoothly, he transferred his own failing onto others. Picked up the phone and asked to have the occurrence file checked. Someone ought to face the music. It turned out that the same two officers had responded to both calls.

Peter Diamond drove back from the golf club thinking dark thoughts about the Lansdown Society. If, as they claimed, they monitored everything that happened on the hill they may well have heard or seen something suspicious connected with the burial of the body. And as guardians of the terrain — vigilantes, whatever they said to the contrary — they might conceivably be suspects. The whole point about vigilantes

130

was that they took the law into their own hands. What if they'd found some undesirable flouting their rules and killed her, maybe by accident? They'd have been well placed to find a burial site.

The substantial fly in the ointment was Georgina.

Diamond had never shirked a confrontation. Noting that the ACC's Mercedes was parked in her reserved space outside, putting her on the premises, he went upstairs to her eyrie. The traffic light entrance system was showing green.

'Troubles, Peter?' she said when she saw him.

'Not really, ma'am. I just want your advice.'

'That must be a first.'

'About the Lansdown Society.'

Her voice took on a defensive note. 'What about it?'

'I was told you're a member.'

'That's right. I do have a life outside the police.'

'They seem to think it's because you're in the police that you're one of them.'

'Who have you been talking to?'

'Sir Colin Tipping and Major Swithin. They said Jamie Fleming was the police member before you.'

'That is true, but I want to make it clear, Peter, that I didn't join in my official capacity. I happen to support the conservation of the countryside. I don't want to see any more building on Lansdown. It's a protected site, which in reality means nothing unless people like me with some influence guarantee its integrity. I know why you've raised this. It's the skeleton, isn't it?'

'Right, ma'am. The society keeps abreast of what's happening on the down. I was hoping they might know something.'

'And do they?'

'Not the two gents I saw this morning.'

'They're the most likely to know. They've been members from the beginning. When was your victim buried?'

'Some time after 1987, when the tree was blown down.'

'Ah well.' She spread her hands. 'The society wasn't formed until 1993.'

'Yes, but we don't know which year she was buried. We have a ten-year time frame.'

'If Colin and Reggie say they can't help, it's no good coming to me. I didn't join until three years ago.'

Colin and Reggie. He had to be careful here. A conflict of loyalties was looming. 'The other founder member is Mrs White, the magistrate.'

132

Georgina was losing patience. 'You don't have to tell me, Peter.'

'I was about to say I might have a word with her as well — unless you would like to approach her yourself.'

She folded her arms and gave a defiant tilt to the most eloquent bosom in Bath. 'Is this your only line of enquiry? I can't see it being very productive.'

'It looked more promising when I started.' He got bolder. 'Forgive me for saying this, but you seem a close-knit society.'

'Perhaps we don't have anything to tell you.'

'It's no easy matter when your victim is dry bones and no one remembers anything.'

'So this *is* your only line of enquiry.'

'I'm speaking to the press this afternoon. We'll see if memories are jogged when the papers get onto the story.'

'That's more like it.' She lowered her chest by at least two inches. 'Are you taking advice from John Wigfull, our new media relations manager? He could probably get some headlines for you.'

'I've discussed it with him.'

'He was extremely impressive at interview. He's well up on all the latest techniques.'

'I'm sure. About Mrs White . . .'

'Well?' The low slung chest became just a

133

memory.

'There's no need for you to do anything, ma'am. I'll speak to her myself.'

He left while he had the opportunity.

To his credit, John Wigfull had marshalled most of the local press and some of the nationals as well. Poster-size photos of the site and the skeleton in its grave formed a backdrop for Diamond's statement. Press-kits stuffed with pictures were handed to everyone.

After outlining the facts and responding to questions, Diamond did more interviews for local TV and radio, stressing repeatedly that the team were waiting to be contacted by anyone with a memory of anything suspicious going on near the fallen tree ten to twenty years ago.

Much of the questioning was about the missing skull. Did he expect to find it?

He admitted that he didn't. The crime scene team had sifted all the loose earth for more evidence and found nothing apart from the metal zip. It was clear that the skull was elsewhere.

One TV reporter pressed him to speculate on whether the killer had removed the head to prevent identification.

He knew better than to go down that road.

'We don't know yet how she died. Murder is a possibility, but we can't discount a fatal accident on the road not far up the slope. Whoever buried her didn't want the body discovered. That much is clear.'

'Are you saying someone ran her over and tried to dispose of the body?'

'That's one interpretation.'

'And decapitated her? In the accident, or after?'

He was trying so hard to stay cool. 'All we've got is a headless skeleton. How could I possibly know?'

'Do you think the head is buried somewhere else?'

'I'm keeping an open mind.' Long experience had taught him how to steer an interview to a close. 'I've told you all I know at this juncture. With your help, we'll carry the investigation a stage further.'

Wigfull was fishing for compliments afterwards. 'I thought it went rather well. These events work so much better with good visuals like the posters.'

'Let's see what results we get,' Diamond said. 'I've done press statements with dartboards as a background and still made the front page of the *News of the World*. Thanks, anyway. You did your job.'

Ingeborg rushed in, bursting to tell them

something.

'Someone phoned in already?' Diamond said. 'That *is* a result.'

Self-congratulation started spreading over Wigfull's features.

'No, guv,' Ingeborg said. 'This has nothing to do with the press conference. A body has been found. The thing is, it's Lansdown again.'

10

The Victorian cemetery in the shadow of
Beckford's Tower would have made an ideal
location for a Gothic horror movie. Weath-
ered obelisks, tablets and carved figures
showed above a waist-high crop of grass,
ferns, brambles, nettles and cow parsley.
Any smaller, more humble headstones were
lost to view, but the grander monuments on
plinths still vouched for the eminence of the
interred, even if the lettering was unread-
able. The Preservation Trust maintained the
site and justified the abundant growth as a
wildlife sanctuary. Only the main pathways
had been kept mown and a cluster of policemen and crime scene investigators could be
seen standing along one of them beside a
trampled section marked with police tape
hung from stone angels and granite crosses.
The main point of interest, a clothed body,
lay face down in the narrow space between
two graves.

Diamond, with Keith Halliwell in support, found a familiar character directing operations.

Duckett, the crime scene man, looked up and said, 'You again?' making his disfavour clear.

'I was about to say the same thing but the cadaver interests me more,' Diamond said. 'Head wound, then.'

'Nothing gets past you, does it?'

It *was* rather obvious. A gash at the back of the victim's head revealed a strip of dented skull between encrustments of blood — as ugly a wound as Diamond had seen in some time. 'Has the pathologist been by?'

'And gone.' Duckett flapped his hand at the flies that were gathering. 'You're late on the scene, superintendent.'

'Did he have anything helpful to say?'

'Only the obvious.'

'How recent was the death?'

'Some hours. You know what pathologists are like.'

'Just a head wound. Nothing more?'

'He wouldn't be drawn.'

Diamond leaned over the body looking for other signs of injury.

Duckett spoke again. 'I can tell you what happened if you like. See the empty beer can over there?' He pointed to a dented

Foster's can lying on the gravel topping of one of the graves. 'He was stonkered, lost his footing and hit his head.'

'How do you know all that?'

Pleased to be asked, Duckett beckoned with his finger and showed Diamond a small patch of dry blood on the raised edging of the adjacent grave. Some had trickled down the side. 'In my job, you can't afford to miss a thing.'

Diamond got on his knees for a close look. 'So why is the wound at the back of the head?'

'He fell backwards. Drunks often do.'

'He's face down.'

There was some hesitation.

'You don't see it, do you?' Duckett said, beginning to bluster. 'He falls backwards, bounces his head on the stone and is thrust sideways, ending up like this.'

'I can't picture it.'

'Okay, he may have rolled over before he passed out.'

'I doubt it,' Diamond said.

'You know better, do you?'

'It's a vicious-looking injury for a simple fall.'

'That granite edge is really sharp. Feel it.'

Diamond ran his fingers along the angle of the stone. Then he got up and stepped over to the next grave and inspected the beer can without touching it. 'There's rust on this.'

'I don't think so. Where?'

'In the angle of the dent. It must have been slung away some time ago.'

'Let's see.' The disbelief was obvious until Duckett had put his face within a few inches, and then he quickly modified his theory. 'Well, he may not have drunk from this particular tin, but there's no denying that he hit his head.'

Deliberately, Diamond crooked his finger just as Duckett had. 'Come and look at this drop of blood you found on the stone.'

'What's up now? Are you saying the blood isn't his?'

'Come on. A close look.'

Some of the other crime scene investigators were getting interested. With an impatient sigh that played to their support, their leader crouched by the grave's edge.

Diamond said, 'What do you make of this?'

A small green blade of grass had adhered to the bloodstain.

Duckett looked and said, 'Well?' It was difficult to tell if he'd missed the significance or was playing cool.

Diamond spelt it out. 'If he cut his head

on the stone I might expect to find a hair, not a piece of grass.'

'The main paths are mown at least once a week. Of course there are clippings about.'

'Yes, but how did this one get where it is?'

'The wind, I suppose.'

Diamond glanced around the cemetery. Not a leaf was moving.

'Show me, then.' Duckett tried to sound unimpressed, but his confidence had taken a knock.

'Blood trickled from the head wound onto the grass. Do you see?' Diamond pointed to a dark brown patch about the size of a beer mat beside the victim's head. 'This looks like an attempt to cover up a crime. He was attacked from behind, fell face down and bled heavily. His assailant dipped the weapon in some fresh blood from the grass and let it drip on the edge of the grave to fake an accident.'

'That's far-fetched, isn't it?'

'It seems to have fooled you.'

'You're suggesting he was attacked? Why would anyone bother to kill a tramp?'

'I can think of several reasons and I'm sure other people would come up with more.'

'A blow from behind, you say? What with?'

'Call it a blunt instrument.'

'That old cliché?'

'You'd better make a search for that old cliché.' He couldn't resist adding, 'In your job you can't afford to miss a thing.'

Duckett made a performance of turning his head, surveying the sea of weeds in every direction. The place would be a nightmare to search. Apart from the few paths, there wasn't a yard of clear space in the cemetery.

'It's got to be done,' Diamond said.

'I'd need an army for a job like that.'

'If it's manpower you want, I can send for more bobbies.'

'I wasn't prepared for this. It's going to take days, even with lots of help.'

'Better start soon, then. Your scene, my friend.' Diamond turned to Halliwell. 'See if you can raise some help, Keith.'

Halliwell used his mobile.

'Who found the body?' Diamond asked Duckett.

'The man who mows the paths. At about eight this morning. Nasty shock. By the look of him he'll need the rest of the week off, poor blighter.'

'And months of counselling,' Diamond said.

This earned a grudging smile.

Diamond looked at what the corpse was wearing, noting the torn jeans and mud-spattered hooded jacket. 'Any idea who he is?'

'No.'

'Have you been through his pockets?'

'We're not total amateurs.'

'What did you find, then?'

'Sod all. He's a vagrant. Get the smell.'

'They usually carry stuff.'

'There's your motive, then. Someone wanted his stash of valuables.'

It was true that the clothes had the smell of the unwashed, but the victim's skin didn't show the deep layer of grime Diamond would have expected. The pores weren't defined by the dirt from years of rough living. He tried ignoring the smell as he stooped for a closer examination. He was starting to question another assumption. The hands were in a reasonable state. The hair was greasy, but had been cut by a professional at some time.

'Okay if I lift the head? I'd like a sight of the face.'

'I suppose.'

Taking care to avoid the area of the wound, Diamond grasped some of the brown hair above the forehead. Although this didn't give him the front view, he could tell a few things from this angle. Some weeks' growth of beard. The nose had bled, but otherwise the features were undamaged. A man of forty or so, he estimated. 'Can someone get a photo?'

The cameraman on the team took several shots before Diamond lowered the head. 'How soon can I get copies?'

'Soon as I finish here.'

'He's not needed here any more, is he?' Diamond asked Duckett.

Another sigh. 'I suppose. It's bloody easy for the rest of you, going back to town and leaving us to this.'

'Cheer up. You don't have to do any digging this time.'

'In this place I wouldn't recommend it.'

Diamond stood up and gave a little grunt of discomfort. 'Tough on the knees, all this stooping. I've seen enough for the present. It's upgraded to a crime scene, agreed?'

'You're the expert.'

'Let me know if you find the weapon.'

The drive down the hill to Manvers Street was thoughtful and mostly silent. They'd reached Broad Street when Diamond said to Halliwell, 'Two suspicious deaths on Lansdown. Is that pure chance, Keith?'

A pause for thought. 'They don't have much in common considering one happened up to twenty years ago.'

'I suppose.'

'One a burial and the other just left in the open to be discovered. One a young woman —'

'All right, I hear what you're saying.' The stress was showing. He'd invited Halliwell to offer an opinion and now he'd shut him down — his loyal deputy. 'You know what's on my mind, don't you?'

'Georgina?'

'Spot on. She won't like me running two murder enquiries if they're not connected. She won't wear it, Keith.'

'We don't know if they're murders yet.'

He took the point, grinned and nodded. 'That's not bad. I could run with that for a while.'

'Difficult to do, anyway,' Halliwell said.

'What?'

'Run two murder enquiries.'

'I'd give it a go.'

Digital photography is a boon to police work. Within the hour Diamond had a series of crime scene pictures on his desk and on computer. They included six close-ups of the dead man's face. Displayed thus, they intrigued him and he rearranged them several times as if playing Patience. Pictures of the dead can be deceptive. Rigor hadn't set in when the shots were taken, so the muscles were slack, giving an appearance that wouldn't be seen in the living.

'Come and look at these, Keith.'

Halliwell crossed the room. 'I saw the face when you lifted the head.'

'Well, I didn't,' Diamond said. 'Not from the angle of the camera. Something is familiar. Don't know what.'

'Do you know him?'

'No, I don't. Never met the guy.' He scratched the patch of hair above his right ear. 'Even so . . .'

'Do you want them on a board where we can see them?'

'Good thinking. Excellent pictures, aren't they? I bet the poor sod never had a snapshot of this quality taken when he was alive.'

'Shall I set up another incident room?' Halliwell was excited. A much more promising investigation was in prospect.

Diamond hesitated. They already had an adjoining room where information on the skeleton death was being processed. He thought about Georgina's likely reaction to two incident rooms. 'Not yet, Keith. Let's see how we go.'

'Up at the graveyard you seemed certain he was murdered.'

'I'm inclined now to soft-pedal on that. It could be manslaughter — the result of a brawl — or even an accident.'

'But you said a second person was involved and tried to cover it up.'

'The drop of blood? Yes.'

'That was good spotting, guv.'

'Bad.'

'Bad?'

'But it was good that it was bad.'

'You've lost me now.'

'The spotting. By the perpetrator, not noticing the blade of grass.'

Halliwell tried humouring the boss by smiling, a forced smile, leaving him vulnerable.

'Make some calls to all the local refuges, the Sally Army, and so on,' Diamond said. 'See if they can throw any light on this. There's a bush telegraph among homeless men.'

'Are you going to attend the PM?'

A casual enquiry, but both men knew what was behind it. Diamond didn't have the stomach for post mortems. Halliwell was inured to them by now, always the police presence there. After years of standing in for the boss, watching a pathologist at work was no ordeal.

'Tomorrow morning, I expect,' Diamond said, as if mentally consulting his diary. 'Pity.'

'What's that?'

'I've got to be here in case of developments. Could you stand in for me on this one, Keith?'

'I was thinking about visiting a refuge.'

Diamond's eyebrows popped up. 'Am I that difficult to work with?'

'A refuge for the homeless, following up on the phone calls.'

'True.' Diamond frowned and then raised a finger as inspiration dawned. 'Ingeborg can do the refuges.'

'Leaving me free.'

'Free to go to the ball, Cinderella.'

Raffles the cat, who had taken to sleeping at the end of Diamond's bed, was roused unusually early next morning. To add insult to injury, his wrong-headed owner then went to the garage instead of the shelf where the cat food was stored and started sorting through the old newspapers stacked for the refuse collection. Ten minutes of leafing through copies of the *Bath Chronicle* brought a result. He'd found the picture feature on the missing cavalier.

'That's my baby, Raffles,' he said. 'And now we'll celebrate by opening a new tin of chicken in jelly.'

True, the portrait of Rupert Hope was just

a mugshot, probably taken for some university ID, but there was a distinct resemblance to the dead man. He read the text again. The age was about right. On consideration, the relatively healthy state of the skin and hands made sense. He'd not been a vagrant for long. From cavalier to corpse in how long? Two to three weeks? The days between took on a new importance.

Raffles was standing beside his empty bowl giving Diamond the glare usually reserved for next door's pampered Persian.

John Wigfull kept to the civilised hours of a civilian and arrived at his office soon after nine. His moustache twitched in annoyance when he saw Peter Diamond seated on the corner of his desk.

'Something the matter?' Wigfull asked.

'Far from it,' Diamond said. 'I've solved your puzzle. I'm here to claim my reward. Was it a brand new BMW or three weeks in the Bahamas?'

'I don't know what you're on about.'

He held up the newspaper. 'The missing cavalier.' With an air of triumph he produced one of the glossy photos of the dead man and held it beside the pictures in the paper. 'If it's all the same to you, I'll take the BMW.'

Wigfull gave the picture a squint. 'Who's this, then?'

'Rupert.'

'Rupert who?'

'Rupert Bear, and I'm Bill Badger. Come on, John. I know it's early in the day, but you can see it's the same guy as the one in the paper.'

'He doesn't look the same.'

'He's dead, that's why.' He was tempted to go into the Monty Python dead parrot routine, which he knew by heart, but it would be wasted on Wigfull. 'We found him yesterday in the graveyard up at Beckford's Tower.'

'You think this is Rupert Hope?'

'I'm sure of it.'

'Dead?'

'Were you hoping for a happy ending? Is that what this is about? Compare the pictures. Look at the hairline, the eyebrows, the mouth.'

'I suppose it could be him,' Wigfull said finally. 'How long has he been dead?'

'Yesterday, or the night before. No longer.'

'Where was he all this time?'

'He wasn't in any condition to tell me. I'm telling you as much as I know. He looked as if he'd been living rough for some days, but it was obvious he wasn't a long-term homeless man.'

'What did he die of?'

'I don't want to anticipate the post mortem, which is happening as we speak, but my money is on the three-inch wound at the back of his head.'

'A violent death, then?'

'You could say that.'

'Pity. I thought he'd turn up alive.'

'Thanks to your press release? You can't win them all, John. What I need to know from you is where the story came from. Who reported it?'

'The university people. The last anyone saw of him was on the day of the battle re-enactment.'

'So he went missing for — what? — two and a half weeks and ended up dead, probably murdered. I'm going to have to find out a whole lot more about this guy. Did you speak to anyone from the Civil War Society, or whatever they call themselves?'

Wigfull shook his head. 'I'm the media relations manager, not a detective. However . . .' He cleared his throat and turned a shade more pink. 'I did speak to a couple of people who responded to the newspaper appeal. They were claiming to have spotted the man up at Lansdown.'

'When was this?'

'One woman said she'd seen him at the car boot sale on Sunday. He helped himself to a meat pie she had for sale and wouldn't or couldn't pay for it. She described him as a down-and-out, scruffy, in a hooded jacket and jeans, but said he had a posh accent. The other witness saw a similar man apparently trying to break into cars.'

'Where?'

'The same place — the racecourse car park — but on a different day.'

'Did she say anything to him?'

'No. She watched him through field-glasses and he went off in the direction of the racecourse.'

'This was . . . ?'

'On the Wednesday before.'

'He was acting suspiciously and she didn't report him?'

'Oh, but she did. Both women did. And there was a quick response from us.'

'Us?'

'Uniform. They seem to have used the softly, softly approach, but that's what they're encouraged to do. These were misdemeanours.'

'They spoke to the guy?'

'At the boot sale, they did, for sure. The pie woman didn't think much of the way they dealt with him. She wanted him clapped in irons and sent to Australia, I think.'

'They must have got his name.'

'Erm . . .' Wigfull looked shamefaced again. 'He said it was Noddy.'

Diamond didn't speak. With a throb of concern, he recalled the evening he'd been at the races with Paloma and seen the drunk almost knocked down by horses cantering to the start.

'I'm only passing on what I was told,' Wigfull said, misinterpreting the silence.

'Who were they, these cops?'

'I didn't enquire. That didn't seem important at the time.'

'Have you told anyone else?'

'No.'

Diamond put it to him straight. 'Basically, John, you were out of order. You goofed. You had no business talking to witnesses. You told me just now you're the PR guy.'

'Media Relations Manager.'

'Call it what you like, you're here to deal with the press. These people are under the impression they reported incidents and we, the police, are dealing with them.'

'It was just a missing person enquiry. I thought CID wouldn't want to be bothered with that.'

'It's murder now.'

'I'll give you their names and addresses.'

'Thanks a bunch.'

The post mortem on the body found in Lansdown cemetery had been under way for twenty minutes and already Keith Halliwell was yawning. He'd worked late last evening on the skeleton case, sifting through missing persons data. Diamond wanted it known by everyone at Bath police station that the murder team were actively investigating, even though the crime must have happened years earlier. And now it had been overtaken by this new discovery.

'Wishing you were elsewhere, Mr Halliwell?' Dr Sealy, the pathologist, asked.

'I'm okay.'

'I know you're okay. You're not going to faint like some first-timer. I'm asking if you're bored.'

'No.'

'Because I can promise something of particular interest when we get to it.'

'Really?'

Up to now all that had happened was a slow disrobing of the dead man. As each garment was removed the police photographer stepped in and took a picture.

'Where exactly are we on identification?' Dr Sealy asked, sipping coffee during another photo interval. 'Do you need any pointers from me, birthmarks, scars, tattoos?'

'My guvnor, Mr Diamond, says he knows the name.'

'Your Mr Diamond is a smart cookie. Isn't he the one who demonstrated that the bloodstaining on the gravestone was put there deliberately?'

'True.'

'He didn't endear himself to Mr Duckett, the CSI man.'

That wasn't the point, Halliwell felt like saying, but he settled for a shrug.

Dr Sealy added, 'Duckett would have found the blade of grass eventually, I'm certain. Quite properly he gave his first attention to the body. Who is the victim, then? You'd better introduce us before I take liberties with him.'

Stripping a man to his boxer shorts was a liberty in Halliwell's book, but he guessed the pathologist meant more. 'The name is Rupert Hope and he lectured on history at Bristol University.'

'He's history himself now.'

'True.'

Halliwell had never been much of a conversationalist. He was here for a purpose and so was the pathologist and he didn't see the need to be sociable. If something of particular interest was about to be revealed he wanted to know what it was. There was nothing obvious.

Dr Sealy peeled off the boxer shorts and dropped them into a plastic evidence bag. 'If I were one of his students I wouldn't sit in the front row. He hasn't changed his underwear for some time.'

'He was living rough.'

'A lecturer living rough? And why was that, do you think? Some sort of field trip experience, seeing how the great unwashed lived in times past?'

'I've no idea.'

'You're the detective, not me. Let's see if this gives you an idea.'

Halliwell's eyes were on the body part just revealed. Nothing about it looked remarkable, let alone capable of inspiration.

But Dr Sealy had taken a step sideways and was standing at the end of the dissection table. 'The interesting bit, the head wound. There's no other external injury, so it deserves our attention. Step closer, Mr Halliwell, and take a proper look.'

The dead man's head was propped on a block, allowing a view of the back of the skull.

Halliwell wasn't squeamish. He eyed the

split flesh and blood-matted hair in a dispassionate way. 'So?'

'You're not really looking, are you? What do you see?'

'A deep wound, deep enough to kill him.'

'Agreed, but there's something else.'

'You've got me there.'

'I think I have.' Sealy pointed with his gloved finger. 'Here, to the right of the laceration, some healing has taken place.'

'After death?' Halliwell bent closer and saw for himself the remnants of a scab with pink new skin forming a line more than two inches long. 'How can that be?'

'You're looking at a wound that was made when Rupert Hope was still alive. A separate wound, just to the right of the fatal blow inflicted later. What we have, Mr Halliwell, is evidence that this unfortunate man was struck on the back of the skull twice within a few weeks. The first time wasn't fatal. The second plainly was.'

11

A fresh corpse, the unfortunate Rupert Hope, had to be a new priority for Peter Diamond. Another press conference, irksome, but necessary. He'd already asked John Wigfull to set it up for 2.30 p.m., in time to make the evening news and morning papers. The story that Rupert was the missing cavalier was a gift to headline writers. With luck, some witnesses would get in touch by tomorrow. Then they'd need interviewing. This new case was going to stretch his resources. Not an insurmountable problem, he thought. He'd ask Georgina to add some manpower.

The Assistant Chief Constable didn't see it his way.

'Peter, it isn't on,' she told him across her great mahogany desk. She was in uniform as usual, glittering with silver braid and buttons.

'What isn't, ma'am?' he said.

'Another murder enquiry.'

He tilted his head as if he must have misheard. 'It's our job. We can't pick and choose. If two come together we have to cope. All I'm asking is that you open another box of bobbies.'

'Not possible.'

'Plenty of keen young coppers are out there wasting their time on binge-drinkers and pre-school kids nicking sweets from corner shops. They'd jump at a chance to work on a murder.'

'You're not listening.' Georgina wasn't listening either, but she outranked him. 'I'm saying we can't take this on.'

'Where's it going, then? We can't walk away from it.'

'Bristol.'

His buttocks went into spasm. 'You're not serious.'

'The victim came from there.'

'Yes, but the killing was on our patch, not theirs.'

She inhaled and her twin emblems of disquiet threatened to surge across the desk and demolish him. 'What do you mean by *"theirs"*? We're in the same constabulary.'

'I've got a crime scene going on Lansdown Hill.'

'Peter, I don't need to tell you, of all

people, that the scene ceases to be of interest after forensics have been through. The body has been removed. All the interest will now shift to Bristol, where Rupert Hope spent ninety-nine per cent of his time.'

A one-man mutiny threatened. 'You're seriously proposing to make them a gift of this?'

'I just told you. They're Avon and Somerset, the same as we are.'

'But I've called a press conference this afternoon.'

'Go ahead with it. Tell them this will be conducted from Bristol. Any calls to this station can easily be transferred.'

'What exactly is the problem here?' he said, trying to stay reasonable. 'Is it the skeleton? That's been buried twenty years. It can go on the back burner while we deal with Rupert Hope.' The imagery wasn't the most elegant, but she knew what he meant.

'It cannot,' Georgina said. 'You've set up an incident room and spoken to the press. Your people are working on the case.'

'They're on the new case as well. Halliwell is at the post mortem as we speak. Ingeborg Smith is checking hostels for the homeless in case the victim stayed there.'

'It's not efficient to have the same officers investigating two unconnected murders. I can't justify it to Headquarters.'

She had a point there. He was running out of arguments. His brain whirred. 'How about this? I hand the skeleton case to Keith Halliwell. The whole bag of tricks. He's got years of experience and he's ready to lead an enquiry. Then I can give all my attention to the cavalier.'

'And have two incident rooms going simultaneously? Not in my police station. I've made a decision, Peter. This is final.'

'I thought you'd have more confidence in me,' he said, forced to play the loyalty card. 'I haven't messed up a case since you arrived here. This isn't such a sticky one. It could be sorted in a couple of days.'

'Why do you always think it's about you?' she said with a sharp intake of breath. 'It's resources. The case goes to Bristol. Now would you go back to work? I have calls to make.'

Desperation drove him to say, 'What I meant when I mentioned Halliwell is that it frees me up to go to Bristol and head the enquiry from there.'

She stared at him as if he'd just performed a pirouette. His dislike of change was known to everyone in Bath. 'You're willing to relocate to Bristol?'

'It's a short drive when the traffic is light.

I'll be getting there early and coming back late.' He could hardly believe he was speaking these words.

Georgina gripped the arms of her chair, unsettled.

He added, 'And Halliwell deserves a case of his own.'

She'd gone silent. She was definitely wavering.

He dangled a real tempter in front of her. 'You won't see me for at least a week.'

That did it.

'If you're that keen, I'll see what can be done. I'll have to speak to colleagues there.' Her eyes rolled upwards. 'They don't know what's about to hit them.'

He left her office wondering if he'd made the right decision. There wasn't time to ponder it for long. The press conference was in twenty minutes and he needed to bone up on the details.

When Halliwell returned from the post mortem Diamond was winding up with the press. He'd made his prepared statement and given follow-up interviews for radio and television.

Ingeborg was outside the briefing room with eyes that had just seen a unicorn.

'What's up?' Halliwell asked.

162

'The boss said the incident room will be in Bristol Central. He's in charge and he's going to be there.'

'That's news to me.'

'It's about resources, he told them. Plus the fact that the dead man spent most of his time in Bristol.'

'Resources? Doesn't sound like the guv'nor talking,' Halliwell said. 'What's got into him?'

Diamond emerged, bouncy as ever. 'There you are, Keith, back from the dead. What's the story?'

Halliwell told him about the partly healed wound at the back of the victim's head. 'Dr Sealy says it could well have caused concussion and loss of memory.'

'Which may explain his odd behaviour.' Diamond rubbed his hands. 'This is good, Keith. We must step up our enquiries here in Bath.' He paused before adding, 'When I say "we" I'm not including you, old chum.'

Halliwell reddened. 'Why not?'

'Don't look so suspicious. I've got terrific news for you. As from this moment you're heading the skeleton investigation.'

'Get away.'

'Check with Georgina if you like. It's official.'

'Bloody hell.'

'That's more like the man I know.' He clapped a hand on Halliwell's shoulder. 'You owe us all a drink.'

'But what about you, guv?'

'I'll be handling the new case — and from Bristol. You don't have to cheer. It's only temporary.'

'What about me?' Ingeborg asked. 'Who am I with?'

Diamond looked over his shoulder to check that no one else was listening. 'For the record, you're with Keith, right? I'm not asking you to come to Bristol. But I need someone here I can rely on, and you may find yourself doing things for me between whiles.'

She frowned. 'Serving two masters?'

'We're not ogres.'

'I'll find out, won't I?'

Diamond let that pass. He needed her good will. 'As a first step, find me the two patrol car officers who met Rupert Hope.'

'Now, you mean?'

'I could be in Bristol tomorrow.'

A remark of Georgina's had stayed with him longer than anything else she'd said. *It's not efficient to have one officer investigating two unconnected murders.* But were they unconnected?

The two sets of human remains on Lansdown had been found within a couple of miles of each other and had little else to link them that Diamond could fix on. They were separated by about twenty years, by the method of disposal and the sex and age of the victims. Lansdown was the one discernible link. It would not be wise to make too much of that.

And yet . . .

The repeated trips up the hill to one crime scene or the other kept reinforcing his hunch that these cases were linked. Over the years he'd often driven along the great limestone ridge and got the idea that it was isolated, a suitable place to commit murder and dump a body. Only in recent days had he become aware that the down buzzed with activity at weekends, not just occasional horse-racing, but golf, football, kites and model aircraft, car boot sales, dog walking and rambling. All this on a site with a proven history dating back to the Iron Age. Maybe the Lansdown Society had a point. Someone needed to keep an eye on things.

Towards the end of the afternoon two nervous-looking constables in uniform were ushered into his office by Ingeborg.

'You're the pair who spoke to the man

whose body has been found?'

The male constable was holding his cap in front of him, twisting it like the steering wheel he would rather have been behind. 'I'm Andy Sullivan, sir, and this is PC Beal.'

'Doesn't she have a name?'

'Pardon?'

'You want me to call you Andy and your sidekick PC Beal.'

The young woman at Sullivan's side said, 'Denise, sir.' She looked straight out of school, with fine, blonde hair pinned up and pale skin of the kind that obviously coloured at the slightest personal remark.

'You were sent to deal with an incident up at the racecourse, right?'

Andy Sullivan asserted his seniority as spokesman. 'Two incidents on different days, in point of fact. It just happened that we got the job both times. The first was suspicious behaviour, tampering with car doors. We met the complainants, a Major Swithin and his wife, but the suspect had already left when we arrived. He was seen heading for the enclosure area. We conducted a search and unfortunately didn't find him.'

Denise Beal cleared her throat. She'd turned beetroot red this time. 'Actually, I did find him.'

Sullivan swung to face her.

'Behind one of the grandstands,' she said.

'You didn't tell me.'

'No. I kept it to myself.'

'Why was that?' Diamond asked before Sullivan waded in.

'I, um, thought he was simple.'

'The suspect — or Andy Sullivan.'

The joke fell flat. Neither smiled. Diamond wished he hadn't spoken. 'You spoke to the man whose body has been found?' he said to get Denise started again.

'I didn't know who he was.'

Sullivan said, 'This is totally new to me.'

She said, 'You were a long way off at the time.'

'You'd gone different ways?' Diamond said.

Sullivan said, 'I was checking the stables.'

'You sent her round the enclosure area while you took a stroll along the racecourse? How long have you been in the police, Denise?'

'Six weeks, sir.'

Diamond gave Sullivan a look and passed no comment. There were bigger issues here. 'So what did you say to the guy?'

'I asked him what he was doing there and who he was. I was trying to keep him talking until Andy arrived.'

'Did he identify himself?'

She bit her lower lip and looked even more the nervous schoolgirl. 'He said he was known as Noddy.'

'Are you sure?' The troubling image returned of the man at the races he'd taken for a drunk. 'Did you ask for a proper name?'

'I tried. He didn't seem to have an answer. That's why I thought he was simple. I couldn't smell drink on his breath. He was smelly from living rough, not boozing. I asked if he'd just come from the car park and he didn't seem to know. In the end I let him walk away. I didn't tell Andy — PC Sullivan — because he'd told me to keep the suspect talking if I met him and I'd failed.'

The hell with Andy Sullivan's hurt feelings. 'Did you notice anything about his speech?'

'Yes. He had quite a nice voice. Educated.'

Definitely the same man. 'But some aftershave would have improved him?'

She smiled. 'Or a shower.'

'So how did you deal with him?'

'I told him to keep away from the car park.'

'Because the major and his wife were still there?'

'Well, yes.'

'You felt sorry for him?'

'He didn't act like a villain.'

'All right,' Diamond said, and brought Sullivan back into the discussion. 'The second time you were called to deal with this man was when?'

'Sunday morning, sir. We were told he'd been nicking food at the car boot sale.'

'I know a bit about this,' Diamond said, to keep it brief. 'This was the hot meat pie.'

'The woman said she'd made a citizen's arrest, but I thought we could deal with it on the spot,' Andy Sullivan said. 'I asked him his name and got the same answer.'

'Noddy?'

'It wasn't as cheeky as it sounds,' Denise piped up. 'He did do a lot of nodding while he was talking to us. I can understand someone calling him that.'

'And you?' Diamond asked Sullivan. 'Did you think he was taking the piss?'

He swallowed hard. 'It didn't come across like that. He was serious. He didn't seem to know much about himself apart from the name. I tried to find out where he lived and didn't get a proper answer.'

Denise confirmed it. 'He said he slept anywhere he could find that was dry.'

'Like a refuge?'

'I don't think he knew,' Sullivan said. 'You

know how you can tell from someone's eyes that they're not all there?'

'What else did you discover?'

'That was about it, sir. Unfortunately, it got out of hand after that because the pie lady attacked another woman and we had to separate them.'

'Both of you?'

'I asked PC Beal to do it, being a woman, handling another woman, like. And when we'd sorted that —'

'When Denise had sorted it.'

'Yes. The suspect had gone.'

'Which saved you a lot of paperwork.'

'We didn't let him go on purpose, sir.'

'I'm not suggesting it. You must have heard by now that your man Noddy has been identified as Rupert Hope, a university lecturer who has been missing for a couple of weeks. His picture was in the *Chronicle*.'

'I haven't seen it,' Sullivan said.

'Nor me,' Denise added.

'You want to listen to what your sergeant tells you at morning parade. This was the man who was murdered in Lansdown cemetery. He was probably suffering from memory loss when you spoke to him. The post mortem showed he took a heavy blow to the head about two weeks before he was killed.'

Shock was written plainly on their faces.

'That's awful,' Denise said. 'He was gentle, no threat to anyone. If we'd arrested him, it couldn't have happened.'

'Don't lose any sleep over that,' Diamond said. 'You did your job. I wouldn't have done any different and neither would Andy here, would you, Andy?'

'Er, no.'

'You won't be playing the blame game, right?'

'Right, sir.'

Sullivan would. He would undoubtedly accuse Denise of disloyalty later, but the sting had been taken out of it. This young woman cared more about what had happened to the victim than her own good record. Diamond liked what he'd seen of her. She'd make a better copper than Sullivan.

After they'd left the office he thought more about his own sighting of Rupert Hope on the racecourse and the shambolic, wayward figure he'd cut. He'd misjudged the man. Everyone seemed to have got him wrong. This investigation was more personal now.

12

Keith Halliwell looked in.

'You don't mind me asking, guv? As I'm running the skeleton enquiry now, I wonder if you've got any pointers for me. Where were you going next with it?'

'You want some tips?' Diamond said, basking in the respect of this old colleague.

'I'd be a fool to let you go without asking.'

'A total idiot.'

Halliwell grinned sheepishly. 'As you know, we looked at the mispers index and there was no one obvious.'

'Plenty of missing persons don't get on that list for all kinds of reasons, Keith.'

'I know that, but I can't see how we can move on until we identify the woman. We know her approximate age and when she died, within a year or two, and that's all. Without the skull we can't use dental records.'

'I doubt if you'll find the skull. The point

of the killer removing it is to hinder identification. You know what I'd do if I was wanting to get rid of my victim's head? I'd chuck it into a reservoir. A skull isn't going to float like the rest of the body. Drop it in deep water and it's gone like a stone.'

Halliwell was frowning. 'I don't have the manpower to go dredging reservoirs.'

'I know. I'm telling you why you won't find that skull.'

'I was looking for encouragement.'

'Okay. Has anything resulted from the press coverage? There are always members of the public who call in.'

'Some have. I'm not optimistic.'

'Have you done a computer search of our own files from the nineties?'

'Unfortunately the time we're interested in is before we went over to computers in a big way. A lot of case notes are still on paper.'

'But retained?'

Halliwell nodded unhappily. Both men knew about the piles of dusty files boxed away in a store room downstairs.

'Still has to be done,' Diamond said. 'And you'll need to go through the local papers of twenty years ago. Crucial witnesses may have moved away, died, or whatever, but a disappearance could still have been reported. Look for mentions of Lansdown in particular. It's hard graft. Let's hope the effort brings a result.' Privately he was relieved it was now someone else's job. 'And there's one other thing.'

'What's that?' Halliwell asked. The encouragement was coming at the rate of a drip-feed.

'The zip fly we found with the body. Is it still in an evidence bag?'

'Must be.'

'Covered in rust and dirt?'

'Yep.'

'Have it cleaned up in the lab. They might find something on it. We assumed she was wearing jeans. What sort — cheap or designer? You sometimes get a manufacturer's mark on the tab.'

'Can we do that? Doesn't it have to be shown to the court as we found it?'

'It's been photographed, hasn't it? And the chain of evidence isn't in doubt. No one can argue that this isn't the zip found at the site. We have a right to make a forensic examination.'

'And will it help, knowing which brand of jeans she wore?'

'We don't know yet, do we?'

Before setting out his stall in Bristol, Diamond had one more interview in mind, one he could do himself. He still believed there was mileage in the Lansdown Society. People like that, self-appointed busybodies dedicated to keeping the place respectable, were the kinds of allies he needed.

Mrs Augusta White, the magistrate, was easy to contact, less easy to approach. 'Yes, of course I know you,' she told him over the phone. 'You're not easily forgotten.'

'Oh?'

'The way you give evidence.' Before he had time to reflect on that, she said, 'But if you think I'm going to sit here and wait for you, you've got another think coming. My dear Mr Diamond, I've spent the whole afternoon in court dealing with pathetic young people destroying their lives with drugs and I promised myself some refreshment.'

'Good thinking,' he said. 'I could do with some myself. May I join you?'

'I suspect you have the wrong idea,' she said. 'Refreshment for me isn't a couple of beers. It's exercise.'

'A brisk walk? I can walk for miles.'

'Not walking.'

'Jogging?'

'Not my style, Mr Diamond.'

That was a relief. 'Whatever. I need to

175

speak to you today, if you don't mind.'

'If this is really necessary you can meet me in the Y.'

'The what?'

'The YMCA fitness centre. Shall we say in three-quarters of an hour? From what I remember of your physique some step'n'sweat would do you good. Wear something light. A T-shirt and shorts will do.'

He hadn't worn shorts since his rugby-playing days. 'I wasn't aiming to work out.'

'You'd better make a show of it. They don't like men standing about eyeing the women and I'm certainly not making an exhibition of myself for your delectation. It's a gym, Mr Diamond. Get there as soon as you can. I'm leaving presently.'

The Y was in Broad Street Place, no great distance from the police station. On the way he called at a sports shop and picked up a white T-shirt, cheap trainers and a pair of shorts that covered the butternut squashes that passed as his knees. He kept the receipt but doubted if he could claim it as a legitimate expense. At the front desk of the Y he asked the price of one session and was shocked, even after the peppy young woman told him it included one-to-one induction with a personal trainer and a lifestyle

176

consultation to devise a training plan and fitness goals.

The anxieties of some days ago resurfaced. Were these people in league with the police doctor who'd said he was overweight and unfit? Augusta White was in touch with Georgina through the Lansdown Society. Surely they couldn't have set him up?

'I don't need any of that,' he said. 'I was just enquiring.'

She looked at him and asked if he was a concession.

'A what?'

'Are you on benefits, dear?'

Annoyed, he leaned closer and showed her his warrant. 'Actually, I'm a police officer . . . dear.'

She said, 'You can get a corporate membership for twenty-six pounds.'

He was tempted to sign up the whole of Manvers Street just to see their reactions, but Georgina would never honour the cheque. 'It's part of an investigation.' He tapped the side of his nose. 'Surveillance. You don't mind if I go through?'

Now it was the receptionist's turn to look worried. 'Is this a sting?'

He thought of saying her prices were, but settled for a shake of the head. 'No one's going to get arrested.'

She sent him downstairs to the gym.

He spotted Augusta White's tightly permed silver hair at once. She was one of several using the cardiovascular equipment, a row of machines facing picture windows with sensational views of the hills around Bath, including Lansdown. In a navy blue tracksuit, she was pedalling steadily on an exercise bike as if confident it would move off and take her Mary-Poppins style over the rooftops. He wasn't the best at estimating women's ages, but he reckoned Mrs White qualified as a concession and was about half his weight. Behind the bench she always looked a formidable figure. Here, she was just a scrap. Good for you, old girl, he thought.

'Why don't you step on the treadmill next to me?' she said when he emerged, kitted and ready to go, from the changing room. 'Be sure to put it on a low setting that you can handle.'

One of the staff showed him how to operate the machine by using the screen mounted at the front of the machine. He started at an ambling gait he was confident he could tolerate for ten minutes or so, by which time Mrs White would surely be exhausted. He was no stranger to fitness apparatus even though it had gone high-tech in the past twenty-five years.

'I can't discuss anything that's *sub judice,*' Mrs White said, continuing to work her legs at the rate of a seasoned user.

'It's all right,' he said. 'This is about your other life.'

'What?'

'Outside the courts.'

'This is my other life — and you've invaded it.'

'You invited me.'

'So I did,' she said in a more forgiving tone. 'But be warned, Mr Diamond, my personal life is off limits as well.'

'It's not personal. It's the Lansdown Society.'

'That's a private club.'

'I've already spoken to Major Swithin and Sir Colin Tipping.'

'Not so private as it should be. Those two.' She clicked her tongue in disapproval. 'Yes, Sir Colin told me you'd interrupted their round of golf. I can't think what you're hoping to get from me that you haven't heard from them. They're about as discreet as a chorus line.'

'You were in at the beginning,' he said, pleased how comfortable he felt on the treadmill. Maybe he was fitter than anyone suspected.

'And so were they.'

'I reckon you have a better memory than theirs. You formed the society in 1993, I was told, to see that the down wasn't mistreated by the people staging the mock battle up there.'

'Correct. And later we put ourselves on a more permanent footing.'

'Public spirited of you.' A genuine compliment from Diamond. Mrs White's contribution to the running of the city was well known to be altruistic and gladly given.

'It isn't a burden. I enjoy walking up there and I might as well check what's happening at the same time.'

'Do you happen to remember if anyone was seriously hurt in the battle? You know why I'm asking?'

'I know about the skeleton you found. It's female, isn't it? Women do take part. They're sometimes in the gun crews. The less adventurous prefer a support role, ministering to the sick or preparing meals at the camp. They call themselves camp followers. Not too nice a description. Personally I'd rather be astride a horse wielding a sword.'

A scary mental image.

'A camp follower could still be hit by a stray cannonball, I expect.'

'I watched the battle,' she said, 'and I'm

absolutely certain real cannonballs weren't used.'

'This woman was minus her head.'

'Lord save us, the explosives aren't that dangerous, or we'd never have sanctioned them. If there had been a serious accident like that, the papers would have been full of it.'

'I know. I'm working on the theory that the death was covered up. She was buried close to the battleground.'

'Surely her people would have raised the alarm: family, friends, workmates?'

'Unless she was a loner.'

'Loners don't join in war games, Mr Diamond — certainly not female loners. Most of them join because their boyfriends or husbands are part of it. I don't know why you're wasting time on this.' She took a hand off the handlebar and raised a finger. 'Ah, but I do. I see it now. You want to link it with the killing of the man found in the cemetery. He was one of the battle people, a cavalier.'

'We can't ignore the possibility.'

'It's far more likely that your skeleton lady had nothing to do with cavaliers and round-heads. My best guess is that she was the victim of a sex crime and the killer disposed of her body afterwards. How are you doing?

Do you want to step off?'

'I'm all right. Is the battle area popular with courting couples?'

'Don't ask me. You're the policeman.'

'Yes, but you people patrol it regularly.'

' "Patrol" is not the way I think of it. We make a point of spending time up there when other commitments allow. I like walking. Reggie and Colin do their golf and Colin never misses the race days. Your boss Georgina is a rambler, like me. Charlie Smart, our vicar, is interested in wildlife, so between us we keep an eye on things. Patrolling, no. We're not vigilantes, you know.'

Speak for yourself, he thought. The major, for one, seemed to think he had a mission to catch anyone who misbehaved. 'So you wouldn't know what people get up to at night?'

She turned her head and gave him a magisterial glare. 'Personally, no. Well,' she said, 'I must correct myself. I haven't seen anything going on personally, but I'm informed what happens. There are several unofficial points where motorists can drive off the road, and do and sometimes throw out their used condoms. Reggie — the major — keeps count for some reason, and will insist on reporting the latest figure at our meetings.'

182

'I didn't think to ask him.'

'I wouldn't. It's not good for his blood pressure. How's yours, by the way? Don't overdo this if it's your first time.'

'The problem with the sex murderer theory,' he said, ignoring that, 'is that he'd need to have a spade with him to bury his victim. If your thoughts are on sex, do you carry a spade in your car?'

A pause while he regretted phrasing it that way.

Then she said, 'My thoughts in that department are not for you or anyone else to enquire about.'

'Sorry, ma'am. I'm speaking of people in general.'

'Drivers sometimes carry spades routinely in case of snow. Or if they're treasure-hunters, or have an allotment. One can think of reasons.'

'Agreed.'

'As you well know, I've had a number of murderers brought into my court for pre-liminary hearings. They can be resourceful when it comes to covering up their crimes.'

'Don't I know it!'

'A magistrate sees the whole spectrum of offenders, from speeding motorists to serial murderers.'

'And I dare say some crimes are committed on Lansdown.'

'Of course.'

'Any habitual offenders up there?'

She laughed. 'You're scraping the barrel now.'

'No. This man Rupert Hope was attacked twice in two weeks. He was living rough. We could be looking for someone with a grudge against him. Maybe someone who gets violent when drunk. You must see a few.'

'Regularly, but not specially linked with Lansdown, except sometimes on race days.'

His calf muscles were aching. He'd need to step off soon. 'No names, then?'

She gave the matter some thought. 'I've seen a man from Charlcombe a few times, a big fellow with the unlikely name of Gentle. Ned Gentle. He's put a few unfortunates into A&E on Saturday nights. I sent him down for six months last time. He'd still be inside.'

'I'll check.'

'If you don't mind me saying so, you've turned rather pink.'

He could feel his face glowing. 'I'm stopping presently. In your rambles over the last couple of weeks did you see Rupert Hope at all?'

'How would I know?' she asked. 'Was his head bandaged?'

'Probably not. How do I switch this thing off?'

'Touch the red button on the screen.'

'I can't see it.' All the controls were a blur.

She leaned right across him and touched the screen.

'Thanks for that. It suddenly got difficult.' He stepped off, panting.

Augusta White continued pedalling. 'You'll feel better after a shower. You don't mind if I continue? I have another mile to go.'

13

He'd arranged to see Paloma at her house in Lyncombe that evening. She'd spent the afternoon in Winchester and would need cheering up, not because Winchester is a depressing city, but because the place she'd been visiting was the prison. As a comforter, he was not much help. Having driven there, he felt a sharp pain in his back when he tried to rise from the car seat. It was ridiculous, but he couldn't get out. He had to sound the horn.

Paloma opened her front door and came out. With her help he got vertical and limped inside, where he explained about the session at the fitness centre.

'What were you on?' she asked. 'The rowing machine?'

'A treadmill,' he said, 'and I was only walking, for pity's sake, and I'm used to that. I felt good at the time, a little wobbly at the end, that's true. I didn't expect this.'

'You must have moved in a way you wouldn't normally use. I can see the pain you're in. You'll need a couple of days off work.'

'Some chance. I'm needed.' He told her about the Rupert Hope investigation.

'Peter, no one is indispensable.'

'That's exactly my point. They can replace me and I don't want to be replaced. The boss is trying to elbow me off the case anyway. She'll hand the whole thing over to Bristol CID. I've got to put in an appearance even if I'm on crutches.'

'Crutches wouldn't look good.'

'You know what I mean. The show goes on.'

'Then we have to get you mobile. Ice and heat.'

He winced at the prospect.

Paloma said, 'If that doesn't grab you, sunshine, I have some wicked-smelling liniment.'

'Ice and heat.'

'Take off your things, then, and I'll get organised.'

She spread cushions from her sofa on the floor and he removed his shirt and trousers and lay face down in his blue striped jockey shorts. He was alone for about ten minutes and the ache eased enough for him to think how ridiculous he must look. His relationship with Paloma hadn't reached the stage when anything goes.

She returned and the ice was applied. His intake of breath was like a rocket launch.

Paloma said, 'This is what they do for injured footballers. It must be effective because they're soon on their feet again.'

'They use some kind of spray.'

'I know, and these are packs of frozen peas, but you have to settle for what you can get. Same principle. If you were a millionaire footballer you'd have a medic and the spray, but you're not, so you've got me and Captain Birdseye. Is it helping?'

'It's going numb.'

'Good.'

'I don't like to think what the hot part will be.'

'Wet flannels heated in the microwave. Take it from me, you wouldn't get better treatment if you flew first class to America.'

'If I was flying first class to America, I wouldn't be half naked on the floor.'

'You'd get a massage if you wanted. Really. It's part of the service.'

'I'll take your word for that.'

Paloma frequently made business trips to Los Angeles to advise on period costume designs for films. She was known to all the production companies out there. It was a mystery to Diamond why a high-earning professional was interested in an overweight Bath policeman who travelled in the tourist section if he ever had a holiday abroad.

She went to collect the flannels.

He wriggled a little on the cushions. The ice had definitely helped and he told Paloma when she came back. Then the first hot flannel was applied and he gave a fair imitation of a peacock screeching.

She said, 'I hope there was a payoff for this. Did you get something out of the session on the treadmill as well as a stiff back?'

'Less than I hoped for. I'm looking for witnesses. The Lansdown Society members spend a lot of time there keeping an eye on things, but they seem to miss all the violence.'

'What's the object of this society?'

'To keep the place peaceful and unspoilt.'

'They don't seem much good at it if a man was attacked twice and murdered.'

'I'm beginning to think it's more about giving the members a sense of importance than making a difference. Let's face it, Lansdown has never been all that peaceful. I wouldn't mind betting the Iron Age saw plenty of brutality.'

'Human sacrifice, according to something

I saw on TV.'

'There you go. Then we know about the Civil War battle, upwards of ten thousand men fighting it out with muskets and artillery. They reckon several hundred were killed, mainly on the royalist side. And in World War Two, the fighter planes were taking off from Charmy Down airfield. Bath had its share of the bombing.' He was breathing more easily. 'That feels better after the first shock.'

'Good. I'd better apply the ice again.'

'Are you sure you're not enjoying yourself?'

'This is the treatment, Peter. By alternating the heat and cold, we stimulate the blood and accelerate the healing. I can tell you something else about violence on Lansdown.'

'You lie in wait up there and attack middle-aged men with frozen peas and hot flannels?'

She laughed. 'Don't tempt me. If you want to know, for centuries there was a fair up there every August. I happen to know about this because of a scene I dressed for a movie. I researched country fairs and found out that Lansdown was one of the biggest. It must have been a marvellous annual treat for the local people.'

190

'Better than a car boot sale, I reckon.'

'I suppose they were the historical equivalent. Trading was done, mainly of cattle, sheep and horses, but the showmen came too, with what we think of as fairground rides, and also fire-eaters, dwarfs, giants, bearded ladies, fortune-tellers, bare-knuckle fighters. Imagine what it was like for country people used to the dull routine of caring for crops and livestock.'

'I liked fairs as a kid,' Diamond said. 'They brightened up our lives.'

'But as children we were treated to any number of amusements like carnivals and fetes, holidays, cinema, television and pop music. In the times I'm talking about this was the one event of the year.'

'And it came to Lansdown?'

'I've got a book upstairs by Lord George Sanger called *Seventy Years a Showman*. He wasn't really a lord. He took it on as a showbiz title. He tells of travelling in the eighteen-thirties with his father James, who owned a peepshow.'

'*What the Butler Saw?*'

'Easy, you're in no state to get excited. Not in your condition. No, the original peepshow wasn't a slot machine. It was a kind of cabinet lit by candles with pictures that were moved up and down on strings

191

while the owner gave a commentary. One set was the battle of Trafalgar because James Sanger had been a sailor on the *Victory*. I have some peepshow illustrations upstairs and they're four feet wide and nearly three feet high, really lurid and painted by an Irishman called Kelley who lived in Leather Lane, Holborn. Why do I remember that?'

'Because you're good at your job, that's why.'

'This should interest you as a policeman. Sanger's peepshow also featured famous murders such as — what was it? — the red barn murder.'

'William Corder.'

'You've heard of it?' Paloma's turn to be impressed.

'Corder was a callous bastard,' he said. 'A rich farmer. The victim was his mistress, a young woman called Maria Marten. He wanted to get rid of Maria, so he told her a secret wedding was all set up in Ipswich and they'd meet in the red barn and he'd arrange transport. She wasn't seen again, but her mother dreamed the girl been murdered and buried in the barn and insisted it was dug up. After a year they found Maria's body. The case passed into folklore. I can well understand it being peepshow material. The story was huge at the time. Ten thousand turned up to watch Corder being hanged. The red barn mystery was turned into melodrama, verse, hellfire sermons, waxworks, even one of those Staffordshire pottery figures.' He didn't add that he had his own small library of famous crimes.

'Anyway,' Paloma said, 'the fair came to Lansdown as usual in 1839, and there was nervousness about coming here according to Sanger because the Bath slums housed the most horrendous bunch of criminals in England.'

This was news to Diamond. '*Bath?* The genteel city?'

'I know it's hard to credit, but that's the way it was at the time, apparently, and they were led by a woman known as Carroty Kate.'

'Go on. I'm enjoying this.'

'She lived in Bull Paunch Alley, which was a no go area for the police.'

'Never heard of it.'

'A backstreet long since demolished and built over. She was huge, this Carroty Kate, built like a navvy, Sanger says, and late in the evening she decided to lead her gang of roughs up Lansdown Hill to the fair. She was half-stripped, as he described it, her red hair hanging loose. They started at the drinking booths, beat up some of the owners and drank themselves into a frenzy, whereupon Kate ordered them to wreck the fair, which they did — or much of it — overturning wagons, smashing up the caravans and the show platforms. They made bonfires with the wood.'

'Where were the police?' he asked.

'Outnumbered and helpless. The destruction went on until dawn and then the mob had sobered up a bit and tramped off down towards the city again.'

'They got away with it?'

'Not for long. Some of the showmen came together and decided this was the time to do something about it. They'd seen their stalls and homes smashed beyond repair and they wanted revenge, so they rounded up their horses and armed themselves with lumps of wood and rode after the gang like a scene out of a cowboy film. They surprised the ringleaders and brought back about a dozen of them with their hands tied, including Carroty Kate.'

'To a warm welcome, no doubt.'

'They called it showmen's law. They tied Kate to a wagon wheel while they dealt with the men. All the show people watched as the terrified roughs were forced down the hillside to a deep pond, where they were lashed together and dragged through the water on tent-ropes time and again until they were close to drowning. Then they were brought back to the ruins of the fair and tied to wagon wheels and horsewhipped.'

'Talk about rough justice.'

'Kate didn't escape either. The women dealt with her. It took six of them to force her over a trestle while two more took turns to cane her using the penny canes sold at the fair.'

No doubt the timing was unplanned, but this was the moment Paloma returned the frozen peas to Diamond's back. His legs kicked up with the shock.

'You were asking about the police,' she said. 'They did round up some more of the mob.'

'That restores my faith a bit.'

'Until I tell you there was a fight in which one officer was hit with an iron bar and crippled for life. The man responsible was taken to court and hanged and several of the others were sentenced to be transported.'

'I don't have any problem with that. It was the system then.'

'So that's the story of Lansdown Fair,' she said. 'I leave you to work out the moral.'

'It's one my mother told me. Stay away from redheads.'

'And have you followed the advice?'

'To the best of my ability. The way you women colour your hair I don't find out until it's too late.'

'It's never too late.'

'I can think of a situation when it could be.'

'But you won't go into that.'

They both laughed.

'Is it easing up at all?' she asked.

'Definitely. I'm grateful.'

She insisted on one more hot and cold application and he manfully allowed it to happen.

'You shouldn't think of driving to Bristol tomorrow,' she said. 'Can't you switch cases and stop in Bath?'

'I'd be stuck with the skeleton.'

'And you want to investigate Rupert Hope's murder?'

'Ideally, both, but as I was forced to choose, yes. The decision is made. Halliwell doesn't have the seniority to lead the Bristol team. I have to get there somehow. A murder investigation can't be put on hold while the SIO gets on his feet again.'

'What's your plan?'

'There are three obvious lines of enquiry: his work at the university and the people there; the battle re-enactment he took part in; and — hardest of all to crack — the possibility that it was a random attack.'

'A lot of hard graft in prospect.'

'You've said it.'

'What about the forensic science? Doesn't that trap most murderers now?'

'You've been watching too much television. It's not the easy ride they make out. We always hope for traces of DNA, but if you can't find the weapon and the victim didn't put up a fight, the possibilities reduce sharply.'

'Footmarks?'

'Nice idea, and the crime scene people will do their best to find some. The trouble is that the cemetery is a public place. You get a fair few visitors walking the paths, especially as Beckford's Tower is there, a tourist attraction.'

'Which reminds me,' she said. 'I must get that book for you.'

'Book?'

'William Beckford.'

'Thanks.' He'd rather hoped she'd forgotten it. 'Coming back to the crime scene, it's a matter of eliminating shoeprints. Not easy.'

'I thought *my* job was tough,' she said. 'How are you feeling now? Ready to think about food? I was planning to send for a Chinese.'

'Suits me,' he said, 'so long as you don't insist on chopsticks.'

'In my house you're at liberty to use your fingers if you want, but I do supply knives and forks as well. I'll find the menu.'

She insisted on driving him to Bristol Headquarters in the morning. The treatment had eased the back pain appreciably, but she wanted to be certain he didn't go into spasm after a few miles in heavy traffic. He agreed it wouldn't make a good start to ask his new team to carry him inside.

She drove his car confidently through the notoriously confusing one way system to Trinity Road. He was able to get out unaided. His mind had been on what he'd say and he hadn't thought how Paloma was getting back.

'The train,' she said when he finally asked. 'I know my way to Temple Meads.'

He nodded. 'This place confuses me.'

'Don't let it show.'

He grinned his thanks and went inside.

14

When Diamond looked in, the day shift had gathered for what was known in the trade as morning prayers, but there was nothing worshipful about it. The duty inspector was reporting on an early morning drugs bust in Bedminster. He stopped in mid-sentence, glared at the visitor, and said, 'Can I help you?'

'I expect so,' Diamond said, and introduced himself.

Some of them straightened up. One actually checked his hair.

The inspector's manner changed from sniffy to servile. 'Would you like to address the meeting, sir?'

'What I'd really like to address is the porcelain, before I meet the top brass,' Diamond said. 'Which way is it?'

The lower ranks enjoyed that. He was off to a good start.

Twenty minutes later he sat down with a

bigger challenge, his CID team, twelve detectives ranging from a muscleman with a silver earring to a veteran with bifocals. He had to be careful here. For all he knew, the owner of the silver earring might be the inspector. You could never be certain in CID. He told them his own name and suggested they started with name and rank when they spoke.

No one did — yet.

He needed an icebreaker. He picked up a set of crime scene photos from the desk in front of him and commented that someone had made a useful start.

A slim black guy gave the slightest of nods.

'And you are . . . ?'

'Septimus Ward, DI, sir.'

'The senior man?'

Septimus Ward nodded a second time. No hint of a smile. It was up to Diamond to win this lot over. Par for the course, he thought. They feel the same way about me as I feel about coming to this place.

'You're the experts here, being local, so I'm in your hands. How much can you tell me about the victim, Rupert Hope?'

Some looks were exchanged. No one seemed willing to say anything.

He added, 'There was nothing found on him. If he possessed a mobile or a wallet or credit cards, they'd long since been nicked. He was a university lecturer, and that's about all we know.'

This was so different from the briefings he gave in Bath. There, Ingeborg or John Leaman would have waded in by now and offered something, if only to hear the sounds of their own voices. Instead, he was doing all the talking.

'Does anyone here know any background?' he asked.

Septimus, the inspector, relented a little. 'He was from these parts, born in Kingswood and went to Clifton College.'

'Not one of the Bash Street kids, then.'

Septimus may not have heard of the Beano. He stayed on script. 'He did his university studies here, took a higher degree at Oxford and then came back as a history lecturer. I don't think he has any close family left living in Bristol.'

But at least there was communication now. A little of the ice had cracked. 'The parents are in Australia,' Diamond said. 'I do know that much. They were concerned about not hearing from him after he went missing so we can assume he was still on good terms with them. He lived in a flat in Whiteladies Road.'

'Alone?' another man asked.

It was such a boost to get another contribution that Diamond ignored his own directive about name and rank. 'Apparently, yes.'

'No relationships?'

'None that we know about.'

'Gay?'

'No one has mentioned it.' Now he sensed what was going on. They wanted to know where he stood on the issue of homosexuality. Fair enough, he thought, but there wasn't time for all that. 'Let's get digging, then, everything we can get on this man: his life history, family, friends, enemies, daily routine, work habits, night life. As well as staff at the university who worked with him, we'll be interviewing students, looking in particular for anyone with a reason to dislike him. I gather he was friendly and good at his job, which means anyone with a grudge should stand out. Septimus . . .'

'Sir.'

'Thanks for that, but "guv" will do. You can divvy up the duties. We need statements from his landlord and neighbours. Anything of note about visitors in recent weeks, changes to the routine and so on. Every last thing they know: where he shops, how he gets about, who cuts his hair, the whole bag of tricks. Another team goes through the flat looking for anything about recent contacts: letters, scribbled notes, phones, address book, computer. The third and fourth team do the university, talk to the other lecturers and students, look in his office or locker, or whatever they have. By tonight I want to know this man better than I know myself; his personal history, friends, contacts and potential enemies.'

'Does it have a name, guv?' Septimus asked.

'Does what have a name?'

'This operation. We'll get more respect if we give it a name.'

He'd heard before about Bristol giving names to everything. 'You can call it what you like as long as you do a good job.'

'Operation Cavalier?'

'If you like. Cavalier it is.'

'Do you want to be out and about yourself, guv?'

A loaded question. Talk about respect. He could earn some for himself by leading from the front. In time, he remembered his bad back. 'No, someone has to get this place up and running. And I'll need an office manager.'

Silence.

Some heads turned. They were looking at the beefy owner of the earring. He said, 'Fair cop. You've got me bang to rights.'

This caused amusement.

'What's your name?' Diamond asked, uncertain where he was going with this. He suspected he was being set up.

'Chaz . . . guv.'

'Can you take this on, Chaz?'

'Sure.'

After the rest of them had quit the room Diamond asked Chaz his rank and learned that he'd made it to sergeant, indicating that somebody rated him. 'Do you know what this involves, Chaz?'

'Common sense, isn't it? We need staff. Someone to take calls, two or three computer operators to file the statements, an indexer, an action allocator and probably an admin officer as well.'

Encouraging.

'And can you get them?'

'We're high priority, aren't we?'

'You bet we are.'

In the first hour, Chaz not only conjured up the equipment, the phones and computers, but the civilian staff as well. He saw them as they arrived and told them precisely what their duties were.

'You've done this before,' Diamond said.

'No, guv. I'm learning as I go along.'

'A fast learner?'

'Born organiser.' Chaz spoke without vanity, simply stating a fact.

Before noon, the first call came in from Rupert Hope's flat, broadcast to all on an amplifier. The search team had found an address book and a diary and they'd started up his computer and begun looking at recent emails. If they expected praise from the management they didn't get it. 'Fuck that for a bowl of cherries,' Chaz said into the phone. 'I'll have a patrol car pick up the tower unit and bring it here. Use your time looking through his drawers.'

Soon a second person was brought in to help with the incoming calls. Steadily a picture of the murdered man was taking shape. He'd been passionate about his subject and an inspiring teacher, regularly taking his students on field trips. History in his eyes wasn't about dead people and forgotten battles, it was the key to enlightenment and the hope for a better society.

'Good at his job,' Chaz said with approval.

'So it seems,' Diamond said. 'We could be looking at jealousy as a motive if he was that special.'

'Some other lecturer?'

'Maybe. As you've probably discovered, Chaz, you can make yourself unpopular by being one of life's achievers.'

'Is that a fact, guv?'

'It's one of those laws, regrettable, but true.'

The team at the flat reported that Rupert Hope must have been keen on personal hygiene, for his bathroom had an impressive array of aftershaves and deodorants. The towels were clean and every surface was immaculate. It was evident that he hadn't been back there while he was living rough. His bedroom, too, was in good order. He'd been reading about the Civil War and left several bookmarks in pages with references to the Battle of Lansdown.

Septimus phoned in from the university with some background on Hope's student days more than twenty years ago. He'd been active in the rag committee and got into trouble for going to Bath with a group and removing a sedan chair from the Pump Room complex and trying to hold it to ransom. They'd achieved what they wanted and got some publicity for the rag at the cost of a roasting from their own Vice-Chancellor. They'd returned the chair the next day, but with a nice refinement thought up by Rupert — a skeleton seated inside.

Diamond's heart rate stepped up by several beats when he heard this from Chaz. He called back to Septimus. 'The skeleton in the sedan chair? When exactly was this?'

'1989, guv, when he was in his last year as a student.'

'Where did the skeleton come from?'

'I don't know. A medical student?'

'You think so?' It sounded reasonable. He'd read somewhere that all medical students had to possess a skeleton. 'Do we know if it was male or female?'

'There's no way of telling.'

'I'm sorry, but there is,' Diamond said from his sure knowledge of forensic anthropology.

'What I mean, guv,' Septimus was at pains to explain, 'is that we don't have the skeleton to look at. All we have is a note in the file that Hope was reprimanded by the Vice-Chancellor for — and I quote — compounding the offence. There's nothing else. Do you really need to know?'

'I suppose not.' Better leave it, he thought. If the skeleton buried on Lansdown *was* a medical student's study specimen, some people including himself were going to look silly. Anyway, didn't they use plastic skeletons these days? 'The main thing here is that he was one of the lads.'

'It's a Bristol tradition, raiding Bath Uni's territory and getting one over them,' Chaz said. 'One year they kidnapped Jane Austen.'

'How did they do that?'

'The dummy outside the Jane Austen centre in Gay Street.'

'Not the biggest heist ever, then?'

'I don't suppose it was reported to Bath CID,' Chaz said.

'Mercifully, no.'

More information came in from some of the current history students. Rupert Hope's inventive brain had been put to more constructive use when he returned to Bristol as a lecturer. He was always looking for ways to bring history to life for his students. He'd taken them to St Mary Redcliffe Church to see the monument to Sir William Penn, the admiral who had captured Jamaica for the British in 1655, and this had led to a project on Penn's son, William. The second year history group had linked up with Penn State University to examine the documentation for Penn's voyage of 1682 when Charles II granted him a lease of land in the New World and he took possession of Pennsylvania.

'This is all good stuff,' Diamond said to Chaz, 'but I'd like to find someone he treated badly.'

'We don't have anything on his love life yet.'

'Did he have one?'

'The emails might tell us.'

'If it was love on email it couldn't have been much.'

The computer tower arrived soon after and one of the civilian staff was given the task of extracting everything of possible use. The dossier on the dead man was growing appreciably without yet providing much for a murder investigation.

'You saw the body at the scene, did you, guv?' Chaz asked.

'I did.'

'Did they find the murder weapon?'

'Not when I was there, and not since. I'd have been told. They've had time to search the entire cemetery by now.'

'Do you know what it was?'

'Something heavy and blunt, more like a cosh than an axe. I doubt if we'll find it now. There's too much on TV these days about DNA and forensics. Any killer with a glimmer of intelligence is going to get rid of the weapon somewhere else.'

Septimus phoned in again. They'd found some photos of Rupert and his students studying the mosaics at Fishbourne Roman Palace.

'Nice work,' Diamond said down the phone. 'You're still in the history department, are you?'

'We are.'

'And able to talk freely?'

'Sure.'

'So you must have met some of the other lecturers. What do they say about him?'

'They're shocked at what happened, that's for sure,' Septimus said, 'and there's a lot of sympathy for him, but no one is saying much. I get the impression he didn't have any particular friends among them. He wasn't disliked. They respect what he was doing with his students. He wasn't looking for close friends among the staff, so far as I can tell.'

'A loner?'

'Not really. I'd say reserved.'

'That could mean secretive.'

'If you want to see it that way.'

Diamond told him to bring in the photos at the end of the afternoon. He and Chaz leafed through the address book brought in with the computer tower. The lettering was in small, neat capitals, more than two hundred names in all. Where someone had moved house, Hope hadn't put a line through the address and added the new one on another page, as most people did. He'd gone to all the trouble of covering the entry with a strip of adhesive paper and writing over it. This was a methodical man, if not a perfectionist, and probably a pain to work with.

There was no way of telling who were the close friends. A long trawl was in prospect, comparing these entries with the email address book. It was a pity Hope's mobile phone had not turned up. Presumably that had been removed at an early stage, after the first attack.

Yet Diamond told the team when they assembled late in the afternoon that Operation Cavalier had brought a good result. 'Thanks to your efforts we know a whole lot more about this guy and his background and contacts. Chaz has drawn up a profile and each of you gets a copy. No obvious leads have emerged, unfortunately, so it's my job to study everything overnight and decide on a strategy for tomorrow.'

While they were leaving he overheard someone say, 'Reading between the lines, he's up shit creek without a paddle.'

15

His sore back was no worse at the end of the day. Lowering himself into the car seat was uncomfortable, but once behind the wheel he felt okay. If he could cope with the nightmare of Bristol's one-way system, he'd be out of here and heading home. It still irked him that the murder enquiry couldn't be managed from Bath.

The main evening rush was over and he was able to switch lanes a few times without mishap and presently found himself on the Keynsham bypass with a chance to think. A sunny evening. He'd call Paloma later and suggest they met for a drink.

Approaching Saltford, an overtaking motorcyclist appeared alongside him wearing the Day-Glo jacket that signified a traffic cop. The bike's blue lights were flashing. Still on duty, you poor sod, Diamond thought.

The sympathy drained away when he

noticed a gloved hand waving him down. The lights were flashing for him. He was being pulled over.

He came to a stop in a lay-by and lowered the window. 'Is there a problem?'

'Switch off the engine, sir, and step out of the car.'

'What's up? I wasn't speeding, was I?'

'Would you do as I ask, sir?'

He turned the key and summoned up a smile. 'Switching off is the easy part. The getting out could be difficult. I've got a stiff back.'

This didn't get the reaction he hoped for. 'Should you be in charge of a car in that case?'

'It only flared up today. Look, I'm in the Old Bill myself.' He remembered as he spoke that his warrant card was in his back pocket and impossible to reach in his present condition. 'Peter Diamond, Detective Superintendent.'

In a situation such as this, rank is supposed to count for nothing. If he'd committed an offence there ought to be no favours. In reality, most traffic cops are lenient when they find they've stopped one of their own.

This one was an awkward cuss. 'If you were the Chief Constable I'd still ask you to step out. The law's the same whoever you are.' Troubling words. Everyone had heard of top police officers brought to court by young cops impervious to persuasion. They even did it to royalty.

He still didn't know what he'd done wrong.

He opened the door, put out a leg and felt a strong twinge in his back. 'Bloody hell, is this necessary?'

The cop folded his arms and said nothing.

'Would you mind giving me a hand?'

Apparently not.

Diamond gripped the roof and heaved himself out, an agonising move. He emitted a yelp of pain.

'The reason I stopped you is that your nearside brake light isn't working.'

A faulty light, for crying out loud.

'I wasn't aware of that. Thanks, officer. I'll get a new bulb.' Biting back his fury he added, 'You're right to bring it to my attention. Now, if you'd like to see my warrant card . . .'

'I'd rather see your driving licence.'

He snapped, 'Oh come on, it's a brake light, not drunk driving.'

'Your tyres look worn to me.'

'Are they?'

'And your tax disc is out of date.'

'Is it?' He turned to see for himself. 'By Christ, you're right.' He'd been sent a reminder weeks ago and it was at home among a pile of junk mail and unpaid bills. 'I overlooked it. I'll renew it on the internet the minute I get home.'

The cop said nothing.

Out of the depths of his humiliation Diamond said, 'Are you based at Bristol? I've been seconded there, which is why I'm on the road. I don't suppose you've heard of Operation Cavalier. A murder case. I'm in charge. It's no excuse, but my thoughts haven't been fully on the car.'

'The licence, please.'

He produced it from his pocket and the cop used his radio to check with the Police National Computer. Then: 'I'm reporting you, sir, for driving an untaxed vehicle. Whether any action is taken is out of my hands. Where were you driving to?'

He didn't like the 'were'. 'Home. I live in Weston.'

There was another stressful delay while the cop considered the options. 'All right,' he said finally, 'you can finish your journey, but don't be so unwise as to use the car again until you get the new disc. And the brake light.'

■ ■ ■ ■

'You can borrow mine,' Paloma said in the Crown that evening. She'd driven out to Weston to meet him.

'I won't do that,' he said. 'I appreciate the offer, but I'm not depriving you of your car just because I cocked up.'

'How will you get to Bristol in the morning?'

'I'll go into Bath and hop aboard a patrol car.'

'I doubt if you'll hop anywhere in your present state. Let me take you.'

'No. I meant what I said.'

'You're like a limpet sometimes.'

'Actually I've thought of a way I can use this to my advantage.'

'What's that?'

'I'll tell you if it works.'

She took a sip of her white wine. 'All told, this hasn't been much of a day for you.'

'Too true. They didn't roll out the red carpet at Bristol, either, but we ended the day on better terms . . . I think.'

'Are you any nearer to finding who killed this man?'

'That's the sort of question I get from Georgina, the boss.'

'Oops. Sorry I asked.'

'We concentrated on the victim today, building up a profile. He's something of a mystery himself. No family in this country. Lived in Bristol all his life, so he must have made hundreds of contacts.'

'For contacts, read suspects?'

'Potential suspects anyway. The problem is that here was a harmless guy who put a lot into his job and didn't make enemies of people. Mind, he wasn't all that popular in the staffroom. They speak well of him — as you do of a dead colleague — but it comes through that he had no close friends.'

'Did the students like him?'

'Apparently. He made big efforts to bring the history to life for them.'

'And in the process showing up the other lecturers? Was that what made him unpopular?'

'With some, I suppose.'

'Enough to justify murder?'

He grinned. 'That would be stretching it.'

'The way you talk about some of the people you work with . . .'

'The bullshit artists and brown-nosers?'

'You've made my point. Resentment can run deep among colleagues.'

'I wouldn't murder them.'

'Look at it another way, then. Your victim

may have been a harmless guy, but he had a knack of annoying people. He seems to have caused an upset at the car boot sale.'

'Nicking stuff because he was hungry.'

'You don't know what else he got up to in those days he was living rough.'

'I know one thing. He was at the races the evening we were there. Remember the guy who wandered across the course when the runners were going to the start?'

'That was Rupert?' She put her hand to her mouth.

'Has to be. He gave his name as Noddy. I took him to be a drunk.'

'And he said something about wanting food. Poor soul. That's awful, Peter. I thought the same as you. How wrong we were.'

He nodded. 'We saw something and we made an assumption, like the people who saw him trying the doors of parked cars. I've been assuming professional jealousy played a part in his death, or some incident in his personal life. It could be much more basic.'

'Someone who caught him misbehaving up at Lansdown and saw red?'

'Exactly. I must find out more about those days when he was behaving erratically. We're short of witnesses. I hoped to get help from the Lansdown Society. They're the resident snoops.'

'They can't be everywhere. You're more likely to hear from someone who happened to be passing by.'

'Walking the dog?' He laughed. 'You're so right. You can bring in helicopters and thermal imaging, you can have a thousand coppers doing a fingertip search, but nothing beats a dog's nose.'

'You wouldn't have found that skeleton without the dog's help, that's for sure.'

He sighed and shook his head. 'The skeleton isn't my case any more.'

She smiled faintly. 'It still rankles, doesn't it?'

'Slightly.'

'Who was it who found Rupert Hope?'

'The guy who keeps the cemetery tidy.'

'Without a dog?'

'I doubt if he had one with him. Dogs don't treat gravestones with the respect that we do.'

They finished their drinks and Diamond said he'd better get home. He'd promised the team an action plan for the morning.

Paloma said, 'That sounds like a dedicated man talking. I suppose it's no use offering you a back massage?'

'I know you mean well, and I'm sure

it would do me good, but I couldn't take it.'

Her face creased in sympathy. 'Are you feeling worse, then?'

'Quite a bit better, thanks to you, but you've no idea what a randy old goat I am. Your touch would inflame me.'

'Get away,' she said, laughing. 'It didn't get you going last night.'

'Frozen peas and hot flannels?'

'Really, Peter, what you're saying hadn't crossed my mind.'

'It crossed mine, and I'm in no state to make a move, more's the pity. It would end in frustration and I'm not nice to know when I get frustrated.'

'Hurry up and get better, then.'

Appreciably more mobile next morning, he took the bus into Bath and arrived early at the police station confident of winning the next round against Georgina. Not much was happening. The desk sergeant was chatting to a MOP — a member of the public — who looked as if he'd lost his wallet. 'Ah,' he said, spotting Diamond, 'here's somebody from CID.'

'Unless it's extremely urgent, I can't help,' Diamond said. 'I'm in a bit of trouble myself.'

'You don't look too good,' the sergeant said.

'Is the boss in?'

'ACC Dallymore?' He glanced at the clock on the wall. 'Before her usual time. Give her ten minutes. If you can spare five to talk to this gentleman — what's your name, sir?'

'Dave.' The MOP turned his gaze hopefully on Diamond. He had the look of a man with a story to tell. Five minutes wouldn't do it.

'To talk to Dave,' the sergeant continued, 'I'm sure he'd appreciate it.'

'What's it about?'

'That skeleton they found on Lansdown,' Dave said.

'Sorry,' Diamond said raising a hand. 'That's Inspector Halliwell's case. I'm on another enquiry. You'll need to see one of Keith Halliwell's team.' He let himself through the door behind the desk and started the painful climb up the stairs to Georgina's lair on the top floor. He paused on each landing and when he reached the top he heard her coming up behind him. She must have been fit because she wasn't breathing heavily.

'Peter,' she said, 'why aren't you in Bristol?'

'That's what I came to tell you about.

There's a technical hitch.'

She swung open her office door. 'Don't tell me they've walked out on you already.'

'No. We're getting on with each other.'

'Are you?' A disappointed note came through. 'That's a relief. Have a seat. You're not ill, are you? You don't seem to be moving freely.'

'That's another story. This is something else, something embarrassing.'

'A personal problem?' A rare touch of pink came to her cheeks. She moved behind her desk as if she would feel safer there.

'You're sure to hear of it,' he said, 'so I thought I'd tell you first. I was booked by a traffic cop on the way home last night. One of my brake lights had gone.'

She flapped her hand dismissively. 'That can happen to anyone.'

'He happened to notice my tax disc was out of date.'

'Oh.'

'Carelessness on my part.'

'Have you applied for a new one?'

'I did when I got home. It takes a couple of days to come through, as you know.'

'Stick a note on your windscreen.'

'My tyres need renewing as well. I'm off the road until I can get it all sorted. What I'm saying is that I won't be going into Bris-

222

tol today.' Chew on that, Georgina, he thought.

'Ah.' She placed her hands palm down on her desk and slapped them several times on the surface. 'Have a word with George Pallant. He'll fix up a ride for you.'

George Pallant was the inspector in charge of transport. Diamond had covered this.

'They're doing a vehicle check on the London Road today. You know what that does to manpower. It's all right. I'll phone Bristol and tell them to manage without me. There's plenty they can get on with.'

Georgina took an audible breath. She was being outsmarted and she didn't like it. 'We can't have that. Where is your car?'

'At home. I came in by bus. I don't intend to spend the day twiddling my thumbs. I can make myself useful to Keith Halliwell.'

'He doesn't need you interfering.' A sound of exasperation came from deep in her throat. She plunged her hand into her pocket. 'Here. Take mine.' She tossed a car key across the desk.

This was a development he hadn't prepared for. 'Your Mercedes? You're lending it to me?'

'I am,' she said with an air of righteousness. 'I have a meeting here tonight of the Crime Prevention Panel and I won't be needing the car until late. Let's have no more shilly-shallying. Get to your duties, Peter.'

He couldn't believe she'd entrusted him with her gleaming silver Merc, a measure of how much she wanted him out of Bath and out of her hair. More than that, she'd outfoxed him. He'd be going to Bristol after all.

His mood was down and he gritted his teeth and swore a few times. Yet he drove carefully, not only because it was Georgina's car, but because he always did. Speed on the roads wasn't in his repertoire. Even though this one was capable of rapid acceleration he wouldn't put his foot down. And somewhere at the back of his mind was a superstition that bad luck comes in threes. First he'd hurt his back and then he'd been booked. If a third mishap was coming it had better not involve the Mercedes.

He tried to be more constructive. An action plan for the day was needed. The information-gathering on Rupert Hope couldn't last much longer. The enquiry needed a sense of direction. Paloma may well have been right when she said that the last days at Lansdown could be the key to the mystery, a spur-of-the-moment killing by someone Hope had upset. Running the investigation from Bristol meant that a different agenda was being set, with heavy emphasis on former contacts and earlier events. Was that all a waste of time?

Somewhere between Saltford and Keynsham his thoughts were interrupted by a loud rumbling from the car. The drive had been blissfully smooth up to now. His first reaction was that his handling of the controls was at fault. He wasn't used to an automatic and he knew they could engage a lower gear by some small movement of the gear shift. Once or twice his hand had gone there out of habit and his left foot had pressed on an invisible clutch-pedal. Had he put the thing in third?

No.

Something else was wrong. The car was slowing perceptibly. He glanced in the mirror and signalled that he was moving over and stopping. Even the steering seemed to be playing up. He braked and put on the hazard lights. This wasn't the ideal place to stop — on a busy dual carriageway with minimal space at the side.

He waited for his chance to get out. He guessed what was wrong: a flat tyre. When he eventually — and painfully — hauled himself out he found he was right. The nearside rear wheel was right down. A perfectly good tyre with plenty of tread had run over a nail. He could see it embedded in the rubber.

I could have done without this, he thought.

What now? He didn't fancy changing the tyre while his back was still giving twinges. Other drivers were zooming past at a rate suggesting he shouldn't count on a good Samaritan. Better phone for assistance.

Fortunately he had his under-used mobile with him. Unfortunately it needed charging. He sighed, flung the phone on the back seat and went to look for the spare tyre and the jack. Lifting the tyre wasn't easy. He managed to stand it upright and rotate it out of the boot and onto the roadside. Georgina's instruction book was in the glove compartment. He had a look and tried assembling the jack. At the sixth attempt he fathomed how to open it and slot it into the jacking point. There was a handle to turn: no problem if your back was functioning normally. But by degrees he succeeded in getting the punctured tyre clear of the ground and faced the next ordeal of using the wrench to loosen the wheel bolts.

No one looked like stopping. He couldn't blame them. It would be dangerous to park anywhere near.

Could have been raining, he told himself to raise morale while freeing the first of those bolts. The raised morale didn't last long. The swearing got stronger as he applied himself to the task, regardless of what further damage it would do to his back. He removed them all and with a supreme effort lifted off the damaged wheel and hoisted up the spare and shoved it into place.

Nice work, Diamond, he said to himself. All it needs now is to tighten the five bolts and lower the jack. For a technophobe this isn't a bad effort.

There was one more hitch. The bolts didn't behave. They wouldn't tighten properly. He kept turning the wrench and feeling resistance but they wouldn't go all the way in.

'Bugger, bugger, bugger.'

A voice behind him said, 'In trouble, are we?' It sounded familiar.

He turned and found himself eye to eye with the same traffic cop who'd stopped him the evening before. The sense of surprise was mutual.

'You?' the cop said. 'I booked you last night. What's this — your second car?'

'It belongs to the Assistant Chief Constable.'

'Oh, yes?'

He recalled that the cop hadn't inspected his ID last night. Probably thought he was a fantasist.

'Is it taxed?'

'Of course. Thanks to you, I had to borrow this one and it got a puncture.'

'On a dangerous stretch of road,' the cop said.

'I couldn't help that, could I? If you'll lend me a hand tightening these bolts I'll be on the road again.'

'The back's giving trouble again, is it?' the cop said with sarcasm.

'That's immaterial. The bloody bolts won't tighten.'

The cop tried and didn't succeed and Diamond felt justified.

'Is that the owner's manual on the ground?'

'Well, it's not the works of Shakespeare.'

'Let's have a look.' The cop thumbed through the pages covering advice on changing a tyre. 'You know what? You're using the wrong set of bolts.'

'No I'm not. They're the ones I took off.'

'These are alloy wheels.'

'And what's that got to do with it?'

'What it says here. "Be sure to use the correct wheel bolt type. Light alloy wheels require different wheel bolts". You're trying to put on the spare with the wrong bolts. I wouldn't mind betting there's a different set for use with the spare. Have you looked in the box where the jack is kept?' He went to the boot and came back in triumph with a set of bolts in an unopened bag. 'These are at least an inch shorter. You know what you've been doing? Driving the bolts into the hub. Wouldn't surprise me if you've done some serious damage. Did you say this car belongs to your boss?'

It took another hour, but eventually a breakdown lorry came out from Georgina's Mercedes dealer in Bath and took the stricken car away. Diamond rode with the driver. 'Any idea what this will cost me?'

'The call-out? About a hundred and ninety.'

'The damage to the hub.'

'Not my job, mate, but I guess you'll need a new sub-frame and with it the flange, angular contact and rim lock. After they've added the tax you won't get much change out of a grand.'

'Jesus!'

'That's not counting the new tyre. You'll want a new tyre by the looks of the old one.'

He didn't ask the price.

16

The good news, he stressed to Georgina when he got back at lunchtime, was that the garage was fixing everything. He would collect the car at five and drive it back to Manvers Street for her to use at the end of the day — as good as new.

She listened to his account in a stunned state. He told her everything and admitted full responsibility and said he'd pay for all the repairs. He was out of the office and on his way downstairs before her mouth closed.

Fish and a double portion of chips went some way to absorbing his own shock.

Now that he'd informed Georgina, he was feeling better about the whole sorry episode. You have to be positive. As his mother had been fond of saying in times of trouble, the sharper the storm, the sooner it's over. Writing the cheque and going deeper into overdraft would be a pain, but, hell, there were bumps along the way in everyone's life.

He'd been right about misfortunes coming in threes. He'd had his three now. He could move on with confidence. He'd already called Bristol and asked Septimus Ward to stand in as senior investigating officer for the rest of the day. There was plenty to keep the team busy.

So he left the canteen with a smile. He felt free to pass on his story to Keith Halliwell and anyone else who would be amused by it. Most experiences are better for being shared.

The incident room was buzzing. Civilian staff he'd not seen before were working computers. A large map of Lansdown was fixed to a pinboard and covered in markers he didn't understand. There were photos of the skeleton hunched up in its grave and laid out later in the lab. Some sort of chart listing events year by year was on another wall. Halliwell was holding a phone to his ear, too busy, it seemed, to listen to stories of Georgina's car.

Ingeborg came in holding a sheaf of papers. She, at least, recognised her boss. 'Hi, guv. I thought you were in Bristol.'

'I was. You seem to be busy.'

'Tell me about it.'

'Are you getting anywhere?'

'Keith thinks so. He's really upbeat.'

'What's happening then?'

'We had a new witness in this morning. He only just left. I don't know what it was about, but Keith and John Leaman took the statement and they seem fired up.'

'I think I met the guy. He was in first thing.'

'You know more than I do, then.'

'No. I stayed well out of it.'

'I'd better get on,' she said. 'I'm doing the map.'

'The coloured pins? What's that about?'

'Locating incidents reported in the press in a five-year period. Everything from a car shunt to an unexploded bomb.'

'What's that supposed to achieve?'

'It's visual, isn't it?'

'Okay,' he said, giving nothing away of his private thoughts. He decided to leave them to it. The story of the Mercedes could wait for a better moment.

In the less frenetic confine of his office, he tried some cautious movements to see if his back had worsened as a result of the tyre change. If anything, the discomfort had eased a little. Encouraged, he placed a hand on the filing cabinet and tried performing a gentle plié, like a ballet dancer at the barre.

Behind him came the sound of a throat being cleared.

He turned to find Halliwell standing in the doorway. 'Am I interrupting, guv?'

'Not at all,' he said. 'You should see my Nutcracker.'

Halliwell didn't get it.

Diamond said, 'I looked in at the incident room a short while back. You were up to your eyes in work.'

'Inge told me you came in. Is everything okay?'

'Why shouldn't it be?'

'I didn't expect to see you here.'

'Car trouble.'

'Ah. Too bad. But as you're here, I can pass on something of interest. We took a witness statement this morning.'

'Dave?'

'You know already?'

Diamond shook his head. 'I met him briefly.'

'Well, I don't know how much he told you, but you might like to read the statement. He was there when they re-enacted the battle and it seems he teamed up with Rupert Hope.'

'My man?' Diamond's interest quickened.

'They were both in the royalist army, as Dave calls it, and they were killed — pretend killed — if you follow me. He offered your man a lager. He'd hidden a six-pack before the battle, buried it at the base of a fallen tree.'

'Our tree?'

'My tree now,' Halliwell was sharp to point out. There were territorial issues here. 'They quit the battlefield for a while and went to look. Two cans were there and they found them and had a drink and then felt in the hole for the others and they'd gone. Someone must have seen him bury them and helped themselves. Dave started burrowing. He didn't ever find the other tins, but he pulled out a bone that seems to have been the femur — my femur.'

'You'd better rephrase that.'

'You know what I mean, guv. The femur from the skeleton.'

'I thought the dog found that.'

'I'm coming to that.'

'Did they know what it was?'

'They worked out that it was human and they assumed, like us, that it was old and probably belonged to some soldier killed in the real Civil War. They agreed that the decent thing was to let him rest in peace, so they buried it again.'

'In the same place?'

'Yes.'

'What did they do then?'

'Both went back to the battle and Dave

never spoke to Rupert again. He didn't know he was dead until I told him. He doesn't read the papers, he said.'

'It's been all over the television.'

'I doubt if he bothers with the box. He's the outdoor type. Likes his riding and shooting and his beer. Someone told him in the pub last night that a skeleton was found and it was part of a murder investigation and that's why he came forward.'

'Are you sure he knew nothing of Rupert Hope's death?'

'It came as a shock when I told him.'

'Do you believe him?'

'He's a bloody good actor if it was put on.'

'What's Dave's job?'

'Farrier.'

'Say that again.' Diamond had heard furrier and it didn't seem to go with the outdoor life.

'Blacksmith. He's got the smithy at Bradford on Avon.'

'Got you.' His thoughts went briefly to blunt instruments and then moved on. 'What's he doing playing soldiers if he's got a smithy to run?'

'Why does anyone play soldiers?'

'Rupert did it for the history. It went with the job. I'd better read that statement. This could change everything, Keith.'

But the change Diamond had in mind hadn't yet dawned on Halliwell.

After speed-reading Dave the blacksmith's statement, Diamond took it upstairs for another session with Georgina.

Her door was open and she was on the phone to her garage, talking about rim locks and flanges, getting their version of the damage. She waved Diamond away and he took a step back but remained in the room. 'And can you assure me that everything is being put right? I don't want any short cuts . . . At his expense, yes . . . And how much for the labour? . . . Very well . . . Yes, he'll be collecting it. Thank you.' She put down the phone.

'Didn't you believe me?' he asked.

'That's not the point, Peter. They're the experts. I wanted to hear it from them. I was thinking of calling my insurance company, but I don't suppose I can claim, seeing that the damage was self-inflicted.'

'You didn't cause it.'

'I was unwise enough to let you use the car, so I must take my share of the responsibility.'

'I don't know about "unwise". You were being helpful.'

'If the truth be told, my motive wasn't as

praiseworthy as that. What have you got there? The estimate?'

'No, ma'am. It's a witness statement taken this morning from a blacksmith by the name of Dave Barton.'

'He saw you changing the wheel with the wrong bolts?'

She couldn't get the damaged Mercedes out of her head.

He tried again. 'This is the murder investigation. May I suggest you read it for yourself?' He held it out.

While she was reading, he idled away the time looking at a black and white photo on the wall of a passing-out parade at one of the police training colleges. A much younger Georgina was saluting in the front row of the march-past. She was probably fifty pounds lighter in weight but she still had the outstanding chest of her year.

'Do you think it's significant?' she said.

'I certainly do,' he said and got his thoughts back on track. 'We've been appealing for witnesses for days without success.'

'There are witnesses and witnesses, Peter. He doesn't appear to have seen anything unlawful.'

'With respect, that isn't the point. He and Rupert found the skeleton — well, a part of the skeleton.'

'The leg bone, it says here. And they put it back.'

'Yes, and some time after that, Rupert was attacked.'

'What are you suggesting — that this Dave was the assailant?'

'That's speculation. I wouldn't be coming to you without proof, ma'am. No, it's more basic than that.'

'What is?'

'Don't you see? We thought the leg bone was found by a dog. We didn't know these two guys found it first. What we have now is a definite link between the skeleton and the cavalier.'

She was frowning. 'There's a difference of twenty years between the two deaths.'

Georgina was intelligent, but there were times when she closed her mind to reason. All of this would work so much more smoothly if she came to her own decision and believed she had made it independently. To encourage the process, Diamond spaced his words. 'Rupert had the femur in his hands and not long after that he was attacked and later murdered.'

'That isn't in dispute.'

She still hadn't cottoned on.

He was forced to spell it out for her. 'Ma'am, I need an operational decision from you. We can't go on treating these cases as separate incidents. They have to be brought together. I'm asking you to centralise both investigations in Bath from one major incident room.'

He didn't say who should be in charge. She may have worked that out for herself.

17

Keith Halliwell would be heartbroken. His first chance as SIO snatched away just when he'd got everything up and running.

Diamond was known to be ruthless in pursuit of the truth, a bruiser who let nothing stand in his way, but Halliwell was the nearest he had to a friend in the team. The first news of the decision shouldn't come from anyone else. Straight from his session upstairs he went to the incident room and asked Halliwell to drive him to the Mercedes garage to collect Georgina's car.

'Guv, I wish I could spare the time, but I can't,' Halliwell said, adding with a companionable smile, 'I'm running a murder case, and you know what that's like.'

'Sorry, Keith, but I do know what it's like and John Leaman can take over for twenty minutes. We need to talk.'

The smile turned to tight-lipped concern. In the privacy of the car Diamond went over the logic of drawing the two enquiries into one, just as he had with Georgina. Through focusing so exclusively on the skeleton case, Halliwell, too, had missed the significance of Dave Barton's statement.

'As I see it now,' Diamond summed up, 'neither you nor I will get a result working in isolation.'

'You're telling me you're taking over again,' Halliwell said, his voice drained of warmth.

'I'm telling you there has to be co-operation. I'm not knocking you, Keith. You've done a fine job already. But it's necessary for me to move back to Bath.'

'And I have to step aside.'

Diamond saw the look and heard the despair. Fortunately the deal he'd done with Georgina had a sweetener. 'Nothing as daft as that. You were appointed SIO for the skeleton enquiry and that's what you re-main, running the show.'

A suspicious frown came with Halliwell's next question. 'So how will you fit in?'

'Not the way you think. There's going to be a new SIO for the Rupert Hope case, an inspector from Bristol called Septimus Ward.'

'I know Septimus,' he said. 'Met him on a firearms course.'

'Like him?'

'He's okay.' But the frown remained.

'Good. He's going to be transferred here with the pick of the Bristol lot. The investigation is under one roof now.'

'Two incident rooms in Manvers Street?'

'Just the one.'

Halliwell shook his head. 'You're joking.'

'I'm afraid that means some rearranging. You'll need to transfer some of the display material to computer.'

'Am I hearing right? Computers have their uses after all?'

A little irony from Halliwell was forgivable. 'You can decide how much of the material needs storing.'

'I prefer it where I can see it.'

'Visual. I noticed.'

'Mine is the hard case to crack, going back twenty years. I'm dealing with masses of information.'

'Yes, and quite properly you're defending your territory. You'll get your share of resources, Keith, I guarantee.'

'So what's your part in this?'

'Me?' Diamond said, striking the first false note, as if he hadn't thought about himself. 'I'm the CIO.'

'C is for chief?'

'Seeing fair play.'

'Keeping your distance?'

'Exactly. At one remove from all the action. You and Septimus are the hands-on leaders.' But even as he spoke, he could see the faint smile playing on Halliwell's lips. Both knew it would go against nature for the big man to keep his distance.

He'd sold the deal as honestly as he was able.

They reached the garage and Halliwell asked, 'Do you want me to wait while you see if the job is done?'

'No need. Wish me luck driving the Merc back to Manvers Street. I've done enough damage for one day.'

Septimus Ward and three others from Bristol CID arrived at Bath Central in the morning looking about as comfortable as the Burghers of Calais. Diamond took them to the canteen for a coffee and explained the new set-up. Their spirits improved when they understood that they'd be heading the Rupert Hope side of what was now a major investigation. 'Presently we'll all drive up to Lansdown and look at the graveyard where he was found, and the other site,' he told them. 'I want you fully in the picture.'

The Lansdown visit had an extra purpose. It gave Halliwell time to clear space in the incident room.

One of the police minibuses had been booked for this and Diamond — sexist when it suited — had invited Ingeborg along as a morale-booster for the newcomers. She was already telling them animatedly about Bath's nightspots.

He injected a more sombre note as they were being driven up the hill. 'You may find this weird,' he told everyone. 'The terrain of Lansdown could be as crucial to this enquiry as the people in the case. I keep asking myself why two bodies should have been found up there. The hill has its own character, aloof from the city, seven hundred feet above sea level, windswept, a place most people drive over without stopping, unless they're golfers, race-goers or boot-sale addicts. What is it about Lansdown that made it suitable for murder? Keep this in mind as we look at the two sites.'

The bus parked in the lay-by closest to the battlefield and the team strolled across the field and down the scarp where the fallen tree was. Septimus appeared at Diamond's side, looking earnest, wanting to confide. 'I heard what you were saying just now, about the landscape.'

'And?'

'We know Rupert was a Civil War junkie.

244

We found masses of stuff he'd downloaded from the internet, maps and battle charts and descriptions of the fighting. It seems to me he must have walked the battlefield a few times.'

'Sounds likely, yes.'

'He was here for some days after he got the head injury.'

'That's correct, but I don't think he was doing the battlefield walk then.'

'He knew the territory, right? You asked us why his killer chose Lansdown. Could the Civil War be the reason?'

'Go on. I'm listening.'

'Maybe his killer was another re-enactment freak. I don't know how seriously they take this rivalry between the armies,' Septimus went on. 'They try to stage the battle as it actually was, as near as they can, but they can't rehearse. Rupert was new to the game. What if he got excited in the heat of battle and did something that wasn't in the script? One of the enemy may have got angry and hunted him down after it was over.'

'Roundhead versus cavalier?'

'Except what it comes down to is more basic. One of their lot taking out one of ours.'

Diamond took stock of what he'd heard.

There was some logic to it. Tribal hostilities accounted for a lot of modern violence.

'Are we investigating these Civil War societies?' Septimus asked.

'That's definitely on the agenda.' He liked the new man's thinking.

They'd reached the fallen oak. The crime scene tape had been removed. The only signs of recent activity were the discoloured turf trampled by many feet and the excavated soil in the burial pit below the roots, sieved to a fineness any gardener would have admired.

'The tree blew down in the great gale of 1987,' Diamond told everyone. 'Most of the ground up here is rock hard, has never been cultivated, drains quickly and gets the full force of sun and wind, but the uprooting of the tree left a large hole and some loose earth where the rain sank in. Some time after, a killer made use of it to bury the body of a young woman, but hacked off the head and disposed of it somewhere else. I can tell you very little about the victim or how she was killed. Under twenty, average height and reasonably healthy so far as you can discover from a bunch of bones. We think she was clothed because we found a zip fly, probably from her jeans. The rest of her clothes had rotted away in twenty years. We don't even know the colour of her hair. We checked missing persons from that time and nobody fits.'

'How can you say that?' Septimus asked. 'Thousands go missing all the time.'

'The local index.'

Ingeborg spoke up. 'Actually, I had the job. It just isn't practical to check the national figures for a five year span.'

'So she could have been a visitor?'

'That's possible. You know how many tourists come through Bath?'

Diamond picked up his thread again. 'Last month, the Battle of Lansdown was re-enacted here and one of the cavaliers called Dave who seems to have been an old soldier in every sense decided to bury a six-pack of lager here. Foot soldiers get thirsty. He says he invited Rupert to join him after they were both supposed to be dead in battle. They'd never met before then.' He turned and pointed. 'They crept away from the fighting up there and found the first two tins and swallowed the lager. But it seemed someone else had helped himself to the other four. Dave was pissed off, as any of us would be. He burrowed up to his elbows in the earth and came up not with his lager, but the femur that belonged to our victim. After some discussion these two decided the bone could very well have belonged to a proper soldier, a victim of the real Civil War. They buried it again and rejoined the action on the battlefield. That's the gist of the witness statement we just had in.'

'Is he telling the truth?' one of the new-comers asked.

'I can't be a hundred per cent sure, but if Dave is the killer he's an idiot to come forward.'

'Why now, and not earlier?'

'He doesn't follow the news. Heard some-one talking in a pub. Simple as that.'

'I'll buy that,' Septimus said. 'Plenty of people don't look at a paper.'

Ingeborg said, 'And some papers don't bother with real news.'

'But do you see the point?' Diamond said. 'Soon after this, Rupert was cracked on the back of the head and in a matter of days he was hit again and murdered. Two victims linked by this spot where we're standing. This is why we're combining the two enquiries.'

Septimus spoke again. 'Could be coincidence.'

'Could be, yes.' He was about to say more, but Septimus hadn't finished.

'After all, these killings are twenty years apart and don't have much in common. The

MO was different in each.'

Keen and intelligent as this new SIO was, he could have used more tact. Best make light of it, Diamond decided. 'If you're right, I'm wasting my time and yours, but you'll find I'm like that, cranky and ready to believe anything. Let's look at the place where Rupert was found.'

Subdued, they retraced their steps and climbed aboard the bus for the short trip to the graveyard.

The terrain around Beckford's Tower had been transformed from when Diamond was last there. All of that swaying vegetation had been scythed and cleared by the search team. Close-packed headstones unseen before stood starkly among the stubble. After such an effort of clearance it was a pity nothing had been found except a few lumps of wood and rock that had no trace of blood or hair.

The immediate site was still taped. 'You can see some staining on the ground where his head was,' Diamond told them. 'We believe he was attacked late in the evening or during the night.'

'What was he doing here at all?' one of the party asked.

'Very likely looking for a place to sleep.'

'Strange choice.' Another note of scepticism Diamond didn't care for. Septimus had set a negative tone.

'He'd been living rough for some days. He could have slept in the dry in the gateway we just came through.' This thought had come to Diamond when he saw the stone benches in the section behind the façade.

The same fault-finder added, 'It doesn't chime in with all we've been finding out about the guy. Here's a bright, outgoing lecturer interested in his subject and suddenly he wants to sleep in a cemetery.'

Ingeborg had heard enough from the Bristol contingent. 'If you'd been cracked on the head so hard you had an open wound in your skull you might behave out of character.'

Diamond nodded. 'I couldn't put it better, Inge, but I didn't explain everything. You and I have been working on this for longer than our new colleagues. All the evidence suggests Rupert was suffering from loss of memory following the first attack.' Exercising tact was almost as uncomfortable for him as getting on and off the bus.

'What's the story of the tower?' Septimus asked in an obvious attempt to lighten the mood, looking across the graveyard to its tall Italianate centrepiece. 'It isn't like your average church.'

'It isn't a church,' Ingeborg said. 'It wasn't built as one, anyway.' She glanced at Diamond. 'Mind if I explain?'

He gave a shrug. 'Go ahead.' He'd got Paloma's book on Beckford beside his bed at home, still unopened.

'There was this millionaire called William Beckford who lived halfway up the hill in Lansdown Crescent. He had the tower built here in the eighteen-thirties and filled it with his treasures and then bought up all the land in between and created his own private walk. Landscaped it specially, like they did in those days, on a massive scale.'

'Capability Brown,' the talkative Bristolian said.

'He's the landscaper everyone's heard of,' Ingeborg said, and then added, 'Dead by then.'

There were smiles all round.

Ingeborg resumed. 'Beckford drew up his own plan. There were little buildings along the way made to look like a mosque or a castle gateway, and so much else to catch the eye: ornamental gardens, a fishpond, archways, an underground grotto, a shrubbery with sweet-smelling plants, an orchard. It was over a mile and he used to do the walk up the hill each morning.'

'And ended up in the cemetery?' Septimus said, and got a laugh, even from Ingeborg.

She capped it with, 'Dead right.' And then added, 'In point of fact it didn't become a cemetery until a few years after his death. When Beckford was alive it was a fabulous garden with shrubs from all over the world.'

'How do you know all this?'

'I was a journalist before I joined the police.'

'An investigative journalist,' Diamond added. 'Gave us a hard time until we stopped all that by recruiting her.'

'Anyway,' Ingeborg went on, 'Beckford's daughter was a duchess and she inherited the tower and decided to sell it but she was horrified when she found that the buyer was about to turn these grounds into a beer garden. She bought it back at a loss and gave it to the Church of England as a cemetery on condition that her father was dug up from the churchyard in Ralph Allen Drive and reburied here. He's in that pink granite tomb behind you, the one on a mound with the ditch around it. As you can see, hundreds of others have been buried since. Beckford's drawing room became the funeral chapel.'

'Instead of a pub,' Diamond said. 'Depressing, isn't it?'

Septimus had other things on his mind. He was looking around him. 'I don't see any recent graves. Isn't the cemetery used any more?'

'Not this part. Not for the past forty years,' Ingeborg said. 'The Church Commissioners sold the ground and the new owners restored the tower and turned it into a museum. It's now owned by the Preservation Trust and left as a wild garden.'

'All done?' Diamond said. 'I'd like to get back to our grubby little murder. As you see, the wild garden was cleared. A fingertip search was made for the weapon and nothing was found. I'm not surprised. This is a crafty killer. Some attempt was made to pass off the death as an accident.' He showed them the bloodstain on the adjacent grave and explained about the blade of grass, which he said was in an evidence bag by now.

'Cool,' Septimus said, and he seemed to be praising the killer rather than the detective work. 'Did he leave any shoeprints?'

'None we could link to the killing.'

'The crime itself looks more like a mugging than a planned murder. They're often the hardest to solve. Was anything of value taken?'

'He had no wallet or cards when he was found. From the way he behaved at the boot sale he was skint.'

'And we don't know where the first attack took place?'

'Unless you have a theory.'

'Somewhere on this hill, I guess.'

'I'm sure you're right. His car was still in the racecourse car park. When it was found, his cavalier costume was inside, so we can be pretty sure he returned with the others after the battle and changed.'

'And got clobbered after that? What do these toy soldiers do at the end of the day?'

'From what I can make out, they hang out among the camper vans and cars. There's a beer tent and a mobile kitchen and Porta-loos. The play-acting goes out of the window. The costumes are sweaty, so they're glad to get them off.'

'If his car was still there,' Septimus said, 'it seems the first attack came that evening.'

'That's my reading of it,' Diamond said.

'It can't have happened in full view of everyone. He must have wandered away when it got dark. My best bet is still on one of the roundheads. Could any of their weapons have made the kind of wound he had?'

'Possibly. We're in blunt instrument territory here. But equally it could have been a car tool or a lump of wood. What's that?'

A beeping sound.

'Sorry,' Ingeborg said, taking her phone from her pocket. She stepped a short way from the group to take the call and then said, 'It's Keith Halliwell. He wants to know if we're on our way back. There's a break-through in the skeleton case.'

18

Changes had been made in the incident room. More work stations and computers were in place and one of the boards had been cleared of data and moved to the far end. But the big change was in Keith Halliwell. He had the face of a lottery winner and his team clearly shared the excitement. He came to meet Diamond, zigzagging between computers like a wing three-quarter making a run for the line. 'Guv, it paid off,' he said, and he was waving a transparent evidence bag. 'Just like you said it might.'

'What's this — the zip?' Diamond said, taking the bag to inspect it.

'Back from the lab this morning. Have a look under the tab. You can move it now.'

Diamond held the bag and its contents under a strip light and saw the silver glint of some of the teeth of the zip. The cleaning had made an appreciable difference, but it had also shown up some damage. 'Am I allowed to take it out?'

'Better not,' Halliwell said. 'They said it's corroded badly and could fall apart.'

He passed the bag back. He'd never been noted for delicate handling of anything. 'Show me.'

Through the plastic, Halliwell manipulated the tiny tab on the slider to reveal the underside. 'There. It's been preserved quite well because it was folded down.'

Diamond squinted at the tiny metal surface. He could just about make out a symbol of some kind.

'Try this,' Halliwell said, handing him a magnifying glass that made him feel like Sherlock Holmes.

He put his face close to the lens and saw a better image. Maybe as a law and order man he was preconditioned, but the figure seemed to him like the upright and crosspiece of a gibbet:

Г

'What is it? A logo?'

'I thought it was just a symbol at first. I've been on it all morning, talking to various experts. It's Cyrillic, their equivalent of a capital G.'

'Doesn't look anything like a G.' He knew

he was being grouchy again, but some devil inside him had to challenge Halliwell's boyish enthusiasm.

'I'm sorry, but that's Russian for you.'

'Cyrillic — the Russian alphabet?'

'Right.' Halliwell sounded quite emotional over his findings. 'We've made a huge leap forward. If the jeans came from Russia — or one of the old Soviet Union countries — there's a good chance our young lady wasn't from Britain at all.'

'Unless we imported them.'

'We're talking about twenty-odd years ago, guv. The Cold War was still on. We weren't doing business with Russia. When did the Berlin Wall come down?'

Ingeborg said, 'November, 1989. Inside our time span. The boss is right. She could have bought them in Oxford Street.'

'No chance,' Halliwell said, so fired up that he wouldn't be persuaded. 'The wall came down and the borders were open and East Europeans flooded into the west. She's a young Russian who ended up in Britain and got into bad company and was murdered. It's not surprising she doesn't feature on the missing persons index.'

'Hold on, Keith,' Diamond said. 'This is all fascinating stuff, but let's not get ahead of ourselves. Cheap Russian jeans with zips like this may well have retailed in our high street shops in the early nineties.'

Keith was unimpressed. 'I hear what you're saying, but . . .' He dismissed the possibility with a shrug.

'Let's work with the facts we have. Have you found out for sure where these zips were manufactured?'

'Give me a break, boss. I only heard about this at ten-fifteen this morning. Most of the time I was trying to work out if the logo meant anything.'

'That's the next step, then. There must be a list of Russian manufacturers out there.'

'I'll go on the internet.'

'You can try. As it happens, I know some-one with a good knowledge of the fashion industry. She may be able to throw some light.'

'Fine,' Halliwell said without enthusiasm. 'I'll still see what Google brings up. Let's use every resource we can. We may pin it down to a particular city.'

While this was being aired, Diamond had almost forgotten Septimus and his three colleagues from Bristol. They had stood in the background, getting their first view of the accommodation and not liking it. When he introduced them to his regular team and showed them their work stations they didn't appear overjoyed. 'Couldn't we have a room to ourselves?' Septimus asked.

'That would defeat the whole purpose,' Diamond said. 'If you're in another room you might as well be back in Bristol.'

The looks that passed between them said it all.

Leaving them to get over their discontent, Diamond picked up a phone and called Paloma and explained about the query over the zip. 'I thought you might have the answer.'

'Off the top of my head, no,' she said, and there was a cool note in her voice that troubled him.

'I'm sorry. Am I abusing our friendship?'

'It's becoming rather businesslike, that's all. Let me think about this. I'll get back to you shortly.'

Halliwell was manically tapping a keyboard.

'Any joy?' Diamond asked.

'Not yet. I'm trying various things. You put in "zippers" or "zip fasteners" and you get so many hits it isn't true. The language is a problem. Even if I knew how to put the letter in, I'd get Russian text coming up. It's a pain!'

'Keep your hair on.'

'God Almighty.' Halliwell clapped a hand

to his head and swung round to face Diamond. 'I forgot to tell you. The woman at the lab said they found a clipping of hair trapped under the tab.'

'A hair? And no one noticed until now?'

'It's small. They're doing tests on it.'

'How small is "small"?'

'A few millimetres, that's all. She said it was dark brown or black and rather coarse.'

'From the victim?'

'How can anyone tell?'

'Fair point. Why should one hair survive, when nothing else was found?'

'I suppose if it was tight under the tab it may have been protected. Hair is supposed to last a long time after a body rots away. Could it be from the killer, do you think?'

'We don't get luck like that,' Diamond said.

'It's probably a pubic hair, being found with the zip fly,' Halliwell said.

'You said it was a clipping.'

'Well, guv, I'm not an expert, but I believe women sometimes trim their bushes.'

'And I was thinking she'd been to the hairdresser's. You're a man of the world, Keith.'

'Let's hope they get DNA from it. They can, you know, even when it doesn't include the root.'

'If it's as small as you say I wouldn't bet your house on it. We can only wait for the science, as always.'

Paloma rang back soon after and asked if he could get to Bennett Street in the next twenty minutes. Now she was sounding businesslike, but he was wise enough not to say so.

'You're a star. Any particular address?'

'The Assembly Rooms, front entrance.'

'We're only identifying a zip,' he said. 'Couldn't we do it somewhere less formal, like a pub or a teashop?'

He could hear the sigh down the phone. 'It's where the Museum of Costume is,' she told him. 'One of the glories of our city. Admit it, Peter — you've lived in Bath all this time and never set foot in the place.'

'You win,' he said. 'See you shortly.'

As he was leaving the incident room he looked over Keith Halliwell's shoulder. He'd stopped working the keyboard and was gazing forlornly at a list of websites. The internet hadn't delivered yet.

Diamond murmured something encouraging, but that devil inside him was hoping Paloma had the answer.

'We're meeting my friend Marcia Martindale,' Paloma said. 'If she doesn't know, nobody in Britain does.'

Disregarding the splendours of the Assembly Rooms where Jane Austen once took tea and found inspiration for *Northanger Abbey*, they went down into the basement and walked rapidly past the tall showcases of the museum ('Promise me you'll come back and see it properly, you philistine,' Paloma told him) to the Fashion Research Centre, a book-lined room where Marcia was waiting. She was over eighty and wore a black hat with a crimson band and long feather. Under the wide brim was one of those pale faces that ought never to be shown the sun. The effect was increased by deep-set intelligent eyes magnified by dark-framed glasses.

'The zip isn't allowed to leave the police station, being evidence,' Diamond said, 'but I made a sketch of the symbol we found under the tab.'

'The puller,' Marcia corrected him. 'We call that the puller. May I see?'

He put the piece of paper in front of her. After being corrected over the puller, he enjoyed airing his new linguistic knowledge. 'It's from the Cyrillic alphabet, their version of a G.'

'I know,' Marcia said. 'I read Russian. Well, if what you say is true, it's rather

263

unusual to have the trademark on the underside, and that may be helpful in identifying the maker. I presume the fastener is metallic?'

'Yes.'

She placed her hand on a book the size of a dictionary she had ready on the table. 'The history of the zip is worthy of study. Elias Howe, the American who also invented the sewing machine, applied for a patent as early as 1851, but he didn't go into production with his "Automatic Continuous Clothing Closure" and we had to wait until 1914 for anything that really worked efficiently to be developed and that was Gideon Sundback's "Hookless Fastener Number Two". Of course it transformed the world of fashion.'

Diamond didn't need the history lesson, but contained his impatience and it was Paloma who gently asked the old lady if the book had anything on Russian zips of the nineteen-eighties.

'I'm sure it does,' she said, slowly lifting the cover. 'This is the *Burke's Peerage* of the zip fastener.' She started turning the pages with an arthritic finger and launched into another lecture. 'The word "zipper", as it is still known in America, was used first in the nineteen-twenties for a brand of galoshes with a zip fastening. All sorts of theories exist as to why the word was coined, but I won't bore you with them. I can see your interest in the subject is limited.' Her finger stopped and she held open the page. 'Here's the section on manufacturers. We'll just have to work our way through the letter "G".'

'Do they show the trademarks as well?' Paloma asked.

'Yes. Give me a moment.'

They watched while Marcia ran her finger slowly down the entries. But unfortunately the *Burke's Peerage* of the zip fastener let her down. She got to the end of the "G"s without a result.

'I'd better try again. It must be here. This is the standard work of reference.'

Paloma started to say, 'If it was just a small company —'

Marcia cut her off with, 'It would still be here.'

But it was not. She reached the end of the list again.

'Could we be mistaken about the symbol?' Diamond asked. 'We took it to be the Cyrillic "G", but maybe it represents something else.'

'Ah,' she said, and snapped her fingers. 'You're cleverer than you look. We'll go through "H".'

Bemused, they waited for her to try again. Working right through the alphabet would take the rest of the afternoon and evening.

Then Marcia gave a little murmur of recognition.

'Got it. "Honta". Here's the logo beside it with a note that it appears on the underside of the puller.'

'So it wasn't Cyrillic,' Diamond said.

'Oh, it is, but it isn't Russian Cyrillic. It's Ukrainian. They pronounce the symbol a different way, as an "H", so it makes sense that it's not listed with the "G"s. Listen to this: "Honta was founded in Kiev in 1991, in the new, independent Ukraine".'

'What a turn-up.'

Marcia was her buoyant self again. 'What you have here is a little piece of history. The choice of logo is an expression of independence. It says Ivan Honta was a leader of peasant revolts in eighteenth century Ukraine. The date when the company was founded, 1991, was of course the year the Ukraine broke free from Russia. You'll recall that the Hungarians and the Czechs were the first to break away and others followed later. Oh, and I see it was a short-lived company. "Honta supplied zips for the Ukrainian Brovary Jeans Company in 1991 and 1992, but ceased trading, as did Brovary, early in 1993 after Levi Strauss set up factories in the former Soviet Union and the Russian Gloria Jeans co-operative began undercutting prices." That's rather sad.'

'Rather sad for them, but good news for me,' Diamond said. 'It narrows the field appreciably. Do we know if Brovary exported to Western Europe? I'm still wondering if the jeans could have been bought by an Englishwoman over here.'

'I doubt it,' Marcia said, 'but we can check.' The misshapen fingers started turning pages again. 'Bratislava, Break Dancer, Bright Boy, Brighton Beach — some of these sound more like racehorses than jeans — Brooks Sisters. Nice sense of humour there. Here we are, Brovary. "Manufactured for the Ukrainian market 1991–3. Exports: n/a." What's that?'

'Not applicable,' Paloma said. 'They didn't export.'

Diamond rubbed his hands. 'Marvellous. That's all I need to know. Our skeleton is almost certainly Ukrainian. Isn't it amazing how much you can learn from one rusty zip fly?'

'What now?' Paloma asked.

'We get on to the Ukrainian Embassy in London and see if they have any reports of missing women from that period.'

'What I meant was do you have time to take Marcia and me for a cream tea?'

Wrongfooted again. Paloma was right. You don't treat friends like staff. Marcia had saved him hours of research. The least he could do was show gratitude. 'What a nice idea. May I borrow your phone?'

'Where's yours?' She'd bought him one as a present last year.

'I always forget to have it with me. I'd like to call Ingeborg.'

'To invite her to join us?'

He blushed. 'Actually, to get this process under way.'

Thoughtfully, Paloma had already reserved a table in the Pump Room. She'd planned to take Marcia there whether Diamond joined them or not. The old lady showed her appreciation by putting away her share of the assorted sandwiches, two scones and three of the fancy pastries. 'Aren't you going to eat your second scone?' she said to Paloma. 'Perhaps Mr Diamond would like it?'

'I'm defeated,' he said.

'In that case . . .' She reached for it.

'More cream?' he said.

'I'd better not,' she said. 'My nephew is

taking me for a fish meal at Loch Fyne tonight. Good thing we don't wear corsets any more. Now *that's* a fascinating topic. Would you like to hear about the history of the corset?'

When Diamond eventually got back to Manvers Street, Ingeborg had contacted the embassy. They'd promised to look at their records and call back. 'Knowing how embassies work, we'll have to put it in writing as well,' she said, 'and that's what I've been doing. The woman I spoke to sounded as if she'd like to help, but wasn't all that confident. With all the upheaval going on in 1991, I wonder if they kept track of missing people.'

'What do embassies exist for, if isn't it helping their citizens in trouble?' he said.

'I'm saying it must have been a chaotic time.'

'Her family would surely make enquiries if they didn't hear from her.'

'It was nearly twenty years ago, guv.'

He shook his head and turned away. 'I keep hearing that from everyone.'

Keith Halliwell looked up as Diamond approached his desk. 'Ukrainian, then? Your friend had the answer.'

'Some of the answer. We've discovered

where the jeans came from and now we need to find out if the woman wearing them came from the same place.'

'It looks certain, doesn't it?'

'Nothing is ever certain in this game, Keith.'

'They were made for the home market. That's what you told Inge.'

'That's true, but I can think of ways someone from outside the Ukraine could get hold of a pair.'

'Okay, we can't be a hundred per cent on this, but I reckon ninety-five, ninety-six. As SIO, I say we should go with this.'

'Leaving the door slightly open.'

'As you wish.' Halliwell played an imaginary piano scale on the edge of the desk. 'You said nothing is certain. There's one thing we can be a hundred per cent sure of. This murder couldn't have happened prior to 1991, when the Honta zip company started up.'

'I can't argue with that.'

'The time frame Lofty Peake gave us was 1984 to 1999. We knocked three years off that by working out when the tree was blown down and now we've knocked off another four.' The start of a smile formed. 'This is where my events chart comes into its own.'

'Yes?' Diamond said, suppressing a yawn.

'Yes. Inge listed every mention of Lansdown in the Bath Chronicle from 1987 to 1999. Now we can erase a whole lot of it.'

'She won't thank you.'

'We're homing in, guv. 1991 to 1993 looks the best bet.'

'What sort of events are these?'

'Take a look.'

The chart had been converted from a visual aid into a computer file that Halliwell opened on his screen.

'This is 1991.'

January 3	Mist causes early end to football
8	Sheep worrying by stray dogs
11	Boot sales to expand
13	Lansdown Road subsidence causes traffic chaos
29	RAF Charmy Down reunion

Diamond peered over Halliwell's shoulder and could only marvel at Ingeborg's staying powers. 'Let's cut to the chase and look at 1993.'

January 1	New Year's Day ramble
3	Motorcycle accident (ice)

'All action, then. Does it go on like this?'

Halliwell took him at his word and brought up February.

'Skip it. I was being ironic.'

'Some would call it sarcastic.'

'Well, I don't need to look at your chart to tell you something of interest to me that happened in 1993 and that was the 350th anniversary of the Battle of Lansdown. July fifth.'

'Yes, but they did the re-enactment over two days at the beginning of August.'

'Why was that?'

'Not sure. Bank holiday?'

'Wrong. August bank holidays come at the end of the month.'

'I don't know, then. Anything else I can tell you?'

'Did anyone have her head blown off?'

'In the re-enactment? Give me a break. According to the *Chronicle* it all took place without a hitch in nice weather in front of a big crowd.'

'Nice weather, big crowd.' Diamond rolled his eyes. 'Did that actually make the paper?'

'It's a local paper. They did a picture feature.'

He yawned at the thought and moved on mentally. 'Another thing about 1993. The Lansdown Society was formed that year. Did Inge find a report of that?'

Halliwell frowned. 'I don't remember seeing it.'

'I'm not surprised. They're a cagy lot. Don't go in for press releases.'

'Are you trying to tell me my events chart is a waste of time?'

He put a hand on Halliwell's shoulder. 'Keith, you're so right about me. I can be a pain. But I say this in complete sincerity. You're in charge of the skeleton enquiry. Be your own man and run it your way.'

19

The next morning was a low point. The Ukrainian Embassy phoned. They were unable to supply information on any of their nationals who may have gone missing in Britain since 1991. Halliwell's mood swung back to almost suicidal. 'We've hit the buffers again. I really believed we were getting somewhere yesterday,' he told Diamond.

'We were — and we did.'

'And see where it led us.'

Diamond knew what it felt like to be moving on with optimism and then have a door slammed in your face. As team leader you took it personally — an experience new to Halliwell. Sympathy alone wouldn't help.

'There are no short cuts, Keith.'

'I'm not asking for a short cut. I just want some movement. Bloody diplomats. Is it political, do you think? Don't they want it made public that some of their people disappeared?'

'It could be sheer numbers. You and I know about human trafficking from East Europe. It's huge — an industry.'

'You think trafficking is behind this?'

'It accounts for a lot of missing people, young women in particular.'

'Sex slaves?'

'There's also the black economy. East Europeans as a source of cheap labour, working long hours without work permits for cash in hand. You've seen it going on. Either way, no one in an embassy is going to have an accurate record of who is here, let alone who is missing.'

'These are illegals you're talking about?'

'Some are for sure, using false travel documents or smuggled in. And some are lured here on false pretences. They come expecting jobs as waitresses or models and find their passports are taken away from them by gangmasters or pimps.'

Halliwell sighed. 'For Christ's sake, if we can't go to the embassy for help on this, we're screwed.'

'No we're not.'

'You just said it's a huge industry.'

'And there's always someone who knows. We have to get to the right person, that's all.'

'Oh yeah, and who's that?'

'I'll think about it.'

The only exit line he could supply. He didn't really have an answer.

He crossed the room to see Septimus, fully expecting another gripe, and instead got a more positive response. The Bristol team, he learned, had now got all the witness statements onto computer. They'd found the canteen and liked the all-day breakfast. They might even survive a few days in Bath.

'I'm overjoyed to hear it,' he said, 'but I'm running a murder enquiry, not a holiday camp.'

'Sure,' Septimus said with the cool of an ocean breeze on a Caribbean beach. 'We have an action plan.'

'Which is . . . ?'

'Item One: we need to question the man who was with Rupert when they found the femur.'

'Dave Barton? He was questioned already. We have a signed statement taken by Keith Halliwell.'

'Yes.' One word carrying such disapproval that Diamond hoped Halliwell hadn't overheard it.

'Are you thinking Barton is a suspect?'

'He needs to answer some tough questions.'

'Such as?'

'Why didn't he come forward when Rupert was reported missing?'

'Keith asked him that. He doesn't look at TV or read a paper.'

'So he claims.'

'You don't believe him? He did come forward finally.'

'After it got serious.'

'Well, he may have got alarmed when he heard about the murder, thinking he'd be an obvious suspect.'

'That's one way of looking at it,' Septimus said, and it was obvious he had another way. 'Equally, if he did the killing himself, he might get away with it by telling us a pack of lies, presenting himself as the good guy who was friendly enough to share his beer.'

'What do you think happened, then?'

Septimus tilted his head and gave Diamond a searching look. 'Do you really want my theory?'

'If it stands up.'

'Seems to me all this had something to do with the bone they found. I've looked at Dave Barton's statement. Suppose he switched roles.'

'What do you mean by that?'

'He claims he buried the beer and offered some to Rupert. Suppose the reverse happened and it was Rupert who hid the beer and quite by chance happened to choose the spot where the girl was buried. Barton was watching. He had a special interest in watching.'

'Why?'

'Because he killed the girl twenty years ago. He's in his forties now. He's old enough.'

The theory intrigued Diamond. 'Murdered her and buried her there?'

'And thought he'd got away with it. A desolate spot on the side of a hill where not many people go and no one does any digging. Then the Civil War society announces it's going to commemorate the battle. Hundreds of people are coming to the part of Lansdown where the body is buried. I've seen the fallen tree. You can't miss it. It's an obvious point of defence, the kind of place where soldiers might dig a latrine or set up camp. Barton gets worried and decides he'd better join the regiment to keep an eye on things.'

'I believe he's been in it some years.'

'Okay, he joined a while ago. It's some years since the first murder. Am I still making sense?'

'Enough to keep me interested.'

'Then Rupert comes along, first to bury

the beer and later collect it. He's a generous guy and when he meets Dave Barton he offers him a drink. To Dave's horror, Rupert finds the bone and decides it belonged to a Civil War victim and wants to excavate the site. Dave persuades him to rebury it, but has his doubts whether Rupert will let it stay buried. He keeps watch and later the same evening he sees Rupert return to the site. He follows him and cracks him over the head, and leaves him for dead. But Rupert recovers enough to wander about Lansdown for days in a confused state.'

'Until Dave Barton finds out and finishes him off?' Diamond rubbed his chin thoughtfully. 'Could it be as simple as that?'

'Can I bring him in again?'

'I think you'd better.'

'Do you want this to be another voluntary statement? No arrest?'

'That would be preferable.'

He wasn't entirely sure that the theory held up, but it demonstrated that Septimus was a thinker. Dave Barton was in for a searching examination.

In the quiet of his office Diamond grappled with the problem of the Ukrainian woman. He'd never had much confidence that the embassy would name her. At the time she went missing her country had been in ferment, emerging from the restrictions of the old Soviet system. They'd probably had a delegation looking after their interests in Britain rather than a fully fledged embassy. All these years later they weren't going to produce a list of missing persons.

There's always someone who knows, he'd said to Halliwell.

Easily said.

Okay, the young woman had disappeared and nobody seemed to have noticed. His remark to Keith — that she may have been trafficked — had something going for it.

The Ukraine was notorious as a source of cheap labour and worse. Young people from the former Soviet bloc had started coming to the west in numbers after the wall came down and temporary work for cash had always been easy to get in Britain, with no questions asked about visas and work permits. Unscrupulous employers were only too pleased to cash in.

Some illegal immigrants undoubtedly were murdered and weren't heard of again. If you don't officially exist, there isn't much of a hue and cry when you go missing.

He called Ingeborg to the office. 'You were a journalist. You know the local scene as well as any of us. Is there a Ukrainian community in Bath?'

'Not that I've heard of,' she said.

'Bristol?'

'Possibly. They do band together in places and keep up the old customs and religion. Ukrainians have always had a strong sense of identity. There's a national association, isn't there? I know there are several thousand in Manchester and they organise events and meet socially.'

'In London, too,' he said, and he could speak from experience after his years in the Met. 'I think the first to settle here in numbers were displaced soldiers after the second world war. The Ukraine has had various political upheavals since and each one saw more of them moving here. I think they have their own cathedral somewhere in London. But Bath . . . ? I haven't heard of it and neither have you, it seems.'

'You're trying to find someone who knew the dead woman?' she said.

'When she first came here, she would surely have looked for some of her fellow countrymen.'

'Unless she was trafficked and had no choice,' Ingeborg said.

He might have expected Ingeborg to think of this. As a socially aware young woman she was well informed about the trade in human beings and keen to see it stopped. 'When did trafficking first become a problem?'

'It started when perestroika came to the old Soviet Union and travel restrictions were eased.'

'When Gorbachev was leader?'

'The late eighties. Young people were looking for an escape and there were crooks only too pleased to take advantage.'

'In Russia?'

'And here.'

'But we know from the logo on the zip that she came in the early nineties.'

Ingeborg nodded. 'Yes and by then they were leaving their country in big numbers, women in particular. Life was hard there. Something like eighty per cent of the unemployed were women. They couldn't earn much at home.'

'So did she land up in Bristol?'

'On the game? Who knows? Montpelier and St Paul's have always had a reputation. You could talk to Septimus.'

'And I will,' he said, 'but I'm still hopeful that she made contact with some Ukrainians here. Common sense tells me she came to London first and we know they have a big presence there. I'm going to call an old friend from the Met. He may throw some light.'

Louis Voss had retired from Fulham CID some time after Diamond left, but still worked in the same nick as a civilian.

'Forgive my ignorance,' Diamond said to him after they'd exchanged greetings and small talk about how their lives had moved on. 'Would you know the part of London where most Ukrainians hang out?'

'Holland Park,' Louis said at once. 'Didn't you get to know it when you worked here?'

'No mate, 'Olland Park was up the posh end,' he said in his cod version of cockney. 'I was stuck down the North End Road. Remember?'

'It's all around that part of town,' Louis said, 'restaurants, clubs, churches, the embassy. You could be forgiven for thinking you're in Odessa. They even have a Ukrainian statue in Holland Park Avenue. Their patron saint, St Volodymyr. They're well dug in.'

'Holland Park,' Diamond said, more to himself than Louis.

'Why? Are you looking for a cheap plumber?'

'Plumber?'

'Lighten up, Peter.'

Diamond explained about the skeleton

and the Ukrainian connection. 'I can't think why she ended up dead and buried in Bath. I'm hoping to tap into her movements before she got here and London seems the best place to start.'

'You want me to put out some feelers?'

'More than that. I want to meet people.'

'Will any old Ivan do?'

'Preferably one who knows what was happening about 1992.'

'Can you drink seven straight vodkas?'

'Never actually tried.'

'There's always a first time. I'll see what I can set up for you. Whether any of them will talk to a Zummerzet plod I can't say.'

20

'Septimus had a brilliant thought,' Ingeborg told Diamond towards the end of the afternoon.

'Oh, yes?' He didn't want to stifle her enthusiasm, but he'd learned to be wary of brilliant thoughts. There was usually a hidden agenda.

'He says if there's a link between our skeleton girl and the killing of Rupert Hope it's got to be that big muster they had in 1993, the three hundred and fiftieth anniversary.'

' "Got to be"? I question that.'

'We know she died about then.'

'Give or take a year or two.'

'It was a huge event, guv, much bigger than the one they put on in July. I read the press reports when I was doing that list for Keith. Sponsored by the Round Table. Plenty of publicity. Oceans of coverage in the *Chronicle.* They staged it over two days in August and ten thousand turned up to watch. Extra police were called in to control them.'

'I believe you, Inge. You don't need to go on.'

'Listen, though. The spectators were all kept behind a rope barrier along the top edge of the field where the main road is. But the fallen tree where the girl was buried is on the far side, on a steep slope.'

'I know this.'

'I'm giving you the picture. You weren't there on the day and neither was I. Whatever went on in the area of the tree was out of sight of most people, right?'

He nodded, beginning to see where this was going. 'That's why Dave Barton hid his six-pack there.'

'Let's stay with 1993 for a moment. What I'm saying — well, what Septimus said to me — is that if a fatal incident happened on one of those two days in front of ten thousand people the obvious place to take the body was down the hill out of sight.'

'But no one was seriously hurt. We know that.'

'How?' she said, her eyes alight with the force of her argument. 'How do we know?'

'It would have made the news, that's why.'

'Guv, it was a battlefield. There were

skirmishes taking place, pikemen fighting, cavalry charges. People were pretending to be dead all over the hill. Who's going to notice if one of the bodies really is dead?' She had a point there and she hammered it home. 'You could kill a person in front of a mass audience and get away with it. Before the end of the show you drag the body out of sight and you can bury it later.'

'Is this Septimus's brilliant idea?' he said.

'Give me a chance. I haven't finished.'

'Go on, then.'

'There were women on the battlefield. I've seen the colour supplement. They dressed the part. Some of them were supposed to be tending the wounded.'

'Camp followers,' he said, recalling what Augusta White had told him.

She snapped back at him, 'That's a pejorative term.'

'Not at all. It's what they're known as.'

'I call them angels of mercy.'

'Call them what you like, Inge. I'm quoting the Sealed Knot. I don't think it's meant to insult women. And since your feminist hackles are rising you may like to know that about a third of the cavalry are women. And your more adventurous sisters sometimes join the gun crews.'

She frowned and went cherry red. 'How

do you know this?'

'Like you, I'm finding out as I go along. But I can see where you're going with this. Our young woman may have died in the battle.'

'Yes, and what a blow it would have been to the whole event — to events like this all over the country. A real fatality, and a woman at that. Would it be it so surprising if she was dragged out of sight and buried?'

'Now you're stretching it, Inge,' he said. 'Asking me to believe the Knot connived at the illegal disposal of a body to save their reputation.'

'It needn't have been official,' she said. 'Probably wasn't. A couple of people could have moved the corpse unknown to the organisers.'

'All right. Let's pursue this for a moment. You're suggesting she was killed during the battle. How? By accident?'

'That's only one scenario.'

'I'm listening.'

'There's a more sinister one, isn't there? One of the soldiers had murder in mind from the beginning.'

'A premeditated killing. It's a possibility. How many took part?'

'The paper said two and a half thousand.'

'As many as that? Inge, you're depressing me.'

'But not so many are women and there's a better chance of them being remembered, particularly if one was from the Ukraine.'

He'd become so involved in her version of the battle that he'd pushed the victim's nationality to the back of his mind. 'Now there's a thing. What in the name of sanity would a Ukrainian woman be doing in an English Civil War re-enactment?'

'Exactly.'

She made him think again. He played his own words back to himself.

'If she was there, someone will know,' Ingeborg said, spreading her hands as if she'd just solved the riddle of the sphinx.

It was a whopping assumption, but he was intrigued. 'So?'

'So Septimus had his brilliant thought.' She waited for him to react. She wasn't going to say another word until he asked.

'And what's that?'

'Why don't I enlist in the Sealed Knot and see what I can find out?'

'Crazy.'

'Why?'

'Because you're a policewoman, that's why.'

'They've all got jobs. They do it in the

evenings and at weekends. It's a free country. I can join if I want.'

'The first thing they'll ask is what your
day job is and you're sunk.'

'All right, I can say I'm a journalist, like I
was.'

'That won't relax anybody.'

'I'll go undercover, then.'

She was not to be dissuaded. She really
wanted to do this.

'What do you hope to achieve?'

'Finding people who remember 1993,
women in particular. When we're in a small
minority, we get to know each other. If
there's anything to be learned about the
murder victim, I'll root it out.'

'I'm sure you're capable,' he said. 'But
there's a downside, isn't there? Someone
murdered Rupert Hope, presumably because he was a threat. You're going down
the same route and you'll be in real danger.'

'I'll watch my back.'

'Not good enough. We can do this the
regular way, letting them know who we are
and taking statements. You'll still be involved, I promise you.'

She shook her head. 'My way is best.
Catch them off guard.'

That was true, but he didn't want her to
take the risk.

She said, 'Guv, if I was a man, you wouldn't hesitate. What happened to equality?'

It was a telling point. Sometimes he treated her as the daughter he'd never had. He'd never fully accepted that she should face the same risks as everyone else. He was happy to make use of her insights into the female psyche, her intelligence and her journalistic experience, but he still didn't want her in the front line.

'I know you mean well,' she said, 'but if I'm going to have a career in CID I have to do it all.'

He said, 'Actually, Inge, this is more than I'd ask anyone to do.'

She was tight-lipped.

'But since you volunteered,' he went on, 'I won't stop you. Just as long as you realise the danger.'

Through the one-way glass of Interview Room 1, he watched Septimus and one of his Bristol DCs pitching in to Dave Barton. The Bradford on Avon blacksmith seemed to be holding up well at this stage. He'd asked to bring a friend with him and she turned out to be a razor-sharp solicitor, Miss Tower, well known to Manvers Street. She was quick to intervene.

'My client answered these questions before, when he was interviewed by Mr Halliwell. You have the signed statement.'

'And I've studied it,' Septimus said. 'But
you must understand that DI Halliwell is
enquiring into the death of an unknown
woman twenty years ago. My investigation
is different, the recent killing of Rupert
Hope. I need to explore areas not covered
in the previous interview.'

'You just asked about Mr Barton's job,
which you know already, and which has no
conceivable relevance to either enquiry.'

On the other side of the glass, Diamond
said, 'Except we're looking for the murder
weapon and a blacksmith's tool kit has to
be of interest.'

'All right, Dave. Let's concentrate on the
hobby, the Civil War thing,' Septimus said.
'How long have you been doing it?'

Miss Tower was quick to say, 'Not
relevant.'

Septimus said, 'I want to find out if he'd
met Rupert at any of the meetings.'

'Then ask him.'

Dave, a strong, smiling man with a beer
gut, said, 'The answer is no. He was a Bristol guy. They have their own branch.'

'He told you he came from Bristol?'

'I found out since. From the university,

wasn't he?'

'That's right. Didn't he mention it at the time?'

'Said he was a historian. The Sealed Knot asked him to give a talk at the lecture day and he thought he'd like to join a muster and find out what we do. He went on a lot about the real battle. He seemed to know his stuff.'

'Are you well up on history, Dave?'

'Me? No, I don't do it for that. I like the action, the fighting.'

'Careful,' Miss Tower advised him.

'I meant the dressing up and all that,' Dave added.

'You're a pikeman?' Septimus said.

'Not always.'

'For this battle you were. And so was Rupert?'

'Foot soldiers really. The lowest form of life.'

'The pikes are long, aren't they? About five metres? What did you do with your pikes when you went for the lager?'

'Left them on the ground where we was supposed to have died. We picked them up later.'

'And you moved down the hill to where you'd hidden the beer? Did anyone see you going?'

'Could have.'

'Other pikemen?'

'Not the living ones. The action had moved on by then. There were some dead and wounded lying about. When you're on the ground it's hard to see much. And there was a few women looking after roundheads, giving them water. Camp followers, they're called.'

Diamond grinned. Whatever happened to angels of mercy? A pity Ingeborg wasn't here.

'Could they have seen you?' Septimus asked.

'I suppose.'

'Were they close enough to have a view of you and Rupert digging out the beer?'

'They'd need twenty-twenty vision. I'd say they were more than fifty yards off.'

'So they wouldn't have spotted you actually finding the bone? That was a strange find, wasn't it?'

Miss Tower said to Dave, 'You don't need to answer that. You're not here to give an opinion.'

But Dave seemed to decide he was on safe ground. 'I was shocked. First I thought it was from some animal. I put it down fast when I guessed it could be human. Nasty. We buried it again.'

'At whose suggestion?'

'I don't remember. We agreed it was the right thing to do, anyway.'

'No argument?'

'No.'

'And you went back to the battle?'

'That's right.'

'Did you see Rupert again?'

He shook his head.

'And after the battle was over?'

'No. I've never seen him since.'

'We'll leave now,' Miss Tower said.

'I haven't finished,' Septimus told her. 'You like a drink or two, Dave?'

'Irrelevant. Don't answer that,' Miss Tower said.

'I'm sorry,' Septimus said, 'but I have every right to ask. Dave is an important witness and we need to establish if his evidence would hold up under cross-examination.'

'Good for you,' Diamond said on his side of the glass.

Miss Tower said, 'He's not in court. He's co-operating and you appear to be about to cast a slur on his behaviour.'

Septimus said, 'He testified to me that he hid a six-pack of lager in the ground before the battle. He also testified to DI Halliwell that he hadn't heard Rupert Hope was missing and this was because he gets out in the evenings, usually to the pub. Now, Dave, let's address this. Did you drink at all prior to joining in the battle?'

'A couple at lunch. I was stone cold sober, if that's what you're asking.'

'Can you be more specific? One pint, two, three . . . ?'

'How would I remember?' Dave said.

'Gotcha!' Diamond said.

Septimus said, 'You seem to remember your meeting with Rupert in some detail, but you can't remember how many you had at lunch.'

'I can handle my drink.'

'Are you quite sure you buried six cans of lager before the battle?'

'I told you. You know what a six-pack is?'

'And at that stage were you aware of anyone watching?'

'Definitely. One of the other army came past. Waller's lot, roundhead, thieving bastard.'

'You think he had the other four cans?'

'I'm certain of it. I've been over it in my mind lots of times. Who else would have known?'

'Do you remember what he was like?'

'Cavalry.'

'Are you certain of that?'

'Come on. He was on a big white stallion,

wasn't he?'

'A pale horse,' Septimus said, more to himself than the witness.

'And he passed really close.'

'Would you recognise him again?'

'I would if I saw him on the horse.'

'Did he say anything?'

'No. He raised his whip, but friendly like. Some friend.'

'And were you in uniform at the time?'

'My red coat and woollen breeches. Not the armour. It was too early for that and too bloody hot.'

'So would he have known you were in the rival army?'

'No problem, and I reckon he had a good laugh, nicking the enemy's beer.'

'He had the decency to leave some.'

'That's what my mate Rupert said, and I told him if that was decent, forget it.'

'When you and Rupert parted, were you still friendly?'

'Of course we were. I'd shared my beer with him, hadn't I?'

'Would it have angered you if he'd returned later to the fallen tree and dug out the bone?'

Dave frowned. 'Why would he do that?'

'He may have thought it was of historical interest.'

'I get you. I'd have been slightly narked, after we agreed to let it rest in peace.'

'Did you go back to check?'

'No chance. After it was over, I was in the beer tent. You get up a thirst in these battles.'

'And did you drive home after?'

Miss Tower slammed her hand on the table. 'Don't answer that.'

Dave stared at Septimus and gave a faint smile. 'You see? I knew I needed my brief with me.'

21

Diamond had been at his lowest point, hunting the murderer of his wife, when he had last seen Louis Voss. His old colleague had managed to trace a crucial contact. If Louis didn't already know what was happening in London, he would know someone who did. Nobody in the Met was better at working the grapevine. Officially Louis was a civilian now, but still at Fulham nick, managing what he called his team of computer cuties. The loss of CID status hadn't cramped his style one bit.

This morning he was in the saloon bar of the Fox and Pheasant, off the Fulham Road, when Diamond arrived about eleven with Keith Halliwell. The lop-sided smile was punctuated by a wink. 'Black Baron, gents? Much needed, I reckon, after the M4. And I bet I know who wasn't driving.'

'We'd still be on the road if I was,' Diamond said.

Louis was right. They'd come in Diamond's car, now roadworthy again, with Halliwell acting as chauffeur.

'Keith, meet my old friend Louis, the wizard of ops, as he's known.'

'Was,' Louis said. 'I'm just a geek now. What's your part in this, Keith, apart from driving him at forty miles an hour, maximum?'

Diamond said, 'He's the main man, the SIO on the case.'

Louis greeted this with a faintly amused look and then went to order the drinks. He could remember every trick Diamond had ever pulled.

'Nice of him,' Halliwell said.

'Don't be fooled,' Diamond said. 'We'll find he's started a slate in my name. I know this guy of old.'

'We can go halves,' Halliwell offered.

'That's all right. We'll need to fill up with petrol on the way home. You can take care of that.'

One more trick. Unfortunately there was no one Halliwell could clobber.

Louis returned with their pints. 'Make the most of this,' he said. 'You'll be on straight vodkas later.'

'Who have you lined up for us?'

'This hasn't been easy. There's a lot of

suspicion. The Ukrainians are charming people, but if they once suspect you're from immigration, you're as welcome as a bowl of cold borsch.'

'They can't all be illegals.'

'I mean it, Peter. Watch your back.'

'Nothing new about that.'

'Don't make any assumptions. They've been through every kind of hardship back home: wretched conditions, ten thousand per cent inflation, rationing, the nuclear disaster at Chernobyl. When independence came, it didn't make the difference they hoped for. There was corruption, organised crime, Mafia killings. It took the Orange Revolution to make a real break.'

'The Ukrainians over here interest me more.'

Louis grinned. 'Fair enough. And you've come to the right place. Waves of them arrived here in the nineties. Life at home was so harsh, particularly for women, that a lot of the young got out. These escapees are mainly the people you'll meet, in their thirties and forties now.'

'The woman we're interested in would have been around twenty when she was killed,' Halliwell said, impatient to get to the point. 'We don't know why she came to Bath.'

'Nice place. Why shouldn't she?' Louis said.

'We think she could have been trafficked.'

'To Bath? For sex?'

'Bristol, more likely.'

'It wouldn't surprise me. Trafficking of Ukrainian women is a big problem. The numbers must run into thousands.'

'Hundreds of thousands actually,' Halliwell said. 'The Ukrainian Ministry of the Interior reckoned four hundred thousand in the last decade of the twentieth century. That's to all countries, not just Britain.'

Louis exchanged a glance with Diamond as if to say gawdelpus, what have you brought with you?

Diamond said, 'Keith does his research.'

Louis gave a nod. 'Okay, but let's remember the majority come here freely and get work permits. What's the background on your missing woman?'

'A Ukrainian zip fly,' Diamond said.

'And a snip of hair,' Halliwell added.

'Teeth?'

'She was headless.'

'You *have* got a problem.' Louis picked up his glass and drank. 'It sounds professional. If you're right about the trafficking, she could have rebelled and been dealt with by her pimp.'

'And if that's the case,' Diamond said, 'her killing will have been used as a threat to keep other women in line. So I reckon someone may remember her.'

'From twenty years ago?' A belch from Louis testified to his reaction. 'You always were an optimist. There's a new generation of working girls now.'

'But the older ones may have graduated into madams.'

'There he goes again. All right, let me tell you who I've fixed for you to meet. Two people at opposite ends of the spectrum. Olena is a pillar of the community and she's been here twenty-five years. She's a *babusya*, a granny, much respected, a kind of church social worker who looks out for vulnerable girls and does her best to link them up with families. Ukrainians are regular church-goers.'

'Which church?' Halliwell asked.

'They have more than one church?' Diamond said.

'The Catholics have their own cathedral in Mayfair,' Halliwell said.

Being well informed wasn't earning Halliwell the credit he craved. He might have come from another planet, going by the look he got from Louis. 'Olena is Ukrainian Orthodox. The church is in Ealing, no great distance from here.'

'We'd like to meet Olena, whatever her religion,' Diamond said.

'Almost any girl who visited that church in the last quarter of a century has been given the once-over by Olena.'

'Thanks, Louis. You've spent time on this.'

'More than I intended.'

'Who else have you lined up?'

'The second contact couldn't be more different. Andriy is a disgrace, an alcoholic who has never done a day's work since he got here. There's a Ukrainian pub in Addison Road called the Crimea and he gets his glass filled up through the day by passing on the lowlife gossip. Amazingly his brain still functions. If anything in the way of scandal is remembered about your lady, Andriy is the man to ask. Treat him with respect. He has powerful friends.'

'So we know where to find Andriy,' Halliwell said. 'How about Olena?'

'Right now she'll be arranging flowers at the church in Newton Avenue, Ealing. I told her to expect you around twelve-thirty.'

Short, slim and with the steady gaze of an icon, Olena met them at the church door and said, 'You will come to my flat.'

'We can talk here,' Diamond offered, trying to be amenable.

'Not in the church, or outside.'

She was the kind of woman you didn't argue with. 'As you wish.'

The flat was in Meon Road, as close to the church as a loyal parishioner would wish to be. Olena lived on the ground floor. 'I prepared *chorni khlib* and salt for you. It is the custom,' she said, unlocking the door.

Unseen by their hostess, Halliwell raised his eyebrows at Diamond, who gave a nod meant to say eat your *chorni khlib* and salt and look happy about it.

Olena had the treat ready just inside the door on a tray covered by an embroidered cloth. She removed the cloth to reveal a black loaf and a small bowl of salt. She offered it first to Diamond.

'Break a piece and dip in salt,' she told him.

He did as asked. The bread had a hint of vinegar, but he swallowed it and thanked her.

'No need to speak. You bow your head, so.'

So he bowed his head.

Halliwell received his portion in the approved way, in silence.

'That is good,' Olena said. 'Now we talk in my living room.'

The room was small, with only two chairs at either side of an old-fashioned fireplace, the mantelpiece crowded with black and white photos in metal frames. In an alcove to one side was a patriarchal crucifix with the extra crosspiece. On a shelf below, a silver-plated vase held some wax flowers.

'You sit,' Olena said, gesturing to the chairs. 'Both.'

She was pouring something from a jug into three wineglasses. There was no arguing with this lady. If she offered you a chair, you sat; and if she said drink, you drank.

'Is called *kvas,*' she said as she handed the glasses to her guests. It looked dark and bubbly. 'After *chorni khlib,* you have thirst so you drink this. Made from black bread and sugar. All Ukrainians drink *kvas.*'

'Children as well?' Halliwell asked.

She nodded. 'No alcohol.'

'Good health, then,' Diamond said, trying not to catch Halliwell's eye. The drink reminded him of cold Ovaltine and he didn't care much for it. 'We came to ask you about a young Ukrainian woman who we think travelled to Bath about twenty years ago and was murdered there. We don't know her name. She would have been about twenty and it's likely she came to London first.'

'Murdered? Why?'

'She must have met bad people, here, or in Bath.'

'With God's help I try to stop girls from meeting such people,' Olena said. 'I would not know.'

'But you may remember a girl who was going to Bath and wasn't heard of again. It would be unusual, wouldn't it, in about 1990, for a Ukrainian girl to be heading for Bath?'

'Or 1991,' Halliwell added, 'when your country gained independence.'

'Regained,' Olena said with a look that put him to the bottom of the class. 'No, I cannot help. I remember nobody like this.'

'It was a time when people gained the freedom to travel,' Diamond said, unwilling to give up. 'Were you already living here?'

'I am here before then,' she said. 'The church helped me to find work here and at home, so I give back. Many who came were young women. In Ukraine so many without job are women. I cannot begin to describe.'

'Can you remember the names of those you helped?'

'Many. Not all. Some we lost to evil men who take them to be Scots.'

Diamond was mystified.

Halliwell said, 'I think you mean escorts.'

'Yes. Scots.'

'And do you keep any sort of record of where they are now?' Diamond asked.

'Record. What is that?'

'Name? Address?'

'Some write to me still.'

'Even from 1991?'

'A few.'

'We'd like to hear of anyone you're still in touch with from that time in case they remember this woman.'

She took down one of the photo frames. 'This is Viktoriya. She arrive here 1991 to be waitress. The men who offer this job are lying. Soon they force her to sell her body. You understand?'

'What happened? Did she go missing?'

'No. Still here, with family now, married to Englishman, living in Barnes, thank the blessed Lord Jesus.'

'She escaped from that life?'

'By his mercy.'

'Barnes isn't far from here,' Diamond said.

'Yes. Sometimes she come to see me.'

He glanced at Halliwell. This was promising. 'Where exactly in Barnes?'

Olena gasped in horror and wagged her finger from side to side. 'You stay away. She will be frightened.'

'Why? You said she's given up the bad old life.'

'That is what she tell me.' But uncertainty remained, even in Olena, who wanted to believe the best.

'All we want is to speak to her.'

'You are secret police.'

'Detectives in plain clothes. Not the same thing at all. Not in this country, I promise you.'

She was tight-lipped.

'We talk to witnesses all the time,' Diamond said. 'We can do this without scaring her. In fact, only one of us needs to chat to her.' He smiled in a reassuring way intended to underline his credentials as Mr Nice.

She shook her head. 'I don't think so.'

He broadened the argument. 'For the sake of the murdered girl and her family. She has a God-given right to be treated properly as well.'

This worked better. They could see the conflict in Olena's eyes. Where did her Christian duty lie? She sighed, a deep heart felt sigh. 'You wait here. I get my address book.'

Now that they were alone, Mr Nice took the opportunity to pour what was left of his *kvas* into a potted plant.

'Are you thinking of dividing forces?' Halliwell said. 'I don't mind going to Barnes if you'd do the booze artist.'

'Sod that. I'm in charge.' When it suits me, he thought.

'What I'm thinking, guv, is that you could handle another *chorni khlib* welcome, but could you handle the *kvas* as well?'

'Ah.' He was wavering. Halliwell had a point.

'You get the straight vodkas, but as I'm the driver . . .'

'You're a devious bastard, Keith.'

Olena returned and handed them a piece of paper with a Barnes address.

Before they split up, Diamond felt in his pocket. For once, he was carrying the phone Paloma had given him. 'Just as well to keep in touch,' he told Halliwell. 'Do you have my number?'

'It's in the memory.'

He blinked. 'Is it? Then it's better than my memory. When did I give it to you?'

'Ingeborg did. She made a note of it last year when she was showing you how to work the thing. She passed it round the office.'

'That woman! Bloody nerve.'

'What's the point of having a phone if you aren't reachable?'

'I have an old-fashioned liking for privacy.'

310

'Is that why it isn't switched on?'

'Isn't it?' He fingered the controls in a clumsy way and Halliwell pressed the correct one. They agreed to meet at the car at 6 p.m. unless they'd been in contact before.

A taxi delivered Diamond to Addison Road and the Crimea, an old-style Victorian pub with a field gun as its sign. To most Brits, the Crimea was a war rather than a place. Inside, blue and green tiles and varnished woodwork made it dark. Some kind of plaintive music from a stringed instrument was being piped through the room. A balalaika, Diamond decided from no expert knowledge.

He approached the two men on bar stools, the only customers he could see. They looked about his age and were speaking in a foreign language. He waited for a pause.

'Excuse me. I'm looking for Andriy.'

'In what connection, my friend?' If this was a Ukrainian, he had a better command of English than Olena.

'I was told if I bought him a drink he might help me find someone.'

'That's always possible.' The speaker had a grey baseball cap pulled well down on his forehead, making his pale blue eyes seem a long way off.

'You know him?' Diamond said.

A nod. 'Two double vodkas would be nice.'

As if by arrangement, a bar girl appeared from nowhere.

'You heard that?' Diamond asked her.

She was already filling a glass. 'And for you, sir?'

He pointed to one of the beer handles. 'That'll do. A half.' He didn't trust himself drinking vodkas. He paid and turned back to the drinkers. 'Which of you is Andriy?'

After some hesitation the second man raised a finger and said nothing. His hunched, comfortable position on the bar counter spoke of many hours of practice. A fine head of black curls sagged between broad shoulders.

'He's your man,' his companion said. 'Knows everyone.'

'Cheers, then,' Diamond said, swallowed hard and told them he was from Bath police enquiring into the death of a young woman, apparently Ukrainian, about twenty years ago. 'She was buried on a hillside a mile or so outside the city. Her skeleton, minus the skull, was dug up last week. It's possible she was known here in London.'

'If she was Ukrainian, she probably was,' the man in the baseball cap said. 'What do you say, Andriy?'

'This is all you know?' Andriy said without looking at Diamond or the other man. 'A headless skeleton?'

He told them about the zip.

Andriy wasn't impressed. 'Hundreds of girls come through London. I don't know where they all end up.'

'This one ended up in another city, dead, probably murdered.'

'So she got in with bad company.'

'Speaking of which,' Diamond said, 'were there any Ukrainian gangs with links to Bath or Bristol twenty years ago?'

Andriy shrugged and looked away.

'She was from your country,' Diamond said.

'He doesn't have an answer,' his companion said.

Yet he was supposed to be a gossip, so why so reticent? Diamond dredged deep. 'Another thought, then. The Cossacks come from the Ukraine, am I right?'

'Cossacks?' Andriy locked eyes with him again. 'What is this talk of Cossacks? Who are you to be speaking about Cossacks?'

'They have a fierce reputation, don't they?'

'What — do you think some Cossack came to Bath and killed this girl?' He grinned at his friend, then said to Diamond, 'Do you know anything about history? The time of the Cossacks was nearly four hundred years ago. They revolted against the Polish oppressors. Smashed them. But it was a long time ago.'

'The 1640s,' the other man said.

'Well, how about that?' Diamond said just to counter the suggestion that he was ignorant about history. 'We had a civil war of our own going on in the 1640s.'

Andriy wasn't impressed. 'I'm telling you the Cossacks are in the past.'

'What about World War Two? There were Cossack brigades fighting on the German side against the Russians.'

'Everyone was fighting and everyone suffered,' Andriy said. 'Poles, Russians, Jews, Cossacks. There isn't a family in the Ukraine without painful memories of the war. Don't lecture me on our history.'

Diamond shook his head. 'I'm making the point that the Cossacks never went away. You can't dismiss them as history. Do they sometimes decapitate their enemies?'

There was a moment of silence. He was in dangerous waters here.

'It's not unknown,' Andriy said finally, and added, 'in past times.'

'Ancient times,' his companion said.

'Right,' Andriy said. 'A long time back. They don't carry swords any more. If I were you, Mr Policeman, I would forget about Cossacks.'

'Thanks for that. Any suggestions where I should look, then?'

'Try the embassy.'

'We already did — and drew a blank.'

'Too bad.'

The man with the baseball cap looked at his watch and said something in Ukrainian to Andriy, and then slid off the stool, grinned at Diamond as if to say you'll be here for ever if you think you're going to find anything out, and left the pub.

'Mafioso,' Andriy said.

'It crossed my mind,' Diamond said. 'Difficult to talk freely with someone like that in attendance.'

Andriy showed him an empty glass. Diamond nodded to the bar girl. She poured another double and then returned to the area behind the bar, despatched there by a flap of Andriy's hand.

'In the nineties, when your dead woman disappeared,' he said to Diamond, 'there were two big groups bringing women to this country. They still operate, and so do others now. He is attached to one such group.'

'Understood.'

'At that time, the competition was strong. Deadly. Two pimps were killed. One of the women, too.'

Diamond leaned forward, all ears.

'But not your woman,' Andriy said. 'This one was given a funeral at the Ukrainian Church.'

'When was this?'

'The year of independence, 1991.'

'Was her killer caught?'

'No. The violence made a strong impression and some of the call girls decided to quit. I'm not sure how many, but they weren't heard of again. If they had any sense they would have got out of London.'

'Do you know of any names?'

He shook his head.

'Surely,' Diamond said, 'if they got away, they would have been replaced. We both know there was no shortage of working girls at that time. They were coming here by the hundred.'

'That is true.'

'If, as you say, the quitters got out of London, would their pimps have gone to all the trouble of hounding them down? I'm thinking of some vengeful bastard following our woman to Bath and killing her and burying her.'

'Depends if she was a danger, I guess,' Andriy said.

'Knew too much? You could be right.' His

thoughts were interrupted by a piercing sound from somewhere close. 'What's that?'

'Do you have a phone?' Andriy said.

'Christ, yes.' He took it from his pocket. This could only be Keith Halliwell.

Urgency bordering on panic was in Keith's voice. 'Guv, I'm in trouble. Can you get here fast?'

22

Of all the team, Keith would be the last to panic. Diamond sprinted along the street, hailed the first taxi he sighted and gave the address Olena had supplied. 'Put your foot down,' he added, ignoring his phobia for high speeds.

'Man, you've got to be hot for it,' the West Indian driver said.

'What do you mean?'

He got no answer except a throaty laugh. While the taxi rattled through the backstreets, he used the mobile to ask Louis to send a response car.

'Say that address again,' Louis said.

'Marchant Street, Barnes.'

'The number.'

'I told you. Sixteen.'

'We know sixteen Marchant Street. It's a knocking shop.'

'Can't be,' Diamond said. 'Olena sent him there. One of her church people lives there with her English husband.'

'Take it from me, Peter, it's a brothel.'

Now he understood the cabby's mirth.

'Is there another Marchant Street?' he asked Louis.

The driver shouted from the front, 'Not in Barnes, my friend.'

'Get someone there, anyway,' Diamond said into the phone.

They joined a tailback waiting to cross Hammersmith Bridge. 'Isn't there a quicker route?' he asked.

'Yeah, you can fly,' the cabby told him. 'What are you on — Viagra?'

He subsided into silence.

Across the bridge, a left turn came up soon.

'Sixteen. Should be on the right,' he said.

'You're not the first I've brought here,' the cabby said. 'It's the one with the blinds down. Shall I wait? I reckon you're gonna be quick.'

'No need.' He got out and handed across a ten pound note. The driver turned the taxi and left, still grinning.

The house was part of a shabby Victorian terrace, three storeys high. The age of smog had blackened the brickwork and this wasn't the class of address that got steam-cleaned. Broken window-boxes spoke of a once-respectable use, but not for some time. Olena the church worker, saviour of vulnerable girls, had been badly misinformed by her protégée, Viktoriya.

The disrepair wasn't total. His attention was caught by a movement above the door. A small video camera had shifted its angle a fraction. Someone inside had seen him coming.

The door worked on an entry-phone. He pressed the control and a woman's voice said, 'Yes?'

'John Smith. May I come in?'

The door buzzed. He pushed it and got inside.

'Upstairs,' called the same female voice.

For all she knew, he was a punter, a new client, and he'd play along with this for as long as it suited. The stairs had a serviceable carpet in brown cord. Presumably Keith had stepped up here, but at what point had he guessed the status of the house?

'In here.'

He pushed at a partly open door and found himself in a room furnished with cheap sofas. A blonde, sharp-featured woman in a black trouser suit stood behind one of them displaying a set of clawlike fingernails painted blue, with silver streaks added. How would those go down at Sunday mass? he wondered. Maybe they were detachable.

She repeated the bland 'Yes?' he'd heard over the intercom.

'My first time here,' he said. 'You were recommended. Would you be Viktoriya?'

'I'm Vikki, yes. Who sent you, then?' Her accent had only the slightest trace of East Europe.

'I didn't catch her name. A Ukrainian lady.'

'Where?'

'Holland Park area.' He was assessing the room, trying to decide if heavies were waiting nearby to deal with troublemakers. If Vikki was the madam, as it appeared, she'd need some back-up. For the present her hands rested firmly on the chair back. 'I'll be straight with you, Vikki. A friend of mine came here an hour or more ago.'

'Who was that?' she said and gave an ironic smile. 'Another John Smith?'

He was through with the play-acting. The response car would be here any minute. 'He was a police officer, wanting information from you. Where is he now?'

'I don't know who you mean,' she said, dropping all pretence of charm. 'No one came here saying he was from the police.'

'He may not have shown you his warrant, but he must have asked you questions about girls who went missing twenty years ago.'

She hesitated. '*That* guy? He left some time back.'

'It won't do,' he said. 'He called me to say he was in trouble.'

Her eyes had turned to the left. He took a step closer and saw the monochrome screen she was staring at. He guessed the police had arrived.

'Come on, Vikki,' he said. 'Do you want cops storming through every room in the building?'

Alarmed, she put a hand to her mouth. 'It wasn't my fault,' she said, playing the innocent through the scary fingernails. 'He came asking questions. Anyone could tell he wasn't a punter.'

'Where is he?'

'I haven't a clue.'

Then a shot was fired nearby, followed by another, somewhere outside the building. He knew gunfire. It wasn't a firework or a car backfiring.

He started down the stairs just as the front door burst open and two uniformed cops from the Met charged in. They were ready to grab him until he pulled out his warrant card and shouted, 'The garden.'

They carried on past the staircase and through a door at the back. Diamond followed them into a small kitchen where unwashed coffee mugs littered a table. One cop flung open the door to the garden, which was more of a concreted back yard than anything cultivated, a poor place to hide. A toolshed stood against a brick wall at the end. The cops went to look, with Diamond following, and the kitchen door slammed behind them. He stopped, turned and tried the handle. The wind must have got behind it, not some inmate of the house, as he suspected, because it opened again.

'No one here,' shouted the cop who'd opened the shed.

His partner had made a leap at the wall and was hanging on by his arms, looking over. 'Here!' he yelled and scrambled up and out of sight. The other cop followed.

For a man of Diamond's build, that wall was a major barrier, but he wasn't giving up while Keith was in trouble. He took a wooden fruit box from the shed and stepped up, got a handhold, hauled his bulk to the top and toppled over. The two uniformed cops were already in hot pursuit of a man who had vaulted over a low garden fence into a neighbouring garden. A dog started barking and another responded from higher up. Suburban Barnes had not seen anything like it in years.

This second garden was heavily over-grown. Diamond hadn't waded far through the sea of grass and weeds when he heard panting to his left. Briefly he thought of the dog and then recognised a human quality in the sound, more like someone gasping for breath. He forced his way through and found Keith lying on his back, his hand to his chest, blood seeping through his fingers.

23

Keith wasn't speaking, but there was plenty of voice in his breathing, a rasp with each struggle for air. The signs were bad. A pink bubble formed between his lips and popped. If his lungs were filling with blood he wouldn't last long.

Diamond took out his mobile and dialled for an ambulance.

He tried giving comforting words without knowing how much Keith understood. He was getting no response from the voice or the eyes.

In all his years in the police, he'd never had one of his team murdered. What could he do? You don't move someone in a state like this, without knowing what damage the shooting has done, which vital organ the bullet may have pierced. The sense of helplessness was overwhelming. He knew about the so-called grace period from thirty minutes to an hour when the shock to the nervous system means that the victim is, in effect, anaesthetised. When that passes, the pain kicks in and can be fatal.

He looked around him. The garden was overgrown and the house appeared derelict. Really he could expect no help until the paramedics came. The two cops were off and away, chasing the man seen running from the scene. If they caught him they wouldn't bring him back this way, over garden fences. They'd take him through the nearest house to the street and drive him straight to the police station.

And no one from inside number sixteen was going to venture into the garden and look over the wall. Any of the inmates who knew what was going on would have escaped by way of the street.

So he waited, powerless to act, and the minutes dragged.

Keith's gasps for breath became shorter and more shallow.

At last came the twin notes of the ambulance approaching Marchant Street. The sound got louder and then stopped, followed by doors slamming. Would the crew find him? He'd tried to explain where he was to the operator who'd taken the emergency call, describing it as the garden backing on to number 16. He had no idea what this parallel street was called.

A voice came from behind the wall: 'Where are you?'

He stood and shouted back.

A head appeared above the wall. 'All right, mate. Stay cool.'

They slung a stretcher over first, and then followed.

He stood back to let the two paramedics assess the injury. It seemed Keith had taken a shot to the diaphragm, just inside the rib-cage. While one was taking the pulse the other said to Diamond, 'Why don't you find the best way out of here? He's in poor shape and we won't want to lug him over that wall.'

Relieved to get any kind of activity, he went to check. Every muscle was shaking.

As he suspected, the house on this plot was empty, the lower windows boarded up. But there was a side gate on a rusty latch that he forced open. It gave access to the street. He jammed it open with a brick.

When he got back, the paramedics had transferred Keith to the stretcher and exposed his arm for an injection that he seemed not to feel at all.

'You'll have to help us get him to the ambulance,' one said, when Diamond had pointed the way to the street. 'Charlie will drive it round.'

So he acted as stretcher-bearer, through the long grass to the gate and outside, where Charlie brought the ambulance in quick time.

'Shall I come with you?' Diamond offered when they'd slid the stretcher inside.

'No point, mate. He's out to the world now and you won't get near when he's in emergency. You're better off chasing the tosser who shot him.'

'Which hospital?'

'Charing Cross. What's his name, by the way?'

By the way. As if it was an afterthought that this was an individual, a good cop, the most loyal of colleagues, a husband and a father. Of course the paramedic didn't mean to sound uncaring. It was just that Diamond was in shock.

He told them. One climbed inside with Keith and the other closed the door and drove off.

The sense of loss was acute.

In the next hour, that neglected mobile was much used. He spoke several times to Louis Voss. He got through to Ingeborg in Bath. He also called Sheila Halliwell and broke the news of the shooting to her, the news every police wife dreads. She said her brother would drive her to the hospital directly. And after her brave acceptance of the emergency came the inevitable question: 'What was he doing, to get himself shot?'

'We don't fully know yet. Probably pursuing a suspect without knowing he was armed.'

'Weren't you with him, then? I thought he was with you.' She may not have intended it to sound like an accusation, but that was how he took it.

'We split up. He was going to interview someone we both thought was harmless.'

'Are they ever? I'd better not say any more, Mr Diamond. I don't trust myself to speak. I'll hang up and get on the road.'

More police arrived, organised a crime scene and called out a forensic team. He said as much as he knew to the team leader and then called the hospital. He was told they'd already X-rayed the patient to assess the damage and he was receiving treatment. His condition was critical.

Somehow, Diamond had to escape from this passive waiting on events. Again he phoned Louis at Fulham Road nick and updated him. 'In all this mayhem I've lost track of what's happening. Did the two cops locate the guy on the run?'

'They nicked him,' Louis said. 'He's here.'

'Thank God for that. Who is he?'

'He's not saying.'

'Not saying anything, you mean?'

'That's right. Silent.'

'Bloody hell. Has he been searched? Doesn't he have anything on him saying who he is?'

'Peter, if he had, I'd have told you, wouldn't I?'

'Has he asked for a solicitor?'

'How do I get this across to you? He's *shtum.*'

'I'm not having that. Who's on the case?'

'DCI Gledhill. He'll want a statement from you.'

'Sod that. We want a statement from the prisoner. Keith is on the critical list. I'm not letting some gun-toting lunatic clam up on us.'

'We think it may be a language problem.'

'Get away!'

'I mean it. He could be a Ukrainian.'

'Christ, yes. Ukrainian. Why didn't I think of that? We must get an interpreter.'

'Don't worry, Peter. Alex Gledhill has it in hand. Our regular interpreter is on his way back from Manchester. We'll get him in tomorrow morning.'

'Like hell you will. I want action. The clock is ticking. I'm sorry, Louis, but I want this pig squealing tonight. I'll find you an interpreter in the next half-hour.'

He switched off. Right off. He didn't want Louis or Gledhill or anyone else telling him what he couldn't do. Mobiles had their merits after all and one was to achieve non-communication.

He knew of a good interpreter. He stopped a taxi at the end of the street and took a ride to the Crimea pub, asking the driver to wait.

True to form, Andriy was at the bar, chatting in Ukrainian to several other drinkers. He grinned at Diamond, recognising him at once. 'My friend from Bath.' He drained the glass of vodka he was holding. 'We were having a nice conversation and you had to leave suddenly. Was everything all right?'

'It's under control, I think,' Diamond said, 'but I still need your help.'

'Cheers, then.' Andriy grinned and pushed the empty glass towards the barmaid.

'For this kind of help, you get vodka by the bottle, not the glass,' Diamond told him. 'I want you to act as my interpreter.'

'Whatever you want, my friend.'

But it took a few minutes more to get through to Andriy that he was required to leave the bar and take a taxi ride somewhere else. The prospect of vodka by the bottle persuaded him.

They were driven to Fulham Road nick. 'How's your head?' Diamond asked in a moment of concern before they went through the front door to meet the desk sergeant.

'Okay,' Andriy said. 'How's yours?'

'Right now it feels like Piccadilly Circus.'

'Maybe you need a drink. Maybe we both do.'

'Not here we don't.'

They went through to the computer room where Louis presided. This evening he was working overtime and most of his team had gone home.

'Any more news?' Diamond asked.

'From the hospital?' Louis shook his head.

'This is Andriy.'

'I know all about Andriy,' Louis said. 'I sent you to him in the first place.' He then asked slowly, to confirm his suspicion, 'Is he your interpreter?'

'Fluent in Ukrainian.'

Louis rolled his eyes.

'And English,' Diamond added. 'So careful what you say. Where's the prisoner?'

Louis hesitated, no doubt thinking what the official line should be on Andriy, and then pointed the way downstairs to the cells. 'On consideration,' he said, 'I'd better come with you.'

Someone must have alerted DCI Gledhill to what was going on, because he rattled down the stairs in pursuit of them, a dapper man with a pencil-thin moustache. 'Can I help you, gentlemen?' he asked in a tone that promised more obstruction than help.

Louis turned and explained who the visitors were, stressing Diamond's senior rank in Bath CID.

'We're about to take a look at the man your boys arrested,' Diamond said, 'and then we'll have him out for an interview. Which cell is it?'

'He's not speaking,' Gledhill said.

'He'll speak to us. Andriy talks his language.'

'I don't think so. I'm the SIO here.'

'Fine. You're welcome to sit in when I interview him.'

'You're out of order, superintendent. This is the Met, not Bath police. We do our own interviewing.'

'I hope I didn't hear right,' Diamond said in a tone that managed to be both subdued and menacing. 'One of my officers, DI Halliwell, is in a critical condition in Charing Cross Hospital, apparently shot by this man, and you're telling me to go to hell.'

'I didn't say that,' Gledhill said. 'I didn't say any such thing.'

'That was the gist of it. You don't have to tell me about procedures in the Met. I served in this nick for five years. If a brother officer came to me from another force enquiring into the shooting of a colleague I wouldn't just offer him full co-operation, I'd shake him by the hand and lead him straight to the perpetrator.'

'It's not about co-operation.'

'Yes, it is, my friend. Here in the Met, of all places, you have to be aware of what's going on across the nation, the inter-force consultation at every level. I'd hate to think Fulham Road has pulled up the drawbridge and refused interviewing facilities to a senior officer in an emergency.'

'That isn't the case.'

'I'm glad to hear it. Which cell?'

Gledhill sighed, defeated. 'The second on your right.'

Diamond slid aside the cover to the Judas window. The man seated on the bed inside was about forty, sallow, with dark, deep-set eyes. His striped shirt looked expensive and his trousers were tailored, evidently part of a suit. The laces had been removed from his shoes, scuffed and muddy from the chase.

A long look didn't help Diamond recognise him, so he closed the window.

'Are we to be allowed an interview room?'

'I'll have him brought up,' Gledhill said. 'This may be a waste of everyone's time. There's no guarantee that he'll talk.'

Diamond grinned faintly and glanced at Louis. In the bad old days, the big man from Bath had more than once been put on report for persuading prisoners to co-operate.

Interview Room 1 was made ready, fresh tapes inserted. 'You can read him his rights, the caution, all that stuff, when he's brought in,' Diamond told Gledhill in a show of altruism. The reality was that he always relied on others to go through the formalities. 'Andriy, we'll have you seated opposite us, next to the prisoner, to do your interpreting. Are you still okay?'

'Thirsty.'

'There's water in front of you,' Gledhill said.

'I can wait,' Andriy said, rolling his eyes.

'We're in shape, then. Let's have him in.'

The custody sergeant brought in the unnamed prisoner, a shorter man than he'd appeared in the cell, with some swelling to his face and left eye. Everything about his demeanour suggested he wouldn't co-operate. He slumped in the chair he was offered and stared at the ceiling.

Gledhill spoke the words for the tape and gave the official caution. Then the focus shifted to Andriy, who appeared as uninterested as the prisoner, probably because he was suffering from alcohol deprivation.

'Over to you,' Gledhill said.

'Andriy,' Diamond said in a sharp tone. He would have kicked him under the table if the space hadn't been boarded in.

It dawned on Andriy finally that he was supposed to do something to earn his next drink. He blinked and turned towards the prisoner. Then he started laughing. He shook with amusement. 'I know this man,' he said. 'What, are you playing a trick on me? Very funny. He's no more Ukrainian than you are. He's English and his name is Jim Jenkins.'

24

'Is this a fact?'

The prisoner reacted with a quick nod. He looked alarmed to be unmasked.

'*English?* We went to all the trouble and expense of getting an interpreter and it turns out you're English?'

And now the Englishman Jim Jenkins found his voice. 'I didn't say I was a foreigner.'

'You didn't say diddley-squat.' Diamond turned to Andriy. 'What can you tell us about him?'

Andriy was looking pensive, with some caginess mixed in. 'Hold on. You hired me to be an interpreter. Two bottles, right? Now you're asking me to be an informer.'

'But you haven't done any interpreting.'

'For informing, the fee goes up. Four bottles.'

DCI Gledhill gave a twitch and said, 'What's this about bottles? I don't understand.'

'It's how he measures his worth,' Diamond said. 'All right, Andriy. Four bottles it is.'

Gledhill was outraged. 'You've no right to make him offers of any sort.'

'I was speaking for you,' Diamond said.

'What? I can't authorise payments off the cuff. There's a procedure.'

'The Met pays two million a year to snouts. We're not going to quibble over two extra bottles.'

'Bottles of what?' the beleaguered Gledhill demanded.

'Never mind. Do you want to talk here, Andriy, or in private?'

'Better in private, I think.'

At this, Jenkins decided to wade in. 'That's out of order. You can't let him make up stuff about me without telling me what it is. I have some legal rights here.'

'Shut your face, Jenkins. I'll tell you every bad thing he says,' Diamond said. 'We'll stop the tape here and adjourn for a bit unless you want to make a full confession. Take him down, sergeant.'

Loudly protesting, Jenkins was removed.

'Now, Andriy,' Diamond said. 'Give us the dirt on that man.'

'James Jenkins? He is a whoremaster, a pimp. You must know this. He is on your files, right?'

Diamond turned to Gledhill with eyebrows raised, and was told, 'I don't personally know every piece of scum in west London. If what you say is true, we probably have him on file, yes.'

'He runs a whorehouse in Barnes,' Andriy went on. 'Before that, for six or seven years, it was managed by a Ukrainian guy called Sergey.'

'Do you know the address?'

'Marchant Street. I can't tell you the number. For myself, I have no need to visit brothels. The madam there is Vikki, former call girl, excellent at her job, never made trouble for Sergey or anyone else. Respected by the girls and the clients. Keeps the house beautiful. Clean bedding and towels, aerosols everywhere, flowers in the rooms.' As an afterthought, he said, 'I know all this from friends, not from experience.'

'Go on.'

'Some time last year, Vikki started going out with an English guy, this Jenkins. Smart, always wore a suit. Sergey didn't object, even when Jenkins started visiting Marchant Street, hanging around the house to chat up Vikki. Then last year in July, when all Ukrainians celebrated *Ivana Kupala,* the midsummer festival, Vikki married Jenkins.

Overnight, Sergey was called to a meeting with the godfather who owns the house and many others and was told he had to move to a low-down backstreet knocking shop in Fulham. No warning, no appeal. He had to go, and he went.'

'And Jenkins was installed there?'

'Do I have to tell you what the Ukrainians thought about it, an all-Ukrainian house taken over by an Englishman? He is not popular in our community. No one can touch him, because he has the blessing of the high-ups. They don't want to lose Vikki, get me? So he lives like a good Ukrainian, goes to church on Sundays, eats our food, tries to speak the language. We think he is using Vikki.'

'That's a dangerous game if he is. Does he carry a gun?'

'He'd be a fool if he didn't.'

'But you say he's untouchable.'

Andriy inclined his head slightly to one side, the Ukrainian equivalent of the Gallic shrug.

Diamond had the picture now, or enough of it to put the screws on Jenkins. The information had been well worth four bottles. With Gledhill's grudging consent, Andriy was driven back to the Crimea on the understanding that the car would call at an off-licence to pick up his payment.

'Cheap at the price,' Diamond said and got only a glare for his economy.

Jenkins was brought back and the questioning started over again. The untouchable pimp was plainly worried over what may have been said while he was back in the cell.

'What am I charged with?'

'Nothing yet,' Diamond said. 'You're being questioned on suspicion of discharging a firearm with intent to kill.'

'That's wrong.'

'Yes, it could be if Inspector Halliwell doesn't get through the night. He's in a critical condition. You'd better pray that he survives.'

His eyes stretched wide in alarm. 'I didn't know the man was a cop.'

'You live and learn. Give us your version of what happened.'

He drew his arms across his body as if he'd suddenly woken up on a Carpathian mountain with a north wind blowing.

'We're waiting,' Diamond said.

A heavy sigh. 'I'd better explain my difficulty. I'm just a businessman, good at my job, reliable. I work for Ukrainians and with Ukrainians. I'm married to a Ukrainian and Vikki is in the business too. But there's hostility towards me because I'm not one of them. It's not just me being paranoid. Vikki notices it, too. I have to watch my back all the time.'

'Is this why you armed yourself?'

'You bet I did.' He paused as if regretting what he'd said and trying to think of a way of qualifying it. 'By "armed", I mean being on my guard.'

'But you own a hand gun?'

'Er, yes.'

'Go on.'

'Today is a bank day. I'm supposed to collect the proceeds from the business, count them, pay the staff and get the surplus to the bank. It's a responsibility I take seriously. Like a lot of businesses we deal in cash and it can amount to a seriously large sum.'

'That I believe,' Gledhill said.

Jenkins rubbed his arms, still apparently feeling the chill. 'I was in the office with my wife Vikki getting the money sorted when there was a caller. We have an entry-phone system for the front door, and CCTV. You have to be secure in these times. There was something iffy about this guy. How would I know he was one of yours? He didn't say.'

'He wouldn't. He'd never get past the door.'

'He asked for my wife by name. That was

suspicious in itself because she looked at the screen and didn't recognise him. We have our regular callers and some of them know Vikki's name, but this guy was a stranger to her. I scooped up the money and my account books and moved into the room next door.'

'Leaving your wife to deal with him?'

'She's experienced. And I would be on hand to help if he caused trouble. As I just told you, we're constantly on our guard from jealous Ukrainians.'

'He wasn't Ukrainian.'

'Put it this way. He spoke English into the intercom, but you can't tell unless they have a heavy accent. We let him in. The office is at the top of the stairs.'

'I know,' Diamond said. 'I was there this afternoon, trying to find what happened to him.'

'He immediately started talking to Vikki about things that happened way back, almost twenty years ago. This was not good. Our clients aren't interested in the past.'

'We know what interests your clients.'

'He talked of some girl who came here — to London, I mean — and went missing. He was questioning Vikki and she was trying to be helpful, telling him things, but it seemed to me she was getting herself — and me — in trouble. Bad things happened in the past, specially in those years after independence when thousand of Ukrainians quit their country. It's safer not to talk about it.'

'You were listening to all this?'

'From the next room, yes, and not liking what I heard. The guy was full of questions about this particular girl whose name he didn't know, and who was dead now. Vikki, being the helpful soul she is, was doing her best to remember her. Then he let out that the girl had been murdered and buried somewhere in the West Country. *Murdered.*' He scraped his hand through his hair and let out a shaky breath, reliving the shock.

'Didn't you know about this?' Diamond asked.

'Very little. I heard there were some killings back then, but it was way before I got involved in the escort business.'

'Two pimps and a working girl,' Diamond said, more for Gledhill's ears than Jenkins'. 'I got that from Andriy.'

'All I can tell you is that it caused one hell of a shake-up. Some girls got so frightened they quit. Nobody knows for sure who carried out the killings, but there are people around today who were minders then. They've risen in the ranks and are big wheels now. Stupidly Vikki was rabbiting on about all of this to a total stranger, all the dirty washing. She spooked me out so much I pulled my gun and stepped into the room.'

'You drew a gun on him?'

'I didn't go in there for conversation. Too much talking had been done already. He took one look at the shooter and was out of there.'

'And you chased him?'

'Down the stairs and into the garden. I wanted to scare him seriously, put the frighteners on him, so he'd be more in awe of me than the people he was snooping for. He must have been across the garden and over the wall like a steeplechaser. I chased him, but that's a high wall and I didn't get over at the first try. When I did get a foothold and drag myself up he wasn't in sight, but I felt sure he was in that next garden somewhere. It's overgrown. The grass is really high.'

'I've been there,' Diamond said.

'I sat on top of the wall. I could see the whole garden from there. It was cat and mouse because I had the high position and the gun. I waited for him to make a move.'

'How long?'

'Fifteen minutes, maybe less. It felt like fifteen. I figured that when he did break from cover I'd take a shot over his head to panic him. Finally I saw the long grass move and I knew exactly where he was lying. Sure enough, he surfaced and started running towards the empty house. I shot over his head and the recoil nearly knocked me off the wall.'

'You missed?'

'Of course I bloody missed. I meant to miss, but then the stupid sod stopped and turned towards me. I pulled the trigger a second time out of pure tension. I saw a hand go out and he dropped and I realised I'd hit him. I jumped down and went over to look and I could see he was in a bad way. I was still trying to think what to do when the police came over the wall. The rest you know.'

'You ran off.'

'I panicked, didn't I?'

'What happened to the gun?'

'I dropped it somewhere in that long grass.'

'You're saying you didn't intend to hit him? We're supposed to believe that? What do you take us for?'

'I've got no experience using guns. You can look at my record. I've got form for other stuff, but nothing to do with firearms.'

'Come on, Jenkins, it's your gun. You

admitted that just now.'

'For self-defence. I'm in a dangerous job, for Christ's sake.'

'You had plenty of time to think if you were going to use it. Cat and mouse, your words. You cold-bloodedly waited for DI Halliwell to show himself and then you loosed off two shots.'

'That's wrong. I want a brief.'

'You're going to need one. And you'd better get praying as well.'

The hospital told them Keith's condition remained critical. He was in intensive care and unable to speak. His wife had arrived and was spending the night at the hospital, but even she was being kept away from the patient.

'Doesn't sound good,' he said to Louis. 'He lost pints of blood. I know that. Do you think I should be with his wife?'

Louis shook his head. 'Right now she'll be blaming you for what happened. It's not personal, it's inevitable.'

'I gave the poor old lad what I thought was the easy option, visiting this gentle couple in Barnes who go to church on Sundays. Olena was really wide of the mark over them.'

'Didn't you say one of the family drove

Mrs Halliwell to London?'

'Her brother.'

'They don't need you, then. Come back with me. I've got a spare bedroom.'

'What time is it?'

'Nearly ten. You look bushed.'

In the morning he heard that Keith had responded to treatment and was out of intensive care. A short visit would be permitted. Elated, he took a taxi there.

In the corridor leading to the ward, his heart sank at the sight of Sheila Halliwell and her brother walking towards him. Situations like this always defeated him. He stopped and turned up his palms in apology.

Sheila stepped forward and offered her face for a token kiss, which he supplied, wishing he'd shaved before starting out. She said, 'He's going to be all right, they say. I'm sorry I was so sharp when you phoned yesterday. It must have been the shock.'

'You've seen him?'

'Yes, and he told me neither of you could have had any idea he was going to have a gun pulled on him.'

'Is he well enough for me to go in?'

'He'll be upset if you don't. He keeps saying there's something he must tell you.'

■ ■ ■ ■

The patient was in a side ward, tubed up for a transfusion. He appeared to be sleeping. He had more colour than Diamond expected, but creases of strain showed in his face, even in repose.

'We can postpone the funeral by the look of you.'

The eyelids flickered and opened.

'Me, being unfunny, as usual.'

'Good to see you, guv.' Keith's voice was not much more than a whisper. 'I messed up big time.'

'You didn't. You're a hero. Are you sore?'

'Full of morphine. Hard to keep my eyes open.'

'Sheila said you want to tell me something.'

'Yes?' Unfortunately he was starting to drift off. The eyes closed again.

'Was it about yesterday?'

'Yesterday, yes.'

'You got to the house and spoke to Vikki. I know that much.'

'Vikki?'

'The madam, at sixteen Marchant Street.'

He opened his eyes briefly again. 'She knows, guv. Vikki knows. You've got to see her.' Then he was gone again.

A hand on Keith's free arm, a gentle squeeze, and he left.

This would not be easy considering he had Vikki's husband in custody and 16 Marchant Street was a crime scene. Police cars would be standing outside and the house would have emptied of girls and clients. Vikki had lost her husband and her livelihood. Even if he caught up with the lady she wouldn't be in a frame of mind to tell all.

He called at the Crimea as soon as it opened and looked for Andriy, thinking he might know where Vikki lived.

No Andriy.

'I don't understand,' the barmaid said. 'Always he is here when I open. I hope he is not ill.'

He guessed what was amiss. 'He took some bottles home last night. Probably sleeping it off.'

His only other contact was Olena. He had to try.

He went first to the church and found her removing used candles from in front of an icon. 'There is nothing I can tell you about Viktorya,' she said, and contradicted herself by adding, 'She is upset. Distress.'

'You've seen her, then?'

'I cannot speak of this in front of St Volodymyr.'

'Shall we go outside?'

'I don't think so.'

'Viktorya is distressed because her husband is at the police station. Did she tell you?'

Excluding him, she opened a new box of candles and set them out neatly in front of the shrine.

He said, 'Would you light one for my friend, Keith Halliwell, who was shot yesterday? I think St Volodymyr will be sympathetic.'

She sighed and walked with him to the main door. On the steps, she said, 'She is at my house. I don't know what happen. You are good man, I think. Be gentle, yes?'

He walked the short distance to Meon Road. Vikki came to the door, opened it a fraction, saw him and slammed it shut. He bent down and talked through the letterbox. 'Vikki, I've come from Olena. Do I have to go back and ask her to leave the church and unlock her own front door?'

After some hesitation, she opened it and glared. No bread and salt welcome this time. The blonde hair was in need of combing and the eyes were red-lidded. She turned her back on him and stepped into the front room where the photos stood on the mantelpiece, including the one of Vikki, or Viktorya, as she was known here. They sat facing each other on the two chairs, overlooked by the crucifix.

'Olena doesn't know what goes on in Marchant Street, does she?' he said.

'She thinks the best of everyone,' Vikki said. 'She is like a mother to me. You don't tell your mother things that will trouble her.'

'But she knows your husband is being held for shooting a policeman?'

'She doesn't know it all.'

'Keith is going to pull through, I think. I saw him this morning. He told me you gave him information. In view of what happened I'm going to have to ask you to repeat it.'

She shrugged and looked away.

Softly, softly wasn't going to work with Vikki. 'We're holding your husband on a minor rap at present. We have to decide what to charge him with. Could be evading arrest, illegal possession of a firearm, shooting with intent to kill. He's lucky it isn't murder. The courts take a hard line on cop killers.'

'He never meant to kill.'

'That's his story. He claims he wasn't aiming the gun, that he's inexperienced at using it.'

'I've never known him to fire it. We've both been under a lot of pressure.'

'Since he took over from Sergey?'

Her eyes widened at how much he knew. She gave a nod.

He judged that she was as ready to cooperate at this moment as she ever would be. 'I expect Keith asked you about the Ukrainian woman we found buried in Bath?'

She gave a nervous, angry sigh, registering that she'd been manoeuvred into this. 'He thought I might know her.'

'From so far back?'

'I was around then. I can tell you what I told him, if you'll leave me alone. We talked about two girls I remember who were trafficked a couple of years after independence.'

'Which was when?'

'Independence was 1991. This must have been 1993.'

'What age would they have been?'

'Late teens. No older.'

'Did they work for you?'

'For me?' She shook her head. 'I was nobody then, just a prossie. We were all trapped in the game, but we knew each other and there was a kind of team thing. I mentioned these two because they got away.

It was a scary time. High summer, which is always the worst. The mob were at war for control of this part of London. Pimps were murdered and at least one girl was shot. These two seized their chance and fled. One of them got back to the Ukraine and years later I had a card from her. I don't know how she got my address.'

'News can travel both ways. You're well known, I gather. And so is your address.'

'Maybe. This girl Tatiana was asking if I knew what happened to Nadia, the other one who escaped. They split up because Nadia didn't want to return to the Ukraine. She had no family to go back to. She'd been raised in an orphanage and left at fifteen and immediately was forced into sex work. That's not unusual. The traffickers take the good-looking girls straight from the orphanages. They leave with just the clothes they're wearing.'

'Did you know Nadia personally?'

'Not well. By sight, I would say. After they made a run for it, her plan was to get out of London. She took a train from Paddington. That's the last anyone saw of her.'

'Paddington? She headed west. She could have made it to Bath or Bristol. Would they have followed her there and killed her?'

'The mob? I doubt it. They were too busy

with their battles here.'

'Later, then?'

She shook her head. 'She wasn't worth the trouble. Girls are just goods, like fruit machines. They get replaced.'

Callous words. He could see that in her terms they were accurate. 'You say you knew her by sight. Can you describe her for me?'

'About my height — average. Blue eyes widely spaced. Straight nose. Even teeth. Good legs, very good.'

He thought of the femur he'd held in his hand.

'Hair colour?'

She smiled faintly. 'We all changed our hair often, to reinvent ourselves. It made us feel better. She could have been any colour. It was straight and long. I know she was an orphan but I always thought she was from Cossack stock. She liked watching the racing on TV, not to bet, just to see the horses. They adore their horses, the Cossacks. And she was confident, believed in herself. If she didn't survive, I'm surprised.'

'Do you know her surname?'

'I didn't at the time. In the trade we use first names and some of them are false, but Tatiana mentioned it in her card. She was Nadia Berezan.'

'Thanks.' He made a note.

355

Nadia Berezan, call girl.

She was still a long shot, but she was Ukrainian and she'd travelled to the West Country at about the right time. And from what he had learned about her origins, no one would have reported her as a missing person.

25

Forced this time to do his own driving, he headed out of London in the slow lane of the M4 at a rate that required everyone else to overtake, even old ladies in rusty Minis. For much of the journey he was reflecting on the shooting of Keith, questioning his own motive in sending him to deal with Vikki whilst taking Andriy for himself. He'd let Keith talk him out of his first intention, which was to go to Marchant Road. He couldn't even argue that it had been about dividing forces according to risk. The decision had been taken on nothing more serious than Keith's offer to cope with another house visit, another *chorni khlib* and *kvas* welcome. Up to then, Vikki had seemed the softer option and, being the guv'nor, he would have taken it as his right — in which case, his conscience would still have plagued him. Face it, Peter Diamond, he thought, either way, you're a selfish bastard.

As another exit sign came up, he forced his thoughts to the challenges still to come, primarily his next skirmish with Georgina. She was certain to hold him responsible for the shooting of Keith and she might well think an enquiry was required. Diversionary tactics were called for.

At Membury services he stopped to fill up and let the team know he was returning. Ingeborg took the call. She ought to have been impressed that he was using the mobile. It merited at least a 'cool'. But no, she was completely focused on Keith.

'He's still in the world of the living,' he told her and then the demon inside made him say, 'I saw him this morning, happy as a pig in shit.'

'No kidding?'

'We'll have to drag him out of there if you want to see him again. The nurses are real babes.'

'Swell,' she said flatly, her concern for Halliwell on the wane. 'Last night you sounded seriously worried.'

'Tired, I expect. The good news is that we have a name to work with.' He told her about Nadia Berezan. 'Do what you can on that miraculous computer of yours to see if there was ever a woman of that name in Bath or Bristol.'

'Wouldn't she have changed her name?' Ingeborg said. 'I would, if I was on the run from the mob.'

'Not so simple as you think, Inge. She'd need proof of identity if she was applying for benefits, as she'd surely need to. A false passport is expensive and takes time to acquire, even if you know where to go for one.'

'I guess.'

'We have to work with what we've got. Or rather you have to work with what I've got.'

'Can't argue with that, boss.'

'How's it going in the incident room? The Bristol boys behaving themselves?'

'They're trying to reconstruct Rupert's last few days on Lansdown, looking for more witnesses.'

'It sounds the way to go. And you? Have you successfully infiltrated the Sealed Knot?'

'I don't know about that, guv. I've started my basic training as a foot soldier. So far it's as exciting as the girl guides. Learning the rules and how to carry a pike. Lesson Three is tonight. We've been promised some swordplay.'

'Where do you meet? I'm tempted to sneak in and have a peek.'

'I'm not telling.'

'I must get on the road again. By the way,' he threw in casually, 'is Georgina on the premises?'

'She was here at the crack of dawn this morning, extremely uptight about Keith. She said she was going to phone the hospital. She thought it best if all of us didn't pester them with calls.'

'Sensible.'

'She'll be over the moon to hear he's recovering so well. I'll tell her as soon as I'm off the phone.'

'I'd rather you didn't.'

There was a pause. He could almost hear her trying to work it out. 'Don't you want her to know?'

'Keep her guessing a bit longer. Sympathy sits better with Georgina than good news.'

He resumed his sedate drive and eventually left the motorway at Junction 18, south on the A46, the busy route over the rump of the Cotswolds and down into Bath. Only he wasn't ready for the city. After Dyrham Park he detoured right, onto a road known as Gorse Lane that links to Lansdown. All the intensity of London and the Ukrainians had left him needing to reacquaint himself with the source of the mystery.

This was a grey, bleak morning and the place names fitted the conditions. Somewhere to his left was Cold Ashton. Looming on the right, Freezing Hill, where the royalists had unwisely formed their battle array in 1643. Ahead were Hanging Hill and Slaughter Lane. He chugged up the steep north scarp of Lansdown and pulled in at the potholed stopping point for the Grenvile Monument. He had it to himself.

Outside, a keen north-easterly chilled the flesh. He wouldn't linger long, just enough to stretch his limbs and remind himself of the terrain that had hosted two unexplained murders. The monument didn't interest him. He wanted the view of the vast limestone plateau. In the foreground lay the battlefield where two great armies had clashed; and where, centuries later, ten thousand had come to watch the first big re-enactment. On the other side the ground plunged into a partly wooded area where the skeleton had been buried. Away in the distance, two miles along the road, the gilt lantern top of William Beckford's Tower marked the graveyard where Rupert Hope had been found.

Between the murder sites lay all those places for recreation: the racecourse, the golf club, sports pitches and the setting for Lansdown Fair and its modern incarnation, the car boot sale. The down didn't have bad associations for everyone. For some it held good memories, outsiders coming in at fifty to one, match-winning goals, holes in one, bargain buys, conquests of every sort. For Peter Diamond it was an adversary; dispiriting, tormenting, defying his attempts to get a rational explanation of two violent killings. He was convinced that the truth of the mystery was here, waiting to be discovered.

Beginning to shiver from the cold, he took a long look at the panorama from the battlefield to the tower. Mainly turf, but with clumps of trees, and the occasional building, the ground was unremarkable, the sort of country you drove through unthinkingly. Yet it had endured since the Jurassic period some 150 million years ago, when a warm, shallow sea covered all of this and deposited the limestone, the source of Bath's prosperity. This ancient hill was the silent witness he couldn't question. He'd hoped that being here would inspire him with a sudden crystal clear revelation, but there was none.

'Bugger you, Lansdown,' he said out loud.

Georgina awaited.

Instead of calling at the incident room he trudged upstairs to her office, bent on getting the worst over first.

'Come.'

The door was open and she was standing in front of her desk with her arms folded. As if that wasn't intimidating enough, the Queen on the wall looked over her right shoulder.

'You're back.'

'That's the size of it,' he admitted.

'What on earth happened to result in Keith Halliwell being shot?'

He gave her his version.

'Didn't anyone know it was a house of ill fame?'

A phrase he hadn't heard in many years. Where had she got that? In the dorm at her posh girls' school secretly reading the *News of the World*? 'We were operating alone at that stage. We didn't have the local police to ask.'

'You used to be in the Met. Wasn't Barnes a part of your old beat?'

'Many years ago, ma'am. It was probably a respectable house in those days. We were given the address by a churchwoman.'

'Who'd been duped, as you were.'

Stung by that, he said, 'Even if we'd known it was a — er — house of ill fame, I wouldn't have expected anyone to pull a gun on Keith. No way could we have predicted anything like that.'

'How is he now? Have you seen him?'

He was more reserved than he'd been with Ingeborg. 'He's off the critical list.'

'That much I found out myself by phoning the hospital. They seem to think he'll be unable to work for several weeks.'

'With a bullet through his middle, I expect so.' He added, making it sound like a throwaway line, 'Good thing we can cover for him.'

Georgina seized on it at once. 'I don't know how. He was one of your SIOs, a key person in the investigation. How can you possibly replace him?'

'I'll do it myself.'

She took a sharp, audible breath. 'I don't think so, Peter.'

He waited for the broadside.

'We agreed you were CIO, an executive role. You don't seem to appreciate what it is to be a senior policeman. You shouldn't have gone to London at all. Your place is here, at headquarters, supervising both arms of the investigation.'

'The trip was arranged through a contact of mine. I had to be there.'

She ignored that. 'This has all worked out very conveniently for you, hasn't it? From the beginning you wanted to run both inquiries yourself. You managed to get the

Rupert Hope case brought back from Bristol on very dubious grounds.'

'With your blessing,' he put in.

'With my compliance. You shoehorned our Bristol colleagues into the same incident room as the skeleton inquiry.'

'Only because you wouldn't provide a second room.'

'And now you want carte blanche to roll up your sleeves and go to work on the case.'

'Someone has to do it, ma'am.'

'What about John Leaman?'

'He's needed to take care of all the other stuff that comes up, knife crime, drugs, domestics.'

'You've got an answer for everything.'

He nodded, and he'd let Georgina have the last word. All in all, he'd come out of it better than he expected.

Downstairs, the team were excited at the possibility that the skeleton had an identity at last. Ingeborg was checking every database she could think of. Others were on the phone trying to prise information from the benefits office, medical practices and women's refuges. Each hoped to be the one who shouted, 'Found her!'

All this energy lifted Diamond's spirits. 'Ukrainians are strong church-goers,' he said, airing his new-found knowledge. 'She may have gone to one of the churches here and asked for help.'

'But which?' Ingeborg said. 'There's no Ukrainian Orthodox church in Bath that I know of.'

'Catholicism is strong over there. She might have looked for a Catholic church.'

DC Paul Gilbert, the rookie in the team, piped up, 'St John's in South Parade, or St Mary's in Julian Road.'

'Are you a Bible-basher?'

'No, guv. I just happen to know.'

'Your job, then. Seek and ye may find.'

From across the room one of the Bristol detectives said out of the side of his mouth, 'Thus spake the Lord.'

Diamond didn't hear. He was looking over Ingeborg's shoulder, trying to make sense of what was on the screen.

'Just thought I'd check the churches,' she said. 'He's right. St John's and St Mary's.'

'Worth a go,' he said. 'You're a young woman. Put yourself in her situation. She manages to escape from a vice ring in London. She's unlikely to have much money. Gets on a train at Paddington and ends up here. The first question is why — what's the attraction?'

'Why did any of us end up here? It's a

nice place to live.'

'She was desperate. I doubt if she was making that kind of choice.'

'She knew someone, then. She planned to join them, thinking they might help her get a new start.'

'That's more like it.'

'But I've tried looking for Ukrainians in Bath, and found nobody. I expect some came, but there's no record of it.'

'This is where the computer lets you down,' he said. 'It stores all those gigabytes of data, but if someone hasn't kept a record of what you want, it's no help. People who stay with friends don't get on computers.'

She laughed. 'Good thing. It would lead to no end of trouble.'

'But you know what I'm getting at? You put a lot of faith in this as an information tool but nothing has yet been devised that gets even close to word of mouth. We're going to have to get out there and ask people questions.'

'About something that happened twenty-odd years ago? Are memories that reliable?'

'Nadia was different. How many Ukrainians have you and I met? I'm sure I'd remember.'

'True.'

'I have a description from Vikki. Average

height. Blue eyes, widely spaced, straight nose, even teeth, good legs, straight, long hair that could have been any colour because she changed it often.'

'Don't get me wrong, guv,' Ingeborg said, 'but half my friends look like that. An e-fit might work better.'

'Do you think so?'

'It depends how good Vikki's memory is and if she's willing to do it.'

'I promised to leave her alone in return for the information I've just given you.'

'We're not asking her to incriminate herself.'

'I'll ask Louis if he can fix it. Personally, I never had much faith in photofits and e-fits aren't much better. They all look like extra-terrestrials to me.'

'It's something to show. The public respond to visual images.'

'I'll get it organised.' He got back on track. 'Any other reason she might have chosen Bath?'

'She heard about it from one of the punters?'

He snapped his fingers. 'Good thought, Inge. Here's a scenario. The guy lives here and visits London on business. Likes to have sex when he's away from home and gets to know Nadia. He's rich and treats her kindly.

She thinks if she can find him he may set her up, but it doesn't play like that. He has a wife and a career and a respectable life here. When she traces him, he gets in a panic. He agrees to meet her late one night on Lansdown and kills her.'

'Not bad,' she said. 'Difficult to prove. How would we ever find him?'

A voice behind said, 'And where's the connection with Operation Cavalier?'

He turned to find Septimus had crossed the room.

'Rupert Hope,' Septimus said, as if memories needed jogging.

Diamond was at his best when a little bluffing was necessary. He hadn't forgotten how important it was to keep both strands of the enquiry linked if possible. 'For businessman read lecturer. Rupert was around in the early nineties, wasn't he?'

'But making regular trips to London?'

'Researches. The British Museum. The Imperial War Museum. The British Library.'

Septimus grinned. 'Quick thinking.'

'It's only a theory. How's your side of the investigation going?'

'We've been working on the days between the re-enactment and his death. We traced a few more witnesses, dog-walkers and car-booters. They all agreed he was acting strangely.'

'From the blow on the head?'

'It sounds like it. He could talk, but he had no idea who he was, or what to do, except he stole food when he was hungry. He slept rough and wandered about the down until his killer caught up with him and finished him off.'

'You're assuming both attacks came from the same individual?'

'It's the most likely explanation. Similar injuries.'

'And in each case the attacker didn't leave the weapon lying about nearby. Is the search of the cemetery complete?'

'All done. A few objects were picked up and sent for testing, but the result was negative. I think the killer was smart. He took the weapon away with him.'

'We're still talking about a blunt instrument, right?'

'Something clean, that left no traces in the head wound. Heavy enough to split the skin and dent the skull, but not to cleave it. Yes, blunt is right.'

26

That evening Peter Diamond stood in shadow at one end of a disused aircraft hangar watching and hearing the clash of pikes as three pairs went through their movements. The ashwood weapons, some sixteen feet in length, looked and sounded dangerous, even though the moves were being choreographed by an expert, an officer of the Sealed Knot. Knowing Ingeborg's steely resolve to be at least as capable as any man, Diamond wasn't surprised to see her wielding her pike with gusto. Like the others she was wearing casual clothes except for a metal helmet and leather gauntlet gloves.

'We'll try that again,' the officer said. 'First positions. Pikes at the advance.'

They stepped back, hoisted the cumbersome staves to waist height and rested them on their shoulders.

Diamond was thinking he wouldn't have

gone into battle armed only with one of those. Engrossed in all this, he failed to notice he was not alone.

'Thinking about enlisting?' The voice at his side made him jerk in surprise. The speaker was a woman with a silver ponytail. Her stylish black suede jacket and pale blue jeans projected self-confidence, as did the voice. Definitely not an interloper, as he was.

'Hasn't crossed my mind,' he said.

'It's good for fitness.' She seemed a fine advert herself, over seventy, he reckoned, yet with the figure of a woman thirty years younger. 'You could do a lot worse.'

'I do,' he said, patting his pot belly. 'All the time.'

She smiled.

He asked, 'Am I in the way here?'

'You're welcome to watch. Is it the young lady who interests you?'

He couldn't get away with anything here. 'Not specially.'

'These days the female recruits insist on doing everything,' she said. 'When I joined more than thirty years ago we delicate creatures didn't think about joining in the fighting. We were angels of mercy, ministering to the dying and wounded. And if that sounds wimpish — is that the word? — it was actually rather bold, wearing low-cut frocks and leaning over fellows. That's how I met my husband.'

'Nice work.'

'The modern generation want to wear armour and carry pikes for liberation's sake. They don't know the half of it.'

'You've been a member how long?'

'Still am. An active member, too, out on the battlefield. The neckline is more modest these days, but I'll carry on as long as my knees allow me.'

'You did say more than thirty years?' People often exaggerate about spans of time. However, this sprightly lady might be a useful witness if she'd been a Sealed Knot member for that long.

'I can tell you precisely when I joined. It got going in Bath in 1971 with a commemorative parade, as they called it, got up by Count Nicolai Tolstoy — handsome man — and his King's Own Army, which was based in Sherborne. I saw them lined up, wonderfully gorgeous and magnificent, with their horses and banners, and vowed to join at the first opportunity. Next year we had a skirmish on the battlefield and I was part of it.'

'Comforting the fallen?'

She laughed. 'They seemed to appreciate it.'

At the end of the hangar another order was shouted. The soldiers lowered their pikes to the horizontal, all pointing to where Diamond and his companion were standing.

'Advancing at point of pike,' she told him. 'It's a fearsome sight in battle. Just imagine.'

'It's pretty scary from here. Are they about to charge us?'

'I don't think so. You're not from Cromwell's lot, are you?'

'Not when I last checked.'

'If you were, you'd be wishing you had your own pikestaff at least as long as theirs and fifty others with you. And even then, you'd probably not survive. The front men are usually impaled, but the others behind them still push. Dreadful for men and horses.'

'You're talking about the real thing. You don't injure each other when you're putting on one of your mock battles?'

'Thankfully, no. The pikeheads look like metal, but they're wood or vulcanised rubber painted silver.'

'You wouldn't want a poke in the eye with one of them.'

'Preferably not.'

The officer shouted another order. The pikes were raised.

'You see?' she said. 'That's the difference between real war and re-enactment. Our pikemen fight with points upwards when they clash. Safety first. We're disciplined. The officers have to pass a series of safety tests, and that goes for the enemy as well as ourselves.'

'And who are the enemy?'

'The parliamentarians, of course. We're fighting for the King.'

'Doesn't everyone want to be a cavalier?'

She shook her head. 'If you're left wing in your politics you probably want to join the other lot. Suits me. I don't want to listen to all that rubbish about the minimum wage and the right to strike.'

He sidestepped the politics. 'And do the roundheads meet in a hall somewhere and drill separately?'

'They use this place on the nights we're not here.' She gripped his arm. 'Ah, now they're putting the pikes away and they'll do some swordplay, just for fun. Our pike-men don't carry swords in battle. The young lady's done some fencing before. I've watched her. She can take on any of the men.'

He could believe Ingeborg was a fencer.

She'd never mentioned it, though.

'It sounds to me as if this is a big part of your life,' he said.

'The best part, believe me. And it isn't only battles. We do a huge amount for charity.'

'So I've heard,' he said, deciding this might be the moment to raise the matter on his mind. 'I dare say you remember most of the women who've enlisted.'

'Since I joined, certainly.'

'Was there ever one from East Europe?'

'In the King's Army? Not to my knowledge.'

'Her name might have been Nadia.'

'Rings no bells with me, dear.'

Disappointing.

Ingeborg had put on a fencing mask and was clashing swords with a young man who had the swagger of one of the Three Musketeers, but without the skill. A parry, a lunge and Inge whipped the sword out of his hand. It clattered on the concrete and slid across the floor, leaving him as hors de combat as Diamond's latest theory.

'If she carries on like this, she'll be picked for single combat,' his companion said. 'That's a massive honour. I'm glad she's joined.'

'She's no angel of mercy, that's for sure.'

She laughed. 'I hope you're not mocking old-timers like me.'

'I'm not. She won't get a husband beating up the guys.'

She turned to look at him 'You're not her father, are you?'

'Lord, no.'

'Grandfather?'

He grimaced at that. Old people lose all concept of age.

'A roundhead spy?' She was not giving up.

'You're safe there. I'm a policeman. Peter Diamond, Detective Superintendent.'

'I wasn't far out, then.' She sighed. 'I should have guessed. You're something to do with that dreadful murder of one of our members, the lecturer from Bristol.'

'A detective on the case, yes.'

Her posture changed. She became defensive. 'I don't think it's anything to do with us. Pure coincidence that he happened to be a new recruit.' Sensing apparently that this sounded unfeeling, she added, 'We're all very upset, naturally. We support each other like family.'

'Did you know the victim personally, then?'

'In point of fact, no. He would have done his arms drill in Bristol.'

'Distant family, then?'

She gave an embarrassed smile. 'I suppose you could say that.'

She'd been so generous with information that he decided to lay out his game plan. 'I came here hoping to find out more about what goes on. Do you keep a list of members?'

'A muster roll. I don't, but I'm sure there is one.'

'What about former members? Are they listed somewhere?'

'I expect so, but it may be restricted information. I'm not a spokesperson for the Knot. I'm sure they have a policy about such things. You'll have to do it the official way and talk to the senior officer.'

'Good advice, ma'am. And is your name restricted information as well?'

She laughed. 'Agnes Swithin.'

Swithin. It clicked into place. 'Married to Major Swithin, golfer and member of the Lansdown Society?'

'And one-time handsome cavalier,' she said. 'Unfortunately the golf took over. You can't serve two masters and I'm sorry to say Reggie prefers the little white ball to good King Charles.'

'So you met Rupert Hope.'

She turned to face him, puzzled. 'Why do

you say that?'

'You and your husband saw him trying to break into cars. You called out the police.'

Her eyes widened. 'Was that the man who was murdered?'

'The same.'

'I had no idea. Didn't make the connection at all. Why was he doing such a stupid thing? We spotted him behaving suspiciously and thought it our public duty to report him.'

'Did you speak to him?'

'No, we kept our distance. At our age you don't tangle with car thieves. I kept him under observation through my field glasses until your people arrived. I had no inkling that he was a fellow Knotter. What on earth possessed him to behave like that?'

'He'd been hit on the head. We think he'd lost his memory.'

She thought about it with a troubled expression. 'Oh dear. You've made me feel guilty for reporting him.'

'No need, ma'am. You did the right thing as you saw it.'

At the other end, Ingeborg was fencing with another of the squad, a young man with a better technique. The exchange was longer this time, the blades flashing under the strip light. She took a couple of steps backwards and appeared to be on the retreat. A sudden forward movement signalled the riposte, a clever feint, drawing the opponent's defence. He'd committed and she lunged again and had the point of her sword at his chest. He lowered his sword.

'Good on you, girl!' Agnes Swithin said, clapping.

The instructor wasn't so delighted. 'It's not meant to be competitive,' he told Ingeborg. 'You could cause damage like that. We're exercising here, not trying out for the Olympics.'

'Sorry.'

Agnes clicked her tongue and told Diamond, 'He's putting her down because she's a woman. They hate it if you show any talent.'

'You've obviously fenced with the foil before,' the instructor was saying to Ingeborg. 'Have you used a backsword?'

She shook her head.

'You'd know it better as a rapier, the Civil War weapon of choice, but you won't get to use one in battle unless you transfer to the cavalry. Can you ride?'

'A bit.'

'You might like to make enquiries.'

At Diamond's side, Agnes took a sharp,

accusing breath. 'There speaks an infantry officer. Doesn't want her showing him up. Actually she'd look good on a horse. At least a third of our cavalry are ladies.'

'Really?'

'Think about it. You see far more horse-women than men out and about, don't you?'

After losing one of his team already this week he wasn't sure he wanted Ingeborg fighting duels on horseback. 'She looks more like infantry to me. Do you have a say in these decisions?'

'No, I'm a minor player.'

'Were you there for the big one, in 1993?'

'All these questions. This is about the skeleton they dug up on Lansdown, isn't it? Yes, I was there for the major muster and I remember it well. I wouldn't have missed it for the world, and I can assure you I didn't see any foul play. I was too busy with my casualties.'

'Real casualties?'

She flapped her hand. 'A few dents and bruises. Nothing serious. If there is, I wave to the St John Ambulance man. There's always one on hand.'

'So you didn't spot anyone behaving suspiciously in the battle?'

'I'd remember if I did. It all passed off very smoothly and we had a lovely write-up in the paper. If you ask me, the Sealed Knot had nothing to do with that skeleton, whoever it is.'

If that's the truth, he thought, I'm wasting my time here and so is Ingeborg. Soon after, he slipped out of the building and drove home.

27

Before ten next morning, DC Paul Gilbert called the incident room and asked to speak to the boss. There was such a rasp of excitement in the young man's voice that Diamond moved the phone away from his ear and still heard everything. 'Guv, I'm at Lower Swainswick with a lady by the name of Mrs Jarvie. She worships at St John's in South Parade. She had Nadia as a house guest for two weeks in 1993. It's proof positive that she came to Bath.'

Diamond wasn't immune to excitement himself. His voice gave nothing away, but his arms and legs were prickling. All the years of experience didn't suppress the adrenalin surge that came with a discovery as big as this. 'What's the address? I'll come now.'

Lower Swainswick is a one-time village long since absorbed by Bath's urban sprawl, on rising ground to the north-east. He kept telling himself to think about his driving as he headed out along the London Road and between the lines of parked cars in the built-up streets of Larkhall, but of course the reason for the trip kept breaking his concentration. This was it. The timing was right — 1993, nicely inside the time span Lofty Peake had given for the death of the skeleton woman. And it fitted what he'd learned in London about the Ukrainian call girl who'd made her escape to the West Country. This local landlady sounded like a terrific find. With any luck she'd finger Nadia's murderer.

Paul Gilbert's car was outside a cottage in Deadmill Lane that was almost entirely covered in clematis. The young constable himself came to the door — the man of the hour, in Diamond's estimation.

He was a shade less triumphant than he'd sounded on the phone. 'I'd better warn you, guv. She's elderly — well, very old, in actual fact — only I feel sure she's all there mentally.'

'That's okay, then.'

'She's also deaf.'

'I can cope with that. Are you going to let me in, or do you want to go over her entire medical history?'

A sheepish smile from Gilbert. He reversed a step and started to lead the way in. Remembering something else, he turned and started up again. 'Incidentally, I haven't told her what happened to Nadia.'

'If you know for sure, I wish you'd tell me,' Diamond said.

He hadn't got far when his eyes started to water. The cottage reeked of cat pee. Or was it curtains in need of laundering?

'Pongs a bit.'

'You get used to it,' Gilbert said, leading the way through a short passage into a back room where the old lady evidently sat by day and slept by night. She was out of bed, dressed in a pink cardigan and blue track-suit trousers and seated in a rocking-chair with a large white cat on her lap. Two tortoiseshells perched on the windowsill and a sleeping Persian had the eiderdown to itself. The odds had lengthened against the curtains as the source of the odour.

Paul Gilbert hadn't exaggerated. Mrs Jarvie was very old. She looked halfway to heaven already. The chalk-white skin hung in overlapping folds under the eyes and below the jaw.

Gilbert introduced Diamond and the only reaction this prompted was some adjustment to the hearing aid. At least she could move her hands.

'He wants to ask you about Nadia,' Gilbert shouted.

The old lady opened her eyes and spoke, and it was only to say, 'You don't have to shout.'

'Nadia,' Gilbert shouted again. To Diamond he said, 'I don't think the hearing aid works.'

Mrs Jarvie said, 'I was ninety-six in July.'

'It takes an effort,' Gilbert said to Diamond, 'but it's worth it.' He moved closer. 'Nadia, the Ukrainian girl.'

'Are you asking about Nadia again?' she said. 'I told you all about her.'

'You said she was here in 1993. Is that right?'

'I gave her the spare room,' Mrs Jarvie said. 'She wasn't with me very long. She was easier than some of my guests because she spoke good English.'

'How do you know it was 1993?' Confirming which year Nadia came to Bath was fundamental to the enquiry and couldn't be bypassed, so after getting a blank look he nodded to Gilbert to come in with his toastmaster impression.

This time the message seemed to get through. 'I had my eightieth birthday the weekend before she came. I particularly remember giving her a piece of my birthday cake and a glass of sherry when she arrived.'

'So which year were you born?' Diamond asked, not entirely convinced.

No reaction at all.

Gilbert rose to the challenge again.

'I just told you,' Mrs Jarvie said with a sigh, as if all the aggravation was coming from the visitors. 'I'm ninety-six. If I get to a hundred I get a telegram from the Queen.'

'Yes, but which year?'

'Guv,' Gilbert said.

Diamond looked to where the young DC was pointing. On a wall above the bed was a framed sampler in needlework with the letters of the alphabet and under it the words *Bless this house. Julia Mary Jarvie, born 23rd July, 1913.*

The mathematics checked. Somebody up there had pity on us, Diamond thought. Bless this house and bless you too, Julia Mary Jarvie. We've got a date to work to.

The old lady had noticed what they were looking at. 'I worked that when I was only eight years old.'

'Marvellous. Would you tell us about Nadia?'

'Who?'

He raised the decibels. 'The Ukrainian.'

'Is it? I hardly ever go outside, and neither do the cats. They hate getting wet.'

This would not have been an easy process for a patient man, and Diamond wasn't that. Gilbert stooped close to the old lady's ear and repeated Nadia's name with more success.

'She was a refugee. What do they call them now?'

'Asylum seeker?'

'She didn't have anything except the clothes she was wearing. I took her in as a Christian duty.'

'For the church?'

'Father Michael was always asking me to take in homeless girls. He's crossed the River Jordan now.'

'Popped his clogs,' Gilbert explained in an aside, in case Diamond had missed the meaning.

Mrs Jarvie continued: 'I must have had more than a dozen staying here over the years. Do you want to know about the others?'

As one, her visitors raised their palms to discourage her.

Diamond said to Gilbert, 'Ask her if Nadia said anything about herself.'

This was a complex question for someone who heard about one word in five and didn't always get that right, but this time there was a result.

'She was working in London before she came here, but she didn't like it there. Someone told her Bath was nice. Well, it is, isn't it?'

'Did she talk about her life in the Ukraine?'

She lowered her eyes and stroked the cat. 'It was all very sad. She didn't remember her mother and father. She grew up in an orphanage and when she got to sixteen a man came and took her away.'

This tallied closely with Vikki's information. Any lingering doubt that they were speaking of the same Nadia could safely be dismissed. He listened keenly to every word.

'He was a stranger, she said, and she had to go to work for him. She didn't tell me what kind of work it was, but I had my own thoughts about that.'

'Prostitution?'

'Did you say streetwalking? I'm afraid it was something of the sort. As I was telling you, they sent her to London. I don't know how long she was there before she ran away and made her way to Bath. Through God's abundant mercy she found our church. We try and help lost souls.'

'But she didn't stay long.'

'I beg your pardon.'

Gilbert did his shouting again.

'No, she didn't stay,' she said. 'She went off one afternoon and I didn't see her again. To tell you the truth, it upset me. She could have told me if she was unhappy here. Sometimes I wonder if it was the cats that put her off. I don't think she was comfortable with them.'

Diamond could sympathise, yet he managed a sweeping gesture that was meant to reassure. 'Did she say where she was going?'

To his great relief, she seemed to tune into his voice, or he was pitching it at a better level. 'I just told you I have no idea.'

'While she was staying, did she ever speak of people she knew in Bath?'

'Never.'

'Did she bring anyone back to the house?'

'Men, do you mean?'

'Anyone at all.'

She shook her head. 'She was no trouble at all while she was here. She was never late coming home, except for the day she left altogether.'

'Which day was that?'

'You want to know which day? You're asking for the moon. How would I know one day from another after all these years?'

He glanced up at the sampler. 'It must have been some time after your birthday on

July 23rd.'

'The beginning of August, then. Or thereabouts.'

'You've no way of telling? You don't keep a diary?'

'A diary — with all the shopping and cooking and cleaning and gardening as well? When you have a house guest you don't have time for anything else.'

He sensed that he probably *was* asking for the moon, so he got her back on track. 'What did you do the night she left?'

She was still tuned in. 'I went to bed at my usual time, thinking she'd soon be coming in. I slept upstairs in those days. I had the front room and hers was the back. She could have got in if she'd wanted. She knew I keep a spare front door key under the flowerpot beside the front door. In the morning I found the door of her room still open and the bed hadn't been slept in.'

'Were her things gone?'

'What things? She didn't have any things of her own. She used my towels, my face flannel, even my shampoo and soap. And her clothes were given by the church.'

'Did you report it? Speak to Father Michael? Call the police?'

'It's a pity she didn't find a little job. They say the devil finds work for idle hands. I do hope she didn't go back to her old way of life.'

He had to repeat his question.

'Report it? Not for some time. I thought she might come back, you see, and it would have seemed inhospitable if I'd reported her missing. In the end I think I told someone at the church, but by then she'd been gone a few weeks and no further action was taken. With people like that, who arrive out of the blue, you never know when you're going to lose them again. Would you like to see a picture of her?'

A picture? Would he just?

'There's a wooden box under the bed.' She turned to Gilbert. 'See if you can reach it, young man. Pay no attention to anything else you might see there.'

Gilbert delved underneath and pulled out a dusty rosewood box inlaid with mother-of-pearl. The cat on Mrs Jarvie's lap was forced to move.

'Now would you hand me my magnifying glass from the bedside table?' She opened the box. It was stuffed with letters and photos. 'The picture I'm looking for should be here somewhere.'

This, Diamond reflected, gritting his teeth, could take some time. Cultivate patience, you hothead. To get an image of

Nadia will be momentous.

She didn't take long. 'Here we are. This was snapped in the garden by my neighbour, Mrs Brixham, now gone to paradise like Father Michael, poor soul. That's Nadia with me preparing runner beans for dinner. It was such a nice day we sat outside. She had a lovely smile.' She handed the photo across.

Although the 6 × 4 colour print had faded, the focus was sharp enough to provide a clear image. It showed a slightly less decrepit Mrs Jarvie beside a young woman on a garden seat. They had kitchen knives in their hands and a saucepan between them.

For Diamond this was a moment to set the pulse racing, the chance to see the face of the young woman whose tragic history he'd been investigating. In the picture she appeared untroubled, no doubt relieved that she'd found this safe haven. She was giving a wide smile to the camera, holding up a bean in her left hand to show what the picture was about. Her hair was blonde and long enough to have been drawn back, gathered and held in place with combs. She was wearing little or no make-up. He noted that she was wearing the expected jeans and a T-shirt. Her face was East European in shape, a fraction too broad to be conventionally pretty, but the smile caught a moment of happiness that gave life to the fading image, a point of contact that moved Peter Diamond more than he'd expected. No doubt he was indulging in sentiment he would have ridiculed in anyone else, yet he felt Nadia's personality lived on in the photo, a young, laughing woman putting her grim past behind her without knowing she had only a few days left.

That photo said more than any e-fit would have done.

'May we make a copy of this?'

No response.

Moved by what he'd just seen, he'd lowered the pitch of his voice. A second attempt got through.

'What are you going to do with it?' the old lady said, frowning. 'I don't want it getting into the newspapers.'

'Why not?'

'I'm wearing an apron, that's why.'

'We'll cut you out of it. We only want Nadia's head and shoulders.'

'I can't think why.'

He wasn't going to enlighten her at this juncture. 'We'd like to find out what happened to her. Nobody has seen her since this was taken.'

'I hope she's all right. She was no trouble to me.'

They left after replacing the box under the bed and allowing the white cat to reclaim its prime position.

'Top result, Paul,' Diamond said, his heart still pumping at a higher rate. It was rare for him to show emotion to a colleague, but he closed a hand over Gilbert's shoulder. 'Full marks for this. Now let's see if the photo jogs some memories.'

There is a stage in every lengthy investigation when the team needs palpable proof of progress. Personally, he'd stayed positive, though he was pretty sure there had been murmurings in the incident room about the lack of suspects. The circumstances had made this case an unusual one. Generally you know from the outset what has happened and why. Most of the team's efforts up to now had been centred on understanding the basics, the nature of the crime. All of that was about to change.

He was humming to himself as he returned to the car.

Hard facts had emerged at last. In London he'd found a name for the skeleton victim and confirmed her nationality and her way of life. And now thanks to Mrs Jarvie he'd discovered the year and the month Nadia had come to Bath and gone missing. Better still, he had the photo in his pocket. He could show everyone what this tragic young woman had looked like in life. The headless skeleton had been reconstructed into a real person.

In this heightened mood, he let his thoughts race on from the facts to their interpretation. Nadia had tried to flee from the hell of prostitution at a time when violence had taken over. Murder was already being done. The vice barons would have thought nothing of ordering another killing. It looked increasingly as if she had been followed to Bath by some hit man and executed, most likely as a deterrent to any other working girl who had plans to escape. The decapitation after death seemed to signify a professional killing. Your average small-time murderer hasn't the stomach for mutilation.

Thinking of small-time murderers, he was forced to admit that the latest developments rather undermined the theory that Nadia's death and Rupert's were connected. If Nadia's was an organised crime ordered by professionals then Rupert's had the hallmarks of a local affair, a casual killing. Did it matter any more? Probably not. Linking them had been convenient at the time, a way of making sure both enquiries were controlled from Bath. Georgina might complain when the cases were solved and the dust settled, but the world would have moved on.

He drove back to Manvers Street deciding on priorities. The first step was to get Nadia's face onto posters, into papers and on television. He'd tell John Wigfull to drop everything he was doing and get the job done fast. After sixteen years was it too much to hope that someone in Bath remembered seeing the girl with her killer? She had left the cottage in Lower Swainswick on an afternoon early in August, 1993. Too long ago? Never underestimate the power of an image.

To his credit, Wigfull didn't demur. He saw the sense in blitzing Bath (Diamond's words) with the picture. It wasn't the highest quality, he said unnecessarily, but fortunately his photographic expert enjoyed a challenge.

'No touching up,' Diamond warned him. 'I don't want any distortions.'

'That doesn't happen these days,' Wigfull took pleasure in telling him. 'You're way behind on the technology.'

Next on the list of priorities was a call to

Charing Cross Hospital. He was given the encouraging news that Keith was breathing normally now and had been allowed out of bed. There was no reason why he shouldn't make a full recovery in a few weeks.

Then a call to Louis Voss. 'I still need help,' he said when he'd summarised what he'd learned from Mrs Jarvie. 'Weren't you working with the vice squad in 1993?'

'I did six years of it,' Louis said before introducing a cautionary note. 'I know what you're going to ask. You think Nadia was murdered to order and the order came from here. You want names. Sorry to disappoint, but you're on a loser, matey. I won't say the vice barons are faceless, but they make damned sure you can pin nothing on them.'

'But you know who they are?'

'It's organised crime, Peter, big business. We don't get near them. We never had the resources to hook a big fish. The trouble with prostitution is that there are no victims.'

'Rubbish,' Diamond said. 'Thousands of women are trafficked. I've seen girls beaten up by ponces. If they're not victims, who are?'

'Okay, I could have put it better. Prostitution works through private transactions, like the drugs trade. Try going to court and you find the sellers and the users are equally unwilling to testify. For me, the vice squad was a reality check. I started out thinking we could make a difference. Some chance. There's no pressure to act except from local residents who complain about kerb-crawlers, and they're not the people with influence. Basically, we turned a blind eye to most of what was going on unless it got really ugly. Occasionally we put away a vicious ponce for a couple of years, and raised a cheer. For how long? Before the case came to court another brute was running the show. We never got near the head honchos.'

'You're saying I should let some hired assassin get away with murder on my patch?'

'I'm saying if he was any good at his job you won't find him. More frustrating still, you won't get the guy who hired him.'

'That's as cynical as anything I've heard in the police.'

'Cynical and true. But let me give you something else to chew on, country boy. I know how the sex industry works in London. At the time you're speaking of, the Wall had come down and London was awash with classy foreign girls willing to turn tricks. Remember the old saying about no one being indispensable? Your Nadia will have been replaced overnight and forgotten.

One little whore making a run for freedom was never worth pursuing to Bath and killing.'

Put like that, the argument was difficult to challenge. There had always been give and take with Louis. That was their way with each other. Deep down, Diamond had a strong respect for his old friend's wisdom. He remembered hearing something similar from Vikki about the girls being treated as money-makers, like fruit machines, and getting replaced. 'If you're right, it means she came to Bath and in a matter of days met someone local who not only murdered her, but removed the head so that we wouldn't identify her.'

'So right,' Louis said. 'What was it Sherlock Holmes said about the smiling and beautiful countryside and its dreadful record of sin compared to London?'

28

'Have you checked your emails today, boss?' Ingeborg asked, breezing into Diamond's office soon after he'd ended the call to Louis.

'What do you think?'

'You're not even switched on.'

'I'm switched on. The computer isn't.'

She smiled. 'Don't you look at your inbox routinely?'

Sarcasm, he thought. This young lady needs reining in. 'I was in London on police business.'

'And of course you don't have a laptop.'

'I'm a detective, not a freak.'

'I think you mean geek. You can access your email from any other computer,' she informed him 'You could have logged on from London.'

'I had slightly more urgent things to deal with, like Keith being shot and almost killed. What did you really want to say to me, Inge?'

'It's high time we heard from the lab about the hair we sent for analysis, the one found under the tab of Nadia's zip.'

She was right. More dramatic events had put the hair to the back of his mind. He would deal with it shortly. He wasn't going to let Ingeborg think she'd caught him out. 'The men in white coats always take an age. They phone if there's anything startling. It's academic now, anyway. We're ninety-nine per cent sure who she was.'

'Just thought I'd remind you,' she said. 'Did you get any DNA from the cottage where she stayed?'

'How would we have got that?'

'Particles of hair or skin.'

Now it was his turn to give a smile, remembering the state of Mrs Jarvie's cottage. 'You're optimistic. Sixteen years have gone by and numerous house guests have gone through that cottage.'

'The girl left unexpectedly. Didn't the house owner keep her property?'

'Nadia arrived with nothing and walked out with nothing.'

'It was only a thought.' She lingered and it was obvious that her real reason for coming in had yet to be aired. 'Did I catch a glimpse of you when I was at pike drill last night?'

He nodded. 'I told you I might look in. You seem to be handling the weapons all right, but are you picking up information?'

'It's a case of softly, softly, guv. I want to get their confidence, so I haven't gone in there firing questions at everyone.'

'I met one of the camp followers,' he said.

'Mrs Swithin? Nothing gets past her.'

'I didn't try. I said straight out that I'm from CID. Of course I didn't let on that you're one of my team. Mustn't blow your cover.'

'She mentioned you later.'

'Favourably, I hope?'

'She was a bit freaked that our local unit of the Sealed Knot is under police surveillance.'

'I told her why.'

'Yes, but the members are proud of what they do and they don't think Rupert's death has any connection with them.'

'You mean Mrs Swithin thinks they're in the clear. She can't know everything that goes on.'

'She has a bloody good try.'

'You know who she is?' he said. 'The wife of Major Swithin, golfer and leading light of the Lansdown Society. The Swithins were the people who reported Rupert trying to

403

break into cars.'

'Didn't she know he was in the Knot?'

'He trained in Bristol. The muster in August was his first appearance on the battlefield.'

'And his last.' She coiled a strand of blonde hair around her finger. 'This is just a thought, guv. Everyone in the Knot takes the soldiering seriously. If Rupert was misbehaving, he was letting down the regiment.'

'So he was cracked over the head? Since when has petty theft been a capital offence? Besides, the military have other ways of dealing with misconduct.'

Still she seemed reluctant to leave his office. 'I don't know if you heard at the drill. My officer said he thought I might get a place in the cavalry.'

There it was, then, out in the open. Nothing to do with emails or forensics. She fancied herself as a cavalry officer.

'Because you can wave a sword realistically?'

'I've done it before.'

'I saw. You're bloody good, but —'

'And I can ride,' she added. 'I used to have a pony.'

'Don't you need your own horse for this?'

'They said they'd find one for me. Some

of the cavalry have stables and several horses.' Her eagerness was transparent.

Women and horses, he grumbled to himself: you didn't have to think much about it to understand the appeal. 'You're not supposed to be doing this for your own pleasure.'

'I can do my job and enjoy it as well,' she said, still pressing.

'The idea is that you lie low and find out what really happened.'

'I know, guv, but —'

'Listen, Inge. You don't have the full picture yet. Mrs Jarvie, this old lady I just saw, has helped in a major way. We're now certain that Nadia came to Bath at the end of July, 1993, shortly after Mrs Jarvie's eightieth birthday on July twenty-third, and she disappeared off the radar shortly after. Let's say two weeks. When do you make that?'

'Early August.'

'Right. Over the weekend of August seventh and eighth, the Sealed Knot held its major muster, the big one, the re-enactment of the Battle of Lansdown.'

'Yikes!'

'This year, Rupert Hope, a new member of the Knot, takes part in another re-enactment and happens to unearth part of

Nadia's skeleton.'

'And is murdered.' Her eyes ignited like the blue flame of a gas-ring.

'Do you see why your role as a recruit could be so useful?'

For once she was lost for words.

'It's why I don't want you prancing around on horseback. The best spies keep a low profile.'

In the incident room he called for silence and gave the team the latest bulletin on Keith Halliwell and then announced that he'd taken over Keith's role as SIO. The whole investigation had a sharper focus now, he said, briefing them on the crucial dates in the summer of 1993. They listened keenly. Even the Bristol contingent left their computers and joined in.

'I've handed Nadia's picture to John Wigfull, our publicity guru,' he told them, 'and he reckons it's sharp enough to make a good enlargement. We'll plaster the town with it, papers, local TV. There's a good chance someone will remember her.'

'The church?' John Leaman suggested. 'That's where she went first.'

Paul Gilbert said, 'The priest who met her is dead.'

'The congregation aren't,' Leaman said.

'Not all of them, anyway. People turn out Sunday after Sunday for years. What you do is this. Ask the priest to mention it at Sunday mass when he's giving his church notices and then have someone ready with a poster and flyers when they all come out.'

He'd walked into it, as usual.

'Good thinking, John,' Diamond said. 'Take care of it, would you?' And more than one of the team mouthed the words along with him.

Septimus spoke in his deadpan tone. 'What's the thinking here? What do you hope to get out of this?'

'Now that we have a narrower time frame, just those few days in the summer of 1993,' Diamond said, 'we're on a similar exercise to the one you've been carrying out for Rupert, reconstructing the days leading up to the murder. Have you made any headway with that?'

'Actually, yes.' Septimus had a way of delivering words to maximum effect. Part of it was his use of the pause. He insisted that his listeners waited, and they generally did. 'Altogether we've traced eleven people who remember seeing Rupert on Lansdown and they all agree that he was behaving in a confused way, turning up at various locations on Lansdown and making a nuisance of himself. I wouldn't put it any stronger than that. He wasn't aggressive.'

'He was hungry,' Ingeborg said.

'Correct. And that was what got him into trouble at the racecourse car park and in the car boot sale. He had no money on him, but he needed to eat. Someone was going through bins at the rear of the Blathwayt restaurant and one night they spotted this figure. We're pretty sure it was him. He ran off.'

'Poor guy,' Ingeborg said.

'It's hard to assess his state of mind,' Septimus continued. 'From what we know he was concussed or brain-damaged from the first attack. He had the power of speech, but he didn't know who he was. Someone called him Noddy and he accepted it. He seems to have hung about on Lansdown the whole time — which we assume lasted twenty-two days, from the day of the mock battle to the morning he was found dead in the churchyard.'

'Living off scraps?' Leaman said.

'Apparently. Until yesterday we were uncertain where he slept. The theory was that he picked anywhere he happened to be when night came, but we found a new witness.' Cue another pause.

'Who was that?'

'A postman who delivers along Lansdown Road. He'd noticed this man early on several mornings near Beckford's Tower.'

'Where he was murdered,' Leaman said.

Septimus gave him the disdainful look that such an obvious remark warranted. 'They didn't speak. It was just a series of sightings, but it was enough for us to order another search. We'd been over the churchyard already, looking for the weapon. Now we wanted to find if he had a base there, somewhere in the dry.'

'The tower?' Leaman said.

'No, that's got a security system. Valuable items are on exhibition there.'

'A burial vault?'

'Are you into horror films?'

There were some sniggers at Leaman's expense.

Septimus added, 'We'd have noticed when we cleared the grass from round the graves.' With eyebrows raised, inviting more suggestions, he looked around the room.

Diamond said, 'I told you my theory when we first went there. He used the front gate as his bedroom.'

'The *gate?*' Leaman said.

'Have you been there?' Septimus asked him.

'Not lately.'

'If you had, you'd know what I'm saying. I'm not talking itsy-bitsy garden gates. This is a building, man, massive, like the gate to a city.'

Diamond nodded. 'I'd call it a gatehouse. Roman in style, I think.'

'Byzantine,' Ingeborg said.

She probably knew for certain, so Diamond didn't contest it. 'Thanks, Inge. That was on the tip of my tongue. A Byzantine gate by the same guy who built the tower; a big solid structure facing the street.'

'Okay, it's a gatehouse,' Septimus went on. 'Behind the front gate is this covered-in part, big, like a room, and with stone seats. Under one of the seats we found a folded blanket.'

'Where would he have got that?' Leaman said.

'Nicked from somebody's car,' Paul Gilbert said.

'Have you sent it for tests?' Diamond asked.

'You bet. There was a plastic water bottle, empty, and some food wrappers. This place is protected from the weather, quiet at night and private. I wouldn't call it a comfortable hideaway, but it was dry. Someone used it recently, for sure.'

'So he may have been brain-damaged, but

he was smart enough to find this,' Ingeborg said.

'If a stone bed in a cemetery on a hill is smart,' Septimus said. 'Personally I would have looked for a Salvation Army hostel.'

'He'd have to go down into Bath for that,' she said. 'I get the feeling he wanted to remain on the hill.'

'God knows why.'

Diamond's thoughts had moved on. 'If the postman noticed him, it's possible his murderer saw him in the area as well. The body was found among the graves — how far from the gateway?'

'Thirty yards, or less.'

'All right. Let's think what may have happened. Rupert makes his way there one evening and his killer is waiting. The blanket was folded, you say, so he didn't get a chance to lie down. He was attacked on his way across the churchyard. Is that the way you see it, Septimus?'

'Pretty much. Or the killer was waiting in the gateway and Rupert ran off and was caught. It seems to have been an ambush, and it happened late. The pathologist said he was killed overnight. He couldn't say what time.'

'Do they ever?' But Diamond wasn't discouraged. He raised a thumb to the Bristol team and then spoke to everyone. 'The more I hear about this Rupert, the sorrier I feel for him. For three weeks he was living rough on Lansdown, not even knowing who he was, and no one understood the trouble he was in or what was going on.'

'What *was* going on?' Ingeborg said.

'With Rupert?'

'With his killer.'

Diamond looked towards Septimus, who shook his head, unable to supply an answer.

'We know this,' Diamond said. 'It wasn't some drunken brawl. He had two goes at killing him. The motive was strong.'

'And are we still assuming a link between Rupert's killing and Nadia's, in 1993?' Ingeborg asked in her journo mode, pinning him down.

'We are.'

'The Battle of Lansdown?'

'Right on.'

'We don't know for sure if Nadia went to the re-enactment, do we?'

'In the next few days we should find out,' Diamond said. 'We do know that the timing was right.'

With that, he drew the meeting to a close and there was a buzz of energy in the room. Nadia was named and pictured. Septimus and his team had moved the Rupert investigation on. As for the link, he'd sounded confident. He had to.

Alone in his office, out of conscience more than confidence, he switched on his under-used computer. Ingeborg had been right to mention emails. He preferred to ignore them and his regular contacts understood and used the phone. But it was possible someone at the forensics lab had tried to reach him that way.

Yawning, he waited for the screen to light up.

He clicked on the mailbox icon, never a move that brought much encouragement. Masses of unwanted stuff appeared that he would have highlighted and deleted at a stroke if he could only have remembered the trick.

Scrolling down, looking at the senders, he spotted one from FSS Chepstow and almost passed it by, thinking he didn't know anyone of that name. Initial letters were a blind-spot with him. But Chepstow was a place, wasn't it, where one of the Home Office labs was located?

FSS.

Forensic Science Service.

The subject title was Test Report.

When he opened the email and read it, he scratched his head and said, 'Oh, bugger.'

This required a rethink.

Ten minutes later, he called Ingeborg in.

'You were right,' he told her. 'The lab report came as an email late yesterday. They had to repeat the test and that's why it took so long. This'll pin your ears back. The hair doesn't belong to Nadia.'

'Her killer?'

'No.'

'How do they know that?' she said, stung into petulance. 'They've got nothing to compare it with.'

'Because it isn't a human hair. It's animal. It comes from a horse.'

'Get away!'

'True.' He handed across the sheet he'd printed. 'They reckon it was clipped. Horses get trimmed sometimes, don't they?'

'Yes, but . . .' She read the report right through. 'Incredible. Can you feature that?'

'There was I thinking we might have got lucky,' he said. 'We end up with a bloody horse.'

'I'm at a loss, guv.'

'So was I when I first read it. But I've remembered something I was told in London by Vikki, the madam at the brothel. She was Ukrainian herself and she knew Nadia. She said she always thought Nadia came from Cossack stock and she justified it by saying she spent a lot of time watching the racing on TV, not for the betting, but the horses. I don't know a lot about Cossacks except they're fierce warriors and they ride horses.'

Her eyes widened. 'Cool.'

'So it's not impossible that when she came here and was looking for a job she thought about working with horses.'

'I guess.' She sounded unconvinced.

'If she heard of an upcoming event involving horses she could well have thought she'd go there in hopes of chatting up some owners and getting work as a stable girl.'

'If you don't mind me saying, guv, there's some heavy speculation here.'

'Sure. I'm trying to link a horse hair to Nadia.'

'Okay. And what was the upcoming event?'

'The re-enactment.'

She took a sharp breath. 'Of course. Plenty of horses there.'

'As you say, Inge, it's all speculation, but we have to work something out and this is the best I can think of. I just wanted you to know I've had a rethink about you joining the cavalry.'

'I can do it?' She gave a scream of excitement and for one alarming moment he thought she was going to fling her arms around his neck.

29

Did Lansdown itself hold the solution to this mystery? In Diamond's thoughts the great limestone hill loomed larger than any suspect. From inside the bowl of the city it appeared disarmingly scenic, a pale green backdrop to the undulating ribbons of cream-coloured buildings. He knew its real character. Up there were places of death, the graveyard and the battlefield, bleak, windswept locations even on a summer day. The battleground had yielded up a bone, and then a skeleton, to set this investigation in motion. Nadia had come to Bath for sanctuary, and been slaughtered and buried on the hill. For three weeks poor confused Rupert Hope had roamed the fields and tracks and slept in the Victorian cemetery until, just as cruelly, his life had been stopped. This was an unforgiving place.

He'd never set much store on intuition, so why was he nagged by this conviction that the down held another, larger secret and it was his duty to reveal the truth? The standard method of probing motive, means and opportunity would not be enough. A bigger, bolder vision was called for. Lansdown both repelled him and tugged at him.

He told Septimus he was going to drive up to the cemetery for another look at the entrance gate where Rupert was thought to have slept.

'There isn't much to see now,' Septimus said. 'Everything we found was bagged up and sent to forensics. We'll know more if they can tell us for sure if he used that blanket.'

'For now, I'm assuming he did,' Diamond said. 'Can you tear yourself away from that computer and join me?'

On the drive up the hill, Septimus seemed to feel he ought to speak up for his team. 'We haven't just been looking for witnesses. We spent a lot of time on Rupert and his life in Bristol. He comes out of it as the kind of guy nobody could hate or feel threatened by. Liked his lecturing and did it well. Always thinking of ways of bringing history to life. Popular with students.'

'Not so popular in the senior common room.'

'The other lecturers respected him. He

wasn't big on socialising, but that was who he was, a quiet guy, maybe a shade too serious for their taste.'

'And outside the university?'

'The same, really. He got on with the neighbours without living in their pockets. People in local shops said he was honest and easy to deal with. He didn't give out much. Some guys don't. That's life.'

'No close friends?'

'Not all that close. Currently he wasn't in a relationship. There seem to have been a couple of girlfriends in the past. He didn't ever live with anyone.'

'Can't hold that against him.'

'We checked his bank statements. Nothing unusual there. Not even a small overdraft. He spent his money mainly on books, DVDs and theatre visits. He could make a bottle of wine last almost a week.'

'I could murder someone like that,' Diamond said.

'Yeah, maybe he was too good for this world.'

'I'm sure you must have checked his computer.'

'Same thing. The downloaded stuff is heavy on history. The emails are mainly to other historians about topics he was researching. He also kept in touch with his parents that way. Got on well with them and was generous with money at Christmas and birthdays. All in all, no trouble to anyone.'

They'd reached the cemetery gate. Diamond stopped the car and switched off. 'You know, it's possible he was just unlucky.'

'Wrong place, wrong time?' Septimus scratched his head. 'How would we ever find out?'

'We have to.' Diamond got out and looked up at the ornate Romanesque façade of the gateway. 'Now show me where you found the blanket.'

They passed through an entrance door to the right of the main gates. 'A gatekeeper could live in here, no problem,' Septimus said as he stepped into the section with the stone seats.

'Where did you find the blanket?'

'Under here.' He indicated the seat to their right.

'What sort of blanket?'

'Deep red, made of some synthetic material. We didn't open it out for fear of losing particle evidence. It stayed folded. I'd say it was large and not too clean.'

'He wasn't too clean himself. You think he nicked it from a car?'

'My best suggestion. The fabric was dry, you see. He hadn't found it lying in the open. And he was seen trying car doors.'

'When did it go to the lab?'

'Day before yesterday, when you were in London.'

'What about the other items? You mentioned a water bottle and some food wrappers.'

'We bagged them all up and sent them for examination.'

'Someone was using this as a base for sure, but we can't take anything for granted. Let me know when you get the lab report.' He tried to imagine stretching out on the stone surface. 'Not the most comfortable bed.'

'Cold, too, these late summer nights,' Septimus said. 'We're two hundred metres above sea level.'

Diamond stepped outside the gatehouse thinking how many more gravestones were revealed than when he'd first come here. They were still close-packed, strangely angled and in disrepair, but the gothic look of crosses and angels poking up from the undergrowth had gone. He wasn't sure which view was the more eerie. 'It can't be more than thirty yards to where the body was found. I'm going to pace it out.'

He didn't count the steps. His mind was with a terrified Rupert late at night, hounded by his killer, dodging between the graves. Or had it worked out differently: Rupert approaching the lodge, crossing the graveyard and being ambushed, like that scene in David Lean's film of *Great Expectations* when Magwitch the convict appears from nowhere?

The crime scene tape had been removed. You wouldn't have known where the body had lain unless you guessed from the state of the ground, trodden to mud by hundreds of footsteps. The only other indication was on the adjacent grave, a faint blue circle enclosing the suspicious bloodstain. He looked at each of the surrounding graves. In the next row was a granite sarcophagus, an ugly grey block a man could easily have crouched behind.

'What's your reading of it, Septimus? Was he chased here, or was the killer waiting?'

'I don't think he was chased. He was hit on the back of the skull. If you're running from someone and they catch you, you turn and defend yourself. I say he walked into a trap and was hit from behind.'

'My feeling, too.'

From above them came a guttural croaking, the caw of a black bird perched on the octagonal balustrade of the tower.

'Carrion crow,' Septimus said.

'More bones than carrion here.'

'I wouldn't spend a night in this place if you paid me.'

Back in the incident room he discovered Ingeborg in seventh heaven. 'I called my drill officer and told him I'd like a transfer to the cavalry and he promised to do what he could.'

'Cool,' Diamond said, straight-faced.

'Yes, and in no time at all I had a call back to say they have a vacancy in Prince Rupert's Lifeguard of Horse.'

'Even cooler, then.'

'What's more, they're doing an event on Saturday at Farleigh Hungerford and they want me on parade.'

'A bit quick, isn't it?'

'Someone pulled out through illness. I have to report for practice tonight. Isn't that neat?'

'Neat, indeed.' He didn't add that she ought to remember why she was doing this. Her joy in being asked to take part was obvious, but she was a professional, too, and he could rely on her to function as a detective. 'Farleigh Hungerford. There isn't much there, is there?'

She said in a crushing tone, 'Farleigh Castle, guv. The scene of a major event in the Civil War. These two half-brothers, Sir Edward Hungerford and John, were on opposing sides. John was the royalist and he held the castle and used it as a garrison. Then some time in 1644 when the royalists were at a low point, Edward made his comeback and secured the place for the roundheads.'

'And you'll be re-enacting this?'

'I'm not sure about that. Apparently the castle was taken without bloodshed.'

'What a letdown. That's no help to you lot.'

'Well, yes. People want to see some action, so we'll take a few liberties with history.'

'Do you have a horse?'

'They're providing one for me — with battlefield experience.'

More than you have, he thought. 'And the uniform?'

'Blue doublet and red sash. I even get to wear the cavalier hat.'

'I'd like a picture of that.'

He stepped into his office and closed the door. Ingeborg's elation was in sharp contrast to his own mood since returning from the cemetery. His confidence was draining away. He couldn't fault Ingeborg or Septimus or Paul Gilbert. They were bright, energetic young officers, committed to the assignments he'd given them. The entire team was among the keenest he'd ever led. Even John Leaman was a beaver with hyperactivity syndrome. And Keith Halliwell had taken a bullet, he was so loyal and brave. How, then, could such an array of talent have failed to produce a single credible suspect? He'd expected by now to have names in the frame and there wasn't one. Not even a strong motive had emerged. Something was seriously at fault with the investigation and he blamed himself. The process they'd followed had been logical and thorough. He couldn't think of any lead they'd failed to pursue. At one stage he'd been ready to point the finger in the direction of London, towards some faceless assassin sent by the vice barons, but wise heads like Louis Voss and Vikki had disabused him of that and he was forced to agree with them. These were West Country crimes requiring a West Country solution.

He had to face the possibility that he'd overplayed the possible connection between the two murders. It remained tentative, speculative. Okay, both bodies had been found on Lansdown, and Rupert had actually sat beside Nadia's grave and handled her bone before being murdered himself.

But coincidences happen. Life is full of them.

Nadia had come to Bath in the month of the Sealed Knot re-enactment. Nothing linked her definitely to the Knot. It looked a possibility and that was the best that could be said. He'd been trying from the beginning to unify the investigation and now he wondered if he was forcing the issue too much.

He feared he'd missed something through trying to link the killings. If he'd investigated Rupert's murder in isolation he might have had stronger suspicions about Dave, who'd come forward long after the original call for witnesses; or Major Swithin, the vigilante who'd called the police to the racecourse; or even the angry woman from the car boot sale who'd made such an issue of Rupert stealing a pie. Because these people had no apparent link to Nadia he'd not rated them as serious suspects. In theory Septimus should have put each of them through the grinder. In the large-scale exercise of reconstructing Rupert's last three weeks of life, had the basics been neglected?

Somebody knocked on his door. Didn't they know by now that when it was closed he was not to be interrupted?

Flushed with annoyance, he walked across

and flung it open. 'What is it?'

Septimus stood there. Ready to confess he'd messed up?

'Sir, I think you should hear about this.'

No one called him 'sir' unless the sky had fallen in.

'I'm listening.'

Septimus took a deep breath. 'The lab just called. They've been examining the blanket I sent in, the one we think was used by Rupert.'

'And . . . ?'

'Something cropped up and they want an explanation.'

'*They* want an explanation?'

'They're saying it's a horse rug.'

'Okay, it's not a blanket, it's a horse rug.'

'They removed a number of horse hairs from it and compared them with the one we'd sent them previously, from the zip fly. They say it comes from the same horse.'

30

He called the lab and asked to speak to the chief scientist. The voice on the line was urbane, well used to dealing with awkward policemen. 'Good of you to call back, Mr Diamond. No doubt there's a rational explanation of our findings and I'm suggesting it must come from your end, not ours.'

'Why is that?'

A definite chuckle was audible. 'Because we're scrupulous in our procedures. We don't confuse samples.'

Diamond held himself in check. 'Before I comment, let's clarify what's in your report, shall we?'

'We haven't made one yet. This was a courtesy call to let you double-check what's been happening.'

'A chance to redeem ourselves?'

'I'm not playing the blame game, Mr Diamond. I'm a scientist looking for an explanation of an improbable result. The horse rug your people sent us contains hair clippings genetically identical to the one you submitted previously. We were led to believe that particular clipping had been buried for up to twenty years.'

'Sixteen.'

'Sixteen, then. And we were told this rug had been used recently by a murder victim sleeping rough. How do you reconcile that?'

'I don't.'

'Well, then. There's only one explanation I can think of, and that's that you muddled the clippings in some way.'

If this wasn't the blame game it sounded remarkably like it. 'You'd better think again because that's not possible,' Diamond said, ready to trade blow for blow. 'Your own scientists found the first hair trapped under the tab.'

'Ah, but how many people handled the zip before it reached here?'

'One only, and he was the crime scene investigator. It was put straight into an evidence bag. We followed correct procedures throughout and I don't much care for these inferences you're making. There's no chance it could have been contaminated.'

'Easy to say, harder to prove, superintendent.'

He was increasingly riled by the man. 'Explain this, then. The zip was sent to you at least ten days ago. The rug wasn't even found until the end of last week. How could there be cross-contamination at our end?'

'You must answer that. It didn't happen here. We'd be sacked for incompetence if it did.'

How tempting was that? He bit back the comment he wanted to make. Instead, he changed tack. 'What's your basis for saying that the hairs came from the same horse?'

'DNA analysis.'

'DNA from a horse hair?'

'Yes, why not?'

'I know about DNA in humans.'

'Animals have their unique profiles, just the same.'

'I'm interested in the science here,' Diamond said. 'Genetic profiling in people is well known. How much data is there on horses?'

'My dear man, it's been going on for years. There's a huge database. All the top racing thoroughbreds have their DNA on record and it can be analysed from hair samples just the same as yours or mine.'

'And you're totally sure the hairs matched?'

'We routinely back up every test and I

430

ordered more when this unaccountable result was reported to me. They came back identical to the first batch.'

Diamond felt as if he needed a cigarette, and he'd given up years ago. 'I'd like to speak to my colleagues about this. I'll get back to you later.'

'Good thinking, Mr Diamond. It's sound science to recheck every damned thing. We do, and we have in this case.'

His blood pressure rocketing, he slammed down the phone. He got up and circled the small office, taking deep breaths to get control of himself. Then he asked Septimus back into the office.

Was the Bristol man blushing under his black skin? He had an uneasy look, for sure.

'You've had time to think while I've been on the phone,' Diamond said. 'How could this have happened?'

'Not our fault.' To the point, and no excuse offered. This was the way Septimus operated. If you wanted alibis, go to someone else.

'Are you certain?'

'We bagged up the blanket — sorry, horse rug — where we found it, in the gatehouse, sealed and labelled it and sent it off directly.'

'If that was handled right, then what about the zip?'

'Not for me to say. If you recall, the zip was already at the lab being cleaned before I came to Bath.'

Back of the net. Septimus was in the clear.

'I can't argue with that.' Diamond hesitated, casting his thoughts back. 'Keith Halliwell sent them the zip at my suggestion. He's ultra-careful. He knows all about the chain of custody and the legal pitfalls if you do anything wrong.'

Septimus gave a shrug. 'Keith was in London with you when the rug was found. It makes no sense.'

But it had to. Diamond leaned on his elbows and buried his face in his hands, locked in thought. After some while he looked up and said, 'How long do horses live?'

'I can't tell you.'

'I'm sure they get to twenty or thirty. It's not impossible that the horse Nadia came into contact with is still alive. Say it was a three year old in 1993. It could be under twenty now.'

'So Rupert happened to find the rug used for the same horse?' Septimus said on a disbelieving note. 'That's stretching it.'

'No, it could be one more link between the cases. You say "happened to". There could be a logical reason.'

'I'm not following you.'

'Rupert the historian had an interest in the Civil War. That's why he joined the Sealed Knot. Agreed?'

'Okay.'

'He was given a pike to carry, but he must have taken an interest in every aspect of the battle, including the cavalry. The horses have got to be battle-trained. What with cannon fire and smoke and all the rest, it's no place for a nervous animal. I reckon they use the same horses again and again. You'd rather have an experienced mount than one that's going to take fright. This was some old warhorse that featured in both re-enactments.'

'Where does the rug come in?'

'Left on Lansdown after everyone went home. Rupert found it and used it for bedding.'

'It must have been left in the dry, then.'

A better idea struck him. 'How about this? The horse is local and kept on Lansdown. I've seen them in fields there. On cold nights they're covered with a horse rug.'

'We're not in winter yet.'

'At that height it's cold most nights. By day the rug is going to be stored somewhere. A shed. The place where they keep the fodder. Rupert breaks in and helps himself.'

Septimus digested this and said nothing.

'Something for Ingeborg to check on tonight,' Diamond said. 'She can take an interest in the horses, find out if there's a veteran among them and where it's stabled.'

Now that the focus was shifting to someone else, Septimus asked, 'Do you need me any more?'

A shake of the head. Diamond was planning the next move. Septimus stepped outside and left him to it.

Presently Diamond reached for the phone and called the lab again. He was put through to the supreme boffin and outlined his new theory. Even as he spoke, his confidence ebbed. He hoped it wasn't showing in his voice.

'The same horse?' the scientist said. 'Each of your victims came into contact with it?'

'We're working on the theory that both of them were involved with battle re-enactments on Lansdown.'

'That's the explanation and you're satisfied?'

'It will do for now. There was no negligence on our part.'

'In that case we'll report to you in the usual way. Mind, it would be helpful if you could find the horse.'

'That's the next step. And it would help

me to know some more about the rug.'

'It's an under-rug. Do you know what that is?'

'I can hazard a guess.'

'And you'd be right. It's made of soft material to protect the animal from friction from the heavyweight rug. They tend to get rub marks and bald shoulders, so they need this softer layer underneath. There's a label. The manufacturer was a firm called Phil Drake.'

'Cheapo?'

'Quite the opposite. Top of the range. Unfortunately the firm over-expanded and went bust eleven years ago. This rug was an expensive product in its time.'

'So if it's at least eleven years old, it's not in the best condition?'

'The original burgundy colour has faded badly and the fabric is disintegrating.'

'Wear and tear?'

He didn't answer immediately. 'Strange you should mention that. There isn't much wear and tear as such. The deterioration is uniformly spread across the rug. It's down to the ageing of the fabric more than use. Materials fade and break down in time, as you know.'

'Not that much,' Diamond said. 'I've got a twelve-year-old suit I still wear.'

'And keep in a wardrobe in a warm house, no doubt. Horse rugs tend to be kept in stables and outbuildings where they're subject to cold and damp.'

'One other question. We've talked about the clippings of horse hair. Did you find anything else?'

'Why don't you ask outright if we found any human hairs that match Rupert Hope's? Actually, we did. We can say for certain that he came into contact with it.'

Finally, something to be pleased about. 'That confirms one theory, then. We know where he went to have a roof over his head. Anything else I should be told?'

'If there is, you'll hear about it.'

Some caffeine-assisted decisions were called for. Diamond went down to the canteen. To top up his blood-sugar he invested in a chocolate chip muffin as well. His thoughts were more positive now.

The horse rug business was intriguing, and made Ingeborg's assignment with the cavalry unit even more of a challenge. What a good thing he'd given way after first insisting she remained a foot soldier. He'd update her and get her ideas where the horse might be found.

By tonight Nadia's picture would be on TV and in the *Bath Chronicle.* If anyone in the city remembered seeing her, the case could be transformed. Had she gone to watch the re-enactment that weekend in August, 1993? Or talked her way into some active role behind the scenes where the cavalry kept their horses?

Encouraging as all this was, the motive for Nadia's murder still eluded him. He'd rejected the theory that she'd been killed on orders from the London vice ring, but that didn't mean sex was discounted as a motive. Here was a young, attractive woman alone and looking for work in Bath, a city she didn't know. She'd needed to meet people. Being experienced in attracting men for paid sex, she may have signalled something she hadn't intended. It didn't require much imagination to see one of the re-enactors, high on the experience of the mock battle and tanked up with beer, deciding she was available, discovering she wasn't, losing control and killing her. An unplanned murder gruesomely covered up and hidden, there on the edge of the battlefield.

The other stock motives didn't look likely in this case. Nadia had just arrived on the Bath scene, so jealousy, that slow, festering cancer, was out. She was homeless and without funds, so theft or any form of financial gain could be dismissed. She wasn't being blackmailed or blocking someone's ambition or giving unreasonable offence. Revenge was unlikely considering she didn't know anyone here.

It had the feel of a sudden, spontaneous killing by a stranger — the hardest of all to investigate. In such cases, the best hope was that someone had witnessed something. His thoughts returned to those self-appointed snoops, the Lansdown Society.

He drained his coffee and went upstairs for a session with their police representative, Georgina.

The traffic light system on her door showed amber. He glanced at his watch. Five minutes, he decided.

No one came out. She was probably on the phone. He put his ear to the door and it opened and he fell into the arms of John Wigfull, who just about held him upright.

'Cheers, mate,' Diamond said.

'What the hell . . . ?'

'We can't go on meeting like this.'

'What?'

From behind her desk, Georgina called, 'Are you unwell, Peter?'

'Not at all.' He sidestepped the startled Wigfull. 'No harm done. I was thrown by the entry system. Thought it was changing

438

to green.'

She wasn't getting into a debate about her entry system. 'We were discussing the publicity budget. Mr Wigfull is going to need a slice of your cake if you continue to demand poster campaigns at the rate of two or three a week.'

An exaggeration he ignored. 'He's welcome to whatever's on offer. I just had a chocolate muffin downstairs.'

She didn't cotton on.

'Slice of the cake,' he said.

His attempts at wit never softened her. 'What are you here for? I'm expected in Headquarters in half an hour.'

'This won't take long, ma'am.' He looked over his shoulder and waited for Wigfull to close the door behind him. 'It's about the Lansdown Society. I see you and your fellow members as potential witnesses, invaluable to the enquiry.'

'You made that clear a while ago and you seem to have spoken to each of us now.'

'Actually, no.'

'Come on, Peter. I know for a fact that you questioned Sir Colin Tipping, Major Swithin and Augusta White.'

'There's another.'

'Me?' She clapped a hand to her chest. 'If I noticed anything I'd volunteer it. You wouldn't have to ask. I don't know what else you hope to discover. We're mere mortals, you know, not all-seeing.'

'Not you. There's somebody else. He's not all-seeing, but he may be halfway there. The sky pilot.'

'The what?'

'The reverend gentleman.'

'Charlie Smart? You've no need to talk to him. He wasn't a member in 1993. He was initiated after me, less than three years ago, when the previous vicar retired.'

Initiated. He was tempted to ask about that. Unfortunately more pressing matters had priority. 'I expect he's still an active member, just as you are? Goes for walks and keeps his eyes open and reports back on anything untoward?'

'We all do that.'

'He may be the witness I'm looking for.'

'I can't think what he could have witnessed.'

'Rupert Hope in the last hours of his life and possibly his murderer as well. Will I find Charlie Smart at St Stephen's?'

'No, you won't. He's not the vicar of Lansdown. His parish is higher up the hill, at St Vincent's on Granville Road, not far from the tower.'

'I don't think I know it.'

'Well, you're not renowned for your piety.' She smiled, pleased to have got in a dig of her own. 'It's tucked in among the government offices. It doesn't have a tower. In fact it looks more like a Nissen hut than a church.'

'Does he live nearby?'

'The vicarage is next door, but you'll be wasting your time. I'm sure if he'd seen anything suspicious, he would have informed us.'

'People can't always tell what's suspicious from what is not.'

'A vicar should.' She looked at her watch. 'I'll phone him and see if he's there.'

The 'government offices' Georgina had mentioned were the squat brick buildings known in Whitehall jargon as 'hutments', originally erected during the Second World War by the Ministry of Works to house a section of the Admiralty evacuated from London. Quite what the present buildings housed apart from civil servants was a mystery to Diamond, except that it had to do with the Ministry of Defence. Yet another Lansdown secret, but not one he needed to unravel. What interested him more was the proximity of the cemetery where Rupert's body had been found, just across the main road. Charlie Smart, living so close, was well placed to have seen something.

Georgina's description of the church hadn't been strictly accurate. A Nissen hut was a tunnel-shaped structure of corrugated iron. St Vincent's was modest in size, but brick built, and looked inseparable from the offices. Diamond would never have identified it until he found a board at the front listing the times of services. The vicarage next door was a similar hutment, fronted by a garden so overgrown that he had to part the foliage to get to the door.

'It's open,' a voice called from within.

He gave the door a push and found himself in the living room greeted by a short, blond man in jeans and a T-shirt with a butterfly motif. 'You must be the myrmidon of the law,' he said, offering his hand.

'I'm not sure what that means,' Diamond said, 'but it sounds roughly right.' He introduced himself.

'Charlie Smart, incumbent,' his host said. 'Would you like a drink?'

'Thank you, but not on duty.'

'Dandelion and burdock cordial won't compromise you,' Charlie Smart said, 'and I speak not only as a man of the cloth but the one who distilled the same. Try.' He picked up a jug and poured some into two tumblers.

In the cause of good policing, Diamond sipped some and found it marginally easier to swallow than Ukrainian *kvas*. 'Tasty.'

'As a society we impoverish ourselves by ignoring the so-called weeds,' the vicar said. 'Speaking of the humble dandelion, did you know that it's a source of rubber?'

'To be honest, no.' He remembered Mrs White the magistrate telling him the vicar was a wildlife enthusiast.

'Nip the stem of one and you get that whitish milk on your fingers. Allow it to thicken and you can rub it into a ball. The plant produces latex, you see.'

'Remarkable,' Diamond said, hoping to close down the botany lecture.

Charlie Smart wasn't finished. 'I have it on good authority that there's an Asian variety of dandelion that was cultivated on an enormous scale by the Russians during the war when their supplies of regular rubber were interrupted. The roots are up to two metres long and produce ten per cent of latex. It's still grown commercially in the Ukraine.'

Diamond became genuinely interested. 'Did you say the Ukraine?'

'I did. It was part of the old Russia.'

'Have you been there?'

'No. Plants are my thing. Preaching and plants — and when the two are combined, watch out. You'd better stop me if you want to talk about anything else.'

'People, actually, as distinct from plants.'

'I shouldn't say this as a man of the cloth, but they're not nearly so interesting. Any particular people?'

'Have you noticed anyone recently hanging about the cemetery across the road?'

'Apart from the people in paper suits, do you mean?'

'Before they arrived.'

'You want to know if I spotted the poor fellow who was murdered?'

'Him, or, better still, his killer.'

'Sorry, but no.'

'Do you get over there at all?'

'Quite often, in my pastoral capacity, conducting funerals on the declivity towards this end where the more recent graves are located. Also, wearing my botanical hat, studying the vegetation. The Victorian section near the tower was a wildlife sanctuary until your levellers arrived and hacked it down.'

'Searching for the weapon.'

'Which I understand they didn't find, so all that destruction of habitats was for nothing.'

'They had to make the effort,' Diamond said. 'Before they arrived, you noticed nobody?'

'Don't look so surprised. I wasn't on a twenty-four hour watch.'

'We believe the victim was sleeping in the gatehouse for a number of nights before he was killed.'

'Sensible,' Charlie Smart said. 'He'd stay dry there and wouldn't be disturbed. I'm sorry to disappoint you, but I can't remember seeing anything suspicious. You get the occasional visitor coming to see William Beckford's grave, but that's by day. It's not the sort of place most people would choose to visit at night. Every so often I'll go there with a lamp to study moths, but not in recent weeks. Have some more cordial.'

'No, thanks. As a member of the Lansdown Society, you patrol the down regularly?'

'I wouldn't put it in those terms. My rambles arise from my interest in the natural world. I'd cover the same ground whether I was in the society or not. However, I support its aims.'

'Do you get up to the battleground?'

'Regularly. You're going to ask me about the skeleton and I'm going to disappoint you again. I know nothing of what went on

445

up there. I've lived here only three years.'

'But you know the fallen tree?'

'The old oak? Yes. It's our success story, that tree. The farmer wanted to saw it up and sell the timber, but the Lansdown Society made sure he didn't. There was a rare variety of lichen growing on it, so they got a conservation order, or whatever you get for trees.'

'Like bats in your loft? It's illegal to evict them.'

'The same principle, yes.'

'What's it called?'

'The lichen? To tell you the truth, I don't know. Whatever it was, it's no longer there. The trunk has a nice shaggy jacket of *opegrapha corticola,* but among the lichens that's about as rare as the cabbage white butterfly.'

'So the conservation didn't work?'

'Apparently not.'

'Will it reappear?'

'I wouldn't hold your breath.'

'Could someone have misidentified it?'

He rolled his eyes. 'I can't answer that, not having been here at the time.'

'The others aren't experts like you.'

'In their own spheres they are. The major with his military know-how keeps a special eye on the war games.'

'And the golf.'

'Yes, indeed, along with Sir Colin, who is a man of the turf and has the racecourse under his wing. Augusta White is our legal eagle. And if Augusta represents law, your esteemed Georgina is the embodiment of order.'

'None of them wildlifers.'

'That's my section of expertise, apart from the obvious.'

'They're fortunate to have you. Was the previous vicar a botanist?'

'Arthur Underhill? No, he was a literary man, a Beckford expert, so he was in his element living here. Beckford wrote books, you know, as well as building towers.'

'Should I have read any?'

'I doubt if they'll assist your investigation. He wrote much about his travels abroad. His novel, called *Vathek* — in French, would you believe? — was set in some Arab country, and he also wrote a peculiar book called *Biographical Memoirs of Extraordinary Painters,* a literary folly, you might say, because none of the painters existed.'

Diamond was losing control of this interview. He'd only asked about Arthur Underhill.

'Beckford is still a cult figure,' the vicar went on. 'People knock on my door asking the way to the tower and some of them know a lot about him. You still get the occasional crank who thinks he squirreled away some of the treasures and masterpieces he stacked in the tower. The auction after his death was a very dubious affair presided over by a crooked auctioneer and his son who absconded soon after.'

'I don't know why Lansdown should give rise to so much crime,' Diamond said. 'It's just one large hill, after all.'

'It's Bath's back room,' Charlie Smart said, 'stuffed with things people want to forget about.'

31

'Where's Ingeborg?' he asked in the incident room.

Septimus looked up from his computer. 'Somewhere on Lansdown by now, looking for an elderly warhorse. I told her your theory and she got really fired up.'

John Leaman said, 'Any excuse to get out of this place.'

'Wishing you'd thought of it?' Diamond said.

'I'm not a horse person.'

'Who's the old nag in here, then?'

There were grins around the room.

Septimus added, 'She was on the phone to someone in the Sealed Knot, finding out where they stable the horses they use.'

'What's she going to do if she finds the right one — interview it?' Leaman asked, not done for yet.

'I expect she'll get a hair sample.'

'To see if it's the same colour?'

'For the DNA,' Diamond said, using his freshly acquired knowledge. 'Didn't you know horses have DNA?'

Leaman went quiet.

'Plenty of horses are taken to Lansdown for the race meetings,' Paul Gilbert said with a charged tone in his voice. He'd been on a high since finding Nadia's landlady. 'Maybe we should make a check up there.'

'Twenty-year-olds, in training?' Diamond said.

He turned a shade more pink. 'I guess not.'

But something was stirring in Diamond's memory. He asked, 'What happened to that calendar Ingeborg made of events that happened on Lansdown? It was on the display board.'

'She transferred it to a computer file, sir,' one of the civilian staff said. 'Would you like to access it?'

'I would if you do it for me.'

'On your computer, or mine?'

'Mine.'

In the quiet of his office, he scrolled through Ingeborg's listings, most of them commonplace and trivial. Her mind-numbing task had been done at Keith Halliwell's suggestion and at the time Diamond had thought it a monumental waste of effort, but had refrained from saying so. What possible relevance could club reunions and cross-country races have to a murder enquiry? Now that the time frame had narrowed to a few days in the summer of 1993 — from Nadia's arrival late in July to the battle re-enactment on August 7th and 8th — the calendar was worth a look.

She had definitely arrived after Mrs Jarvie's eightieth on July 23rd. He watched the pages roll like film credits and stopped them at the end of July, 1993.

July 24	Rare red kite sighted over Kingswood School
July 28	Lorry sheds its load and causes two-mile traffic jam
July 31	St Stephen's Church Fete
August 1	Car boot picture said to be Rowlandson print
August 2	Sheep savaged near Upper Langridge. Big cat theory
August 4	Four-hour power failure after thunderstorm.
August 7	Battle of Lansdown re-enactment Day 1
August 8	" " " " " " " " " " " " Day 2

Disappointing. A few suggestions of summer, but nothing to link to Nadia except

the re-enactment — and that was only
because she'd been buried close to where
the fighting took place As for the rest, rare
birds and big cats were staple items for
newspapers in the so-called silly season. A
traffic jam and a power failure didn't spark
the vague recollection he thought he had of
something significant.

He scrolled on a little.

August 9   Metal-detectorist finds Roman
            brooch, Charlcombe
August 12   Hang-glider stolen
August 13   Travellers moved on from
            Charmy Down site
August 16   Car-boot 'Rowlandson' was
            forgery
August 20   Hole in One at Ladies' Golf
            Tournament

He couldn't imagine Nadia metal-
detecting or hang-gliding or golfing like
some leisured Bathonian. She'd be trying to
get work. Yet he had a sense that the information on the screen mattered to the case.
Elusive thoughts were trying to connect in
his brain. He scrolled back and started to
study the list again, from the red kite onwards.

His phone beeped.

Wigfull's voice. 'Just to let you know that

your Ukrainian girl is in tonight's *Bath Chronicle*. I've got an early copy if you want to see it. And the story will be on Points West and HTV News tonight, so the phones should start ringing soon. You'd better not go home early.'

His train of thought had derailed. 'Nice work, John. Do you want to be part of the excitement?'

'No, thanks. It's my positive thinking night.'

He didn't ask.

He took one more look at the screen before stepping into the incident room to see who was willing to do overtime. The practicalities of managing a team had to be gone through. Paul Gilbert was game and so were a couple of the Bristol team and three civilians. Not Septimus: he'd worked more than his share of late evenings in recent days and wanted a night off.

'Fair enough. We'll cope,' Diamond said.

A high profile appeal to the public always brings in responses. Most are made in good faith, even if a high proportion prove to be mistaken. Wanting to help is a human instinct. Sometimes the offers are driven more by the wish than the reality. It's easy to convince oneself that certain events took place and fit the facts of the appeal, particularly after a long lapse of time. Additionally there are callers not so altruistic, who see an opportunity of profit. They'll have heard about payments to informants. Usually their information is worthless. Finally there are the nuisance callers, the equivalent of the idiots who make bogus 999 calls.

Out of all this the police must sift the genuine witnesses. Diamond went over the procedure with his volunteers, stressing the known facts about Nadia: that she was Ukrainian, under twenty, a Roman Catholic, had lived for a time in London as a prostitute and was in lodgings in Lower Swainswick. She spoke good English, had been orphaned, so had no family, and she would have been wearing jeans and a T-shirt. 'The trick is that you don't give out any of this. You listen to the information coming in and see if it checks. Be sure to get the contact details of the informant before they tell you their story.'

As if on cue, a call came in, but it was only Ingeborg. 'I've spent the entire afternoon checking on horses, guv.'

'I was told. Any joy?'

'Joy? I saw some adorable animals, but none that were old enough. And now it's got so late I'd better get straight to my evening session with the cavalry, so I won't come back, if that's all right.'

'It's okay. You don't want to be late on parade.'

'God, no.'

'One thing, Inge.'

'Guv?'

'Don't lose sight of what you're really there for.'

In the short time Diamond had been speaking to her, the first call had come in about Nadia. Paul Gilbert was taking it. After a few seconds he started shaking his head. He thanked the caller and rang off. 'Wrong year. They said the Olympics were on in Barcelona. That was 1992.'

'Good thinking,' Diamond said. 'Did you watch it on TV?'

'I was only two at the time.'

'There's a sobering thought. I was working here. Same job, same rank. *Barcelona.* I used to drive up Wellsway singing along with Freddie Mercury and Montserrat Caballé. And you were just a toddler at the time. Unbelievable.'

More calls started coming in. One was a definite sighting, but only at Mass at St John's and the caller couldn't recall which Sunday it was. Nadia had covered her head with a dark scarf, but otherwise she was wearing the T-shirt and jeans.

'Must have borrowed the scarf from Mrs Jarvie,' Diamond said.

After six, when the local news was screened on HTV, a flurry of calls came in, but none proved to be of obvious help. It seemed everyone had memories of young foreign girls asking directions in Bath or enrolling for English as a Foreign Language at the Tech. The problem was that enrolment didn't start until September. By then Nadia was almost certainly dead.

'I'm starting to lose confidence,' Diamond said. 'I wish I'd joined John Wigfull for some positive thinking.'

He helped man the phones for another two hours. The results were disappointing. Three would be worth following up, but they appeared to offer little new information. Someone had spoken to a Ukrainian girl at the station on the day she arrived. Two had seen someone who looked like Nadia walking into town from Lower Swainswick.

The evening shift could be left to take any more calls. He thanked the team. 'You never know,' he said. 'Someone may call us tomorrow.'

Before leaving, he made a call of his own, to Paloma, inviting her for a drink and a bite to eat. She said she'd eaten already, but she'd be pleased to join him. He suggested meeting at the Blathwayt. The pub-restaurant was right at the top of the hill, a long-established watering-hole for racegoers, golfers, car-booters and travellers on the South Downs Way.

'On Lansdown?' she said. 'Can't you leave your work behind?'

'I've heard they have a good chef.'

'Be honest, Peter,' she said. 'You're not going there for the food.'

'All right, I'm combining business with pleasure, but the pleasure will be paramount.'

'Smoothie. I don't believe a word.'

He'd suggested 9 p.m., and made sure he arrived early enough to walk through the Blathwayt's several dining areas checking who was there. A chat in this relaxed setting with one of his vigilante friends from the Lansdown Society wouldn't have come amiss. The bar was doing a brisk trade, but he recognised nobody there or in the restaurant. Outside, under the patio heaters, was a candlelit section he hadn't seen before — a development pubs everywhere were favouring since the smoking ban came in. Seeing some people leave, he moved smoothly into a seat at the table. He'd ordered his lasagne and the drinks before Paloma drove up.

'I seem to be losing my aura of mystery,' she said after they'd kissed. 'You even know what I want to drink.'

'Is that bad?'

'I've *got* a drink and it's the right one, so I'm not going to complain. This is nice, being outside.'

'I don't know if you've been inside lately,' he said. 'It's had a makeover since I was last here. I remember it as dark and seedy.'

'In keeping with its past,' she said.

He smiled. If there was background on any Bath location, Paloma knew it.

'Back in the eighteenth century, it was a highwaymen's pub called the Star. The road to Bath was perfect for hold-ups. They'd rob people at gunpoint and then spend some of the money here before moving on.'

'There's no end to the villainy on this bloody hill. Only this afternoon I was hearing about a firm of bent auctioneers.'

'English and Son. Absolute crooks. How did they come up?'

He told her what he'd learned from Charlie Smart.

'He's right,' she said. 'It's all in the book I lent you. The pair of them disappeared owing a fortune in debts and were never traced and neither were some of William Beckford's treasures. He had one of the finest private art collections in the country, paintings by Raphael and Bellini, Claude and Canaletto. And there were other treasures of gold and silver.'

'A secret hoard?' Diamond thought about it as the possible mainspring for two murders. 'Now you're confusing me. I was coming round to sex as the motive for Nadia's death.'

'It sounds likely,' Paloma said. 'She had nothing worth stealing.'

'But if she happened to have found a stash of valuables, that could have made her a target.'

'Beckford's lost treasures? Don't you think all the likely places have been checked long ago?'

'Right. I'm way off beam.'

She thought about it, turning her glass. 'There have been other finds up here. Have you heard of the Lansdown Sun Disc?'

Amused once again by her fund of local lore, he shook his head. 'Tell me.'

'A gilded bronze model of the sun over three thousand years old, excavated in one of the Bronze Age barrows. It's now in the British Museum. Quite a treasure.'

'I can cap that,' he said. 'What do you say

to three tons of gold bullion in ingots so pure you could mould them in your hands?'

'I say yes, please, if it's legal.'

'It isn't. The trail for the biggest robbery in history went cold on Lansdown.'

'Get away!'

'You've heard of the Brink's-Mat heist in 1983? Twenty-six million in gold bullion from a warehouse at Heathrow?'

'Of course.'

'There was a local guy, a millionaire, who came under suspicion. He lived in style at the Coach House at Battlefields, the hamlet beside the Civil War site. A snatch squad raided the place and found a smelter, ingot moulds and two gold ingots still warm to the touch. Also shotguns and a rifle.'

'I do remember reading something now.'

'The people doing the smelting were minor players. The owner was in Tenerife. Eventually he was deported and put on trial and acquitted on all charges.'

'Acquitted? How was that?'

'He claimed the smelting was part of his legitimate business. Among other companies, he owned a Bath jeweller's. He went on to create the largest timeshare company in Europe, worth many millions. Eventually it was exposed as a scam and he got an eight-year sentence.'

'What about the gold?'

'No one knows. About a thousand kilos are still unaccounted for. Our people dug up the floorboards at the Coach House. They went at the area around the pool with a digger and drills. Nothing else was found.'

'Lansdown's a big area.'

'And full of secrets.'

His food arrived. He unwrapped the knife and fork. 'Care for a taste?'

'No, thanks.' She took a long sip of her spritzer. 'I saw the picture of Nadia on Points West. She looked happy enough when it was taken.'

'She'd just escaped from the London vice ring. Bath was a new beginning. This is a lasagne to die for.'

'I hope not. Has the picture jogged any memories?'

'Not enough. I'm interested to know if anyone saw her at the re-enactment.'

She looked doubtful. 'In the cavalry?'

He smiled. 'These East Europeans are second to none at getting work. No, you're right. I can't believe she was taken on by the Sealed Knot within days of arriving here.'

'It's unpaid, isn't it? They dress up and play soldiers for the fun of the thing. What Nadia needed was a paid job.'

He told her about the lab report on the horse rug. She listened keenly and weighed his theory. 'You think Rupert found a rug belonging to the same horse Nadia came into contact with all those years ago?'

'Sixteen years. It's possible.'

'Theoretically,' she said in a voice already thinking something else. 'You said the rug had deteriorated through age, rather than wear and tear?'

'That's what they told me.'

'Isn't it more likely that it hasn't been used in many years and was stored in some outbuilding and found by Rupert? He was scavenging for stuff all the time.'

He nodded. 'That makes sense, too. We can't dismiss any scenario.'

'So Ingeborg got out today visiting the horses?'

'And riding one. She's at cavalry training as we speak.' He glanced at some people entering the restaurant, two women in conversation and a bearded man tagging on behind, all of them probably in the forty to fifty age group.

'Someone special?' Paloma asked.

'The dark woman in the blue suit is familiar.'

'How familiar is that? An old flame?'

'You did ask. No, I don't believe I've ever

spoken to her, but I've seen her recently. Can't think where.'

'On one of your "wanted" lists?'

He shook his head.

'She's attractive . . . for her age,' Paloma said. 'I expect she's on someone's wanted list.'

'The guy with the beard?'

'No, he looks like extra baggage. He's there on sufferance. Staff, probably. She's the boss lady.'

'They don't look dressed for a night out.'

'My guess is that they worked late and she's invited them for a drink.' She clicked her fingers. 'I've seen her, too, and I know where. At the races. She was the woman in the peacock-coloured hat we saw getting the prize.'

'Spot on,' he said. 'Davina Tipping, daughter of Sir Colin. He told me she owns her own practice as a vet.'

'And the others work for her, I expect. The bearded guy looks as if he could tell one budgie from another. I'm not sure I'd trust him with a pregnant cow. Davina, on the other hand, looks well capable. She may be able to advise you on the local horse population. I bet she knows where a lot of them are stabled.'

'I hadn't thought of asking a vet,' he said.

He liked the suggestion. 'They're heading for the bar.' He pushed his plate aside. He'd eaten most of it. 'Let's join them, shall we?'

Paloma gave a resigned smile and followed him. The 'pleasure' part of the outing was over.

Davina and her party had taken their drinks to a table near the open hearth in the centre of the room where a genuine log fire blazed.

'Pardon me for butting in,' Diamond said, 'but you're just the people who can help me. I'm correct, am I not, in saying you're Davina Tipping, the top vet in Bath? I'm Peter Diamond of Bath CID, and this is my friend Paloma Kean. We watched your filly winning the trophy a week or two ago.'

'My Stylist,' Paloma said trying to soften his none-too-subtle interruption. 'We backed her. These drinks should have been on us.'

Diamond refrained from mentioning he'd backed another horse and not won anything.

'That's generous,' Davina said. 'I started a tab. I haven't paid yet.'

'Peter will see to it,' Paloma said.

There was a strict rule in Bath nick that pub expenses had to be authorised in advance by Georgina. This would come out of his own pocket.

'What sort of help are you wanting?' Davina said. 'I hope you haven't got a sick animal under your jacket.' She introduced her companions. True to expectation, Sally and Wilfred worked in the practice.

Without going into specifics, Diamond said he was currently involved in a case linked to the re-enactments of the Battle of Lansdown and trying to get information on a horse that could have taken part in the 1993 event and might still be kept somewhere local.

'It would be getting on a bit,' Paloma added. 'We think about twenty.'

'Is that too old?' Diamond asked.

'Horses, like people, live longer these days,' Davina told them. 'Twenty isn't unusual. You can get insurance up to twenty-five and some breeds, like Morgans, live well into their thirties.'

'I expect they need more treatment as they get older,' he said. 'As a vet, you may know of an elderly horse like this.'

'What colour?'

'Black or dark brown.'

She smiled. 'Any other markings?'

'I wouldn't know,' he said. 'We've only got a few hairs as evidence. If it's any help, they were found on a burgundy coloured under-rug made by a firm called Phil Drake.'

'That's going back some,' Davina said. 'I haven't heard of Phil Drake equipment for years. Where was this rug found?'

'In the entrance gate to Beckford's Tower, being used by a man sleeping rough. Where he found it is a mystery.'

'Out of a stable, I expect,' she said. 'There are more than you might think on Lansdown and I know of two that supply horses for these battle events.'

'I expect this old warhorse would be retired.'

'Not necessarily. You wouldn't want young or highly strung animals taking part, so older ones are preferred because they aren't troubled by the gunfire and drums. A mock battle isn't demanding on agility, a few short gallops, that's all. It doesn't compare with steeplechasing or showjumping.' She spoke with the calm authority that comes with giving expert advice.

'That's so helpful to know,' he said, his ideas moving on. 'Puts a whole new slant on the case. Would you mind giving me the addresses of those stables?'

'Not a problem. I'll write them down if we can find a pen and paper. You should speak to the Sealed Knot people. They know more than I do.'

'One of my team is with them tonight.'

He took a pen and notebook from his pocket and handed them to Davina. 'While you're doing that I'll get more drinks. Same again, everyone?'

It was a cheap round. Sally and Wilfred said they were leaving for home shortly and Davina had promised to meet her father at the golf club.

Whilst waiting to settle his bill, Diamond found himself thinking about Sir Colin Tipping and things he had said that morning at the golf club when they rode in the cart ahead of Major Swithin. Some part of the conversation was niggling at his brain and he couldn't grasp the relevance.

'Are you a vet, sir?' the barman asked.

'God, no.' He was still struggling to remember.

'My mistake. Saw you with the others.'

'No problem. I'm sure you get all sorts up here: golfers, racegoers, ramblers.'

'The world and his wife, sir.'

Then the connection was made. He realised what he'd missed when scrolling through Ingeborg's calendar of events. Now it was vital that he spoke to Davina's father.

He was about to impose even more on Davina's good nature — and Paloma's. The opportunity had to be seized. The chance of an off-the-record chat with Sir Colin was too good to miss.

'I don't know if you'll get any sense out of him,' Davina said when he told her what he wanted. 'He'll have sunk a few whiskies by now. My job on a Friday night is to get him home.'

All the better if the whisky is talking, Diamond thought.

32

'Not the evening you expected, was it?' he said to Paloma as they walked to their cars.

'I had my suspicions, if you remember,' she said.

'And you were right.'

She smiled. 'I'm going to leave you with your horsey friends. You'll do better on your own at this stage — unless you want me to call reinforcements.'

'Send for the cavalry?' He grinned. 'I don't think.'

They embraced and he promised to make it up to her.

In the car, he picked up his disregarded mobile phone and gazed at it in his palm. What was the hour now? If he knew which buttons to press, the thing could tell him. No doubt it could supply the latest cricket scores and the state of the pound against the dollar. All he used it for was to make the occasional phone call. Ingeborg was about to rue the day she had set up the menu for him and put her own number in the directory. Wherever she was, he reasoned, she should be capable of answering. Her evening training session would be well over.

'Inge? It's me — Diamond.'

'I know, guv. You're on my display.'

He had no desire to be on anyone's display.

'I can always tell who's calling,' she said.

'Right, and it's late.'

'Must be important, I guess.'

He could hear a background buzz of voices and canned music. 'Are you in company?'

'Sure. Guess who I met at the drill.'

He didn't have time for guessing games. 'I was looking at that list of events on Lansdown, the one you compiled for Keith.'

'Not only for him,' she said. 'It's for everyone to use.'

'Do you happen to remember working on July to August, 1993, the time we know for certain Nadia was in Bath?'

'Now you're asking. I just plodded through the years. At the time I didn't know 1993 or any other year was important. I simply went through the *Bath Chronicle* jotting down anything I found.'

'Mainly headlines?'

'They were only meant to be a quick reference.'

'Fine — like the re-enactment, which is on the list, both days, among lots of other stuff.'

'Don't ask me, guv. It's a blur now.' Her tone of voice told him she was having a good time and wanted to be shot of this call.

'But I am asking. On one of the days, not long after the battle, you made a note that went "Hang-glider stolen".'

'Did I?'

She wasn't usually this vague. He could picture her shrugging and smiling at her friends in the bar. 'Are you listening, Inge? What I need to know — and it's important — is if you meant a hang-glider as such, or the racehorse with the same name? At some point — and it could have been 1993 — a young stallion called Hang-glider belonging to Sir Colin Tipping was driven away and never seen again — like Shergar.'

'Like what?'

'Never mind.' The kidnapping of Shergar must have happened before she was born. 'A hang-glider or a horse?'

'You've got me there,' she said. 'The horse that went missing made big news for some days, but offhand I couldn't tell you its

471

name or which year it was. I can check and call you back.'

'There isn't time. I'll be with Tipping directly.'

'Put it this way, guv. I have mental pictures of most of these incidents, but I can't remember anyone nicking a hang-glider. I'm ninety per cent sure it must be the horse.'

'I'll go with that,' he said.

He had to. Davina was getting into a sports car close by. The roar of her engine rattled the keys in Diamond's car. He threw down the phone, started up and followed her the short distance up the road to the front of the club house.

'I can't say what state Fa will be in,' she called as they both got out of their vehicles. 'It's my job to collect him so that he isn't breathalysed. He used to collect me from parties when I was a kid, so I suppose I owe him this. Are you coming in?'

'I'd rather see him apart from his friends when he comes out.'

'Give me time to root him out, then.'

The notion of the golf club members being collected like kids after a party amused him, particularly when he saw two other women drive up and go inside. A couple of taxis were waiting as well.

Then a group of four emerged from the

472

club house in loud conversation and he saw that Davina had accomplished her mission. Sir Colin looked reasonably steady on his feet. The others were Major Reggie Swithin and his wife, Agnes, the redoubtable woman Diamond had met at the pike drill. The noise was coming mainly from the major. 'The night is young and I know of several excellent hostelries in the city,' he was saying. 'Where's your spirit of adventure?'

'You've had all the spirit you're getting,' his wife told him. 'Come along, Reggie. Time to go home.'

There were more protests, but it became obvious that Agnes would get her way. She steered the major to their Land Rover, leaving Sir Colin and Davina in conversation near the entrance. Sir Colin looked across the car roofs to where Diamond was waiting. It didn't take detective work to deduce what was being said.

Diamond went over. 'Just happened to meet Davina in the Blathwayt,' he said. 'She mentioned she was driving you home and there was something I forgot to ask when we spoke before.'

'My daughter's hand in marriage?' Sir Colin said, straight into his music hall routine. 'So what are your prospects, young man?'

'Fa, that'll do,' Davina said. 'Mr Diamond doesn't have time for fun and games.'

'I don't know about the "Mr". He's not what you take him for.'

'It's all right. He told me he's a policeman.'

'Policeman, be blowed. He's the genie of the golf course. You never know when he's going to appear, but instead of granting your wishes he asks questions.'

'Fa, that's his job.'

'Don't I know it? He put me through the third degree the other day and ruined my chance of a decent round. Well, superintendent, what did you forget to ask?'

'You told me about the horse that went missing.'

'Hang-glider. Don't remind me. I get tearful.'

'Was that in August, 1993?'

'You're asking me for details like that at this end of the evening? Really, I can't recall.'

Davina said, 'It was definitely 1993, the year you met the Queen at Ascot, her fortieth since the Coronation.'

'You're right. He'd just won the Prince of Wales's Stakes. What a win that was.'

'Tragically his last,' Davina said to Diamond. 'His trainer noticed a slight limp in the near foreleg and felt some heat below the knee. Ultrasound revealed an injury to the tendon and Fa had to retire him, just when he was ready to take on the world. We were all devastated. Which was when Sheikh Abdul made his offer. Talk about genies. We thought Fa's magic moment had come, but it wasn't to be.'

'May I ask what the offer amounted to?'

'It's on public record,' she said. 'Half a million up front and fifty per cent of the stud fees. He was expected to cover more than a hundred mares in a season at a stud fee of fifty thou a time.'

'So the money would continue to flow in?'

'For as long as the horse did the business,' Tipping said. 'I reckon he was good for five to ten years. Compared to that, the insurance payout was a pittance, under a hundred thou, and I had to wait three years and get my solicitor onto them before they paid up.'

'I suppose they needed to be sure he was dead,' Diamond said.

'No, that wasn't the issue.'

'What was he insured against?'

'Accident, foul play or death. The claim was foul play. Bloody obvious when the horse had vanished.'

Diamond came to the point. 'The reason I asked about the date is that 1993 appears to have been the year that the young woman whose murder I'm investigating was buried on Lansdown. There was a horse hair found with her skeleton and it's just possible it came from your horse.'

'Good Lord! What makes you think that?'

'I said it's a possibility. Did you employ a girl to groom the horse?'

'Personally, no. You'd have to ask my trainer, Percy McDart, at Lambourn. He looked after all that. He's still in business there.'

'Lambourn? Is that where the horse was stabled?' This was not what he wanted to hear. He knew of Lambourn, one of the centres of racehorse training, at least forty miles off, the other side of Swindon. 'I was thinking Hang-glider was trained locally.'

'Well, you'd be wrong. Any half-decent horse is kept at Lambourn, Highclere or Newmarket.'

'I'll contact McDart. We'd like to check Hang-glider's DNA.'

'How can you do that when he's not been seen since 1993?' Davina asked. 'They didn't keep DNA records then.'

'If anything was kept as a souvenir — let's say a saddle, or a rug — we might get hairs or skin particles, from it. Do you possess anything like that, Sir Colin?'

Tipping shook his head. 'All I have are photographs and racecards and a fat file of correspondence from the damned insurance company. You're welcome to see those any time.'

'And some silver cups in the trophy cabinet,' Davina said. 'You still have those, Fa.'

'That's true, but they won't help the police. They get polished regularly.'

'His rug?' Diamond tried again.

'I collected cheques and trophies, not horse rugs. You'll have to ask McDart.'

'And did you ever hear from the people who stole the horse?'

'Not a word. They didn't demand a ransom and they couldn't race him. I believe I told you my theory.'

'That he was secretly put to stud?'

Davina said, 'I don't believe that one.'

'He'd have produced damned good foals,' her father said.

'Not necessarily. There are no guarantees in horse-breeding. Many great stallions and mares have produced only moderate offspring. You know the saying: breed the best to the best and hope for the best.'

'Sheikh Abdul thought he was a good investment and so did the blighters who took him.'

'But if the matings were done secretly the foals would have no pedigree.'

'Doesn't matter. When you know something and other people don't, there's money to be made.'

'Not enough,' she said.

'What's your theory, then, Miss Wisenheimer?' Tipping asked.

'I've never said this to you before, Fa, but if you really want to know, I think it was done from personal spite. Someone heard you were about to cash in and they chose that moment to bring you down.'

He looked quite shaken. 'I'm not one to make enemies. I've always treated people decently in business and in everyday life.'

'You don't know the effect you have on others. Ask Mr Diamond.'

For one awkward moment Diamond thought he was being invited to say what a boring old fart the man was, but Davina went on to say, 'Isn't jealousy one of the main motives for crime?'

'It's one to consider, yes,' Diamond said. 'If you're right, what do you think happened to the horse?'

She gave him a glance that made him wish he hadn't asked. 'I'd rather not say. He was my father's pride and joy.'

33

Ingeborg was waiting to see Diamond when he arrived next morning, her eyes bright as sword blades.

'Something happened?' he asked.

'It's Saturday, guv.'

'Even I can work that out,' he said.

'Farleigh Hungerford Castle. The muster this afternoon. I'm wondering if I can leave early.'

'Your performance. Right.' With the focus shifting to the missing racehorse, he had nudged Inge's frolic to the back of his thoughts. 'What time?'

'Well, as soon as possible. They want us on parade at one p.m. — that's in full uniform, us and our horses.'

'You've had only one rehearsal, haven't you?'

She gave him a pained look. 'Drill, guv. We call it drill. Yes, I'm making up the numbers, one of the extras, but I still have to look the part.'

'Like a bloke, you mean? They didn't really have women in the cavalry, did they?'

'Do you mind? I expect they did. Only I'm not trying to pass myself off as a guy.'

'Before you go, did you find out anything last night?'

'About Hang-glider?'

'No, I cleared that up. Anything on Rupert?'

She shook her head, a fraction too fast for Diamond's liking.

'You forgot?' His eyes continued to read her face. 'There's something, isn't there?'

A sigh, blaming him. 'I tried to tell you this last night. The surprise was the officer in charge, our drill instructor. I must have done a double take when he rode up in his buff coat and feathered hat. It was Dave.'

'Dave who?'

'You know. Dave Barton, the man who was with Rupert when they found the femur.'

He paused, taking this in.

'Inge, are you sure?'

'Hundred per cent.'

'He's a foot soldier, not cavalry,' Diamond said. 'He shouldn't be on a horse.' Even as he spoke, he recalled Keith Halliwell telling him Dave liked the outdoor life and went out riding.

Ingeborg flushed scarlet. 'You don't know what you're saying. Believe me, Dave could teach Butch Cassidy a trick or two. I don't know what he was doing the day of the re-enactment, but he's a cavalry officer, and a good one. I'm not kidding, guv.'

'He's not the officer type.'

She clicked her tongue in annoyance. 'It's not the real army. You don't have to go through Sandhurst to do the job.'

Fair point, he thought. These people were playing at soldiers. He'd been caught making assumptions.

'He's just your average guy, except he's a top horsemen,' she said to soften her petulance. 'He makes it all seem simple.'

'I believe you. I'm surprised, that's all.'

'Maybe his horse was injured when they had the muster. He'd still want to take part, wouldn't he?'

'Did he recognise you as CID?'

'I don't think so. I saw him the day he came in, but we didn't speak. He's okay. No side to him.'

He allowed her to leave directly. Much else was on his mind.

John Wigfull was the next to look in and he, too, appeared uncommonly cheerful. 'I hear there was a very good response to my

481

press release. I expect you've solved your case now, or you're on the point of doing so.'

'It's not the number of calls. It's the quality of the information.'

'The story was on the late news on television. You'll get more take-up this morning, I guarantee.'

'I'll let you know, John.'

For the next few precious minutes he was not interrupted. The previous night's conversation with Sir Colin Tipping had almost persuaded him that the theft of Hang-glider in 1993 was the key to the case. Up to then he'd been assuming Nadia's murder was connected to the re-enactment, that she'd been killed during or shortly after the battle and buried hurriedly. The discovery that the race meeting took place four days later and a serious crime was committed opened a new possibility. Could she have witnessed the theft of the horse and been shot simply because she was there? They could have bundled her body into a car or van and driven her a short way up the road and buried her.

Wouldn't it be marvellous if Wigfull's publicity had produced an eye-witness who remembered seeing Nadia at the race meeting? He stepped back into the incident room and asked the receiver for the latest batch of notes from callers.

Wigfull had been right about one thing. Enough people had phoned to raise expectations. A glance through the material was less encouraging. He found the usual mix of guesswork, wishful thinking and imprecision. Any foreign woman of almost any age was liable to have been reported. Some callers were under the illusion that Nadia was still alive and working in a shop. There was another sighting from Sunday Mass in August, 1993, but otherwise the result was negative.

He picked up the phone and asked the operator to get a line to the Lambourn trainer of racehorses, Percy McDart. She called back to say McDart wasn't listed under his own name and could Diamond kindly supply the name of the stables he worked for?

A job for young Paul Gilbert. 'What's that paper the punters buy — the *Racing Post*. They're sure to know. And when you reach McDart, make an appointment for later this morning, say about noon. You can say who we are, but not what it's about. I want to see his reaction for myself.'

'Will you need directions, guv?'

'You will. You're doing the driving.'

From across the incident room, Septimus called out, 'Something you should know, boss.'

'What's that?'

'Remember the lager that was buried before the battle?'

'By Dave Barton?'

'We finally caught up with the guy who nicked it.'

He shimmied around the desks to hear more. 'Nice work. Who is he?'

'A parliamentarian, he calls himself, named Bert Pope. He was exercising his horse on the battlefield an hour before the fighting started and he saw this soldier in royalist red burying a six-pack by the fallen tree. As he tells it, this was one of the enemy, so he thought it was fair game to return there later and help himself and that's what he did. But seeing as it was a hot day and everyone knows how thirsty you get, whichever army you're in, he left two of the cans. He said he read about the skeleton being found there later but he didn't come forward because he couldn't see that the lager had anything to do with it, and anyway he felt a bit mean for what he'd done.'

'How did you find him?'

'He shared the drink with some of his friends in the roundhead army and told them where it came from. At the time, they enjoyed the joke. When one of them saw the stuff in the paper, he told Pope he'd better fess up. And he did, eventually.'

'Good. It chimes in nicely with Dave Barton's statement.'

'It doesn't mean Barton is in the clear,' Septimus said at once. His suspicions of the blacksmith had not gone away. 'He was in no hurry to come forward himself.'

'So don't you believe the rest of his story — that the last time he saw Rupert was after they finished the lager and returned to the fighting?'

The only response was a tightening of the lips.

'What's your take on it?' Diamond said.

He remained edgy. 'It's one of those things you can't prove. He comes across as an okay guy.'

'Inge agrees with you. He's her cavalry officer.'

Septimus blinked and drew himself up. 'That didn't come out at the interview.'

'If I recall it right, when you asked if he was a regular pikeman, he said not always, or something similar.'

'Evasive.'

'Perhaps he'd been demoted for some misdemeanour. He's a captain of horse according to Ingeborg.'

'That makes sense now. When I asked him about the cavalryman who saw him burying the lager, he said he'd know the horse if he saw it again.'

Diamond nodded. 'A white stallion.'

'A pale horse.'

'Same thing.'

'You don't get it, do you?' Septimus gave him a gaze burnished with zeal. 'The Book of Revelation. "And I looked, and behold a pale horse: and his name that sat on him was Death." '

For much of the trip along the motorway, those words resonated in Diamond's head. The Bible wasn't often quoted in Bath CID. Was it stereotyping to suppose Septimus, as a member of the black community, was a churchgoer, used to hearing high-flown texts from the pulpit? Some of the Pentecostal churches in Bristol were well known for the power of their preachers and the involvement of their congregations. He could picture Septimus, a man with a solemn presence, letting go as he joined in the responses. Had the phrase about the pale horse come to him automatically, or did it give voice to a genuine apprehension?

To do the man justice, he had been consistent in his suspicion of Dave Barton. He'd worked out that ingenious theory that it had been Rupert who had hidden the six-pack, chancing on the very place where Dave (the supposed killer of Nadia) had buried the body all those years before. Dave (the theory went) had been compelled to silence Rupert by murdering him. The tough inter-rogation, when Dave had brought along his lawyer, Miss Tower, had been insisted on and carried out by Septimus. The truth should have emerged. Either Dave was very smart or Septimus was barking up the wrong tree. Nothing conclusive had come from it.

And now new witness Bert Pope had torpedoed the theory. Dave had been seen in the act of burying the lager. His story was corroborated.

Septimus was reduced to quoting doom-laden stuff from the Bible.

Unsettling, even so.

Paul Gilbert said suddenly, 'If you don't mind me asking, guv, I'm not too clear how this racehorse trainer fits in.'

'Right. I'll tell you.' It was a relief to talk about something else. He hadn't briefed the team since his meeting with Tipping and his daughter. Taking his time, he told Gilbert precisely why it had become necessary to get the trainer's version of what had happened the evening Hang-glider had been stolen.

Before he'd finished, they ended the steady climb into the Cotswolds and joined the motorway. Stone buildings gave way to vast stretches of pasture covering Wiltshire's chalk downs. Nowhere in the south offered longer views, or such a sense of the past. Gilbert was driving at a speed Diamond approved, content to use the slow lane along with the Saturday traffic of caravans and campers returning from holidays in Cornwall.

It wasn't long before they passed Swindon and started looking for their exit. Gilbert had the Sat-Nav working — just one more gadget Diamond had resolved he didn't need in his own car.

'We're close now,' Gilbert said as they made the fourth prompted turn in under a minute and started up a narrow lane rutted with mud and cow manure.

'I've heard that before. You couldn't bring a horsebox up here.'

'It's the direct route for us.'

Sure enough, it opened into a wider, better maintained road and only a short way along they had to pull in for a string of horses on their way to the gallops. Gilbert pulled down his window to ask and the leading rider pointed behind him.

In two minutes they were driving towards a complex of stables and outbuildings. Security, Diamond noted, was all around them: CCTV, high walls topped with razor wire, double sets of gates. They had to speak into an entry-phone to gain admission.

'They call this a yard?' Gilbert said, marvelling.

'A yard and then some. It's a multimillion business.'

Inside, they drew up outside the brick-built admin section, two storeys high. Mr McDart, they learned from a high-heeled, white-suited receptionist, was at the main stable block.

'Mucking out, I expect,' Diamond said to Gilbert.

His eyes widened. 'Do you think so?'

'No.'

Even so, they found the trainer seated on a bale of hay at one end of the block, short, silver-haired and in a padded waistcoat and flat cap. His brown eyes assessed them as they approached. The hay was his throne and they were expected to show deference, if not actually to bow.

'You must be the long arm of the law.'

'Something like that,' Diamond said,

showing his ID.

'Is this another complaint about my horses holding up the traffic?'

'Actually, no. It's about Hang-glider.' Diamond watched for the reaction.

It wasn't panic. Not even concern. Expectation best described it. 'Have you found him after all these years?'

'Unfortunately, no,' Diamond said. 'But we want the facts about his disappearance. It's possible a murder was committed at the same time.'

'Murder? I know nothing about that.' McDart was still in control, unfazed, heels kicking idly against the hay.

'But you were there for the races?'

'I was. Hang-glider wasn't. He'd popped a tendon and retired. He was the star guest, making a final appearance in front of his fans. They regarded him as a local. He had his first outing on Lansdown.'

'Trained here?'

'From the beginning. The owner, Sir Colin Tipping, paid a small fortune for him as a yearling. That's a gamble, you know. Some of them never race, they're so useless. This colt was the real deal from the start. Full of pluck and class.' He looked away, remembering, and there was pride in his voice. 'In his short career, he was ahead of

490

everything. He took the Irish 2000 Guineas by four lengths and the Prince of Wales's Stakes and he could have done much, much more.' He gave Diamond another gimlet gaze with the brown eyes. 'Murder, you said?'

'That's our suspicion. Would you mind telling us your memories of that day?'

'Nothing I can say. I didn't see anything. I drove the horse here myself with my son Charles, who was learning the business in those days, as a stable lad, like I did.'

'You drove what — a horsebox?'

He nodded.

'Was that safe — driving an injured horse?'

A frown. 'What are you suggesting? He was three months over the injury. He'd had ultrasound. You wouldn't have known there was anything amiss except that he'd have torn it again if he was raced. All we did that evening was walk him in front of the grandstands.'

'You said "we".'

'Charles, actually. I watched from a box in the stands with the owner. It was rather moving. Cheering all the way.'

'So did your son return the horse to the box?'

'That's right. Locked him in securely and joined some of his friends.'

491

'Where was the box parked? Among all the others?'

'No, that's a secure area for the racing. We were away from them. As he wasn't racing, we asked for a different spot near the premier enclosure.'

'When did you find out that the horse was stolen?'

'The end of the evening. I was among the last to leave, yarning with a couple of other trainers. Charles came to collect me and we went back to the box. I saw straight away that the doors had been forced and Hangglider wasn't inside.'

'Wasn't there an alarm system?'

'Neutralised. They knew what they were doing. We alerted security and they checked the boxes that hadn't been driven off already. He must have been moved to another box and transported that way. By this time it was dark, of course, over an hour since the last race, and most people had left.'

'Did you tell Sir Colin?'

'After he got home. He'd already left. He was shattered when I told him. That horse was worth well over a million to him in stud fees.'

'I heard,' Diamond said and moved on to a matter that had mystified him for some time. 'What I can't understand is why it didn't become a police matter. I was on the stength then. To my recollection, CID had nothing to do with it.'

McDart gave a shrug. 'Racing is like that. We have our own security through the British Horseracing Authority. We're pig-headed enough to think we know more about horses than you do, and if you think about it you'll have to admit we're right.'

'I might — if your people had solved the mystery. What's your theory about it?'

He expelled a long breath. 'With this amount of money involved, there will always be criminals out to abuse the system for their own ends. Hang-glider was a valuable property as a stallion, even though his racing days were over.'

'But you can't breed with a stolen horse?'

'Why not?'

'It's all about pedigrees, isn't it? Anyone buying a foal wants to know who sired it.'

'Speaking off the record, if I'm sent a foal that can run well, I won't care what sired it. The paperwork can be forged to make it appear right. I've never got into anything like that myself, but fiddling registration papers must be easier than forging banknotes, mustn't it?'

'So could Hang-glider still be alive under some other name?'

'At this distance in time? I very much doubt it.' He stopped and shouted at one of the lads who had been silently going about their work, 'You! You're spilling feed all over the yard. Get a broom and clear up your bloody mess.' Then he resumed with Diamond in a mild tone: 'You still haven't told me who was murdered and what the connection is.'

'A young Ukrainian woman called Nadia. She was killed about the same time and buried on Lansdown Hill. She was in the area and she may have been seeking work with horses.'

He shook his head. 'Means nothing to me. I don't employ casuals on the racecourse. That's an offence. I could lose my licence for that.'

'I wonder if your son may have met her that evening.'

'You can ask him,' McDart said.

'Is he about?'

He rocked with laughter. 'No.'

'What's the joke?'

'He could have had a good career with me, but he didn't stick at it. He joined your lot.'

Diamond opened his eyes wide. 'The police?'

'Bristol CID. I hardly recognise him now.

The silly mutt shaves his head, goes to the gym, wears an ear-ring. He doesn't even use the name we gave him. Calls himself Chaz.'

34

'I've worked with Chaz,' Diamond told Paul Gilbert on the drive back. 'He's a good copper.'

'Disappointment to his father.'

'I expect he got pissed off being shouted at.'

'He'd get some of that in our job, too.'

'But not from his old man. There's a difference.' He reached for his mobile phone. The thing had its uses after all. He might even get to like it one day. 'Let's see if he's at work this morning.'

Getting through to Bristol Central meant first calling Septimus at Bath for the number: an opportunity to get another opinion on Sergeant Chaz McDart. Salt of the earth, Septimus affirmed, a good colleague and a man you could depend on.

'Then why isn't he in your team at Bath?'

'Because I needed someone to look after the shop.'

The switchboard operator confirmed that Chaz was in and asked if Diamond wished to speak to him.

'Not over the phone,' he said. 'Tell him him I'm on my way to see him.'

Up to now, Paul Gilbert had been a model of tolerance, driving at the slow speeds Diamond preferred and acting as the sounding board for the big man's theories. Suddenly a manageable trip was being extended into a grand tour. 'To Bristol? Now?'

'Junction nineteen,' Diamond said. 'I didn't fix a time. You don't have to put your foot down.'

They were on the long stretch between 16 and 17. Gilbert gritted his teeth and said no more about it.

There wasn't much for Diamond to see outside the window. Pleased that so much could be achieved from inside a car, he continued to hold the mobile in his hand. He'd come a long way to mastering the little monster, dialling the numbers with his thumb, like the teenagers did. Soon he'd progress to texting . . . Soon? Who am I kidding? he thought. Eventually, perhaps. Toying with it, he pressed the menu key and found the phone book. Not many names were listed.

He'd try Ingeborg and see if she'd got to

her event in good time. She'd almost certainly be waiting around for her two minutes of action.

He highlighted her name and pressed the key.

It rang a few times and a recorded voice, not Inge's, asked him to leave a message.

'Funny,' he said to Gilbert. 'I called Ingeborg and she isn't answering.'

Gilbert gripped the wheel a little harder.

'I said Ingeborg isn't answering.'

'She's at the jousting, or whatever it's called,' Gilbert said. The longer this journey went on, the more this young man was sounding like one of the more cynical veterans of the murder squad.

'Better not be jousting. I don't want her knocked off the horse.'

'She's more likely to knock the other guy off.'

'She's just a recruit.'

'They'll go easy on her, then.'

'I don't know. Dave Barton is in charge. Not sure I trust him.'

'The blacksmith who found the leg bone?'

'He's her commanding officer. I wonder why she doesn't answer.' He tried again, with the same result.

'I expect she's wearing gauntlet gloves,' Gilbert said.

He had to think about that. 'Difficult to use the phone. Good point.'

'And she wouldn't want her mobile going off. It's not very Civil War, is it?'

That also made sense to Diamond. He told himself not to fret.

Another mile of green hills went by.

'Which way is Farleigh Hungerford from here?'

'Your side,' Gilbert said. 'Fifteen to twenty miles from the next exit. You're not worried about her?'

'Not in the least.'

'Barton isn't a serious suspect any more, is he?'

'No. He's in the clear.' Shielding the phone from Gilbert's view, he tried one more time, pretending he was adjusting the safety belt. Still the recorded message.

A disturbing thought was forming. All along, Septimus had clung to his theory that Dave Barton was the killer. Even after the interrogation, Septimus remained suspicious. The new witness, Bert Pope, the roundhead who had watched the lager being hidden and gone back and dug it up, had appeared to confirm Dave's story and prove Septimus wrong.

But had he?

The version Septimus had relayed to

Diamond was that Bert Pope had seen 'the soldier in royalist red' burying the six-pack.

They'd assumed the soldier was Dave. It now struck Diamond that he could equally have been Rupert.

Septimus could yet be right.

'We'll take the turn to Farleigh,' he told Gilbert.

'I thought we were going to Bristol.'

'Farleigh Hungerford Castle. And put your foot down.'

Gilbert grasped that this must be an emergency. He steered into the fast lane and powered forward at a heart-stopping rate while Diamond, averting his eyes, called Septimus again and told him his concerns.

All Septimus could find to say was, 'Oh, man,' several times over.

'So we're on our way to Farleigh Castle,' Diamond told him. 'Put out a call. Get some manpower there. He'll be armed with a sword at the very least. If he suspects Inge is police I don't like to think what could happen.'

'I'll come myself,' Septimus said.

'Quick as you can, then.' He looked up and spotted the sign for Junction 17. 'We're ten to fifteen minutes off.'

This was wildly optimistic, given the amount of slow, heavy traffic on the road.

Paul Gilbert added to the suspense by steering with one hand and keying FARLEIGH into the Sat-Nav.

'Couldn't I do that?' Diamond said, and got no answer. On reflection, he didn't need one. His technophobia would have meant reaching across and getting it wrong several times over. Instead, he said, 'Don't you know where it is?'

'I want the quickest route.'

The machine asked DO YOU MEAN FARLEY?

Gilbert persuaded the microchip that his first choice was correct. They took the Chippenham by-pass and then diverted briefly to the A4 before turning onto a B road at Corsham.

'It's taking us through Bradford on Avon,' Diamond said. 'That's a bottleneck any day of the week.'

'Tell me how to avoid it,' Gilbert said through his teeth.

There were ways, but they would add desperate minutes.

'I'd better shut up,' Diamond said.

Gilbert didn't comment.

Winding roads, steep hills, tractors crossing: they suffered it all. Mercifully Bradford didn't delay them by much. Once they were through the little town the system brought them onto ever narrower lanes.

'We must be close now.'

'Thank God for that.'

Ahead were flags and the two ruined towers of the castle, strategically positioned above the River Frome. They crossed over two small bridges. Cars were being diverted down a slope into a temporary park in a field.

'We don't have time for that,' Diamond said. 'Put me down here.'

A police patrol car came from the opposite direction with its blue beacon lights flashing. Diamond was already scrambling up a grassy bank into the area below the castle where the crowd had gathered. Things were being said over a public address system, but he was too concerned to stop and listen. The hairs on the nape of his neck bristled. In the roped-off area where the display should have been taking place was an ambulance with the doors open and someone was being stretchered inside.

'What happened?' he asked the first person he met, a man with two children.

'One of them copped it,' he was told. 'Fell off the horse and didn't move. Looked serious from here.'

He ran on towards the ambulance. An official tried to stop him crossing the rope.

'Police,' he hissed.

The ambulance doors had closed before he got there.

'Who is it?'

'Sorry, mate,' the paramedic told him. 'We've got an emergency here. Talk to the police.'

He felt a hand on his shoulder and turned.

'Guv, what are you doing here?' It was Ingeborg, unhurt, radiant in her royalist uniform.

His relief was overwhelming. He would have hugged her if she hadn't been holding the reins of a large black horse. 'I thought that was you in the ambulance,' he said. 'Are you all right?'

'Sure. I told you I can look after myself. It was Dave who bought it, poor guy.'

'Dave Barton?'

'He lost his balance and came off his horse very awkwardly. He seems to have knocked himself out.'

'Was he in a swordfight, then?'

She nodded. 'The roundheads were down on numbers, so he was asked to switch sides. Anyone in the crowd will tell you I never even made contact. I swung my sword and he ducked and that was it.'

35

It doesn't get much worse than a police officer being questioned about a murder. To avoid the rumour merchants, Diamond had brought Sergeant Chaz McDart out of Bristol Central to one of the few locations where a quiet exchange is possible on a Saturday afternoon, the harbourside. They'd picked a table under the trees in front of the Arnolfini Gallery. True, this agreeable setting was a lot less secure than an interview room, but with Paul Gilbert's support it was workable. If Chaz tried to make a break for it, the two of them could surely grab him.

For the moment, their man appeared docile, even allowing that the shaven head and muscled torso suggested he wouldn't come off second best in a fight. When they'd first spoken in the reception area at the police station, he'd said with an air of resignation he knew why they were there and they could count on him to co-operate.

Now, over coffee, looking out at the glittering water, he said, 'I'm glad you came for me, really I am. Where do you want me to start?'

'We spoke to your father in Lambourn this morning,' Diamond told him. 'That's why we're here.'

'He doesn't know the whole story,' Chaz said in a sharp tone eloquent of a history of family tension. 'He'd have given me a thrashing if I'd told him. They have old-fashioned discipline in stable yards, or at least my dad does. I was only a kid at the time, seventeen or thereabouts, son of the boss, serving an apprenticeship. He was tougher on me than the other lads, not wanting to show favouritism. It was impossible to talk to him — really talk, I mean.'

'What part of the story doesn't he know?' Diamond asked, in control, yet eager for information.

'The evening we went to Lansdown Races with Hang-glider. Did he tell you much about that?'

'You and he drove the horsebox there and parked it away from the secure area, somewhere near the Premier Enclosure.'

'That much is right. And it was my job to parade the horse in front of the two grandstands and return him to his box and see

505

that it was properly locked. I did all that. I gave him water and hay and fitted on his travel boots, tail guard and rug. He was strapped into his stall. I told all this to the HRA people several times over, the same evening, the next day and when they had the enquiry. I wasn't lying.'

'Economical with the truth?'

He hesitated, then grinned and nodded. 'Sums it up. I could have said more and I didn't. All they were interested in was what happened to Hang-glider and they got their answers. It was obvious I wasn't the horse thief. I had sod all to gain. So they didn't question me except for the boring stuff about what I did with the horse. And if they had, it wouldn't have told them anything. A stable lad and a woman. What's wrong with that?'

'This was Nadia?'

He nodded.

Diamond remained outwardly calm while his heart-rate quickened. The case was moving to a conclusion. This was what he'd needed for so long — proof positive that Nadia had been on the racecourse that night in August, 1993.

'After I'd settled the horse in its box I had some time on my hands. Dad was sure to be in the owners' and trainers' bar with his friends. I went to the marquee. It's a trick known to all the lads. Parties of race-goers get drinking at tables and then someone hears an announcement about the next race and they're up and away. Some carry their drinks with them, but not all. Plenty of glasses get left behind more than half full. If you don't mind drinking from someone else's glass, you've got it made. Pimm's, champagne, G&T — take your choice. I picked up some drink or other and looked up and this gorgeous babe was smiling at me.'

'She was already there?'

'Standing alone by another table. I could see straight away she was older than me, in her twenties, and she wasn't dressed up for the racing like most women are. She was in jeans and some kind of top. They wouldn't let someone into the premier enclosure dressed like that at most courses, but this was an evening meeting at Lansdown and they're not too strict there. I went over and introduced myself and she was great — friendly, ready for a chat, standing really close to me. I couldn't believe my luck.'

'Did she give her name?'

'Yes. I could tell she was a foreigner by the accent. I asked if Nadia was a Russian name and she laughed and said not in her case and we had a bit of a guessing game and she still didn't actually say which country it was. She'd been in Bath for a week or two and was in lodgings at Swainswick, down in the valley. She'd come to the races because she loved horses.'

'So you told her about Hang-glider?'

'Well, I wanted to impress her, didn't I? I wasn't sure if she'd seen me doing my lap of honour bit in front of the crowd and it turned out she hadn't. I told her about my job and my dad and she said would I mind showing her this famous horse. The way she said it, curving her mouth, I took as a coded way of saying she fancied me. I gulped down my drink as if it was water. Outside, she slipped her hand round my arm and I thought I'd got it made. The horsebox was parked some way out on the grass at the end of the enclosure, well away from the crowds. I playfully told her it would cost her a kiss to see Hang-glider and she laughed and took me into a clinch right away.' He released a sharp breath at the memory. 'I don't know where she learned how to kiss like that.'

Diamond refrained from telling him. 'Did it go any further?'

'I'm coming to that. At this stage she wanted to get inside the horsebox. I un-

508

locked and helped her up. The box was small compared to some of them, what we called a two-box, with room for a second horse. I wondered if Hang-glider would get nervous, but he didn't. He let her stroke his neck and feed him some titbits. It was obvious she was used to horses, like she claimed. She said he was adorable and she'd really give anything to work with him, and then repeated the word "anything" in a way that left no doubt what she really meant. I was in two minds then.'

'Nervous, you mean?'

'Right. I stalled a bit, and told her he was being sold for stud.'

'What did she say to that?'

'She didn't mind. What she really wanted was a job with horses.'

'She told you that?'

'Asked me straight out if I could help her get work with my father. I said it wasn't so easy and he liked his stable lads to have the right paperwork and serve an apprenticeship. She didn't let up at all and said she'd sign anything. I was getting jumpy, thinking what my dad would make of this. Then she turned away from the horse and said something about persuading me and the next thing she was kissing me again and groping me at the same time. I'd had girlfriends before and done some heavy petting but none of them had made the first move.' He glanced at Paul Gilbert. 'You know what I mean? I was really turned on.'

Gilbert nodded as if from a rich store of experience.

Diamond asked, 'Where did you do it? In the horsebox, with the horse beside you?'

'No, we used the front cab. Plenty of room in there.'

'Locking the box first?'

'You're damn right. My dad would have roasted me if I'd put the horse at risk. Even with the offer of sex, I thought of that.' He looked down at the empty coffee cup. 'So I did it with Nadia and it was sensational. The first time I'd gone the whole way. You've probably worked that out. You've got to remember I was just a kid.'

And she was a professional, Diamond thought, and stopped himself saying it. 'What happened after?'

'She said some stuff about how good I was. How good! I shudder to think what I was really like. In the same breath she told me I could have her any way I wanted if I persuaded my dad to give her a job.'

'What did you say to that?'

'I don't remember. By this time I'd had my big moment and the excitement was turning to panic. All I could think about was how to get out of this without Dad finding out.'

The account rang true. Diamond had listened with understanding — and it wasn't just because Chaz was a brother officer. He had chastening memories of his own initiation into full sex as a teenager, woefully inept. But the empathy only went so far. All the elements for an unpremeditated killing were present here: the powerful youth, eager for sex without a thought of what it might cost him; the ex-prostitute desperate for a new start; and the domineering father terrifying the boy.

'How did you deal with it?' he asked, uncertain of what was to come.

'Not well. I couldn't just ask her to clear off. I played for time, telling her I'd try and work it with my dad if she'd come to Lambourn in a week or two. She got a bit stroppy, saying that was no bloody use because she didn't have the money to get there and didn't know where it was. She needed to meet my father now — the same evening. Time was going on and I was shit-scared he'd suddenly appear and find me with her in the cab. I told her I'd better go off and talk to him right away. She wanted to wait inside the cab, but I persuaded her that wasn't a good idea. I locked everything up and left her waiting outside.'

'You went back to the race meeting?'

'The races were well over by then and it was getting dark. Most people were leaving. Dad was always one of the last to go home. He was still in the bar with a few of his cronies. He doesn't actually drink much. It's the shop-talk he likes. I wasn't in any hurry to root him out of there.'

'You had a problem on your hands.'

'Did I just! I was hoping she'd get tired of waiting and simply walk away. A bit unrealistic.'

'Totally, I'd say, knowing her situation. Did you go back to her?'

'No.'

Diamond leaned closer. 'Is that the truth, Chaz?'

'Gospel. I hung about for almost another hour. Finally Dad came out and he was in quite a good mood.'

'Did you tell him about Nadia?'

'No chance. I was hoping she'd given up and left. If she hadn't, I was counting on Dad to deal with her. He can shoot anyone down in flames. She might have decided she wouldn't want to work for a mean sod like him.'

'I doubt it. What happened next?'

Chaz shrugged. 'You know, don't you? Dad and I returned to the horsebox and found it broken into and Hang-glider gone. The sky fell in on us.'

'Was Nadia there?'

He opened both hands. 'Gone. I've never seen her since.'

Was it staged, or could he be believed? The gesture was a touch too contrived, Diamond thought, but then Chaz had no doubt been visualising the impression he would make.

'Your father said you alerted racecourse security.'

'Yes, it was mayhem. Cars, vans and horseboxes leaving. Searches at the exits. People getting angry, wanting to leave. Whoever had done it had got clean away before the search began. They should have contacted the police and made road blocks, but they didn't. The racing world likes to handle its own wrongdoings.'

'Do you think Nadia was in on it?'

He shook his head. 'I've thought about it many times. I was fearful that she'd tricked me. I can't see how.'

'Is it possible the box was broken into while the pair of you were making love in the cab?'

'No. We'd have heard. You can hear any

move the horse makes. Besides, I checked that the door was locked. I swear it. Even with the offer of sex I couldn't forget I was responsible for Hang-glider.'

'And after? You didn't unlock the box for any reason?'

He shook his head. 'Everything was secure when I left Nadia there. Anyway, the door was forced by the robbers, which proves it had been locked.'

'You know what really happened — that Nadia was murdered?'

He swallowed hard. 'I do now.'

'When did you find out?'

'Only last night when I saw the poster of her. A batch of them were delivered to Bristol Central.'

'Why didn't you get in touch last night?'

He lowered his eyes and sighed. 'I was shocked rigid. Scared, too. I'd kept this secret — about having sex with her — for all these years. I didn't say anything about it to the security people. I couldn't see how it affected the theft of the horse. Then, last night, this bombshell. My first instinct was to see if I could ride the storm like I had before. I was asking myself if anyone really needed to know. I decided to sleep on it and come to a decision today.'

This sounded credible, if reprehensible.

People in a spot behave like that, trying to convince themselves nothing has changed. 'Didn't it occur to you when the skeleton was found on Lansdown that it might be Nadia?'

'It crossed my mind, but I thought of all kinds of reasons why it could be someone else.'

'As a serving police officer, you had a duty to speak out.'

'I know. I should have reported what I knew in case it had a bearing. I'm a bloody disgrace.'

'You worked with me on the Rupert Hope murder — briefly, I know, but you did.'

'At the time, I couldn't see any connection, and since then I've been running CID here, covering other cases.'

Diamond wasn't dishing out blame. There was a bigger agenda here. 'You heard that a horse rug was found with hairs attached to it that matched the single horse hair discovered with the skeleton? Rupert found this rug, an under-rug with the Phil Drake label. We don't know where. Do you recall if Hang-glider had such a rug?'

Chaz looked up, his eyes brighter. 'He did, yes. It was on his back in the horsebox. I put it on him myself. How the hell could it have turned up after all this time?'

'That was my next question.'

'God knows. I can't begin to get my head round that.'

Diamond knew when a witness was going cold on him, and it wouldn't be allowed to happen here. 'I need your help on this. You've lived with this mystery longer than anyone in the police. What do you think happened that night?'

Chaz glanced towards the glittering expanse of water between the harbour walls. 'Obviously it happened in that hour or so after I left Nadia standing by the horsebox and when I returned with my father. There must have been more than one person involved, but I doubt if she was part of it. I guess she was killed because she got in the way. They were there to steal a valuable horse and she would have been a witness.'

'Physically, how do you think it was it done?'

'The horse-thieves seem to have transferred Hang-glider to a trailer hitched to another vehicle, probably a four by four. There were tyre tracks found by the security team. That way, they would have got on the road before the mass of cars were leaving the racecourse. They could have gone anywhere.'

'And Nadia?'

'Must have been taken with them.'

'She was found on the battlefield, buried,' Diamond said, as the interrogation became more of a consultation. 'They couldn't have buried the horse there without a mechanical digger. Anyway, we'd have found evidence that the earth had been excavated. So the horse was taken elsewhere, sold on to breed secretly on some criminal stud farm, if Sir Colin Tipping's theory is right. He was the owner. Did he hold you and your father responsible?'

'He was gutted when Dad told him. He lost a million or more in stud fees. The deal with Sheikh Abdul was all agreed and wasn't signed.'

'Was it really worth as much as that?'

'Dad swore it was. There was going to be money on signing and then a percentage of every stud fee the horse earned.'

'Did your father take it out on you?'

'Actually, no. He blamed himself for the lax security. I'd followed his instructions. Of course he knew nothing about Nadia.'

'How long was it before you quit?'

'A matter of months. I was through with being treated as a fourteen-year-old. I left home, dropped out for a while, did some part-time jobs and then joined the force. These have been good years. Now that I've messed up, I guess I ought to resign before they sack me.' He was red-eyed.

'I'd wait and see if I were you,' Diamond said.

36

'We'll drive back over Lansdown.'

Hearing this from his superior, Paul Gilbert took a sharp breath. He'd had a testing day as Diamond's chauffeur. 'How do you mean?'

'Like I said. Over Lansdown.'

'Bit out of our way, isn't it?'

'Take the A431 and turn off shortly after Bitton. If you don't trust me, you can use that satellite gadget of yours.'

'I trust you, guv.' Said with a faint sigh.

This would add at least twenty minutes to the journey, but it was futile to protest. Much as Gilbert was looking forward to getting home (and out) for Saturday night, he'd learned that the working day wasn't over.

'Being driven like this, at a sensible speed, has given me a chance to think,' Diamond said, deciding after all to say more. 'We know Rupert found that horse rug somewhere on the hill. I've got a new thought where it might have been.'

So instead of the fast route home they took the old Bath Road and diverted up Brewery Hill and through the village of Upton Cheney, swinging along the western side of Hanging Hill to climb the steep western ridge where the royalist army had once fought its way to the top at such a cost in lives.

Gilbert's little Honda chugged steadily upwards until Lansdown's battlefield came into view, benign, tinted gold by the evening sun. You wouldn't have guessed at its savage history.

'Are you thinking of stopping here?' he asked.

'I'll say when.' Diamond was preoccupied with a piece of information he'd learned days earlier. Once more it was from the calendar of events Ingeborg had put together for Keith Halliwell when he was briefly in charge of the case. One of the first entries he'd seen scrolling down the screen had not made sense. He hadn't questioned it at the time because it didn't have any obvious relevance to the investigation. He was interested now and he could picture it. The date would have been early in 1991, the year he'd first looked at.

Lansdown Road subsidence causes traffic chaos

Subsidence on Lansdown? He didn't know of any mining under Lansdown Road. In centuries past, there had been open quarrying for Bath stone towards the top of the hill, but nothing underground. All the local mines below the surface, some of them notorious for caving in and alarming the residents when sudden craters appeared, were on the south-east side of the city at Combe Down and Odd Down and all the way out to Corsham and Bradford on Avon.

They motored in silence past the racecourse where Hang-glider had been paraded and the golf club where Swithin and Tipping outdid each other in bending the rules. A mile or more ahead, the landlocked lighthouse that was William Beckford's folly appeared on the horizon. The gilded cast-iron columns of the lantern were catching the low sun.

'That's where we stop,' Diamond said.

'The tower? Will it still be open?'

'We're not going inside.'

Considering how productive the day had been, he was subdued, locked into his own thoughts. Paul Gilbert, uncertain how to deal with the man, chose to say the minimum.

They approached the tower and parked in the space in front of the gatehouse where poor Rupert Hope had passed his nights on a concrete bench with the horse rug as his covering.

Diamond spoke again. 'Do you carry a torch?'

'A flashlight, in the boot.'

'Bring it with you.'

While Gilbert rummaged through the clutter in the boot, Diamond opened the gate and went in. Relieved to find that the flashlight still worked, Gilbert followed, stepping through the cheerless little room.

The stone memorials of the Victorian cemetery appeared theatrical in the orange sunset glow, taller than before, casting long shadows. Gilbert glanced up at a wind-blown, crumbling angel, its arm pointing heavenward. This was not a comfortable place to be so late in the day — or any time, he thought.

Diamond was a short way ahead, stock-still, looking towards the tower. In a low voice, speaking more to himself than Gilbert, he started on a barely audible monologue. 'People have been telling me about Beckford from the start. I was even given a book to read. Stupidly I didn't open it. No, that's not quite true. I looked at the pictures. It seemed to me he was extra lumber and now I'm not so sure. Do you know anything about him?'

Realising he was being spoken to, Gilbert uttered a feeble, 'Not much.'

'He was rich, filthy rich, and full of himself. Strutted around Bath in a pea-green tailcoat with his four dogs and a dwarf in tow. Building towers was his thing and this was the last of them. Am I boring you?'

'No, guv.'

'You have to know this stuff, or you could miss the very thing we're looking for. In the eighteen-twenties Beckford buys a house in Lansdown Crescent. Smart address, hundred metres above the city. Quite a stiff climb. Any idea why he chose to live so high?'

'The air was nicer?'

'You've got it. A dirty great cloud from hundreds of coal fires hung over the city most days. Being Beckford, he also buys a house across the street in Lansdown Place and has a bridge built to link them. Do you know it?'

'I think I've seen it.'

'Then he builds this, his tower, a mile up the hill, with a view to die for. Not content with that, he buys all the land between his house and here and shuts off the footpaths and makes this private walk. Landscaping, they called it in those days. If you had pots of money that was what you did. These days he'd buy an airline or a football club. Down the bottom near the house he puts up weird buildings like a mini-mosque and a gateway dressed up as a castle. He steps through the gate with his dwarf and his dogs and heads across country to the plantation. Come on, I'll show you.' He set off at a brisk pace down the path through the cemetery, with Gilbert a couple of yards behind. Below them to their right, the crimson disc of the sun was directly over Bath.

At a point where the trees permitted a view, he stopped. 'In that book I was telling you about there's a plan of Beckford's walk and I'm trying to work out where we are. Below us would have been a shrubbery, bushes and plants from all over the world chosen because they smelled nice. Lower down in that middle area was an open quarry that he didn't change because it reminded him of some ruined baths in Rome.'

'The Caracalla Baths, I expect,' Gilbert said, the first intelligent response he'd managed.

Wrong-footed, Diamond turned to face him. 'What do you know about it?'

'Where the three tenors did their first big concert.'

'Is that so? You're taking this in, I hope.' He stepped out again, and the Victorian cemetery gave way to rows of more modern graves. 'Good thing we didn't leave it any later,' he said. 'Another half-hour and we'd be tripping over this lot. The walk got fancy again this side of the quarry with more gateways leading you through flower gardens and an orchard. He brought in fifty-year-old apple trees, would you believe? They blossomed all right, but never formed fruit. Keep up, will you? I'm not talking to myself.'

But for an interval he stopped speaking and marched purposefully down the slope.

'Isn't this private land?' Gilbert asked.

'I expect so.'

'I don't think we'll get much further.'

They were blocked by a dense patch of brambles more than head high, sprouting a few pathetic blackberries, as if all their strength had gone into creating sturdy, vicious-looking shoots.

'This wasn't here in Beckford's day,' Diamond said. 'The walk must have gone straight through this. Check the road, will you? See how close we are to the Granville Road turn. Is that Charlcombe on the other side?'

'I'll find out,' Gilbert said, glad of a break. The boss in this tour-leader mode wasn't easy to take, particularly when the tour party consisted of only one individual.

He didn't need to go far to the left to see the lights of a car moving along Lansdown Road. On the other side were the offices used by the Admiralty. He also spotted a road opposite.

Returning to Diamond, he reported what he'd seen.

'This is the place, then. Somewhere in this area, Beckford sunk a large pond filled with gold and silver fish.'

'Is that what we're looking for?'

'Quiet, I'm getting my bearings. Nearby he came to a major obstruction in the shape of a lane leading to a farm. It was one right of way he couldn't ignore. To continue the walk he was forced to go underground. So what did he do? He made a virtue out of necessity and created a seventy-foot grotto. You know what a grotto is?'

'Like a cave?'

'Except this one had to be a tunnel. That's what I hope to find if it's still here. Where's the flashlight?'

Gilbert switched it on and passed it over.

Diamond swung the beam this way and that, patrolling the margins of the thicket. 'Some time in 1991 there was subsidence along the road and it caused major traffic problems. My hunch is that it happened around here due to Beckford's tunnelling. The walk went very close to the road at this point.'

The significance of the grotto wasn't lost on Gilbert. He could see what was coming. He didn't fancy plunging into the brambles and getting scratched all over just to satisfy a theory of Diamond's.

'I think there's a gap here,' Diamond called from the other side. 'I can't get through myself, but you might.'

Resigned, Gilbert joined him and saw where the beam was picking out a space between the long, prickly shoots. 'What am I looking for?'

'I'm not sure. Hole in the ground. Steps, maybe. Mind you don't fall in. Take the flashlight.'

More intent on avoiding injury than finding anything, Gilbert dipped his head and edged under a vicious-looking branch. If he showed willing, he might get a reprieve. 'Can't see much,' he said, rubbing spider-webs from his face.

'There's a way through. There has to be,' Diamond told him.

A thorn pierced Gilbert's trousers and dug into his leg. 'I think I've reached my limit, guv.'

'You're shining the light the wrong way. Look to your left. Isn't that a way through?'

Gilbert turned and got his face scratched. Wrestling with brambles would have been unwise by day. In this light it was madness. He was about to say so when he noticed something he was bound to report. 'Some of these are bent right over. It looks as if someone else has been here before me.'

'We must be close, then.'

We? Gilbert thought. There's only one of us getting scratched to pieces.

Easing to his right to duck under an arch of thorns, he felt his foot against a hard, straight edge. 'There may be something here.' Gingerly he pushed his leg forward into a space above a flat, solid surface. 'Steps, I think.'

'Give me some light. I'm coming in,' Diamond said, then swore as the first thorns made contact. By attacking the bush like a rugby forward he powered through to Gilbert's side regardless of discomfort. 'What I'd give for a chainsaw.'

With a probing foot he located the step

for himself. 'Let's get down there.'

Together they battled the last of the prickles and forced their way down a flight of about ten steps.

'Flashlight.'

They had reached an impasse. The light shone on a mass of ivy with branches like cables.

'What's behind it?' Diamond thumped the butt end of the flashlight against the surface.

'That's the only light we've got,' Gilbert warned him.

'If we could rip some of this away . . .' He tried getting a grip on the ivy. It didn't yield.

'Can I have the flashlight a moment? I think I can see what's in the way.'

Low down, the beam showed what looked like vertical indented bands, largely covered in moss and creepers, but recognizable as corrugated iron.

'Find the edge,' Diamond said.

Not only did the light show them the limit of the iron barrier. It revealed a gap wide enough to squeeze through.

'Someone has definitely been here.'

Gilbert went through and forced the gap wider for Diamond to follow.

'Bloody hell.'

There was no longer any doubt that they'd found Beckford's grotto, a tunnel stretching ahead for about twenty feet to where the roof seemed to have collapsed. There was rubble, too, immediately in front of them.

'Take care,' Gilbert said.

Diamond wasn't listening. He stumbled inside, picking a way over the debris with the flashlight and intermittently pointing the beam ahead towards a tall structure blocking the way.

Coated in dust, at first it looked like an extension of the rock all around it, but then he saw the faint gleam of metal and recognised the obstruction for what it was.

A horse trailer.

37

Without the flashlight, Paul Gilbert struggled to keep his footing while crossing the rubble. Up ahead, Diamond was oblivious to him, squeezing between the side of the trailer and the flints on the grotto wall.

'This is what Rupert found,' his voice carried back. 'God knows how. Picking blackberries, maybe.' He reached the back end where the door was. 'A cheap little one-horse trailer, not the transport a top racehorse is used to. Do you carry a handkerchief?'

Gilbert edged along the wall and joined him. 'Will tissues do?'

Diamond took what was offered and used it to avoid direct contact with his hand as he pulled open the door and shone the lamp inside.

Neither man spoke. The sight that confronted them demanded an interval of respect.

The remains lay along the left side of the trailer floor, pathetically like the proverbial bag of bones, recognisably equine, manifestly long dead, part skeleton, part leathery tissue. The legs, reduced mostly to bone, were bent under the torso and still covered to the knees in padded travel boots made from some artificial fabric. Anything left of the tail was entirely enclosed in a matching tail guard.

Diamond finally said, 'No dignity in death, is there?'

'Is it Hang-glider?'

'Must be.'

'Well preserved, considering.'

'Partial mummification,' Diamond said. 'In conditions like this, cool and dry, it can happen, especially if there's a through draught.'

'So Rupert took the rug off a dead horse,' Gilbert said, the distaste clear in his voice.

'Shows how desperate he was. Give me a hand up. I'm going to check the head.' Diamond climbed into the trailer, moved to the front and crouched down. 'Not pretty, but more skin than bone,' he informed Gilbert. 'The bridle still fits snugly. Ah — and I see how it was done. The hole is precisely where it should be, front of the skull, just above midway between the ears and the eyes. They knew what they were doing.'

'Destroying a champion,' Gilbert said. 'That's what they were doing.' He was in danger of getting emotional — not advisable in police work.

'Don't let it get to you, lad.'

'I can't see the logic in it.'

'There's a reason. There must be. Whether it rates as logic is another question.' Diamond stood up and passed the light beam across the rest of the interior, looking for anything else that would yield information. 'How the heck did they get the trailer in here?' Automatically they'd slipped into speaking of more than one perpetrator. A set-up as complex as this was too much to have attempted alone.

'You could drive an SUV across the field, no problem,' Gilbert said without realising Diamond was steering him back to practicalities. 'If the brambles and the barrier weren't in the way, you could reverse the trailer part way down the stairs and then unhitch it and let it roll down. I'm assuming they killed the horse above ground?'

'Seems likely.'

'And after it was done they must have sealed the tunnel opening to cover up the crime.'

'I doubt if anyone else did.' He clambered out and joined Gilbert. 'Let's hope we haven't buggered up the crime scene. I'll have to call in Duckett and his layabouts. They made a picnic out of the human skeleton. I wonder what they'll do with a dead horse.'

'Do you want to wait for them?' Gilbert said, despairing of his Saturday night out.

'No.'

'So we're going back to the nick?' His hopes revived.

'I am. I'll borrow your car, if you don't mind.'

'What about me?'

'Sorry, Paul. I'm not waiting, but someone has to. Give me a call when Duckett shows up and I'll send a car to pick you up. Shouldn't take long.' He took out the mobile, called Duckett and ruined his Saturday evening. 'You heard me right the first time,' he said. 'A horse. But there's a definite link to the two murders. Even if you don't start work tonight, you'd better get there and seal the place. Don't be long. My man is waiting for you.' He ended the call and said with a smile, 'Shame, I forgot to mention leather gloves.'

Buoyed up, he did more phoning. 'I don't care if you have to break your date, miss your dinner, turn your car round halfway up the motorway,' he said into the phone. 'Get to Manvers Street fast. There's work to do.'

'Who was that?' Gilbert asked.

'John Leaman, moaning as usual.'

He was less abrasive with Ingeborg and Septimus, but the message was essentially the same. Crunch time had come. 'You wouldn't want to be left out, would you?' he said to Septimus.

If there was an answer, it wasn't audible.

'Are you going to inform the ACC?' Gilbert asked.

'Georgina?' Diamond just laughed. 'I'm off now. You did a fine job today, lad. Bangers and mash for supper when you get back to the nick.'

'Thanks,' Gilbert said bleakly. He added, as the big man turned away, 'May I have the flashlight?'

'Sorry, lad. I don't fancy that graveyard in the dark.'

All the key members of the team were at Manvers Street to be briefed within twenty minutes of his return. He updated them fully and set out his plan of simultaneous arrests and house searches. 'It isn't just about question and answer, or even confessions. It's an evidence-gathering operation. Let's remember we're building a case for the prosecution. We've done the ground-work. We know the perpetrators. They're clever, manipulative and they may yet have more tricks to pull. Now let's nail them.'

He and Septimus drove to a street of detached houses on the side of Lansdown Road opposite the Royal High School. The lights were on inside and security lights beamed down outside, yet there was a delay before the sound of unbolting relieved the tension a little. The door opened a few inches on a safety chain and Major Swith-in's voice said, 'Yes?'

They were admitted and shown into a large sitting room smelling faintly of cigars. Brown leather armchairs, standard lamps and gilt-framed prints of hunting scenes. It put Diamond in mind of a club room.

In a knitted cardigan, cords and carpet slippers, the major looked and sounded out of sorts. 'What do you want with me?'

'Actually, we want your wife.'

'Agnes? What does she have to do with it?'

'We're about to find out. We'll speak to her alone, if you don't mind.'

'I most certainly do. I object, in fact.'

'In that case, we'll arrest you now and put you in the car outside.'

'On what grounds?'

Septimus, quick as one of those hounds in the pictures, said, 'Wilfully obstructing a police officer in the execution of his duty under section eighty-nine of the Police Act, 1996.'

The major gave a nervous twitch. 'You're not planning to arrest Agnes?'

'I was referring to you, sir.'

'Yes, but if you need to see her alone . . .' He did an about-turn, literally and figuratively. 'Damn it, I'll fetch her.'

Diamond exchanged a high five with Septimus.

Agnes Swithin came in, frowning. She had a towel round her head and was wearing a pink dressing-gown. 'I was washing my hair,' she said in an accusing way as if they'd deliberately picked this inconvenient time.

Diamond turned to Septimus and asked him to speak the words of the official caution to Mrs Swithin.

'What on earth . . . ?' she said, and was silenced by the officialese.

Diamond took over again. 'We've spoken before about your part in the recent re-enactment of the Battle of Lansdown —'

'I did nothing to be ashamed of.'

'You were an angel of mercy, you told me. Was that right?'

She opened her mouth to confirm it, stopped herself and sighed. 'Strictly speaking, the term may not be historically accurate. The regiment prefer "camp follower", but that has vulgar connotations I don't care for.'

'Whatever you call yourself, you go out on the field of battle and pretend to be dressing their wounds and looking after them?'

'That's what women have done for centuries in warfare, picking up the pieces, ministering to the wounded and dying. We also search for our menfolk among the slain.' Agnes Swithin was over the first shock of policemen invading her home, and starting to give back as good as she was getting.

'Right, and to carry out all these duties you need supplies.'

'Of course.'

'Which you carry in a shoulder bag?'

'A knapsack, or a snapsack, to use the authentic term.'

'And it doesn't get inspected by the officers, so you can carry some modern items as well as rolls of bandage?'

'I suppose that's true.'

'Did you have a mobile phone with you?'

She shrugged. 'Doesn't everyone these days?'

'So the answer is yes. Did you also have

your binoculars?'

An impatient sigh. 'To save us time, I also carried my purse, make-up, comb, glasses, deodorant, camera and certain pills I take for a medical condition. Is there anything else you want to know?'

'Did you confirm the binoculars?'

'The re-enactment is a spectacle. One likes to enjoy it.'

'That's a yes?'

'It is.'

'We've come to the nub of this,' Diamond said. 'After the fighting moved up the field, did you see two of the cavaliers going the other way, down the slope?'

'There was a lot going on. I don't recall everything.'

'Men on your own side acting like deserters? They must have caught your attention.'

'At the time, possibly.'

'Anyway, they stopped by the fallen oak tree, an important landmark to the Lansdown Society because of its rare lichen.'

'I'm not a member of the society.'

'But your husband is. And you keep the major informed of everything you see through those strong binoculars of yours. I'm suggesting you watched the two men acting oddly, burrowing in the earth, and you decided the Lansdown Society should be informed immediately. Your phone company keeps a record of the calls, you know.'

She caught her breath. 'You've been checking my phone calls? That's outrageous. Anyway, we could have been talking about anything.'

'If you don't want your actions to be misinterpreted, Mrs Swithin, I suggest you stop this stonewalling and give me the truth. One of those men was beaten over the head and later murdered.'

She'd gone as white as the towel on her head. 'I didn't witness that. What are you trying to pin on me?'

'Tell me exactly what did happen.'

'I didn't see any violence. Just as you said, I saw what was going on by the fallen tree and phoned Reggie.'

'Where was he at the time?'

'The golf club.'

'With Sir Colin Tipping?'

'You'll have to ask him.'

Diamond nodded to Septimus, who stepped to the door and jerked it open. Predictably, the major was there, eavesdropping. 'Step inside, major,' Diamond said, 'and let's hear it from you.'

38

The moon was the only source of light and there wasn't much of that. Paul Gilbert, still on duty in the field below the cemetery, was having doubts. Doubt One: would Duckett, the forensics man, bother to come out on a Saturday night to look at a dead horse? From all he'd heard, Duckett was an awkward type who'd clashed with Diamond and might well ignore the call, or leave it to the next day.

Doubt Two: would Diamond remember his promise to send a car? The boss had more urgent matters on his mind, like arresting suspects and bringing the whole investigation to a climax. Would he give another thought to the most junior member of the team, stuck on this godforsaken hill?

This could be a long night.

Get a grip, he told himself. Give it an hour at most and then phone the nick and ask them to send a replacement. If someone has to stand guard all night, it's a job for uniform, not CID.

He felt better for that — until he checked his back pocket and remembered he'd left his phone in the car.

Idiot.

Somewhere on the hill came the hoarse triple bark of a dog fox, answered by a vixen's scream, a hair-raising sound.

A short way off, vehicles were going by intermittently, each set of headlight beams offering the faint hope that Duckett was imminent. Faint indeed. What was the point of Duckett coming out here after dark? Once he took over the scene he and his people would be responsible. There were rules about continuity of evidence. Someone had to be on watch all night because of the remote chance that an intruder or one of the suspects would visit the place and corrupt the evidence.

Let an intruder come, Gilbert thought. Let *someone* come.

Preferably not the killer.

His thoughts turned to the victim, who'd lived up here for a couple of weeks, concussed, off his chump, not knowing he had a car and a home. What threat had poor old Rupert Hope presented in his pathetic state? Finishing him off in the graveyard had been a heartless act. This killer had no mercy.

The cool of early evening had turned in a matter of minutes to shivery cold. What else could you expect on an exposed hill seven hundred feet above sea level? The luckless Rupert had at least found himself a rug and a place to lie down. There was nowhere in this field except the grotto itself, and Gilbert didn't fancy that, but he was starting to understand what had driven Rupert to rob the tomb.

A twig snapped nearby. His self-pitying stopped.

He looked where he thought the sound had come from, straining to detect a shape or movement.

Then he heard what sounded like short gasps for air.

'Who's that?' he said.

No answer. Only an animal, he tried telling himself. The breathing was too heavy to be a fox. Were there deer on Lansdown? He'd never seen one.

He had nothing to defend himself with. Should have thought of that.

In his heightened state, he started to see shadowy shapes closing in. He looked over his shoulder and they were all around him. Bushes stirred by the breeze, or attackers closing for the kill?

'I can hear you,' he said aloud. 'I know you're there.'

A beam of light shone directly into his face, dazzling him. 'Stay still, absolutely still.' The voice was male, high-pitched, yet authoritative.

Gilbert obeyed.

'What's going on?' the voice asked. 'What are you doing here?'

'My job.' Gilbert managed to add, 'I'm a police officer.'

'You're not dressed like one.'

'I'm CID. Plain clothes. I can show you my ID. Who are you?'

The man with the torch had the advantage and intended to keep it. 'What's a police officer skulking around in the dark for?'

He was cautious. 'I can't say. I'm on duty.' He fished his warrant card from his back pocket. 'See?'

The beam shifted down and Gilbert took his opportunity, grabbed the arm holding the torch, hauled the man towards him, at the same time thrusting out a leg and toppling him over. It wasn't the sweetest of judo moves, but it worked. They both hit the ground heavily. The torch flew out of range. The advantage had swung to Gilbert. Bearing down with all his strength, he clung to that arm and twisted it behind the man's back.

'You're breaking my arm.'

'Who the fuck are you?' Gilbert demanded.

'A man of God.'

'What?'

'Charles Smart. I live in the vicarage across the road.'

If this was a try-on, it was a clever one. If not, Gilbert was wrestling with a vicar. Now that the name was sinking in, he remembered seeing Charlie Smart's name listed on the display board in the incident room. 'What are you doing here, then?'

'I saw the light earlier.' This, from a vicar, would have been laughable in other circumstances. 'I came over to see what was going on.'

'You were taking a chance.'

'If God be for us, who can be against us? Do you mind? The pain in my arm is unspeakable.'

Gilbert let go, made a grab for the torch and shone it on his adversary. The man had wide blue eyes and a shock of blond hair. True to his claim, he was wearing a strip of white across his throat, a clerical collar. He propped himself up with difficulty and massaged the top of his arm, saying, 'That really

545

wasn't necessary.'

'Creeping up on me and shoving a torch in my face wasn't necessary,' Gilbert said.

'I'm in the Lansdown Society. I made a solemn promise to keep an eye on things up here.'

That was the connection.

'And if you're about to ask me if I witnessed the murder, save your breath,' Charlie Smart continued. 'Your superintendent already covered the matter and I couldn't help at all.'

'Did you see the victim roaming around here?'

'We covered that, too. No. The first suspicious behaviour I've seen was yours tonight. Lights in the field. A car parked up the road. Very dubious, after all that's been going on. As a responsible citizen, I dialled 999 straight away. They should be here any minute.'

'Thank God for that,' Gilbert said.

In the incident room, Diamond checked with his team on the results of the house arrests. The suspects were in custody and the evidence had been gathered, labelled and sealed. 'Nice work, people,' he said. 'That was the easy part. The real job starts now and I'm not expecting any favours from the suspects. We'll take them one at a time, using the interview room with one-way glass, so the rest of you can see how we do. Cavalry Officer Smith, I need you with me for the first one.'

Excitement was written large on Inge's face and no one seemed to mind that she was the first choice, particularly as the suspect was female.

The custody sergeant brought Davina Temple-Smith to the interview room. White-faced and with a sullen stare, she was a different incarnation from the radiant winning owner at the races. She had the consolation of appearing in her own clothes — jeans and a red sweater — rather than a zipper suit. A personal search hadn't been deemed necessary. Her DNA sample and finger-prints had been insisted on as routine procedure following an arrest.

She had her own solicitor seated beside her, a woman new to Manvers Street interviews.

After Ingeborg had gone through the preliminaries of place, time and who was present, Diamond took over.

'We found Hang-glider this afternoon, what's left of him, the neat hole in his skull where he was despatched with a vet's equipment, the penetrating captive bolt gun.

Expertly done, right on the spot, humanely, I don't doubt.'

Shocking her with the discovery was worth a try. He might not have said a word for all the reaction he got.

He reached for an evidence bag containing a bolt gun and dropped it on the table. 'There's no telling if this was the one, but we picked it up from your surgery in case. The big question I asked myself many times was why anyone needed to destroy a marvellous horse worth over a million to your father. The deal with Sheikh Abdul was drawn up and ready to sign.'

Davina continued to stare ahead.

This wasn't meant to be a monologue. Diamond gave her the chance to say something that wouldn't incriminate her. 'Your father bought Hang-glider in the yearling sales at Newmarket in October, 1990. Remember how much he paid?' He knew, of course. It was on public record.

'Two hundred thousand,' she said in an expressionless tone.

'Pounds?'

Her lip curled in contempt. 'Guineas.'

'He must have had great faith in the colt.'

'Great judgement,' she said. 'It was a half-brother to a Prix Lupin winner who lost the Irish Derby in a photo.' Diamond was outside the racing fraternity and she wanted him to know it.

'Still a risk, wasn't it?'

She shrugged. 'The whole of the sport is risky. Some expensive yearlings never do anything.'

'I mean he could have lost his investment through the choice he made.'

'If you want to invest, put your money in National Savings. He was buying a horse.'

'You speak as a successful owner yourself,' he said.

'In a different league.'

'What made your father spend so much?'

'He'd talked about owning a thoroughbred for years. It was his life's ambition. He'd raced horses before, but they never had the breeding. Let's give him credit. He picked a champion.'

'At a cost,' Diamond said.

'Tell me about it.' The bitterness cut through. Was this a factor in her behaviour — father blueing her inheritance on a horse?

'Two hundred thou was just the beginning,' she added. 'A top trainer like McDart doesn't come cheap, and then there were all the extras. Stabling, race fees, transportation, jockeys.'

'Vets.'

She gave a cautious nod.

549

'He could save on vet fees by using you.'

'He didn't,' she said, spotting the trap. 'McDart uses his own Lambourn vet.'

'All this outlay on Hang-glider,' he said. 'Was it funded from his surveying business?'

'No chance. It was private money. Look at his company accounts if you don't believe me.'

'Family money, then?'

'His savings, and he took out a loan as well.'

'Good thing it was such a fine racehorse. Did it earn back the money?'

'Hardly,' she said. 'Another season might have made a difference, but it got the injury and that was it. That's why you have to treat racing as a gamble. Things go wrong.'

'But you insure against accidents.'

'Insurance. That's another expense I didn't mention,' she said. 'It's massive in the case of a racing thoroughbred. They base the premium on the value of the animal by looking at the bloodline, the price paid and so on. You're shown a portfolio of options and you have to decide which you can afford.'

'He must have bought medical insurance.'

'It covered the cost of treatment, not the loss of income.'

'But all was not lost . . . yet,' Diamond

said. 'Hang-glider's stud value as a classic winner was considerable, and along came the sheikh with an offer that would make light of all these costs you've talked about. Half a million, wasn't it, with an extra fee for every mare Hang-glider covered?'

'That's what I read in the *Racing Post*.'

'Didn't your father let you in on it?'

'He wasn't counting on anything until the money was in the bank,' she said. 'Rightly, as it turned out.'

'The agreement was drawn up, but not yet signed by Sheikh Abdul. Then this ill-fated farewell to Lansdown was arranged, parading Hang-glider for his admirers to see him one last time.'

'It was home territory,' she said. 'His debut win was at Bath. The racegoers knew him and they knew Fa. He deserved his tribute.'

'They didn't know he was about to be put down.'

'No one knew.'

'That isn't true, is it, Davina? Where were you that evening?'

'Delivering twin calves at Upper Westwood.'

The answer came pat, as if she'd expected the question. Westwood was the other side of Bath. Difficult to prove or disprove at this distance in time.

'I thought as a lady of the turf, you wouldn't miss an evening meeting at Lansdown.'

'Nobody explained that to the cow.'

'Do you keep some sort of diary or appointment book?'

'For 1993? I threw it out years ago.'

'Yet you remember where you were that evening.'

'Of course. It was a huge, horrible day for our family.'

'Your father lost a fortune. He told me he got something back in insurance that he described as a pittance. Under a hundred thousand. It still sounds a lot to me.'

'It didn't cover the outlay,' she pointed out. 'And it was way below the offer he had in writing. He's never owned a horse since.'

'When we question him, as we will shortly, do you seriously expect him to confirm your version of events?'

There was a telling moment of hesitation before Davina said, 'Certainly.'

'Because we all know this isn't only about the killing of the racehorse. We're investigating two murders and we have evidence that incriminates you both.'

'A stun gun that I bought last year?' she said with contempt.

552

Her solicitor put a restraining hand on Davina's arm. 'If there's evidence of the sort you're describing, superintendent, we wish to be informed about it.'

'Forensic tests need to be completed before we can release any details,' he said. 'Meanwhile, we'll have a word with Sir Colin.'

Outside, he said to Ingeborg, 'We'll let that sink in. It's time to talk to the father.'

She said, 'She's got an answer for everything.'

'Up to now.'

39

On the other side of the observation window Diamond asked where Septimus was. The shrewd DI from Bristol was the obvious choice to have beside him for the second interview. John Leaman said Septimus was using his computer in the incident room.

'Doing what?'

'Checking stuff from way back, he told me.'

'Ah. Should have remembered. A task I set him.'

'Do you want me to fetch him, guv?'

'He'll come when he's ready.' He looked around the room to see who else was there. Paul Gilbert was in the back row cradling a mug of coffee. 'You made it, then. Did Duckett actually appear?'

Gilbert shook his head. 'There's a lad from uniform guarding the site.'

'Bit of luck came your way?'

'Charlie Smart came over to check up on

me and I borrowed his phone.'

'Good initiative. You slipped my mind, I have to admit. Have you had supper?'

'Not yet, guv.'

Diamond took a fiver from his back pocket. 'For you. I meant it, about the bangers and mash. You did well today.'

There was an awed silence. Such generosity from the main man was rare.

'Inge did well, too,' Leaman said.

'Putting a witness in hospital?'

'Fortunes of war,' Leaman said. 'She could have been the one who was hurt.'

'Okay. Inge gets supper, too.' He felt in his pocket again and peeled off another note.

Amazing.

'Nice to know the front line people are appreciated,' Leaman said. 'The boys in the back room may get a chance to shine some time.'

'Bloody hell,' Diamond said. 'All right, team. It's supper for everyone when this job is done.'

'Me included?' a voice behind him said.

He swung round in surprise. Georgina had come in.

'I thought it was your choir night, ma'am.'

'I heard there was singing in prospect here.'

'It hasn't begun yet, unfortunately.'

Not long after, Septimus appeared with a piece of paper in his hand.

'Was I right?' Diamond asked him.

A nod. 'It took some finding.'

The two of them took their places in the interview room, Sir Colin Tipping now occupying the seat his daughter had, with an elderly pin-striped Bath solicitor at his side.

'We'll begin with the game of golf,' Diamond said after Septimus had spoken the formalities for the tape.

Tipping rubbed his hands. He had a confident smile. 'What a splendid idea.'

'I'm referring to the game you were playing with Major Swithin on July seventeenth, the date of the battle re-enactment.'

'That's put me on the spot straight away. We play almost every day. If you're asking the score, I doubt if I can recall it, but I'm usually the winner.'

This would be his defence then, making light of the interview in his jocular style. Better than silence, Diamond thought. 'You'll recall this one because the major took a call from his wife.'

'It wouldn't be the first time. Agnes never lets the poor fellow off the leash.' He turned to his solicitor. 'Don't you agree that pocket telephones are the curse of the modern age? One sounded off at morning service in the Abbey the other day. Colonel Bogey in the Bishop's sermon. It isn't on.'

Diamond kept to his brief. 'What Mrs Swithin had seen through her binoculars was two soldiers in royalist uniform up to their elbows in earth by the fallen oak tree your society has vowed to protect. They unearthed a bone, a human bone that they reburied. The major tells me he shared this information with you, as a fellow member of the Lansdown Society.'

'Do you know, I sometimes think Agnes Swithin suspects Reggie of being with some floozy when he's out of her sight? She finds these silly pretexts to call him unexpectedly.'

'Except you didn't treat this as a silly pretext. You completed the round — it was almost through when you took the call — and broke with your usual habit of a drinking session afterwards in the clubhouse. You made some excuse about an appointment and left immediately.'

'Doesn't sound like me. At my age you don't do anything immediately.'

'I spoke to the major at his home this evening.'

'He said I left without having a drink? Or

without *buying* one?' He grinned at his solicitor.

'You had reason to be alarmed about what you'd heard, and we'll deal with that presently. You're going to tell me you got in your car and drove to the battlefield on behalf of the Lansdown Society, to check the tree, which was supposed to be off limits to the Sealed Knot.'

The solicitor raised a finger. 'Have a care, superintendent. You know very well you shouldn't put words into my client's mouth.'

'Did I get it wrong?' Diamond said, pretending to be mystified. 'Did he go there for another purpose?'

Tipping looked from one to the other. Suddenly the questioning had turned serious and he was uncertain how to proceed. 'What if I tell you I didn't go there at all?'

Diamond countered with, 'What if I tell you we have a sighting of your car at the side of the road?' Actually they hadn't, but if Tipping wanted to trade in speculation, so could he.

'All right, I was testing you out. Your first assumption was correct, old boy. I take a particular interest in that tree. It's treasure trove to a botanist, host to one of the rarest lichens in Great Britain.'

'It isn't,' Diamond said. 'And I doubt if it

ever was.'

Tipping took a sharp, surprised breath that he was forced to account for. 'What's this? A policeman with some knowledge of botany? I think he's about to tell us lichens don't grow on trees.' He shook with amusement.

'I'm quoting one of the Lansdown Society. Your botanist member, Charlie Smart, told me the only lichen on that fallen oak is a common variety found everywhere.'

'Charlie hasn't been with us long. Probably doesn't know where to look.'

'Neither does the British Lichen Society, it seems. They have no record of it on Lansdown. Could you be mistaken?'

A climbdown was called for. 'I'll look pretty damn silly if I am. The identification was done years ago by one of our members who passed on. Let's hope the rare lichen didn't hop the twig as well.' He chanced a smile at Septimus and got a cold stare in return. 'Why don't we talk about something we all know more about?'

Diamond nodded, encouraged not from scoring a point, but from teasing out a major admission from the suspect: he'd definitely visited the tree. 'We'll turn to Rupert Hope, then — one of the men Mrs Swithin saw unearthing the bone, a history lecturer with an interest in the Civil War. That bone could have been of historical interest if it belonged to a soldier in the real battle. Although Rupert agreed to put it back in the soil, he appears to have gone back secretly after everyone left the field. He thought he'd made a find, you see.'

'We're in the realm of speculation again,' Tipping said, more to his solicitor than Diamond. 'They don't have a clue what happened. "He appears to have gone back secretly." That's a stab in the dark, wouldn't you say?'

'Does it matter to you if we get it wrong?' Diamond asked.

'It does if you're accusing me of crimes I didn't commit.'

'You're ahead of me. I haven't accused you of anything. We know Rupert was attacked that evening because he didn't return to his car. He'd changed out of his battle armour. He was struck on the back of the head with a blunt instrument. It wasn't enough to kill him, but he was left for dead. He wandered Lansdown in a confused state, suffering memory loss, for over three weeks. Then he was hit again, fatally.'

'Nothing to do with me, old chum.'

'You carry a blunt instrument in your car. In fact, you have a selection of them — your golf clubs.'

'Is this a joke?'

Diamond turned to Septimus and nodded.

'What on earth . . . ?' Tipping said, as the colour rose in his cheeks.

Septimus had stooped down and lifted a bag of golf clubs.

'The nerve of it. Those are mine,' Tipping said.

His solicitor leaned close and spoke to him in an undertone, no doubt informing him that the police are permitted to enter and search the house of a person detained for a serious arrestable offence.

It was a lightweight bag of the sort golfers without caddies can carry themselves. Septimus unzipped the top.

Diamond asked him to count the clubs.

'Thirteen.'

'Unlucky for some,' Diamond couldn't resist saying. 'According to the laws, which I've checked, you're allowed a maximum of fourteen. A dedicated golfer such as yourself won't carry fewer. Where's the missing club, Sir Colin?'

For the first time, he didn't have an answer.

'I expect it's a heavy one,' Diamond said. 'An iron, going by the shape of the injuries to the dead man's skull.'

'Are you accusing my client of murder?' the solicitor asked.

'I haven't yet,' Diamond said. 'I'm waiting to hear what he did with the fourteenth club.'

There was still no response from Tipping.

'If you are,' the solicitor said, 'I must insist on an adjournment.'

'Painful as it must be to a golfer to destroy one of his clubs,' Diamond said, 'that seems to have happened here. I don't see how he could have lost it.' He thanked Septimus and told him to put the bag aside. 'Rupert survived one crack on the head, but the second really did for him. Why the delay? For a few days he was missing. Then he was seen trying car doors; foraging, in effect. The amnesia had set in. He didn't even remember his own name. The danger for his killer was that Rupert's memory would come back. Worse, he'd taken to sleeping in the gatehouse, a short distance from Beckford's grotto.'

'Beckford's what?' the solicitor said.

'An underground tunnel with a secret of its own that your client knows all about.'

Tipping gripped the desk with both hands and still said nothing. All the colour had drained from his face.

'It's a matter of record that Rupert Hope was hit from behind and killed in the cemetery near the tower. He'd found an under-rug last seen strapped to the race-horse Hang-glider's back. We've done the tests. This afternoon we went into the grotto and found the remains of the horse. Are you listening, Sir Colin?'

A nod. All the fight had gone out of him.

'I've interviewed your daughter and discussed how it was done. You couldn't have managed it alone. Each of you brought your professional skills to the job. In your case, it was knowing the existence of the grotto. You're a chartered surveyor dealing in major civic works. DI Ward, would you take over?'

Septimus was ready. 'In January, 1991, a section of the Lansdown Road collapsed near Beckford's tower, due to subsidence. A survey of the immediate area was commissioned.' He took from his pocket the printout he'd shown Diamond and passed it across the table. 'From the council planning department website. You'll see that C. Tipping and Associates carried out the survey. You identified nineteenth century excavations as the cause, an exploratory dig for the grotto. The tunnel itself was a short way off and you located that as well. Two years later, this knowledge would come in useful. Disposing of a dead racehorse can be a problem.'

'That was your contribution,' Diamond said. 'Davina supplied the veterinary skills, obtained a horse-trailer and drove it to the races the night Hang-glider was paraded there. You knew McDart would be in the owners' and trainers' bar until late. You saw that the stable lad had returned from the horsebox. You went there, broke in and transferred the horse to the trailer. But there was an unforeseen problem in the shape of Nadia, a young woman waiting by the trailer in hope of getting a job with McDart. She would have ruined the scam. She had to be disposed of, and quickly. Correct me if I'm wrong. You held her and Davina killed her with the bolt gun and you bundled the body into the back seat of the Land Rover before driving off with the horse.'

'No comment,' Tipping said.

'We insist on an adjournment,' his solicitor said.

'No,' Tipping said in an abrupt change of tactics. 'Let's nail this now for the bullshit it is.'

'I'm advising you not to say any more.'

'They can't stitch us up like this. There's no motive, for Christ's sake. Why would I go to all this trouble to destroy my own

564

horse when I was on the brink of the biggest deal of my life? I lost a fortune when that horse was stolen.'

Diamond refused to be sidetracked. He was telling it his way. 'With the horse in the trailer and the dead woman in the Land Rover you drove to the grotto, right into the field and up to the entrance. Davina used the stun gun on the horse and you reversed the trailer to the steps and let it roll inside and out of sight. That was enough for one evening. The next night, working together, you buried Nadia's body in a place you knew, the hole left by the fallen oak's root system, first removing the victim's head. Why? Because the bolt-hole in the skull would have revealed the form of death and led us to suspect a slaughterman or a vet. I expect your daughter carried out that necessary task and also disposed of the head. Murder is gruesome, however clinically it is done.'

'You've missed the point,' Tipping said. 'We had no motive.'

'The motive in both cases is the same. These unfortunate people strayed into your danger zone. The only thing you had against them was that they would give you away. With the help of the Lansdown Society you kept watch on the burial site and you were compelled to act when Rupert returned there. He survived one clubbing and had to be given another. The attempt to dress up his killing as accidental was pretty inept. I suppose you hoped we'd think he'd died in a brawl. I won't pretend it was easy to track you down. Casual killings of strangers are the hardest of all to investigate.'

'Have you finished?' Tipping said. For all the revelations, he'd recovered some of that air of infallibity. 'We'll award you A+ for invention and B for effort, but I'm afraid you fail on the argument. You could have saved us all a lot of time if you'd addressed the simple fact I raised just now. I had no reason to kill my horse. Quite the reverse. He was going to make me very rich indeed.'

'You're talking about your motive for killing the horse?'

'The penny drops. Yes, Mr Diamond. We're on tenterhooks to hear your theory on that.'

Diamond locked eyes with him. 'I'm not giving you that satisfaction.'

'So this great hypothesis comes tumbling down.'

'No. It's as safe as any house you ever surveyed. Charge him with murder, Septimus.'

40

Diamond's offer of supper in the canteen was interpreted by all but himself as free drinks in the Sports Bar of the Royal, the hotel at the east end of Manvers Street. He had little choice but to join the party and start a tab. Someone bent on mischief — probably John Leaman — got busy on the phone and in the next half-hour familiar faces kept appearing through the door, civilian staff, wives and partners. Paloma arrived — proof that their private life was an open secret — and there was a huge cheer when Keith Halliwell, pale, but smiling broadly, walked in with his wife.

Even Georgina had joined the party and was drinking lemonade with John Wigfull.

Diamond told Paloma, 'This started with an offer of bangers and mash to one deserving case. I'll need to take out an extra mortgage.'

'It's no bad thing to let them feel

appreciated,' she said.

'They get that all the time from me.'

And for that evening, you might have believed him. There was a moment when the din was hushed and Leaman raised his glass and said. 'To the guv'nor.'

'The guv'nor.'

Ingeborg shouted, 'Speech.'

With reluctance he hauled himself upright. 'Apart from thanking you for a job well done, I don't know what to say.'

Georgina said, 'I'll tell you what. We watched and listened through the glass and there isn't any doubt that those two are guilty of murder, but you didn't answer the question about the racehorse. Why, in the name of sanity, did they kill it?'

'For the insurance,' he said. 'It was insured for a hundred grand.'

'But that's a fraction of what was on offer.'

'From the sheikh? Didn't you work that out?'

'Come on, guv. Spill it,' Ingeborg said.

He took a long look around the room. No one seemed to have got it. 'Even a billionaire sheikh isn't going to buy a horse for stud without proof of fertility. The agreement required an independent guarantee that Hang-glider was up to the job. The trainer's regular vet wasn't eligible, so Tipping asked his daughter's firm to do the necessary and when Davina had the sample tested she discovered to her horror that the sperm count was negative. The horse was sterile. The deal was scuppered and they hadn't insured against infertility. The insurance they had was for illness, foul play or mortality. They were left with a horse that couldn't race and couldn't breed. Between them they decided on the fake kidnapping to activate the foul play option. A hundred grand was better than nothing.'

John Leaman said, 'How many years' salary is that?'

'But Tipping had paid out much more, and he felt entitled to some return. All he had was a pensioned-off horse requiring feed and care for the next twenty years.'

'Can we prove this?' Georgina asked him.

'Davina destroyed all record of it, as you'd expect. Fortunately, she wasn't the only one with a copy of the report. There aren't many labs in our part of the world that offer equine sperm analysis. The second one I checked was able to confirm a test it conducted in July, 1993, for DTS Animal Care, Davina's company. The horse wasn't named, but the result was notable: a negative count.'

'And that's rare?'

'Rare enough to make our case, ma'am.'

Georgina sighed. 'I'm impressed — genuinely impressed.'

John Leaman said, 'You speak for us all, ma'am. Don't you think our guv'nor deserves some recognition?'

She frowned. There were limits. 'What did you have in mind?'

'An honour, ma'am. As a result of all this isn't there a vacancy in the Lansdown Society?'

ABOUT THE AUTHOR

Peter Lovesey is the author of ten mysteries in his best loved Peter Diamond series as well as two in the Hen Mallin series and eight in the Sergeant Cribb series, and several others, all available from Soho Press. He has been awarded Silver, Gold, and Diamond Daggers by the British Crime Writers' Association, and in the United States he has received Edgar® and Dilys nominations, an Anthony Award, and a Macavity Award, as well as the Ellery Queen Reader's Award. Malice Domestic's Lifetime Achievement Award was given to him in 2008. He lives near Chichester in West Sussex, England.